heartless

heartless

TALES OF GOLDSTONE WOOD

ANNE ELISABETH STENGL

BETHANY HOUSE PUBLISHERS
Minneapolis, Minnesota

Published by Bethany House Publishers
11400 Hampshire Avenue South
Bloomington, Minnesota 55438

Bethany House Publishers is a division of
Baker Publishing Group, Grand Rapids, Michigan.

Printed in the United States of America

Library of Congress Cataloging-in-Publication Data

Stengl, Anne Elisabeth.
Heartless / Anne Elisabeth Stengl
p.   cm. — (Tales of Goldstone Wood)
ISBN 978-0-7642-0780-8 (pbk.)
1. Magic—Fiction. I. Title.
PS3619.T47647675H43   2010
813'.6—dc22
2010006229

To Dean and Jill Stengl

PROLOGUE

Two children, a brother and a sister, played down by the Old Bridge nearly every day, weather permitting. None observing them would have guessed they were a prince and a princess. The boy, the younger of the two, was generally up to his elbows in mud due to his brave exploits as a frog catcher. His sister, though significantly more prim, was often barefoot and sported a few leaves and flowers stuck in her hair. She thought these romantic, but her nurse, when she brushed the princess's hair at night, called them "common," and said it with a distinct sniff.

This never stopped the princess, whose name was Una, from weaving daisies and wild violets and any other forest flower that fell under her hand into garlands and coronets, with which she festooned herself, thereby transforming from an ordinary princess—which was rather drab—into a Faerie Queen of great power and majesty. Felix, her brother, was never a Faerie. He, by dint of a few expert dabs of mud in the right places, made himself her gremlin guard instead and waged war against all her imaginary enemies.

The Old Bridge was the perfect place for these games for a number of reasons. Most important, none of their entourage of servants and tutors, not even Una's intrepid nurse, dared follow them there, for the Old Bridge was located in Goldstone Wood, outside the boundaries of Oriana Palace's seven-tiered garden. Plenty of stories were told about Goldstone Wood, and its history was strange enough to ward off most people. But Una and her brother liked the stories—the stranger and more superstitious the better. So they often made their way to the Old Bridge and did their utmost to disturb the ancient quiet of Goldstone Wood with their laughter and games.

Una was not so fond of mud as Felix; thus she would invent adventures to occupy him while she sat on the planks of the bridge and scrawled thoughts and ideas in her journal.

"Faithful gremlin," she declared one fine afternoon as they made their way down the side of Goldstone Hill toward the bridge, "you must seek the fabled Flowing Gold of Rudiobus, lost somewhere in this raging river." She indicated the stream that trickled down the side of Goldstone Hill. Raging river it was not, but facts never stopped the course of Una's imagination. "You must bring it back to me before the sun has set, or all my kingdom will be lost in darkness without end."

"Righto!" Felix hurtled headlong through the foliage and splashed into the stream. He grabbed a pebble and held it over his head. "Is this it, Una?"

"Does that look like *flowing* gold?"

He studied the pebble, shrugged, and tossed it over his shoulder before plunging on down the stream, wallowing with all the joy of a boy set loose in the mud.

Una wove a crown appropriate for her Faerie Queen status, placed it on her head, and took a seat on the middle of the Old Bridge. Removing her shoes, she dangled bare feet over the stream, turning up her toes so that they did not quite touch the cold water. Taking from the pocket of her full skirts a nub of pencil and a small journal, which she pressed open in her lap, she wrote a few scrawling lines, frowned, and scratched them out.

"Is this it, Una?" Felix bellowed from farther downstream.

She looked. Her brother held up a ragged handful of waterweeds, brown and dripping and slimy. "What do you think?" she called back.

"Well, it's *flowing*!"

"Is it gold?"

"Bah!"

He tossed it away and continued his search, and his sister returned to her writing. She scribbled uninterrupted for some time, and the noise of her brother's questing faded away as she pored over the little journal. At last she smiled, held up the page, and read her work.

Then she frowned and crossed it all out with vigorous strokes.

Sighing, she chewed the end of her pencil. A wood thrush sang somewhere far away in the forest, and Una allowed her gaze to wander to the trees on the other side of the Old Bridge.

The far forest began only a few steps away—two, maybe three at most. It looked much like her side of the bridge: stately trees, new spring growth, last year's leaves damp on the ground. Perhaps the sun did not shine as brightly on that side, perhaps more shadows lurked along the ground.

Una had never crossed the Old Bridge. It was an unwritten law that had been imprinted on her mind: No one crossed the Old Bridge. Not once in all the years that she and Felix had escaped their nursemaids' clutches and run to this very spot had either of them actually crossed the narrow wooden planks and stepped into the forest on the other side.

She frowned around the pencil nub.

Miles and miles of forest lay beyond the bridge. Goldstone Wood was the largest wood in all the kingdom of Parumvir, so large that no one had ever attempted to map its mysteries. And here Una was, a girl of imagination with a taste for adventure, and she'd never even thought to cross over! Wasn't it strange—

An icy splash of water down her neck shocked her from her reverie. Una dropped her pencil with a scream. "Felix!" She watched the pencil swirl out of sight in the muddy water, then snapped her journal shut and whirled about.

Her brother stood on the bank, his hands cupped and dripping. He laughed. "Wake up!"

"I was not asleep!"

"You weren't awake either." Still laughing, he scrambled up the steep embankment and around to the bridge. He flopped down at her side, grinning, and held a glob of mud under her nose.

"Eeeew, Felix!" She pushed his hands away. "Stop it!"

"It's all that was left," he said.

"All that was left of what?"

"The Flowing Gold," he said. "I think it got melted by a dragon."

"Melted gold doesn't turn into muck."

He let the mud dribble between his fingers and plop into the stream beneath them, then sneaked a peek at her journal. "What are you writing?"

"Nothing." Una glared at him.

"Are you composing verses?"

"Maybe."

"Can I see?"

"*May* I see."

Felix rolled his eyes and made a grab for her book, but she pulled it away, leaning back across the bridge. "Let me see!" he demanded. Feigning reluctance, she opened her journal. She turned her shoulder to keep him from reading and flipped through to find the most recent page, full of her scratched-out work. She could still discern the words, and she read them aloud, half singing:

> *"I ask the silent sky*
> *Tell me why*
> *As I look so high*
> *Into the leaf-laced sky*
> *You do not reply*
> *So I—"*

"So I flop down and cry in a muddy pigsty!" Felix flung his arms wide and burst forth in a squeaky falsetto. "Then I go bake a pie out of apples and rye! O hey, nonny-ni and a fiddledee—"

Una closed her book and smacked him in the stomach, then knocked him again on the back of the head as he doubled up, laughing wickedly.

Resisting the urge to push him into the stream after her lost pencil, Una instead grabbed her stockings and buckle shoes from behind her, pulled them on, and got to her feet. Tucking her journal into her pocket, she stepped away from Felix to the middle of the bridge. "I'm going to cross over," she said.

Felix, still rubbing the back of his head, looked up. "What?"

"Yes," she said, nodding. A determined line settled between her brows, and she took a few more steps across the bridge, the heels of her shoes clunking on the planks. "I'm going to cross over."

"No, you aren't." Felix swung his feet up onto the bridge and leaned back to support himself on his hands. He watched her, his head tilted to one side as she stood looking into the far forest extending down Goldstone Hill. "You aren't," he said again.

"I will."

"When?"

She did not answer for several long moments. Felix pushed himself to his feet and went to stand beside her. They gazed into the leaf-shrouded shadows.

Goldstone Wood waited.

A breeze darted between them, dragged at Una's skirt, and skittered off into the forest beyond, rustling leaves as it went. The trees laughed quietly together, and their branches seemed to point at the brother and sister standing solemnly on the Old Bridge. Somewhere far away down the hillside, a wood thrush sang again. The breeze darted back, carrying the silvery song to their ears—a song of mystery, of secrets.

"Now," Una whispered at last. "I'll go right now." She took a step, then another.

A horrible caterwaul filled the air, startling her out of her skin. She leapt back, stumbling into Felix, and the both of them nearly went into the stream. Clutching each other in surprise, they stared into the trees beyond.

A cat stepped into view.

"Ha!" Felix burst out laughing and pinched Una. "You were scared of a kitty cat!"

"Was not!" Una glared at him and pursed her lips, then looked back at the cat.

It was a large golden animal with a plumy tail, but its fur was a mass of burs and snarls. It appeared from among thick-growing ferns on the far side of the bridge, picking its way carefully, as though hurt.

"What's wrong with it?" Una said as it made its way down the steep embankment of the stream. At last it reached the water's edge, where it put its nose down and lapped. Then it raised its face to them.

It had no eyes.

"Oh, the poor thing!" Una cried. "The poor little cat! Do you see that, Felix?"

"Poor little cat, my foot." Felix snorted. "He's ugly as a goblin. A regular monster."

"She's blind!" Her venture into the Wood forgotten, Una scrambled back to the familiar side of the bridge and down to the stream. She stood across from the cat, which seemed to watch her without eyes, the tip of its tail twitching slightly. "Kitty-kitty-kitty!" she called, holding out an inviting hand.

It began to groom its paw.

"Felix!" she called to her brother, who still stood watching on the bridge. "Felix, get her for me."

"Why?"

"She needs help!"

"No, he doesn't."

"She's blind!"

"Not my problem."

"Felix." She huffed. Then a sudden inspiration struck. "She's the Flowing Gold, Felix. Don't you see? The gold fur . . . the flowing, um, tail?"

Felix rolled his eyes, but this persuasion worked its magic. He swung down from the bridge into the stream and waded across to the cat. It raised its nose, gave a polite "Meeaa," and made no protest when the boy scooped it up. "He's heavy," Felix grunted, splashing back across to his sister. "And his claws are in my shoulder. Right to the bone!"

"She needs help," Una declared staunchly, holding out her arms.

"The Flowing Gold to save your fair kingdom, my lady." Felix deposited the cat into her keeping. It began purring as soon as she held it—a loud purr that Felix declared obnoxious but Una thought sweet.

"We'll take her home," the princess said, turning and beginning the long walk back up Goldstone Hill. "I'll brush her fur and give her a good meal—"

"He doesn't need a good meal. He's heavy!"

"She's blind and lost," Una snapped. "She needs a good meal. Isn't she lovely?"

"He's ugly."

So with the cat draped over the princess's shoulder, the children returned home, leaving the Old Bridge uncrossed and the far forest unexplored.

Goldstone Wood watched them go.

1

FIVE YEARS LATER

D O YOU THINK they will come before the year is out?" Princess
Una asked her nurse.

"Who will come?" her nurse replied.

"Suitors, of course!"

Though the sun was bright, the air blew chill through the open window that spring morning, and Una wrapped a shawl around her shoulders
as she sat waiting for Nurse to finish the awful business of preparing her for
the day. Nurse, who had long since ceased to function as a real nurse and
these days played the part of maid and busybody to her princess, wielded
a brush with the tenderness of a gardener raking last year's dead leaves,
making every effort to tame Una's honey-colored hair into an acceptable
braid. One would have expected that, with many years' practice, she might
have acquired rather more gentleness. Not so Nurse.

She paused now, mid-tug, and scowled at Una's reflection in the glass.
"What brings on this fool talk?" She raised a bushy eyebrow and gave
the braid an extra tug, as though to wrest all the unruliness out of it in

one go. "You keep your mind busy with your lessons and deportment, just as always, and leave that messy business of courting and arranging marriages to your father, as is right."

"But I'm of age!" Una winced again and tried not to pull away from the vicious brush. She twisted her mouth into an unattractive shape as pain shot through her scalp. "Papa always said that he wouldn't accept a single inquiry from a single prince or single dignitary in a single realm of the whole Continent until I came of age."

"As is right."

"Well, now that I'm eighteen, shouldn't he start receiving them? When will they come to pay their respects?" *To pay their respects,* according to the definition given the phrase by the courtiers of Oriana Palace, was a tactful way to say, *investigate marriage possibilities with the resident princess.*

"That's not for you to be speculating, Miss Princess," said Nurse. She pronounced it "speckle-ating." Una dared not laugh. Though Nurse had not been brought up to speak an elegant dialect, her ideas on what was and was not proper behavior for a princess went far beyond anything Una had ever learned from her decorum instructors.

"Suitors indeed! Why, in my day, a girl never put two thoughts together concerning a boy—not till her father gave her the go-ahead."

"Never?"

"Not once!"

"Not even when—"

Nurse whapped the top of Una's head with the back of the brush. "No more! There, you're tidy as mortal hands can make you. Get you gone to your morning tutorials, and I don't want to hear another word of this romantic drivel!"

Rubbing the top of her head, Una gathered herself up, grabbed an armload of books, and made her way to her chamber doors, muttering, "I like romantic drivel." She stepped from the room and, just as the door swung shut behind her, called over her shoulder, "Your day was a singularly unromantic one, Nurse!"

The door clunked, and Nurse's voice came muffled from behind. "You'd better believe it!"

Una glared at the closed door. A demanding "Meeeowl?" at her feet drew her gaze, and she looked down at her cat, Monster, who sat before her, his tail curled elegantly about his paws. He seemed to smile all over his furry face, despite his lack of eyes.

She wrinkled her nose at him. "Don't look so smug."

With that, she turned on her heel and marched down the corridor, the blind cat trotting behind, unlike a dog in every way because, of course, he wasn't truly following her. He merely happened to be going her way.

"Nothing in life is as romantic as it should be, Monster," Una said as they made their way along the white hall and down a graceful staircase. She nodded civil acknowledgements to members of the household who greeted her as she passed. "Here I am, a princess, of age to be courted and married, and where am I? On my way to another history lesson! Then there'll be a tutorial on the proper ways to address ambassadors from Beauclair as opposed to dignitaries from Shippening. Then dancing. And not a single respects-paying gentleman of certain birth as far as the eye can see." She sighed at the heaviness of the world. "Nothing ever *changes*, Monster."

"Meeaa?" the cat said.

Una looked down her nose at him. "You're not just saying that, are you? Trying to make me feel better?"

"Meeaa."

"I knew it." She sighed again. "Someday, Monster, won't you express an original idea? For me?"

Felix waited for her in the large but nonetheless stuffy classroom they shared, doodling caricatures of their tutor in the margins of an essay he was supposed to be composing. He scarcely looked up when Una entered. Monster took a moment to rub a cheek against the young prince's knee before dodging Felix's backhand and arranging himself on the windowsill to catch the sunlight.

Una took a seat and opened her book just as the tired-eyed tutor shuffled in. He fortified himself behind his desk, attached a pair of spectacles in place—which made his eyes seem still more tired—and looked upon his students with the air of a man resigned to his fate.

"At what are you so diligently working, Prince Felix?" he asked. His voice never varied from a mournful drone.

Felix held up his essay full of doodles.

The tutor winced. "Most amusing, Your Highness."

"See how big I made the nose on this one?"

"A remarkable likeness, Your Highness."

"Doesn't look a thing like him," Una said.

Felix made a face. "Not supposed to. This one's you."

The tutor closed his eyes during the ensuing argument and let the storm pass. When at last calm returned, he slowly creaked his eyelids back up and dared face the world again. "Prince Felix, do you recall at what passage we left off our reading yesterday?"

"I do," Una said.

"He was talking to me!"

She continued, "We were studying the rise of Corrilond in the year of the Sleeper's Awakening during the reign of King Abundiantus IV—"

"Know-it-all!"

The tutor shoved his glasses up onto his forehead and rubbed his eyes. It was a day like all others, a mirror of yesterday and a foretelling of tomorrow: The prosperous sameness and drudging boredom of lives placidly spent proceeding as endlessly as the mind could conceive. Nothing ever really changed, and as far as anyone in Oriana Palace could surmise, nothing ever would.

But then, something did.

For two hundred years they had not been seen.

They first appeared as deeper shadows among the shadows of the Wood, all staring eyes and sniffing noses, as wary as children dipping a toe in deep water, fearful to take a dive.

Then one stepped forth, and he, with a smile, beckoned to the others. A huge creature with eyes as wide and white as the moon and skin like craggy rocks followed with a strange grace of movement; behind him walked another who was black as a shadow but whose eyes shone like the sky. After these came the others. Out of the Wood they streamed in parade—carrying with them the scent of dusk, the sound of dawn—and they arranged themselves upon the lawn outside the walls of the city of Sondhold, in the shadow of Goldstone Hill.

A shepherd boy saw them first. His heart leapt with fear at the sight, though not because of their strangeness, for such strangeness he had witnessed a thousand times in dreams. Rather, he feared that he dreamed them now and that, as soon as his old dad caught him snoozing at his watch, he'd fetch a hiding and perhaps be sent to bed without supper. So he pinched himself, and when that did not work, he pinched himself again.

His lazy flock all lifted their heads, regarded the oncoming throng a moment, and then returned to their grazing. But the quick-eyed herding dog let out a joyous bark and left the shepherd, left the flock, and ran to greet the strangers as though welcoming long-lost friends.

Then the boy jumped up and ran as well, shouting as he went. But he ran the opposite direction, down the dusty path toward Sondhold. Though he had only ever seen them in dreams, he recognized those who came.

"The market! The market!" he cried. The guards at the gates let him through, calling derisively after him, but he paid them no mind. "The market!" he shouted, gathering too much speed so that he lost his balance and scraped the skin from his palms and knees. But he was up again in a flash, shouting all the louder. "The Twelve-Year Market is come from the Wood!"

The very oldest grandmama in all Sondhold could only just recall her old grandmama talking about her grandmama's visit to the Twelve-Year Market. Many families in the city boasted prized heirlooms, strange oddities handed down from father to son, mother to daughter, for generations. A silver spoon that never tarnished; a kettle that sang familiar old tunes when the water boiled; a mug that never let the tea grow cold; a pair of boots that, if polished with the right stuff, would carry a man seven leagues in a step—too bad the polish ran out ages ago. The items once purchased at the Twelve-Year

Market were rare and wonderful indeed, items of Faerie make and ever so expensive. But the Twelve-Year Market was the stuff of stories.

Until it showed up on the lawn below Goldstone Hill that day in early spring, soon after Princess Una came of age.

A washerwoman hanging up her second load of the day to dry paused in her work, her wrinkled white fingers momentarily still as the shepherd boy ran by. "The Twelve-Year Market!" he bellowed as he went, and she dropped the clean shirt—dropped it right in the dust—brushed off her apron, and hitched up her skirts to hasten from the city, out to the green lawn.

The boy ran on, shouting, "The market! The market is come!"

Merchants by the docks closed up booths and locked away their wares.

"The market!" the shepherd boy cried.

The cobbler's wife and the baker's sister ceased their gossip, blinked startled eyes, and joined the merchants.

The boy went on, shouting until he was too hoarse to make himself heard, but by then his work was complete. The folks of Sondhold streamed through the gates: the washerwoman, the merchants, the cobbler's wife and her brood of children, even the guards who were supposed to stand at the gates. They all made their way down the dusty track from the city to the lawn below the hill. There they beheld the Faerie bazaar.

They stopped on the fringes, afraid to go forward.

The first to hail them was a man so incredibly ancient that his upper lip nearly reached his chin. His skin was like a walnut, and his eyes like acorn caps. A big black sow pulled his rickety cart, on which two enormous pots of alabaster hummed, as though some musical instrument played the same three notes again and again inside. Water sloshed as he lifted them down, and the city folk could hear the creak of every joint in his body, a crackling percussion accompanying the humming.

When he saw the gathering crowds his acorn-cap eyes winked twice, first with fear, then with a smile. "Come!" he cried, raising a gnarled hand, beckoning. "Come, folk of the Near World! Come inspect my wares! Unicorn fry, fresh from the sea, caught just this morning—or last century, depending on your view. Learning to sing; hear them for yourself! Come hear the sea unicorn young as they sing!"

The folk of Sondhold looked from him to each other, afraid to move closer, unwilling to leave.

Then the cobbler's wife took hold of her youngest son and strode boldly to the lawn, her chin set in defiance though the baker's sister called a warning to her. "I'd like a look," she told the old man with the acorn-cap eyes.

He grinned and lifted the lid of one jar. The strange humming filled the air, only three notes dancing in the ears of all those near, but the sweetest three notes ever played together.

The cobbler's wife stood on tiptoe to peer inside. "Coo!" she breathed. Then, "May I show the boy?"

The old man nodded, and she lifted her littlest one to peer into the alabaster jar. The child made a solemn inspection and finally declared, "Pretty."

"Unicorn fry!" the old man cried. "Caught fresh this morning! I'll sell them at a bargain, good dame, and you can raise one at home, hear sweet music every day!"

With that, the market truly opened. The crowd standing on the edges of the lawn could not bear to miss whatever wonders lay just before them, and they flooded in to inspect the hundred colorful stalls. The lawn below Goldstone Hill was suddenly as merry as a festival, as noisy as a circus, as frantic as a holiday. Music sang from all corners, outlandish music on outlandish instruments played by even more outlandish people. But although the songs were different, somehow they blended into each other in cheerful harmonies, often underscored by a low, melancholy tune that heightened the curiosity and the fun of those who browsed the many stalls.

Word spread fast. Soon all of Sondhold was bestirred. Working girls feigned sickness to be excused, and schoolboys made no pretense of attending classes. The washerwoman let the dirtied white shirt lie untouched, and the smithy allowed his fires to die. How could anyone attend to mundane things on the day of the Twelve-Year Market?

The hubbub bubbled all the way to the crest of Goldstone Hill and flowed on into the palace, where Princess Una sat with her nose in her history text, wallowing in academic misery. Dates and battles and dead kings' names swam before her eyes while spring fever, cruel and demanding, picked at the back of her brain. She and her brother had ceased their squabbling for the time being, and their tutor's voice filled the room in one long, endless drone that commanded no one's attention, least of all the tutor's.

Monster stood up on the windowsill. He stretched, forming an arch with his body, and flicked the plume of his tail. Then, after a quick wash to make certain his whiskers were well arranged, he interrupted the lecture.

"Meaaa."

The tutor droned on without a glance at the cat. "Abundiantus V was never intended to sit upon his father's throne, being the second son—"

"Meaaa!" Monster said, with more emphasis this time. He unsheathed his claws and scratched the window, a long grating noise.

"Dragon-eaten beast." Felix threw a pencil at the cat's nose, missing by inches.

"Princess Una," the tutor said, "we have had this discussion. Would you kindly remove that creature from the room so that our studies may continue uninhibited?"

Una huffed and went to the window. But when she reached for him, Monster made himself heavy and awkward, slipping through her grasp. He landed back on the windowsill with another "Meeeaa!" and pressed his nose to the glass.

Una looked out.

She saw the colors. She saw the movement. She saw the dancing far below, as though she was suddenly gifted with an eagle's eyes and able to discern every detail even at that great distance. Wonderingly, she opened the window, and music carried up Goldstone Hill and filled the room.

"Oh," she said.

"Meeeea." Monster looked smug.

Felix was on his feet and at her side in a moment. He too looked down. "Oh," he said.

The tutor, frowning, came around from behind his desk and joined them at the window. He looked as well and saw what they saw. His mouth formed an unspoken "Oh."

A clatter of hooves in the courtyard drew their gazes, however unwillingly, from the sight down the hill. Una and her brother saw their father, King Fidel, mounting up with a company of his guard around him. Brother and sister exchanged a glance and bolted for the door, falling over themselves in a headlong dash from the chamber, down the stairs, and out to the courtyard, heedless of the tutor's feeble attempts to restrain them. Monster trailed at their heels.

"Father!" Una burst into the courtyard, shouting like a little girl and hardly caring that she drew the eyes of the stable boys and footmen standing by. King Fidel, upon his gray mount, looked back at his daughter. "Father!" she cried. "Are you going to see?" She did not have to say what.

"Yes, Una," Fidel replied. "I must make certain all is well below."

"May we come?" Una said, and before the words were all out of her mouth, Felix was shouting to the stable boys, "My horse! Bring my horse!"

King Fidel considered a moment, his eyebrows drawn. But the day was fine, the air was full of holiday spirit, and his children's faces were far too eager to refuse. "Very well."

Una and Felix rode on either side of him as he descended the King's Way, the long road that wound down Goldstone Hill to the teeming lawn. The breath of the ocean whipped in their faces, carrying the spice of other worlds up from below.

Sheep left neglected trailed across the road as the riders came to the bottom of the hill. The animals trotted out of the way, lambs scurrying behind their mothers. Una saw a man leaving the market with a great embroidered rug over his shoulder, and children ran hither and yon eating golden apples. A juggler tumbled just in front of Felix's horse, tossing what at first looked like knives, but then seemed to be silver fish, and then, Una could have sworn, shooting stars. A dancer with eyes as large and wet as the moon on water, with pupils like a cat's, too strange to be either beautiful or ugly, twirled past trailing what could have been iridescent scarves or perhaps wings. A man with green-cast skin sprang alongside Una's mount and held up an empty hand. Flowers bloomed from his fingertips, and he smiled hugely, bobbing and bowing.

"Blossoms for the lovely lady? A fair price! Always fair! I do but ask for a strand of your hair. Is that not fair? A single strand of hair!"

Una urged her horse closer to her father's, uncertain whether or not to be frightened. But the green-cast man darted away into the crowds, shouting as he went, "Prices always fair! Blossoms to share!" She could hear his voice amid the din long after he vanished from sight.

Fidel's guards called out in large voices, heralding the king's arrival. But their words hardly carried over the music of the market, and the crowds did not part. The people of Sondhold, their eyes wide and wondering, scarcely spared a glance for their king or his children. King Fidel smiled as he looked around, for despite the noise and the otherworldliness of it all, it was impossible to remain unmoved by the wonders and the excitement. He called the captain of his guard to him and said, "Try to find out who is in charge here, will you?"

Before he had quite finished speaking, a path suddenly emerged in the crowds, and the most enormous person Una had ever seen stepped forward. He stood at least seven feet tall and was terribly ugly. He so exactly fit the image of a goblin she'd held since childhood that, at first sight of him, she felt all her limbs go atremble. But despite his craggy skin that looked as though it would turn sword blades and arrowheads, his face was welcoming.

He raised a hand and called a greeting to the king. "Fidel of Parumvir," he said, "welcome to the Twelve-Year Market."

Fidel raised an eyebrow and inclined his head, and because he was king he showed no sign of fear if he felt it. "And welcome to Parumvir, stranger," he said. "You make yourself quite free in my lands without so much as a by-your-leave." His voice was not unfriendly, but he spoke as a king not a friend. "What is your name?"

The goblin-man, now near enough for Una to see that he stood taller than the ears of her father's horse, bowed low. He was clothed all in white, with a golden belt and a long knife at his side. "I am Oeric," he said when he straightened, "knight in the service of the Prince of Farthestshore."

"Farthestshore?" Fidel repeated.

It was a name from ancient days, from tales so old they were no longer called history but relegated to legend; and even in legends, these tales were mentioned only as myths believed by heroes of long ago. Yet the name of Farthestshore was deeply imbedded in the earth of Parumvir and all the nations of the Continent. When she heard it spoken, Una caught again that strong scent of the sea that she had smelled as she rode down the King's Way. It came to her in a rush, overpowering the thousands of foreign spices and perfumes that misted the air of the market.

Odd, for she had grown up just a few miles from Sondhold Harbor, where tall ships sailed to and from far-off countries, and she had grown so used to the smell of the ocean that she no longer noticed it. But she caught it now, that whiff of wildness and salt and sun and storms, and she wondered how she could ever bear to sit long hours over textbooks or tapestry when that smell beckoned so?

Her father's voice brought her back to the present. "Has the Prince of Farthestshore placed you in charge of this bazaar?"

Sir Oeric answered, "The Prince himself has led us here. Many would not have dared come otherwise. He is near at hand, and you shall meet him anon."

"And in the meanwhile, you and your folk make yourselves at home upon my lawn?"

Sir Oeric bowed again. "It is an ancient and time-honored tradition, Your Majesty, that the people of the Far World visit the Near every twelve years so that we do not too soon forget one another. This very lawn has been kept clear and clean for that purpose. We apologize if we disturb you, but we of the Far World do not so swiftly forget agreements."

Fidel considered this a moment, his face quiet so that Una could not read it. "You're rather late, don't you think?" he said at last. "You have not come to Parumvir in the time of my father or that of his father. If I am not mistaken, it has been two hundred years at least since a Twelve-Year Market was recorded."

"But only twelve years as my folk count it."

"Then your years are much longer than ours."

"Shorter too, Your Majesty. And also wider and narrower, if you will." Sir Oeric smiled, and Una glimpsed sharp fangs. "Time is rather friendlier with the people of Faerie." Then his smile vanished, and his moon-wide eyes were serious. "We bring goodwill, Your Majesty, and wares to delight your kingdom. The Prince himself will assure you of this when you meet him. I know he wishes only to please you with our presence."

"I am eager to meet him."

"Until that time, Your Majesty, would your children like to explore the market?"

Fidel looked at Una and Felix. The prince was already scrambling from his horse, and Una was no less excited. "Very well—" he said, and the two were off like a shot.

All fear overwhelmed by curiosity, Una followed her brother deep into the gathered throng. The people of Sondhold were at first too enchanted with the strangeness surrounding them to take notice, but by and by they recognized the faces of their prince and princess and edged away so that Una and Felix had a circle of distance around them everywhere they went. As she trailed behind her lanky younger brother, inspecting the wares presented before her eyes, Una could not believe that only a short hour before she had been locked away in that den of a schoolroom. The world had taken on a sudden romance and adventure, and anything was possible.

A woman with feathers in her hair—whether she had put them there or they grew right from her head, Una could not guess—beckoned her near to look at fine cloth. "Woven from all the scents of summer," she whispered in a voice like wind-stirred trees. Una reached out to touch it, but the woman snatched it back. "For a price," she said. "Only for a price."

"The lady is not interested in such nonsense as yours!" said the vendor of the next stall over. He was a dwarf with a red face and slanting eyes that disappeared behind the folds of the most enormous grin Una had ever seen. "Step this way, damsel fair. Step this way and see what Malgril has to offer!"

She obeyed, and he pulled back a cloth to reveal silver statues of intricate work—little animals set with jewels for eyes. "Lovely," she said.

"But wait," said the dwarf. "Watch closely."

She smiled and looked again. The animal statues were of the most exquisite workmanship, the bodies engraved all over with delicate scrollwork. They were of creatures she did not know or beings she recognized only from stories: a cat with a woman's head, a snake with wings, a centaur, and a gryphon.

She blinked. Then she gasped.

The little figures had moved. Or had she imagined it? She blinked again, and sure enough, the woman-cat's tail twitched, the gryphon's mouth opened, the centaur turned his head.

"The scrollwork," said the dwarf, "was wrought by my brother, the great Julnril himself. These are powerful charms, like those of the ancient golems. Do they please your ladyship? Would she hold one in her hand?" The dwarf picked up the winged snake and held it out to her, but when Una looked at it, blinking fast, it seemed to writhe in his fingers. She stepped back, smiling again but shaking her head.

Felix's voice caught her attention. "Are you sure these are my size?"

"Standard size, my lord," someone replied, and Una turned to see Felix sitting before a cobbler's bench, shoving his foot into a boot made of old leather. It was a tough fit, and Felix made faces in his efforts to pull it on. The cobbler, rubbing his hands together, nodded and smiled and spoke encouragingly. With a final tug, Felix's heel slid into place, and the prince stood up. "And these are seven-league boots, are they? They kind of pinch—"

"Don't stamp your feet!" the cobbler cried, but too late.

Una yelped. Her brother had vanished.

Immediately the cobbler began ringing a bell and shouting at the top of his lungs, "Thief! Thief! Stop, thief!"

The next instant, huge Sir Oeric appeared, shaking a fist at the cobbler. "You shouldn't insist your customers try them on if you don't want them to run off!"

"He must pay! He must pay!" the cobbler insisted.

"Give me a pair, and I'll fetch him back."

"But, sir—"

"At once!"

King Fidel was there by now with the guardsmen, along with a great hustle of people, all shouting. "Which way did he go?" "He'll be halfway to the Red Desert by now!" "You certain he didn't step toward the sea?" "Fool boy, won't know enough to turn around and come back!"

"I'll get him for you, Your Majesty," Sir Oeric declared, pulling on another pair of the cobbler's special boots. Amazingly, they seemed to grow to fit his enormous feet. The next moment he vanished as well, and the yells of the market-goers doubled. The cobbler, grinning from ear to ear, was suddenly blessed with the best business he'd managed that day.

Una watched it all, laughing to herself and feeling a bit jealous of the fun Felix was having. She turned back to the silver statues but found herself instead looking into a pair of huge white eyes in a face like gray stone.

"My lady, would you have your fortune told?"

The man before her was the ugliest she had ever seen, uglier even than massive Sir Oeric. He was small, smaller still because he huddled into himself, and when he smiled he also displayed rows of sharp fangs. But then again—and here she frowned, for surely her eyes were lying to her one way or the other—he was also beautiful. Like the silver statues that moved only when she blinked, so this shrunken man seemed to change his face for hairbreadth moments, as though a veil wafted over his features and then away again. In those moments, he was beautiful.

He bowed to her. He was dressed in red robes, his head covered with a golden cap edged in intricate embroidery. With a sweep of a long sleeve, he indicated a tent, also red and worked with gold. Glittering beads hung over the opening, and all was dark inside.

"My lady," he said, "you are newly come of age; I read it in your eyes. Are you not curious to know what fates await you this day, this week, this month and year? Catch a glimpse perhaps of your future lover; see the smiles of your children? Torkom of Arpiar is no charlatan. Torkom of Arpiar knows the secrets, and he will tell you."

The ugliness faded more and more as he spoke, and his face grew ever more trustworthy. After all, had not Sir Oeric declared that the people of the market brought only goodwill? If she was going to trust him, a goblin, why should she not trust this beautiful being?

She followed him into the tent. The beads shimmered like so many stars as the tall man held them back, and she stepped into a room full of warm, rosy light. Curtains of gauzy fabric, embroidered and beaded, hung suspended from the center bar, and she had to push them aside as she stepped deeper and deeper into the tent. It was bigger inside than she could have guessed from looking at the outside; curiously it seemed to grow as she went. But the rose-colored light was beautiful, and the smell all around was too sweet for her to feel afraid.

At last Una pulled back a final drape, which felt like fine milkweed to her fingers, and found a low cushioned stool and a wooden box so dark that it looked black.

The fortune-teller appeared beside her and, taking her hand, gently led her to the stool. "Sit, lady, sit," he said. "Torkom will tell you your secrets. Trust him to know. Trust him to tell."

She trusted him. The sweet smell made it impossible not to. The perfume of the roses intoxicated her, though she did not recognize the scent. She allowed the man to seat her upon the cushioned stool. For a moment he remained bowed over her, holding her hand so close to his face she thought he might kiss it. But instead his large eyes inspected the ring on her finger.

"Such a lovely piece," he said. "Opals, yes?"

Breathing in roses, Una nodded. "My mother gave it to me. Before she died. I wear it always."

"Ah!" Torkom's smile grew. "Such a gift. A gift of the heart. Not one to part with too soon."

"I wear it always," Una repeated and drew her hand from his grasp. She put both her hands in her lap, covering her ring.

Torkom bowed himself away and knelt to open the dark wooden box.

Fascinated, Una watched him put his hands inside and lift out a strange object. At first she thought it was a shield, for it was the right size and shape, wide at the top and narrowed to a point at the bottom. But it was subtly concave, and the outside was black and rough, a natural roughness like rock. The inside, however, gleamed gold, and the air shimmered around it as if with heat.

Torkom, his teeth showing in what was almost a smile but might have been a grimace of pain, held the strange object out to Una. "Lady," he said, his voice hissing. "Lady, if you dare, behold your future. Look inside." He held the black shield out to her, and Una leaned forward.

Hot air rising from the golden surface hit her face. Inside she saw her own reflection, wincing but curious. Nothing more.

"Take it," Torkom whispered. She could not see him through the haze of heat and the glare of gold, but his voice worked like magic in her ear. "Take it, lady."

She put out her hands and took hold of the shield.

Heat seared up her fingers, through her arms, and wrapped about her head like a fiery vine. She gasped but could not take her eyes from the bright surface, which writhed suddenly like melted gold.

A face took shape. Black eyes ringed with flames, bone-white skin, and teeth like a snake's fangs. It looked at her, and she could not tear away her gaze. A voice flared in her mind, speaking not in words but in a language of heat and smoke that burned in her mind:

Beloved of my enemy! I played for you, didn't I? I played for you and won! Are you not the one I seek?

Una could not answer, could not break his gaze. The heat from the golden shield was like strong arms pulling her down, drawing her face closer and closer, and the fiery words rolled about her, a thunderstorm.

Where are you? Where are you?

Then another voice spoke.

"Stop!"

2

Hands grabbed Una's shoulders and pulled her to her feet, and the heat fell away from her like a shriveled cocoon. She dropped the shield; the vision shattered. Weakness filled her body, and she would have fallen, but strong arms held her up. She blinked several times before her vision cleared and she found herself looking up into the pale face of a strange man.

He was glaring fiercely, but not at her.

"How dare you?" His voice was quiet, but it rang in her head with both menace and authority.

Una stepped back, uncertain of her feet. The stranger seemed unwilling to let her go, but she pushed his hands away. Her fingers burned in searing lines where she had touched the shield. She turned and saw the fortune-teller, ugly as sin, rubbing his hands together and smiling obsequiously.

"*Eshkhan!*" The way the man said the word, Una wondered if it was a curse. "*Eshkhan,* I do but sell my wares."

"How dare you?" the stranger repeated. "You turn my market into a devil's carnival."

"I do but sell my wares!" Torkom repeated. "I asked, and the lady agreed to glimpse her future."

The stranger said nothing but turned to Una. He was young, she realized, though older than she, and his earnest eyes frightened her. She drew back from him.

"Lady," he said, "come away, please. Touch nothing more in this den."

Her hands tingled. "I . . . I don't see what business it is of yours, sir." She spoke more sharply than she meant to, but the words spilled out like fire from her tongue. "How I deal with this gentleman is my own affair."

The stranger put out a hand to her. "Come away, lady," he said. "Come out of this place."

She stared at him without seeing him. Her mind desperately tried to recall the vision she had just witnessed: the voice, the face. But it was gone like a dream, leaving behind only the heat. She tried to speak but could find no words, so she swept past the stranger, parting curtains with her arms, stepping into the labyrinth of embroidered drapes. Immediately she was lost, uncertain where to find the entrance, uncertain how to return.

Someone grabbed her arm. She looked and saw Torkom's gray claws.

"My lady must pay," he said. "My lady must pay for the vision." He lifted her hand toward his face, licking his lips as he drew her fingers toward his mouth. Her ring gleamed in the rose-colored light, reflecting back into his white eyes. "Worth so much," the fortune-teller said. "Worth so great a price—"

"Torkom."

The fortune-teller trembled at the stranger's voice and dropped Una's hand. "Courtesy of Arpiar," he muttered. "First vision is free."

The stranger stood beside Una once more, a hand under her elbow. "If you dare lure another into your lair, Torkom, I will personally see you returned to Arpiar. And this time you will not leave it. You have my word. Now, pack up and get you from this market."

The ugly man bowed deeply, closing his great eyes, and once more muttered, *"Eshkhan."* The next moment he was gone, and Una found that she stood just inside the beaded entrance.

The stranger lifted the beads and allowed her to step out ahead of him. The sun was garishly bright after the rose glow of the tent, and Una put up a hand to shield her eyes. She drew a great breath, missing the scent of roses, and turned to the stranger, who emerged just behind her. In natural light, he seemed even paler, though his eyes were dark. His features were neither handsome nor ugly, merely ordinary. In truth, he was the most unnoticeable man Una could recall ever seeing. Though, a reasonable side of her added, she might have seen one without noticing.

He met her gaze. "My lady—"

She held up a hand, once more aware of the burning line across her fingers. "My good man, you are possessed of a singularly impertinent nature that I find most . . . most . . . *Dragon's teeth!*" It was the most unladylike phrase she knew. Nurse would have exploded had she heard it, but Una was pleased to see surprise cross the stranger's face. "You have no right putting your nose into my dealings. Do you have any idea who I am?"

"You are not yourself," he said quietly. "The incense of Arpiar and the vision—"

"My good man!" she interrupted again. "I am Princess Una of Parumvir, and you will speak when you are given permission."

To her irritation, he smiled as though he was trying not to laugh. Then he bowed. "And I am the Prince of Farthestshore."

Of all the curses upon Una's young life, the very worst, she believed, was her tendency to break out in red blotches across her face when flustered or embarrassed. Especially on her nose. This was enough in and of itself to make her believe in Faeries, bad ones, who were neglected on dinner party lists and showed up at christenings full of vengeance and cackling, "She shall burst forth in blotches, brilliant glowing ones, at the least provocation."

Una could feel the blotches developing now, little red flags signaling for all they were worth. "See! See, she's gone and put her foot in her mouth again! Right in, heel and all!"

Without a word she turned and marched back through the market the way she had come.

The crowds had spread out once more, no longer clumping about the cobbler's stall. This probably meant that Felix was safely back, the purloined boots restored to their proper owner, and the attraction dissipated. Una had no eyes now for vendors, no matter how determinedly they shouted, jostled, or cajoled; she made her way back to where her docile gray mare was tied, not far from the old gentleman selling unicorn fry.

Her father and brother were both there—King Fidel giving a shamefaced Felix a scolding while the guards stood a few paces off, pretending not to hear, their heads tilted just enough to seem disinterested yet still able to pick up every word. One of them hid a laugh behind an unconvincing cough.

Sir Oeric, also near, bowed to Una as she approached, but she did not acknowledge him. Instead she walked up to her father, ignoring Felix's scowls, and said, "I'm ready to go home now."

"Una!" Fidel turned to her, relief on his face. "I was beginning to wonder if you'd rushed off seven leagues as well. What am I to do with you two?"

"Take us home," Una said. "I am done with this market. It's a silly place full of silly people."

Fidel was nobody's fool. He gave his daughter a critical once-over. "What have you been up to?"

"Nothing, Father! I—"

"Do not be angry with your daughter, King Fidel," a gentle voice said. "It was I who detained her."

Una closed her eyes and wished that the ground would open and swallow her up. The nature of the universe seemed to be against her, however, and no sudden chasms rifted the turf beneath her feet. Instead she had to listen to her father ask in a stern voice, "And who might you be, sir?"

The stranger bowed. "Forgive me. I am Prince Aethelbald of Farthest-shore."

Prince Felix muttered, "*Aethelbald?* I don't think we can forgive that."

Una shot him a quick glare, silently promising a dire future, but Felix made no effort to hide his mirth.

Thankfully the Prince of Farthestshore did not seem to notice. "I had intended to introduce myself to you first, Your Majesty, but circumstances transpired otherwise. However, let me now humbly express my joy at once more finding myself in your fair kingdom."

Fidel stared. Una could not remember ever seeing her father, whom she imagined had been born a king complete with a beard and a gold crown on his head, at a loss for words. But as he regarded the strange prince, his expression implied that he was mentally considering and discarding any number of responses. At length he settled on "You are lord and master of all these peoples, then?" He indicated the assortment of beings milling about on the market lawn.

"I am their Prince," he responded. "But many here do not call me master."

"Ah."

A pause followed—one of those pauses in which everyone feels the need to insert something profound, but no one can think of anything more profound than "So, yes. Anyway." Una used the pause as an opportunity to sidle closer to her father, though this necessitated turning and facing the Prince of Farthestshore, which was no more comfortable, she found, than standing with him just behind her. She studied the toes of her shoes to avoid looking at him.

"So, yes. Anyway," Felix said, stepping forward and extending a hand to the other prince, who shook it warmly. "I'm Felix, crown prince and all that, heir to the throne, though Una's older. Don't let her fool you. She'll pretend she's all right with the royal succession being what it is, but you get her in the right mood and—"

"Felix!" Fidel and Una said, though in rather different tones. Felix let go of the other prince's hand and backed away, still grinning.

King Fidel stepped forward, determined to once more take charge of the situation. "I bid you welcome to Parumvir, Prince A . . . Apple—"

"Aethelbald."

"Prince Aethelbald. Should you wish to dine at my table this evening, your presence would be well received."

"Indeed," said Prince Aethelbald, "such was my hope. Though I traveled with the market, my first desire was to pay my respects to you, Your Majesty, and most particularly to your daughter."

Una blinked.

Her father said, "Pay your respects?"

"Indeed, Your Majesty."

Fidel cleared his throat. There are many expressive ways a king may clear his throat; this one expressed keen interest. "Just how great would you say your kingdom is?"

"How great can you imagine, King Fidel?"

"Rather great."

"Mine is greater."

"Ah."

Another pause. Una's mind had reached a mental wall several sentences back, and was only just now getting up the speed to vault it. But instead of making a graceful leap, her mind crashed headfirst into the wall, scattering bricks and uttering one long, silent *Nooooooo!*

Because she was a princess, however, her face remained serene.

"Do, please, come to supper this evening, then, Prince Aethelbald," King Fidel said. With these and a few more polite words, king and Prince made what arrangements were necessary. Then Fidel signaled his guard, bade his children mount their horses, and Una found herself riding back up the King's Way in a numb daze.

Felix urged his horse up beside hers. "Applebald!" he whispered.

She took a swipe at him with her riding crop, not caring if the guardsmen thought her common.

"I *so* dislike the name Aethelbald!"

Nurse, busily tying Una's hair into an awesome if precarious tower on top of her head, clucked without sympathy.

A buzz of activity percolated through Oriana Palace as hasty preparations were made to feast the Prince of Farthestshore and his entourage, due to arrive at sundown. The best silver was polished, the chandelier was refitted with new candles, and even the great tapestry in the King's Hall was taken out into the courtyard and beaten until the guardsmen standing at their posts were coughing and filmed over with dust. To crown it all, Princess Una had been stuffed into her best dress, a much-hated creation consisting of three layers of silk, two layers of chiffon, and wire structures beneath that made things stick out in odd but highly fashionable places. Then Nurse had sat Una down before her vanity, and the real work, the task of taming the princess's flyaway hair, had begun.

"I mean it!" Una said, shaking her head so that her hairstyle fell in a long flop down one side of her face. Nurse growled, cracked her knuckles, and firmly twisted her princess's chin straight again. She set to with her brush more vigorously than ever.

"It sounds stodgy," Una said.

"Stodgy, Miss Princess?" Nurse took a pin from between her teeth and rammed it into place with more force than efficiency.

"You know." Una frowned. "Pudgy and flat-footed. Heavy. Hard to digest."

"Mmm-hmm." Nurse plucked another pin from her mouth and took aim. "This Prince Aethel-whatsit. He's stodgy, is he?"

"Ow! Prince Aethelbald is nothing if not stodgy."

"Is he heavy?"

"Well . . . no."

"Flat-footed?"

"Not exactly."

"Hard to digest?"

"Stodginess is as much a state of mind as anything, Nurse."

"I see."

"No, you don't see! Ouch. Are you *trying* to draw blood?" Una sighed as she watched Nurse in the mirror, fixing a twist of fake, honey-colored curl in place so that it dangled, as the Parumvir fashion experts put it, "fetchingly" down the side of her face. "Stodgy princes," she said, "have no sense of romance. They sit around making practical decisions about economics and trade and things."

"Sounds worthy in a man who'll one day rule a kingdom," Nurse said, closing one eye as she inspected her work. Nurse was a practical woman to whom a romantic gesture equated picking up one's own dirty socks and washing one's hands before dinner. And while there was perhaps a certain romance in these, Una failed to appreciate it.

"Stodgy princes," Una said, pulling at the fake curl until it sprang back into place, "wouldn't know the first thing about poetry and next to nothing about music."

"The poor souls." Nurse selected a large white feather from an assortment of accessories, held it up for effect, and then tossed it aside in exchange for a larger purple one.

"They wouldn't recognize moonlight if it hit them between the eyes, and they never notice the stars."

"Blind too, eh?"

Una slumped with her chin resting on her other hand, her eyes crossing to watch a spruff of feather gently wafting down to land on the vanity. Monster sprang into her lap, purring and flicking his tail under her nose. Absently, she ran her knuckles down his head and back. "Stodgy princes don't stand under a lady's window in the dusk of evening and sing songs about her virtues, comparing her beauty to summer days and their love to the high seas."

"I should hope not!" Nurse stuck in a final few pins, twisting them to be certain they held. "A real prince—stodgy, pudgy, or otherwise—wouldn't be caught dead standing under a lady's window after dark!" She sniffed. "And Aethelbald seems as good a name as any to me. Names are just as good as the folks what bear them. I had an Uncle Balbo who was teased like nothing else 'bout his name, yet he was the finest pig-keeper in all the country. Why, he had an old boar that weighed twice as much as I!"

This was quite an accomplishment on Uncle Balbo's part, for Nurse's proportions were impressive. Nevertheless, her words did little to inspire Princess Una's young mind. "Oh, Nurse! You are utterly lacking in romance!"

" 'Nough of that whining, Miss Princess," Nurse said and, with surprising gentleness, patted the top of Una's head. The gentleness was for the hairstyle rather than the girl, but Una tried to appreciate the gesture. "You're as beautiful as Lady Gleamdren herself, and your flat-footed prince won't fail to fall in love the moment he sets eyes on you."

"Meeeaaa!" Monster said.

"Fall in love?" Una wrinkled her nose. The two feathers on either side of her head drooped like the ears of a hound dog. She pulled the fake curl one more time for good measure. "Somehow, I don't think so."

"Now who's lacking romance?"

The sun set, burning red as a dragon's eye before it disappeared behind the horizon and left the world in twilight.

One by one, the vendors on the market lawn packed up their wares. The man with acorn-cap eyes placed lids on his great jars, muffling the songs of the unicorn young, and lifted them onto the rickety cart. With a "He-hey!" to his pig, they rattled across the flattened grass and disappeared into the shadows of the Wood. The woman with feathered hair folded her fabrics and glided away as gently as a leaf on the wind. Jugglers pocketed their balls and knives; dancers wound up their scarves like birds drawing in their wings.

In a long, steady line, they streamed back into Goldstone Wood as quietly as they had come, until all that remained to give testimony to their presence were a few glowing baubles no bigger than marbles, a flower worked in silver that wilted and budded and bloomed again and again as you blinked, and other forgotten trinkets. A faint scent of roses lingered in one corner of the lawn. As the night deepened, even these disappeared, fading into memory as distant as the oldest myths.

But the Prince of Farthestshore, followed by ugly Sir Oeric and two other tall knights, climbed the King's Way to Oriana Palace, and the guards at Westgate trembled as they admitted him to Fidel's household.

3

FIDEL'S DINING HALL was older than the rest of Oriana Palace. It had been built in the days of King Abundiantus V many hundreds of years ago, in the old style with enormous doors opening to the east and to the west. In the middle of the hall, on a dais, stretched the long table of the king.

The king himself sat in a gilded chair, his back to the north wall, upon which hung a fantastic tapestry of a maiden and a unicorn—which, incidentally, looked nothing like the unicorns seen in the market that morning, being rather more of the classical horse-and-horn nature.

Felix, suffering agonies in a collar that stuck out like a peacock's tail behind his head, sat at his father's right hand. Una, hardly any happier, took a place on the other side of Felix, partly because precedent required it, partly because King Fidel expected her to keep her brother on his best behavior, an expectation Una found rather difficult to bear at times.

The elegant chair on the king's left remained unoccupied. Once upon a time, Una's mother had presided over all the great feasts of Parumvir from that place; but that had been years ago now, and the seat had remained empty ever since the queen's death. Una, when she took her place beside her brother—the wires supporting her petticoats creaking dangerously as she arranged them—allowed herself one forlorn hope that perhaps Prince Aethelbald, once he arrived, would be invited to sit on her father's left side. It would, after all, be an honor suited to a prince of so purportedly great a kingdom.

But no, the practical side of her insisted, that would be too much to hope. She was fated, she knew, to have him seated beside her for the entire evening. She eyed the empty place conveniently located on her right with a sigh that gently puffed one of her hair plumes.

"Why the long face?" Felix asked with a smirk. Being stuffed into his best clothing always made him disagreeable, and Una chose to ignore him, expressing through straight shoulders and an icily set jaw an unwilling-ness to talk. But Felix wasn't one to pick up on nonverbal signals. "Any suitor is better than no suitor at all, right?"

"Felix," Fidel said in a warning tone.

The prince slouched into silence and pulled at his collar. Una took a moment to scan the assembly up and down the hall. Lower tables below the upraised one at which she sat were filled with all the various courtiers of Oriana Palace, the visiting nobles of Parumvir, barons and dukes and ladies of high rank, all the dignitaries and ambassadors from other king-doms and provinces, from Milden and Beauclair and Shippening. Every one of them had come to welcome this prince from the Far World.

And every one of them was watching her.

She hated that.

"Pssst!" Felix hissed and nudged her. She turned sharply and regretted it when the tower of her hair swayed threateningly. She put up a hand to steady it and glared at her brother. "What?"

"You want to know something fishy about this lover of yours?"

"No," she said. "He's not my lover."

"You're not curious?"

"Not in the least."

But she was, of course, so Felix went on. "People are saying he's magical and has cast a spell on us all." He looked smug even as he pulled at his collar. "What do you think of that?"

Una frowned, her thoughts darting back to the man who had stood so quietly before her father. Of all the remarkable sights she had seen that day, Prince Aethelbald had surpassed them all simply by virtue of being so remarkably unremarkable. The notion of that soft-spoken gentleman casting spells on anybody was a stretch even Una's limber imagination could not make.

"Don't be daft, Felix," she said, turning up her nose. "I think if there'd been any spell casting done, I would have noticed."

Felix smirked and wiggled his eyebrows. "And that's not all."

Una maintained a cold silence for nearly three seconds before giving in. "All right, what else do you hear?"

The prince leaned closer and lowered his voice to a whisper. "Just look at the way he steps out of nowhere, declares himself a prince, and everyone believes it. He says, 'I'm the Prince of Farthestshore,' and we respond, 'Oh, splendid, come to dinner!' How can we know for sure that he is who he says he is? When have we ever heard from Farthestshore before, beyond nursery stories?"

Una blinked. Felix had a point. Yet not once that afternoon when she had listed to herself all her reasons for disliking Prince Aethelbald—beginning with that name—had she considered the notion he might be untrustworthy. His face, plain as it was, just wasn't a face one could mistrust. But she couldn't explain this to Felix.

"Well," she said, "he did come out of the Wood. And we all of us saw those strange people down on the lawn, and we've never heard of them but from stories either."

"Did we actually see them?"

"Of course we did! What nonsense are you talking?"

"That's just it, Una. Mightn't it all have been an illusion? Something this so-called prince magicked to make us believe his story?" Felix nodded sagely. "I'm telling you, Una, your wooer is an enchanter, and much more dangerous than he looks."

Una rolled her eyes. "Since when were you gifted with all this insight?"

"I've always been the bright one."

"Oh, is that—"

Her retort was cut off by the booming of the east doors opening. At the sound, all the assembly save for the king and his children rose, and a herald's voice intoned: "Aethelbald, son of the High King of Farthestshore, Prince of the Haven Peoples."

Una, despite herself, craned her neck to see the Prince again. Felix's talk, though she insisted to herself that it was all nonsense, excited her. After all, this man *had* come from the Wood, which was known to be enchanted—or at least mysterious, which is almost the same thing—and maybe there was some truth to this notion of his magical quality. If so, he could not help but be suddenly rendered in Una's mind a far more romantic figure, and she wondered if perhaps her first impressions of him had been too hasty.

Three men passed through the doors ahead of the Prince. First was Sir Oeric, resplendent in green and white, but terrible in his bulk and ugliness. Following him was another clad in similar garments, but this man was much smaller, with red-gold hair. Behind him came one whose black skin gleamed almost blue under the chandelier's candles, and his eyes were like the sky on a summer day.

After them came Prince Aethelbald.

"Well," Felix whispered, "maybe not so enchanting."

Una sighed and leaned back in her chair. Perhaps it wasn't the Prince's fault. Following three such splendid men as his knights, he could not help but seem narrow and pale and unprepossessing, despite his elegant clothes. Perhaps in a different context he would appear dashing and exciting and full of inner fire. To Una's eye, however, he was stodginess personified.

But what could one expect of a man named Aethelbald?

The courtiers of Parumvir bounced their gazes back and forth between the Prince and Una. She wished they'd all go cross-eyed and stared down at her plate. From the corner of her eye, she saw Aethelbald approach and bow before the king.

"Greetings, Prince of Farthestshore," Fidel said, extending a gracious hand across the table. "You are welcome in my house. Do, please, bid your knights sit where there are places readied for them. And you yourself must sit at my table. There, beside my daughter."

Una closed her eyes. Yet another faint hope dashed.

"Thank you, Your Majesty," Prince Aethelbald said and nothing more, which did not, Una decided, speak volumes in favor of his imagination. She refused to raise her gaze as he came around and took his place beside her, but instead made a detailed study of her fork.

King Fidel clapped his hands, and musicians began to play while servers scurried about bearing their great silver platters. Una twisted the ring on her finger, sucked in her lips, and felt Prince Aethelbald's gaze on the side of her face for what seemed like ages, though it was probably less than a minute.

At last he said, "I trust that—" just as she began, "I hope your—"

They both stopped, and Una darted a glance his way. He was smiling, which irritated her. "Please continue," he said.

"I . . . I've forgotten what I was going to say." Bother those red blotches! She could feel them creeping forward, but she set her chin, hoping to force them back.

"Then allow me to inquire," said the Prince, "after your hands."

Her hands? The red blotches burst forth in full glory, and no amount of chin setting could drive them back. Was this some awkward form of proposal? Was Nurse right and he'd already fallen in love with her? Despite the feathers?

She glanced at him again, hoping the droop of the purple plume would hide most of her reddening face. "Sir?"

Aethelbald was smiling still, but his eyes were serious. He reached out and touched one of her hands, which was resting just beside her fork. She removed it hastily, wondering how many eagle-eyed ladies of the court had spotted the gesture, and folded both hands tightly in her lap.

"I believed you burned them earlier today," Aethelbald said in an even quieter voice, drawing back his own hand as well.

"Burned?" Una frowned down at her lap. When she said the word, a brief memory shot across her mind's eye, a memory of heat and the scent of roses. But, now that she put her mind to it, she couldn't quite say where that memory had come from. Was it something she'd seen? She opened her hands and looked at them but could discern no trace of a burn. "You are mistaken, sir," she said.

He did not reply, and when she dared raise her eyes to his face once more, he was no longer smiling but earnestly studying her. Heaven help her, this was going to be a long dinner!

Felix, on her other side, had placed his elbow on the table and leaned in to hear their conversation. She forced herself not to pinch him; he knew it and grinned from ear to ear. Desperate to break the silence, she managed a brave, "Are you intending to stay long in Parumvir?"

"A *very* long time," Felix said.

"I wasn't talking to you!"

"Oops."

Aethelbald smiled again, and Una wished she could take both the plumes from her hair, flap them hard, and fly away. But the Prince of Farthestshore only said, "I do not yet know how long I shall enjoy your father's hospitality." He took a sip from his goblet, then, setting it back down, added, "That depends on many things."

Felix snorted. Before Una had a chance to jab her elbow between her brother's ribs, in a voice that carried across the room, he piped up, "What, pray tell, brings you to Parumvir this fine spring, Prince Aethelbald? Did I understand you've come to pay your respects?"

Una's eyes widened. *Felix!* she screamed inside but kept her mouth shut in a tight line.

"To my sister, yes?"

The court murmured. From his place beside Felix, King Fidel cleared his throat meaningfully. But Prince Aethelbald sat a moment, contemplating his goblet. "None here need pretend ignorance of my purpose," he said in his quiet but authoritative voice. "I, for one, am not ashamed to announce it."

The next moment, to Una's horror, right there before the entire assembly, before soup had even been served—which somehow made it more horrible—Prince Aethelbald pushed back his chair and got down on one knee beside her. She found herself staring down into his kind, boring face. She looked away, mouth open, for some sign of help, but all the court of Parumvir was watching with held breath.

"I love you, Princess Una," Aethelbald said. "It would be my honor and my joy if you would consent to be my wife. Will you have me?"

4

"YOU REFUSED HIM?"

"Of course I refused him, Nurse!" Una sat once more before her vanity as Nurse undid her work of the afternoon, pulling curls and feathers from their places and letting Una's hair fall down her back. "How could I do otherwise?"

"Umph," Nurse said.

"What's that supposed to mean?"

"Nothing at all, Miss Princess, nothing at all."

Una turned on her seat to look up at Nurse, who was scowling like a storm cloud. "You think I should have accepted him."

Nurse stepped back, a bristled hairbrush clutched in one hand like a battle standard. "A match like that, and you up and said, 'No, thank you.' " She shook her head, and the brush quivered in her hand. "The Prince of Farthestshore, by all accounts the greatest and richest kingdom ever heard tell of, asks for your hand . . . and you refused him."

Una rose from her stool. A feather still in her hair drifted around to tickle under her nose, and she brushed it aside. "He's saying he loves me when we've hardly even spoken. That doesn't make any sense!"

"It's romantic."

"It's ridiculous."

"Look who's talking."

Una frowned, considering the irony of role reversal. Then she shrugged. "I don't even know him."

"He's prince of a mighty kingdom," Nurse replied, pointing the hairbrush at Una's nose. "And you, my dear, are a princess. What more knowing do you need?"

Una swept away, her dressing gown trailing behind, shedding more feathers as she went. Monster batted at them as they drifted by his nose. "I won't marry him for his rank, and that's that."

"You are a princess. What else do princesses marry for?"

Una flung open her tall window door and stepped out onto the balcony. The spring breeze was cool, biting at her face, but she hardly cared. "I won't marry that man, Nurse." Her chin rose imperiously. "I won't marry him, never, and nothing you can say will convince me otherwise!"

She slammed the door, rattling the glass, and stepped to the rail of her balcony. Her chambers on the third floor of the palace overlooked the gardens, which were edged with the light of a bright crescent moon. She leaned against the rail and took a deep breath, closing her eyes. Standing there in the quiet of the evening, she could almost imagine that she heard the murmur of the sea far below the hill. But when she opened her eyes again, it was not the ocean she saw but the dark expanse of Goldstone Wood, which began at the edge of the moonlit garden and swept its way down the hill and off into acres of impenetrable forest beyond.

"Meeaaa?" said Monster, sitting at her feet.

Una looked down at her cat. "I won't marry him," she whispered. The wind blew in her face, and she turned once more to gaze at the Wood. The dark treetops swayed, rippling the moonlight across their leaves. "It's my choice. And I won't."

Goldstone Wood watched her in silence until at last she gathered up her cat and went back inside. A wood thrush, which long since should have been roosting, threw its voice to the moon.

That night, the room was too hot. Una's coverlet was heavy, and even with her bed-curtains open, the air suffocated.

Una lay in bed, staring up at her embroidered canopy. The embers in the fireplace cast a dull glow. The window curtains were drawn, but a tiny sliver of moon broke through, and by its silver light combined with the bloodred gleam of the embers, she could make out the picture above her.

Her mother had embroidered it soon after Una's birth. She had made it especially for Una, and if only for that reason, Una loved it. Bold threads of gold, which picked up light from the fire, depicted the contours of Lord Lumé surrounded in a glowing aura. He wore robes like those worn by the old singer who sang at all royal christenings and weddings, though those in the embroidery were much grander and fanned out like flames.

Lord Lumé was the sun, and he sang the Melody.

Across from him, picked out in delicate silver threads, was his wife, Lady Hymlumé, the moon, and she sang the Harmony. She wore robes such as Una had never seen anywhere else, and she wondered how her mother had dreamed them up. Una thought she would much rather wear the silver garments of Hymlumé than all the brilliant fashions into which the royal tailors stuffed her.

Many sleepless nights throughout her childhood, Una had studied the faces of Lumé and Hymlumé as worked by her departed mother, and wondered about the songs they sang. The Sphere Songs, as they were called, had once been known in Parumvir, her tutor said. But that was long, long ago, back when people were foolish enough to believe in myths about the sun and his wife, the moon. They were pretty stories to be told and woven into tapestries, but nothing more.

Some nights, however, if the windows were left open wide and she heard the whisper of the Wood and the occasional song of an evening bird, Una could imagine that she heard the strains of a song, the faintest memory of a tune that suns and moons might sing.

Not tonight. Tonight Una stared at the embroidered faces, and her imagination could not dwell on songs or myths. It was too hot.

Monster heaved a heavy sigh. He slept on the pillow by her head, and she felt him twitch in his sleep. Suddenly his head popped up and he started grooming his paws. The movement annoyed her. She shoved him off the bed, counted to ten, and felt him hop back up again. He returned to the pillow, plopped down, and flicked his tail over her nose. She pinched the end of it. He tucked it around his body, and that battle ended for the night.

She stared again at the embroidered faces above her.

It was too hot. Far, far too hot.

She considered getting up to open the window, but her limbs were too tired. Too tired to move, too tired to sleep, Una was slowly roasting to death. Sweat beaded her forehead. Her mother's ring was tight on her hand—so tight she thought perhaps the finger would fall off. Lumé's face gazed down at her, his arms outspread so that the flames of his robe flared about him. He burned her with his unrelenting glare. She wished she could cover him somehow, wished she could escape his heat.

The air shivered with vapors. She saw them moving in the moonlight, and even the moonlight boiled. She closed her eyes and tried to draw a full breath, but could not.

When Una opened her eyes once more to look up at Lumé and his wife, they were gone. The night consumed her vision and pulled her into a dream.

The Lady waits in a colorless world all her own. She sits alone on a misty throne—expecting no one, hoping nothing. Her world is silent but for a soft, subtle sound that she alone hears.

It is the weeping of dreams that are no more.

Long ages pass, and she listens and waits, her patient eyes downcast. Her eyes are the white of emptiness, the white of nothing, and her face is a mask of onyx. No one dares speak her true name.

The rush of wings on the threshold of her world disturbs the silence, drowning the sighs of the weepers. The Lady does not raise her gaze but hears the heavy tread approaching and feels the heat of fire. A smile twists her mouth, the first movement she had made in an age.

"Sister," a burning voice speaks, "I am here to play the game."

"Brother," she replies, "I am glad."

She raises her eyes to meet his, which are as dark as hers are white. He is a dragon, vast and black, but as he approaches her throne he dwindles into the figure of a man. A flame smolders deep within the pupil of each eye.

"It is a woman this time," her brother says.

"Man or woman, I care not which," she replies.

"I want her for my child."

"Did you bring the dice?"

He raises a hand. The skin is leprous pale, stretched thin over black bones, and each finger is tipped with a talon. In his palm he holds two dice, their faces marked with strange devices.

"I want her for my child," he repeats, and smoke licks from his forked tongue. "She is beloved of my Enemy."

"Roll the dice," says the Lady, her eyes not breaking gaze with his.

"I want her, sister."

"Roll the dice."

He clatters them together in his hand, then sets them rolling across the mist-churned floor. Her gaze does not move from his face as he follows the progress of the dice. When at last they are still, she sees the flash of triumph pass over him.

"The game is done," her brother says. "I have won."

"She is yours, then," the Lady replies. "Take her. But 'ware, brother! You've not won yet."

Her brother snarls, revealing sharp teeth blackened by fire. "When I have through, it will not matter whether I win or lose! My Enemy will hurt with a pain that cannot be comforted. The heart of his Beloved will never be his."

The Lady makes no reply to this, but her empty eyes flash one last time, meeting the burning coals of her brother's gaze. "Take her, then, my brother. But touch not those who belong to me."

"I shall honor our game, my sister."

With those words, the Dragon withdraws and becomes once more his true self as he flees the borders of his sister's land.

Una awoke to pain.

Something rough grated the skin of her hands, and she opened her eyes with a start to find Monster grooming her fingers as determinedly as he ever groomed his own paws. She sat up, pulling her hands away. "Dragons eat you, Monster!" she hissed. But she spoke with relief.

The dream was already almost gone from her memory, but the heat remained.

She sat with her hands close to her chest for a long moment, staring down at her cat, who sat with his tongue out, his sightless face upturned to her. Then she looked at her hands.

They were red. A searing burn mark ran across the fingers of both, as though she had grabbed a hot fire iron. Her fingers throbbed. What could she have touched that had burned her so badly?

Though the room was still stuffy, Una found herself able to move. She slid out from under her coverlet and staggered across the room to her washbasin. Grimacing when her seared fingers brushed the cold porcelain, she poured water from the pitcher into the bowl, then plunged both hands in. The cool water helped, but the pain did not go away.

Muttering, she reached up to pull the curtains aside and open the window. A breeze wafted through the chamber, and the moon, now unhindered, poured light onto the floor. Una, bleary-eyed, gazed up at the night sky. On impulse she lifted her hands, dripping water from the basin. The red marks glowed as bright as the brands in her fireplace.

But even as she looked, they faded. As though the moonlight itself were a soothing ointment, the burning cooled, the redness dissipated and then was gone. The pain was a memory, and even that evaporated so that she wondered if she'd dreamed it.

The air on her face pleased her. The world was wet from an earlier spring shower, and the night was chilly, which had motivated Nurse to close the window before retiring. It was too early in spring to leave it open.

Yet the room had felt near to roasting just a few moments before.

Leaving the windows open and resigning herself to a scolding from Nurse in the morning, Una climbed back into bed and pulled the coverlet up to her chin. Monster sniffed her cheek, his whiskers prickling against her skin, and she swatted him away. Then she closed her eyes.

The cat perched on the pillow beside her, silent as a statue, hardly moving save for the occasional twitch at the end of his tail. When at last he was certain she slept, Monster hopped off the bed, padded to the window, and slipped out into the night.

Despite the lateness of the hour, in another wing of the palace, a fire still blazed bright in a marble fireplace. Prince Aethelbald sat before it, his back bent, his elbows resting on his knees, studying the moving flames, or perhaps gazing into the shadows behind them. The room was silent save for the snapping of embers, until a scratching outside his window drew his attention.

"Meea?"

Aethelbald rose from a chair and crossed to the window. The scratching increased, along with a persistent "Meea? Meeeowl?"

Drawing back the curtains and opening the latch, Aethelbald came face-to-face with a pink nose on a whiskered face. The cat slid gracefully into the room, took a seat on the comfortable chair where Aethelbald had just been sitting, and set to work grooming himself. Aethelbald folded his arms, watching the cat and waiting several patient moments before he said, "Yes?"

The cat gave his coat a last lick, then turned his ears to the Prince. "My lord," he said, "she dreams of him."

Aethelbald did not answer. He paced to the fireplace, resting his hand on the mantel as he gazed down into the flames. "Are you certain?" he asked at last.

"I smelled him," the blind cat said. "I smelled death. I smelled burning."

The Prince closed his eyes and nodded.

The cat hopped down from the chair and rubbed around the Prince's ankles, purring and flicking his tail. "Must it be this way, my Prince?"

"Yes."

"He has not found her yet." The cat stopped purring, his nose twitching as he considered his words. At length he said, "I've become fond of the girl. I'd hate to see her . . ."

"No," said the Prince quietly.

The cat lashed his tail once, then stalked a few paces away, keeping his ears trained back on Aethelbald. "I know," he said. "I know you love her more than I could. I just wish . . . I wish I understood."

"I will do everything I can for her," Aethelbald said. "Everything." He looked at the cat, his eyes full of compassion.

The cat felt the expression that he could not see and relaxed under the Prince's gaze, purring once more. "Do you know what has brought on these nightmares?" he asked.

"Torkom was selling visions in the market today."

"That old goblin?" The cat bristled. "What's he doing so far from home?"

"The usual mischief." Aethelbald's face became hard. "She touched a dragon scale."

"Torkom dared sell . . ." His lip curled back in a snarl. "Dragon-kissed fiend!"

Aethelbald turned back to the fireplace. The flames danced and played across his vision, writhing hungrily over the logs. The light shone off his cheekbones and brow but cast his eyes in shadows. "The fire stirs already, Sir Eanrin," he said in a low voice. "Soon it will wake."

He closed his eyes and made a quick motion with his hand. "Please return to the princess. Guard her dreams as best you can."

The cat bowed after the manner of his kind, haughty and respectful at once. Then he whirled and leapt out the window, swallowed by moonlight and darkness.

5

Felix disliked few things in life more than sparring by himself in the practice yard. But his father's guard never found time to practice with him, and his own attendants were hopelessly inept with a sword, or at least pretended to be whenever they sparred with their prince. Therefore, bright and early in the morning, Felix made his way alone to the barracks yard, his wooden practice sword strapped to his side, and began the basic stretching exercises.

He did not need to come here to practice, of course. Oriana Palace furnished a room where noblemen and their sons could study the arts of fencing and swordplay. But Felix did not feel that it was authentic to learn weaponry surrounded by gold-framed mirrors and stepping on a polished wooden floor. He visited that room only to take lessons with his fencing master, a tight-faced old man who emphasized in a reedy voice that fencing was an *art*.

"What good will *art* do me on the battlefield?" Felix had once demanded.

The fencing master refused to answer. His mouth had squeezed into a severe wrinkled line across his face as he slapped the prince on the wrist with the flat of his sword and told him to assume first position.

Felix never practiced in that room unless absolutely necessary. Much better the dirt and grit of the guards' practice yard, where real men pitted their skills against those of their peers and learned what it meant to prepare for war and battle and glory and honor. None of which had anything to do with *art*.

But the guards refused to spar with him. Felix suspected that they laughed at him behind his back when he practiced by himself against one of the wooden dummies suspended on poles at intervals across the practice yard.

Felix flexed his fingers and stretched his arms and legs, a scowl souring his face. He'd quarreled with his senior attendant before venturing out to the yard that morning, for the man had once more tried to insist that he should go to the noblemen's room and practice with one of the barons' sons or some such nincompoop. Felix had stood his ground, but on his way down to the yard he had been obliged to listen to whispers among his three attendants trailing behind him, and he suspected they were discussing his swordsmanship in unflattering terms.

Felix glared at the dummy before him, drew his wooden sword, and assumed first position before it, saluting first as he'd been trained. A snort of laughter exploded behind him somewhere, and he turned to glower over his shoulder, but none of the off-duty guardsmen in the yard were looking his way. No others were practicing at that moment, though a few men stretched their muscles near the fringes of the yard. Felix faced his inanimate opponent once more, raised his sword, and lunged. The dummy swung around on its pole, its own wooden sword flailing uselessly through the air. Felix jumped away, carrying his leading foot back behind his rear foot and touching on the balls of his feet. He executed the maneuver perfectly, he thought, and wondered if any of his father's guard would notice.

His attendants, clustered by the small north entrance of the palace, whispered among themselves and refused to look his way. The boy's scowl deepened until it threatened to form permanent creases across his face. He assumed first position again and advanced, carrying the leading foot forward, toe pointed, setting it down heel first and bringing the rear foot up beside it—planting it ball first, as his master taught him. He lunged again and struck the dummy in the shoulder.

It rocked about, its blank face spinning balefully before him, and Felix suddenly wanted very badly to whack it a few times over the head. His grip tightened on his sword, and he had to force himself to back away and assume first position again rather than take out his frustration on the inoffensive dummy. He wished one of his attendants swung on that pole.

"Bad form."

Felix jumped and spun to his right. Prince Aethelbald stood a few yards away, his arms crossed over his chest. "What's that?" Felix asked, frowning at him.

"You presented your exposed back to your opponent," Aethelbald said. He shook his head, his eyebrows quirked reprovingly. "You are, by all rights, dead. That was no retreat."

Felix rolled his eyes, swinging his sword through the air as he shrugged. "It's a dummy."

"It's your opponent."

"I highly doubt he's going to take a poke at me." Felix turned from Aethelbald back to his dummy and lunged again. He knocked it squarely in the stomach, and it spun in a complete circle. It was a satisfactory hit, and Felix felt better for it. But when he glanced Aethelbald's way, the Prince of Farthestshore was still eyeing him critically. "What?" the boy demanded.

"He would have disarmed you."

"What?"

Aethelbald nodded to the dummy. "Were he alive, he would have disarmed you."

Felix sneered at him. "Everyone's a critic."

"Yes," Aethelbald said, "but no one else, I gather, has bothered to voice his criticism."

Both Felix and Aethelbald looked around the practice yard, and once more Felix had the sense that everyone had been watching him but had just in that instant turned away and now pretended otherwise. He glanced toward his attendants, who yawned and leaned against the wall, dozing like so many cows in a pasture.

Felix turned back to Aethelbald and shrugged. "I've been trained," he said. "And by the best fencing master in the kingdom, I'll have you know."

"Not a soldier, I would venture," Aethelbald said with a smile.

"Common soldiers don't train princes."

"Common soldiers would advise you not to drop your guard. Unless you wish to be skewered, of course."

Felix huffed, exasperated, and indicated the dummy with his wooden sword. "It's not alive. It's not going to skewer me."

"Which is why you should practice with someone who might." Aethelbald uncrossed his arms, and Felix saw that he held a wooden practice sword in one hand. He stepped forward and stood beside the dummy, his arms limp at his sides, no more lithe and mobile than a dummy himself. But his eyes twinkled. "I can see by your face, Prince Felix, that you're itching to hit me a good one."

Felix eyed him up and down, his eyes half closed. "You say *my* form is bad. Look to your own!"

Aethelbald shrugged but otherwise stood still. "Hit me," he said.

Felix adjusted his grip on his wooden sword. "Will you salute first?"

Aethelbald smiled again. "I'm a dummy, Prince Felix. Has a dummy ever saluted you?"

Gritting his teeth, Felix assumed first position. He executed his attack with precision—his feet placed dead on, his arms extended in opposite directions, the point of his sword perfectly parallel to the ground. He was quick as a dart flying toward its mark, and even his fencing master should have been proud.

But an instant later he found himself stumbling forward empty-handed, his arms spinning to catch his balance, and Prince Aethelbald stood behind him, motionless save for his sword arm, which slowly dropped back into place at his side. Felix whirled around and immediately shot glances across the yard. None of the guards looked his way, but who could say how many had watched the engagement? He turned on Aethelbald, trying to mask his anger. "How—"

"Where is your sword?" Aethelbald asked.

Felix cast about for it and saw it had landed a good three yards away. He ran to fetch it, but Aethelbald called out, "You're exposed again, prince."

Felix swept up his sword and stood with it before him, point at the ready. "I was getting my weapon!" he snarled.

"Do you think your opponent will always give you that opportunity?" Once more the Prince of Farthestshore stood like a wooden doll, his feet rooted to the gravel. "Hit me."

Felix went on guard, his arms extended in a straight line in opposite directions, and lunged again. It was perfect, an artistic movement like a dancer's performance on stage. Yet at the end of it, he stood disarmed once more, glaring in unconcealed fury.

"Your weapon?" Aethelbald said.

Felix retrieved it and lunged again. A third time he was disarmed. He grabbed up his sword, attacked, and lost. Glaring daggers Aethelbald's way, he shouted, "You don't fence by the rules, sir!"

"Neither will your enemy," Aethelbald replied.

Felix took in the man's horrible form. Aethelbald's stance screamed inexperience, yet Felix noticed suddenly something in his posture that hinted otherwise. Though Aethelbald stood like a wooden block, his knees were ever so slightly bent, and something in the set of his shoulders implied strength and quickness. One might not notice such details if one had not experienced, in four successive encounters, being disarmed by a single stroke.

Felix lunged again and was once more disarmed, but this time he snatched up his sword in an instant and attacked without preamble, forcing Aethelbald to move out of his wooden stance and actually engage him. But at the end of the engagement, Felix stood empty-handed.

"What are you doing?" he cried, but now his voice held less anger and more curiosity. "You're doing something I haven't seen. What is it?"

Aethelbald smiled, but though Felix looked for it, he detected no smug amusement, only pleasure. "I'll teach you. Fetch your weapon. Watch your back, prince!" He slapped Felix lightly across the shoulders as he retreated. Felix rolled his eyes and groaned but took up his weapon again and whirled into a defensive stance.

"Teach me," he said.

That morning Una woke freezing. Nurse scolded her, saying it was her own fault for letting in all that unhealthy fresh air when sensible people would have left the windows shut. Monster refused to leave his nest beneath the covers at the foot of the bed, obliging the maid to make the bed around him. Una wished she could join the cat there, keeping the quilts pulled tight over her head all day. She was cranky and ill-rested. Vague impressions of dreams haunted her, but she could remember nothing specific.

It was all Prince Aethelbald's fault, she was sure. She hoped he burned his tongue on his morning porridge.

No lessons were scheduled for that day due to Prince Aethelbald's visit. Una planned to while away her time in the gardens, penning odd thoughts in her journal as she thought them. But following a private breakfast and before Una could make an escape to the gardens, Nurse caught her and made her sit down to her tapestry stitching.

"It'll steady your nerves," Nurse said.

"I'll impale myself." Una's skill with a needle was feeble at best and worsened by her strong dislike of the pastime.

"Nonsense," Nurse replied. Against this argument there could be no rebuttal, so Una took her place at one end of the large tapestry—which depicted a gory scene from the epic poem *The Bane of Corrilond*—and Nurse settled at the other end.

A stony silence followed, for they had not yet forgiven each other for yesterday's argument. With nothing but tedious stitching to occupy her, Una could find no relief for her mind, which skittered back every chance it got to revisit that awful scene at dinner the night before.

I did the best I could, she told herself over and over. *I handled the situation with the most grace possible. What else could I have done?*

Clear as a bell, she heard Felix's snorting laugh while the rest of the court had exploded in a flurry of whispers, all drumming her ears at once.

Una shook her head, trying to drive out the memory, but she could still see Prince Aethelbald's face as he'd knelt before her with such hopeful uncertainty in his eyes.

What else could I have done? she asked herself again, poking violently at her tapestry. She stitched a troop of soldiers and townspeople fleeing the fire of a monstrous red dragon, which Nurse was busy working in the opposite corner. Una's people looked more like beans stacked on top of each other, with twig arms and legs sticking out on all sides. She stabbed a bean man through the heart with her needle.

She had babbled. In front of everyone, absolutely everyone, she had babbled! All the dukes, all the counts, all the ambassadors had listened to her stammer, "Um, yes . . . well, I mean, I'm sorry."

With those words she'd had the good sense, thank heaven, to close her mouth, take a deep breath, and try again.

"Thank you, Prince Applebal—Aethelbald." She had spoken slowly, getting the words out as neatly as possible. "I cannot accept your . . . your kind offer at this time."

Una winced at the memory.

Aethelbald had risen from his knees, his face unreadable, and bowed again. "Thank you, Princess Una," he had said. "I hope we shall come to know each other better. Perhaps you will think more kindly of my offer in the future." With that, he had pulled his chair back up to the table and sipped his wine.

That dinner would go down in history as the longest of all time.

Una huffed through her teeth and yanked at a knot in her thread, which refused to pull through the fabric. She glanced up at Nurse, who was pointedly ignoring her.

"I give up!" Una threw aside her work and marched through the room to her adjacent bedchamber, calling for a maid as she went. "Bring plenty of hot water!"

Nurse sat up and lowered her own work. "Where do you think you're going, Miss Princess?"

"I'm going to give Monster a bath." Una flung back the coverlet of her bed, exposing her snoozing pet, and before he had finished yawning, grabbed him by the scruff.

If anything could distract her mind, bathing her cat would.

Aethelbald and Felix stood side by side, Aethelbald demonstrating and Felix copying his motions. The steps were more complicated than any he had before attempted, yet as Aethelbald explained, Felix saw the underlying simplicity. At last, after many attempts, he understood; yet even so could not get his muscles to do what he told them.

"In a true engagement," Aethelbald said, "there is no room for artistry. No posing, no choreography. There is attack and defense, and you must be prepared at each moment for either or both."

Yet Felix watched in awe when the Prince of Farthestshore once more demonstrated the complicated steps that allowed him to transform instantly from wooden statue to breath of wind, avoiding Felix's lunge and disarming him at the same time. If that wasn't art, Felix couldn't guess what was. Again, the boy stood beside Aethelbald and mimicked his motions.

The sun slowly rose in the sky, and soon sweat dropped down every inch of Felix's body. Yet he went on. Aethelbald took the offensive and lunged, and Felix attempted to put into play what he'd been taught. Time and again he failed and found himself disarmed and sputtering. But at last his motions were right, his timing correct, and he watched in triumph as Aethelbald's sword flew through the air. He whooped and raised his sword above his head, twirling it to the sky. The next moment he was flat on his back, the Prince of Farthestshore kneeling on his chest and the wind completely knocked out of him.

"Even disarmed, your enemy is dangerous," Aethelbald said. "Remember, Felix." He stood and helped the boy up. "You have earned a rest, my friend. Come."

Felix was flushed and exhausted as he followed Prince Aethelbald to the barracks. He realized suddenly that they had an audience. A lineup of guards stood along the fringes, whispering among themselves and pointing like so many gossiping ladies. Felix blushed, thinking what a fool he must have looked, but Aethelbald slapped him on the shoulder. "They're impressed," he said.

"With you, perhaps," the boy replied.

"With you, Prince Felix. They've not seen such a soldierly performance from you before, I would wager."

Aethelbald led him to a bench against the outside wall of the barracks, and the two of them sat and stretched their feet out before them. Every muscle in Felix's back and shoulders throbbed, but it felt good—in a painful sort of way. He closed his eyes and let his breath out in a puff. "Is that how they teach swordplay in Farthestshore?"

Aethelbald chuckled quietly beside him. "You could say that."

Felix opened one eye and squinted up at the other prince. "Do your knights all fight like that?"

Aethelbald leaned his head back against the wall. "My knights bring individual skills and fighting styles from their own countries."

"Your knights aren't from Farthestshore?"

"They are the Knights of Farthestshore. But their homelands are many and varied."

Felix pondered this a moment, thinking of the three strange men who had accompanied this unprepossessing prince into the palace dining hall the night before. "Where is Sir Oeric from?" he asked, remembering the enormous knight with the saucer eyes and rocklike hide who had greeted his father at the market.

"You wouldn't believe me if I told you."

"Yes, I would."

"No, you wouldn't."

"Try me!"

Aethelbald smiled sideways at the young prince. "Sir Oeric hails from the realm of King Vahe of the Veiled People, the far land of Arpiar."

Felix frowned. "You're teasing me," he growled. "Arpiar isn't a real place. It's a story. Arpiar is where goblins are . . ." He paused as his brain caught up with his words. "Is Sir Oeric a goblin?"

"No."

"But stories say Arpiar is the realm of goblins. If anyone ever looked like a goblin—"

"And yet, Oeric is no goblin."

Felix sank into silence, pondering several thoughts as they spun through his head. A minute or two passed, and he became aware suddenly of voices just around the corner of the building against which he and Aethelbald leaned.

"Stranger than I like," the first voice said. "I'm not in favor of mysteries; I won't deny it."

"Who are these people?" another voice asked. "They come from the Wood without a by-your-leave and take up residence in our king's home. . . . How are we to know they're trustworthy?"

"They're not our kind," the first said.

"That they aren't."

"My grandmother told me," the first voice went on. "She said, 'Nothing good comes from the Wood.' "

"And we all know the fount of wisdom your grandmother was."

"Well, I trust the old biddy!"

The next moment two guards came around the corner. They stopped when they saw Felix and Aethelbald. Aethelbald remained where he sat with his eyes closed and his head back, looking soundly asleep. But Felix saw the guards exchange worried glances, then scurry past without even a bow for their prince.

Felix nudged Aethelbald with his elbow. "They don't like you."

Aethelbald grunted.

"Where are you from, Prince Aethelbald?"

"From the Wood, they're saying," Aethelbald replied.

"But where are you *really* from? You say you're the Prince of Farthestshore, but is Farthestshore a real place?"

"Just as real as Arpiar."

"That helps a lot!"

Aethelbald yawned suddenly and stretched his arms over his head. "People fear the unknown, Prince Felix. They fear what they cannot understand."

"They fear you," Felix said. "You and your knights."

"Just so."

Felix crossed his arms. "I'm not afraid of you."

Aethelbald raised an eyebrow, looking down at him again. "Perhaps you should be." He got to his feet. "Come. Let's see if your muscles remember what you've been trying to teach them this morning."

Felix groaned but got up and followed the Prince of Farthestshore into the middle of the yard. He drew his sword and swung his arms to loosen up his shoulders. But before he took position, he said, "You really intend to marry my sister, Prince Aethelbald?"

Aethelbald swung his sword arm in an arc, then did the same with the other. "I hope to."

"She won't have you," Felix said.

"Perhaps not."

"She doesn't like you."

Aethelbald smiled wryly and took up his wooden sword. "I'd gathered as much last night."

"She won't change her mind."

"Perhaps not."

"No, I know my sister." Felix emphasized his words with a jab of his sword. "She doesn't like you, and she won't change. She's stubborn as anything."

"But I am steadfast," Aethelbald replied. "We'll see who prevails in the end."

Felix snorted. "I'll put my money on Una."

"As any loyal brother should. On your guard, Prince Felix!"

Felix hardly had a moment to react before his sword was knocked from his hand and sailed across the yard. Yelping in surprise, he scampered after it and had just enough time to swipe it up and place it between himself and Aethelbald before the Prince lunged for him. He parried weakly, and the next moment Aethelbald's sword swung around and froze a fraction of an inch from his neck.

Felix's breath caught in his throat, and his eyes locked with those of the other prince. Aethelbald's gaze was unreadable, and his eyes seemed to look not at Felix but inside him. They penetrated deeply, behind whatever masks he wore, down into his soul.

Felix looked away.

"You should have tried the maneuver I taught you," Aethelbald said. "In combat it would have saved your life. Again, Felix."

This time when Aethelbald lunged, Felix's feet seemed to move on their own, performing the steps he'd been practicing all morning. His reaction was imperfect, but it was good enough, and he knocked Aethelbald's sword from his hand. No whoop of victory escaped his lips this time. His sword whipped through the air, and its point rested just before Aethelbald's heart. They stood like statues for a long moment.

"Good," Aethelbald said at last.

Clattering hooves drew their attention. Both turned to look toward Westgate across the yard. A troop of horsemen stood just outside the gate, all astride sorrel horses but for their leader, who rode a black charger taller and more powerful than the rest. The leader exchanged a few words with the captain at the gate, and a moment later he and his men were waved inside. They were at least twenty strong.

"I know who that is." Felix wiped sweat from his brow as he watched the horsemen enter the courtyard and dismount. "Word arrived a few days ago of their coming. That's the emblem of Beauclair on their cloaks, and their livery is of the royal house." He turned to Aethelbald, a wicked grin spreading across his face, and waved his sword at him. "I think you have a little competition now. That's Gervais, Crown Prince of Beauclair."

Aethelbald said nothing but watched as stableboys came out to take the horses, and as the palace steward appeared at the great front door to greet the newcomers. The tall leader, whose cloak was blue and shot with silver threads, did not return the steward's bow but allowed himself to be escorted inside.

Aethelbald quietly stepped over to pick up his sword. Then he turned to Felix. "On guard, friend."

"What? No!" Felix watched his own sword spin through the air once more.

6

A CERTAIN AMOUNT OF WHISPERING and Nurse's exclamation of "What?" in the nearby hall were not enough to distract Una's attention from the work at hand. She knelt beside a basin brimful of sudsy bubbles, holding Monster in a death grip by the back of the neck with one hand, wielding a scrub brush with the other, which was difficult to manage while wearing heavy leather gauntlets. Her tongue poked into her cheek in concentration. Monster's caterwauls had diminished into low, seditious growls that boded ill for the future. She scrubbed for her life while she had a chance.

"Princess!"

"Oi, wait! Bad kitty, no—"

Una screamed, lost her hold, and watched her flailing cat escape her erstwhile paralyzing grasp. Monster's claws found several exposed places, including the tip of Una's nose, and the next moment he disappeared under the bed, leaving a trail of bubbles behind. Una sat back on the floor with a thump, wiped blood from the end of her nose, and fixed an irritable eye on Nurse. "If you don't—"

"Get yourself up off that floor, girl!" Nurse cried, her hands flying in flustered gestures. "What in the moon's name do you think you're doing?"

"I was bathing my cat, just like I told you," the princess said coldly, watching her nurse dart across the room to the wardrobe, yank the door open, and start rummaging. "I can't remember the last time Monster had a— What are *you* doing? Why are you . . . Oh, Nurse, no!"

Nurse pulled the much-hated best dress from the closet and flung it across Una's bed, then returned to the closet to dig out a pair of awful pinching shoes.

Una clambered to her feet, putting her arm in the basin of water up to her elbow in her haste. The gauntlet filled with dirty bubbles. "I'm not wearing that dress, Nurse. I don't care if Prince Aethelbald dines with us tonight, I will not—"

"None of your smart talk, Miss Princess." Nurse tossed the shoes out over her shoulder and emerged herself a moment later. Her ruddy face was a shade redder than usual. "Prince Gervais of Beauclair arrived not ten minutes ago. He's come to pay his respects!"

Una's mouth dropped open, closed, and opened again wordlessly.

"Gervais?" she managed at last. "Prince Gervais?"

Her mind danced over a hundred different thoughts at once. None other in all the kingdoms on this side of the Continent had a reputation half so exciting as that of Prince Gervais. The kingdom of Beauclair was located just south of Parumvir and famed far and wide for its music and for the splendorous balls and entertainments hosted in Amaury Palace, whereat King Grosveneur held court. The prince, rumor had it, was the most brilliant dancer and singer in the kingdom, a great favorite with the ladies, young and old alike. His very name conjured up notions of romance wherever it was mentioned.

Una snatched off the gauntlets and the kerchief she had tied over her hair and rushed to the vanity to inspect the scratch on her nose. It was still bleeding. "Bother it all, why didn't Father *tell* me he was expected?"

"Probably to prevent an entire week of the nervous tizzy you're now working yourself into—"

"Did you see him, Nurse?" Una dabbed her scratch with the handkerchief. "What's he like?"

"I only just glimpsed him in the hall downstairs. Oh, he's grand, very grand!" Nurse flung panniers and petticoats about with unprecedented abandon. "They say he rode up with a retinue of twenty, all bedecked in blue, with bells on the horses' bridles. I do believe he winked at me."

"*Winked* at you? Nurse!" Una fumbled with a petticoat, trying to do up the buttons at her waist, but her fingers, wrinkled with hot water, shook too much to manage them.

Nurse blushed like a schoolgirl. "I could be mistaken. Here, let me fasten that for you. Gracious, you've put it on inside out! Turn around."

"Did he say anything?" Una asked.

"I heard him ask to be presented to His Majesty, and your father's steward asked if he would wish to wash and rest himself first, and he just laughed. 'Twas such a musical laugh."

"Nurse!"

"Well, it was, and I don't mind saying it. I may be old enough to be your grandmother, but I'm not dead yet, Miss Princess. There. Now put this on." Nurse helped Una step into the voluminous skirts of her dress, chattering all the while. "You're to go to the receiving hall immediately and be introduced to the prince. Then the king has ordered a supper for him, a fine one, to which all his most powerful nobles will be invited—Beauclair being our strongest ally, you understand. Not even Prince Aethelbald received such a welcome as this! Sit and let me do something with your hair; you're not half presentable. Can you not stop that bleeding?"

A quarter of an hour later, once again powdered and tweaked into the height of Parumvir fashion, Una descended the staircase, one hand trembling on the stair rail, the other desperately attempting to lift her heavy skirts so that she could walk.

"Prince Gervais," she murmured to herself. "Now that's a fine name, I must say. Nurse didn't say whether or not he's handsome. But he must be, by all accounts. I wonder if he'll think me pretty. Oh, Monster, you goblin cat, why'd you have to nick my nose?"

She touched the developing scab and sighed ruefully just outside the receiving hall door. Taking a deep breath and lifting her chin, she nodded to the herald to announce her.

Prince Gervais was not a handsome man.

But it did not matter. He possessed an air of graciousness with perhaps the smallest hint of disdain about the corners of his mouth, which was altogether alluring. And when he smiled, one forgot any flaws in his face or figure.

He turned a glittering smile on Una as she entered the receiving hall, for he stood already before Fidel, having been presented a few moments before. Una blinked under his gaze and felt suddenly dizzy. The curious stares of all the courtiers around her withered away in the light of Prince Gervais's brilliant grin.

"Princess Una," Gervais said after Fidel had made the introductions and everyone who was supposed to had bowed or curtsied. His accent was thick and smooth as velvet. "I had heard rumor of your loveliness long before now, which incited my curiosity to meet you. But no rumor, however extravagant, came close to touching the true radiance of your presence!"

Una knew that whatever Gervais meant by that remark, it probably wasn't entirely honest—her best dress added about thirty pounds to her frame in unflattering places—and she felt the onslaught of red blotches on her cheeks. Princess Una was a pretty girl, but few would have guessed it at that moment. Still, Prince Gervais's face expressed pure dazzlement, and how could Una know better? Her heart thudded not unpleasantly in her breast.

"Crown Prince Felix and Prince Aethelbald," the herald boomed across the hall.

Una felt the blotches multiplying. She turned and saw her first suitor crossing the room in company with her younger brother. Both looked flushed from exercise, though their clothing was fresh.

"Ah, there you are," Fidel said, waving a hand in greeting. "Gervais, allow me to present my heir, Felix. And this is Prince Aethelbald of Farthestshore, newly arrived from afar."

"Ah! Delighted." Gervais flashed another brilliant smile and bowed.

"Good day, sir," Aethelbald quietly replied.

It was just as Una had expected—standing beside the shining prince of Beauclair, Aethelbald disappeared into obscurity.

King Fidel rarely hosted meals for his court. Once in a great while, for holiday feasts, tables would be set in the great dining hall, courtiers and dignitaries would be invited to join, and the royal family would display themselves in proper pomp. But these occasions were few and therefore much more impressive when held.

Magnificent banquets two nights in a row without a holiday in sight were enough to try the patience of all the cooks and servers in the king's service. But in honor of Prince Gervais's arrival, no extravagance could be spared. After all, as Fidel encouraged his staff, they would not wish the Crown Prince of Beauclair to compare the hospitality of Oriana Palace to that of Amaury and find it wanting, would they? No—no Parumvir cook would see those trifle-making dandies from Beauclair held up as his superiors. So the feast was one of special eminence, outdoing even the dinner served in Prince Aethelbald's honor the evening before.

The great dining hall was opened up, and all those counted of any note in Parumvir sat at long tables with golden placeware before them and dined in the presence of the king. The men from Beauclair and Farthestshore mingled with the counts and barons of Parumvir, and at the king's table in the center of the room sat Fidel, his two children, and Princess Una's two suitors, along with a handful of dukes and noblemen.

Una found herself beside Gervais, which both delighted and distressed her. She found it difficult to eat with his gaze constantly sliding to rest upon her, and she desperately hoped the red blotches faded under candlelight. She spent most of the meal rearranging the food on her plate, unable to transport any of it to her mouth. A subtly scented Monster sat at her feet under the table, grooming himself and sometimes touching her leg with one paw to beg, but she resisted slipping him tidbits in the present company.

To make matters worse, Prince Aethelbald was seated on her other side. He did not speak to Una, nor did she bother looking his way. But consciousness of his every movement made it difficult at times to focus her attention on the Prince of Beauclair.

Gervais was infinitely charming. He spoke in a voice clear enough to carry across the room, and many of those who did not sit at the royal table turned to listen to whatever he might say. One could hear the singing voice behind his speaking voice, Una thought, and both must be equally pleasant to hear.

Felix, who sat beside Gervais and just to the right of his father, asked around a mouthful of bread, "What sport do you find in Beauclair, Prince Gervais?"

Sport! Una thought with disgust. Surely the musical, talented prince before her wouldn't find time for such boyish games. She rolled her eyes at her brother, who covertly made a face back. But Gervais leaned back in his chair, raising his wine goblet, and declared, "Sport in Beauclair is as fine as any in all the world. In season I hunt deer, bear, even wild boar."

"Boar?" Felix asked, impressed. Boar hunting had not been practiced in Parumvir for several generations now.

"Indeed," Gervais said. "You'll rarely find a beast fiercer or more satisfying to chase." He tossed his head back in a short laugh, and Una found she agreed with Nurse; his laugh was musical. "But that is nothing," he said, "compared to the quarry I pursued just this last autumn."

Felix leaned forward in his seat, eager as a puppy. "What is fiercer than a boar?"

"Dragon, young Felix," Gervais said.

A hush settled around the hall at his words, and people from all the surrounding tables looked up.

"Dragon?" Felix breathed.

"Dragon, my boy." Gervais adjusted his seat so that he could cross his legs off to one side, his wine goblet still cradled in one hand. "One day last autumn—late afternoon, I believe it was—I hunted with my men on the borders of Gris Fen. We gave chase to a boar, an ancient and grizzled old thing, but wily with age. It had killed two of my dogs already and maimed one of my men. But I was determined that I should not be put off, that I should not rest until I saw the creature's head mounted on my wall. Such was not to be its fate, however."

He paused and sipped his wine while Una and Felix both leaned forward, their faces eager. Gervais set his cup down. "As I came under the shadow of the swamp trees, intent upon the trail of this boar, my attention was suddenly arrested by a great and hideous roar!"

His eyes flared, and in the candlelight his face looked frightening and at the same time terribly fascinating. "A roar so vicious," said he, "so bloodcurdling that I and my men froze in place, too frightened for the moment to go on.

"But that moment passed for me, and while my men yet stood in mortal terror, I cried, 'Wait here!' for I did not wish to put them at risk. I rode on ahead, following that gruesome bellowing, which sounded again and again at regular intervals. I told myself as I went that nothing in this world could make a sound so terrible save a dragon."

Una nodded solemnly, her lips parted, and Prince Gervais flashed another smile her way before continuing.

"All afternoon I hunted deep into the swamp, on foot after a time, for my good horse could not carry me into the deeper mires. Snakes swam past my feet, poisonous and deadly, but I pressed on, determined to find and rid my lands of the beast, wherever it may be. The sound swelled to so mighty a roar that I knew the monster must be near."

The warm lump of fur sitting at Una's feet growled when Gervais said "monster." Una nudged her cat, and he slipped out from under the table and skulked from the dining hall.

"At last," Prince Gervais said, "I felt certain the beast was just beyond the next rise. I thought it odd that no smoke or flame or scorch marks came into view, but I comforted myself that it must be a young dragon . . . though I would have hunted it no matter the size! I drew my sword." He picked up the knife beside his plate and raised it dramatically in the air. "With a mighty cry, I sprang over that final rise!"

He clanged his fist down on the table, causing those seated around him to jump and the glasses and silver to rattle. The courtiers at the next tables strained their ears to listen, waiting in breathless silence.

"Well, what did you find?" Felix demanded at last.

"Nothing." Gervais flung up his hands and leaned back in his chair with a laugh. "There I stood, ankle-deep in swamp muck, surrounded by miles of nothing. Disgusted, I turned to go, when I heard that great bellow again. 'GRAAAAAUP! GRAAAAAUP!' " He opened and closed his mouth comically. "I looked down at my feet, and what did I find?" He held up a fist. "A bullfrog, no bigger than my hand, puffed up like a child's balloon!"

Nearly everyone burst into laughter, and Gervais, shaking his head, finished with, "Of course, I tried to step on it, but the fell beast hopped away, and all my heroic efforts were for nothing. No bounty for that dragon's head!"

"Oh, but you were brave," Una said and blushed at her audacity, quickly looking down at her plate. "I mean, well, you didn't know what it was, yet you hunted it anyway. Alone too! That takes courage." She boldly raised her eyes and received a wink that knocked the breath right out of her.

Gervais leaned back so that his chair balanced on two legs, and took up his wine goblet. "How about you, sir?" He turned to Aethelbald, who sat quietly cutting his meat. Una had forgotten he was there. "I have heard stories of your kingdom since I was a small boy no higher than my nursemaid's knee. Surely you have had your adventures as well. Have you hunted dragons before?"

Aethelbald went on cutting. "I have," he said.

"Indeed?" Gervais paused and sipped his wine, a line appearing over his brow. But he smoothed it out with another smile directed briefly toward Una. "Do tell, good Prince," he said. "Is it a tale of might and daring comparable to my own?" He laughed.

Aethelbald paused and looked up from his plate, his fork halfway to his mouth. "No," he said and took a bite.

"What? Come, man, there must be a story here somewhere. Did you lead a band of thirty strong? Did your sword taste dragon blood?" Gervais placed an elbow on the table and leaned closer to Aethelbald. "We're all eager to hear the tale, Prince of Farthestshore."

Gervais's eyes were bright and intent upon the other prince, so Una tried to put an expression of interest on her own face. Inside, however, she wished Gervais would stop trying to draw conversation from a block of wood and go on talking.

Aethelbald glanced at Una. Candlelight cast strange shadows across his face. His expression, Una realized, was sad, deeply sad. She felt a pang in her heart and looked away. *Is it my fault?* she wondered. *He knows I don't want him. It is my choice. I have every right to fall in love with whomever I choose.*

"Come, Aethelbald," Felix prompted. "Let's hear your story."

Aethelbald set down his knife and fork and placed his hands flat on either side of his plate. "It is no fit tale for such company," he said and rose from his chair. "Nor do I wish to tell it." He nodded to the king. "If you'll excuse me?" Bowing to those present, he exited the hall. Servants hastened to clear his place.

"I like him," Gervais declared and lifted his glass to salute the door through which Aethelbald had just disappeared. "Humility is a rare quality in a man, and one I respect." He drank to this little toast and smiled again at Una, his smile only a touch sardonic.

7

S HE DREAMED AGAIN THAT NIGHT.

Nurse firmly closed the windows, and Una climbed under the covers, believing there could be no chance of sleep for her. Her imagination was lost in a romantic whirl, dancing and twirling faster than any music the court musicians could play. "Good night, Miss Princess," Nurse said as she left the room, but Una did not bother to answer.

Prince Gervais was so handsome! Prince Gervais was so charming! Prince Gervais was come to pay his respects!

Two princes in two days! Who would have thought?

Not that she cared about Aethelbald's suit, of course. Nor would she concern herself with the sorrowful look he had given her just before leaving the banquet. What cared she for somber eyes, no matter how kind, when Prince Gervais was present and so attentive?

Thus Una's thoughts continued, and she tossed fitfully as the light of her fire dulled and dimmed. She plumped her pillows so many times that Monster gave an irate squawk and stalked to the foot of the bed, curling up like a chipmunk with his tail wrapped over his nose.

Then the heat came.

It began the same as it had the night before, and with it came sudden remembrance of the dream she had forgotten. The two faces—one black, one white, one ice, and one fire. She remembered the clattering dice, and her heart began to race. The desire to leap from her bed and flee the room filled her, but once more her limbs were like stone and she could not so much as blink. Her mother's ring on her finger tightened, and her hands throbbed with burning.

The two faces in her mind blended together into one enormous face surrounded by fire, and Una sank into her dream.

There is nothing but fire, and within the fire, a voice.
"Where are you?
"Five years I have searched. Five years I have wasted.
"Beloved of my Enemy, I played for you, didn't I? I played for you and won! Are you not the one I seek?
"Where are you?"

Una woke early the next morning to a dreadful prickling against her cheeks.

Opening one eye, she found herself gazing up Monster's pink nose. Though he could not see her, he sensed she was awake and immediately said, "Meeeaa!" in no uncertain terms, placing a velveted paw on her nose.

Una tossed her pet aside and climbed out of bed. Without knowing why, she glanced at her mother's ring. The clustered opals, when tilted to the light, glowed deep within their centers. Twisting the ring about with her thumb, Una opened the palm of her other hand, not certain what she looked for. Some memory of a burn tugged at her mind. Had not Prince Aethelbald said something about one?

Well, she certainly wasn't going to think about Aethelbald on a morning like this! She closed both hands into fists. Prince Gervais was come to Oriana Palace, and she must prepare herself for more respects-paying at once.

Deciding to dress herself before Nurse came and determined her wardrobe for her, Una put on a simple, nonconstricting gown, tied her hair in a braid down her back, and slipped her little journal into her pocket.

"I need some air," she told Monster, who twined himself about her ankles, purring madly. "Ask the maid to feed you when she comes. I'm going for a walk."

She felt a bit wicked as she slipped from her room and down the hall. Nurse disapproved of princesses going anywhere unattended—or making any independent decisions at all, for that matter. But servants and footmen abounded in every passage and around each corner, and Una hardly felt unattended even as she slipped out into the gardens. Gardeners were already busy pruning bushes and caring for various beds of seedlings. They bowed to her as she passed by, and she nodded.

Her mind spun away onto the same thoughts that had disturbed her rest the night before. "Will he ask for my hand?" she whispered, gazing earnestly into the face of a marble statue standing in a bed of perennials. It was an odd statue, a depiction of her great, great, many-times-great grandfather, King Abundiantus V. Carved in white stone, he stood with one hand on the hilt of his sword and the other resting upon his breast, fingering a pair of incongruous spectacles on a chain. His marble face scowled severely down upon Una as though to say there were far more important things to consider on a spring morning than love and romance.

Una did not believe she and her great-grandsire would have seen eye to eye on many subjects.

She moved on down the garden path.

Surely Gervais would ask for her hand. He could not have come to Parumvir for any other purpose. "But what if he doesn't like me?" Her face wrinkled with worry. "He's such a favorite with all the ladies by everyone's account. He could have his choice of any woman! Why should he consider me?"

She kicked a stone out of the path and watched it skitter off into the lawn. "I am a princess. He'll consider me for that reason if nothing else. But would he think of me otherwise?"

Music drifted to her ears. Una paused and looked around. The soft strumming of a stringed instrument floated down the path from the garden higher up the hill, nearer the palace. It was called the Rose Garden, though no roses had bloomed there in over twenty years. Today, instead, it bloomed with peonies and clematis, a poem of color. Una turned, gathering her skirts, and retraced her steps. As she entered the Rose Garden, she heard a voice, a deep voice, smooth and rich, singing:

> *"Oh, my love is like the blue, blue moon*
> *Floating on the rim of June!*
> *Oh, my love is like a white, white dove*
> *Soaring in the sky above!"*

Una put a hand to her head and wished to heaven that she had waited and let Nurse style her hair before she went out that morning. Too late now, so she went on, following the lovely voice.

> *"Oh, my love is like a sweet, sweet song*
> *That never seems too long!"*

She turned a corner in the path and saw an arbor festooned in clematis, under which stood Prince Gervais. He strummed an elegant lute, and his eyes locked with hers the moment she stepped into view. He smiled, and she feared her heart had stopped for good this time.

> *"Oh, my love is like a fine, fine wine*
> *If only she'd be mine!"*

He played a few more chords, then placed his hand on the strings to silence their humming.

"Don't stop," Una said. "That was lovely."

"Do you like it?" Gervais asked. He strummed another chord. "It is a song of the great Eanrin of Rudiobus, dedicated to his one true love, the fair Gleamdren, cousin to the queen. By tradition, it is a song meant to be sung only to—" he set the lute aside and bowed to her—"a woman of rare beauty."

Red blotches burst forth in wild cavorting across her nose. Una turned away, one hand pressed to her heart, and looked about for the gardeners. The nearest worked several plots away and had their backs discreetly turned. She thought desperately, hoping some witty or clever remark would suggest itself, but the backs of the gardeners presented her with no inspiration. "I . . . I hope you are enjoying your visit in Parumvir," she managed.

Prince Gervais stepped up beside her, and she could feel his gaze on the side of her face. "Princess Una," he said, his voice low and soft, "did you know that your eyes shine like the stars?"

Where the star analogy might have come from so early in the morning, Una couldn't guess, but that hardly mattered at such a moment. She bit her lip and forced a nervous smile. "Oh?"

"Could I lie to one such as you?" He chuckled softly at the thought. "The first moment I gazed into the limpid blue depths of your eyes," he said, "I knew I might drown there and die a happy man."

Some small part of her deep inside winced that he'd gotten her eye color wrong. But Una silenced that thought and glanced up into the not-very-handsome but so-very-fascinating face of Beauclair's prince. "I think I . . . I think I'd rather you didn't die," she admitted bravely.

"Truly, Princess Una?" Gervais lifted a hand and reached out as though he might touch her cheek, but restrained himself at the last moment.

"I think so," she said. Why must she suddenly wish so badly that the gardeners would turn around?

"Princess," Gervais murmured. "Una, I was wondering if I might . . . speak with your father?"

Una blinked. "My father?"

"Yes."

She frowned. "I suppose so. I mean, I see no reason why you might not. You're his guest after all. . . . "

Gervais cleared his throat and moved a fraction of an inch closer. "I meant about a delicate subject."

"Delicate?"

"Yes." He reached out and took her hand. Her eyes widened and her mouth dropped open. "Do you understand me, Una?"

"Oh!" she gasped, then inwardly kicked herself when the next word from her mouth was a resounding, "Uh!"

Crunching footsteps on the gravel path shot through her ears like cannon fire. Una pulled her hand from Gervais's and spun about to see Prince Aethelbald striding up the garden path. He saw them at the same moment and paused. A sharp expression flashed across his face, then vanished the next moment behind a complete mask. He bowed and went on his way without a word, disappearing around a bend in the path.

Una backed away from Gervais and curtsied. "Thank you, prince, for . . . the lovely song," she said, then turned and all but ran from the garden, clutching her skirts in both hands.

"Oh dear," she whispered as she retreated, wishing her thudding heart would ease. She glanced back and saw Gervais shoulder his lute and walk from the clematis arbor. "I think I'm in love— Oh, *dragon's teeth*!"

With that unladylike phrase she landed in a heap on the garden path. In her flight she had not watched where she went and failed to see Aethelbald when he stepped out in front of her.

"Princess Una," he said, offering her a hand, "are you all right? I'm sorry. I didn't mean to startle you."

Really, the blotches had earned a holiday for all the extra time they'd been putting in these days! She refused Aethelbald's proffered hand and scrambled to her feet on her own, brushing gravel from the back of her skirts. "Sneaking up on people," she snapped. "Really, sir, there are proprieties to maintain!"

"I was standing in plain sight."

"It couldn't have been that plain since I didn't see you!"

"You might have seen me had you been looking where you went."

"I was looking where I went right up until I stopped . . . looking. . . ." She crossed her arms, then uncrossed them because Nurse said that princesses should never cross their arms. But then she didn't know what to do with them, so she crossed them again. "What do you want?"

Was he *smiling* at her? Did his rudeness know no bounds?

"Princess Una," he said, "I merely wish to inquire after your hands."

She glared at him. "My what?"

"Your hands."

He reached out and, much to her surprise, took one of her hands. Too taken aback to know how to react, she watched as he turned it palm up and drew it closer to his face for inspection. His smile was gone now, replaced by a solemn expression. She stood, mouth agape, watching him study her fingers and desperately trying to remember what was considered a seemly response to this sort of situation. None of the etiquette books Nurse had shoved in her face had covered spontaneous hand inspection.

At last Aethelbald raised his gaze to meet hers. "You are badly burned," he said.

She drew her hand back and studied her fingers herself. There wasn't a mark to be seen. "I'm not."

"I see what you cannot," he replied. She looked up to meet his gaze again. His eyes were dark, flecked with gold about the edges. And somehow, as she looked at them, she felt as though they weren't quite human. All the wildness of the Twelve-Year Market, the breath of great distances, and the smell of the sky lay hidden in that gaze. For just a moment Una believed him.

"Will you allow me to tend to your hurts?" he asked.

The moment passed.

"You have plenty of nerve, Prince Aethelbald." It didn't come out as regally as she had hoped. In fact, she thought she sounded like Nurse, which galled her. "I don't know what you're hoping to achieve by ordering me around so!"

"Ordering you around—"

"First bursting in on me at the market!"

"Bursting in—"

"Then embarrassing me in front of the whole court!"

"Princess, I—"

"And now all this rot about invisible injuries and interrupting Prince Gervais as he and I don't see what business it is of I can do what I like and I think you're simply and that's that!"

Una paused there, wondering if what she'd just said had made a lick of sense. Judging from Prince Aethelbald's face, it hadn't. "Well, now you know," she finished, and took fistfuls of her skirts, preparing to sweep grandly past him.

But he sidestepped to block her way. "Princess," he said gently, "please believe me when I say that I care for you and am only concerned for your well-being."

"You can stop concerning yourself. My being is well enough, thank you. Good morning."

To her relief, he let her go. She crunched on up the path to the palace, telling herself that she wouldn't look back. Heaven help her, she would *not* turn around to see whether or not he was still watching her!

But she did.

And he was.

Grinding her teeth, Una fled to her chambers, determined never to leave them again.

8

TRAILING ATTENDANTS BEHIND, Felix hunted for Aethelbald in the practice yard. He saw the Prince of Farthestshore standing near the barracks, talking to one of his knights. His wooden sword slapping against his leg as he ran, the boy hurried across the yard. As he drew near, he realized that the knight standing before Aethelbald was not one of the three he remembered seeing at the banquet hall a few evenings ago. This one was tall and slender, with hair as golden as a dandelion. He turned as Felix neared, and the young prince came to a halt in surprise.

The knight's eyes were both covered by silk patches.

Felix remained frozen where he stood, and the blind knight turned back to the Prince, speaking in a voice bright and merry but with an underlying edge. "Can't say that I trust him a great deal, my Prince," he said. "Begging your pardon, but he doesn't have the most dependable reputation."

"I'm not sure you're one to talk," the Prince said. "Gambling, Sir Eanrin!"

"Call it a bit of surreptitious research, my Prince," the knight said. "All in your service, of course."

"Of course."

"But I don't mind saying I'd like to get what he owes me. I won a good deal off that scoundrel and have not yet heard the clink of gold."

"I'll take care of it immediately," Aethelbald said. "Return to your duties. And, Eanrin?"

"My Prince?"

"No more surreptitious research for my benefit, please."

"Your wish is my command, my Prince!" The blind knight gave an elegant bow and, after turning his face momentarily toward Felix and wrinkling his nose, swept from the barracks yard.

Aethelbald looked down at Felix.

"Who was he?" Felix asked. "What was that about?"

"No one and nothing concerning you, Prince Felix," Aethelbald replied. He looked at the sword at Felix's side. "Have you come to practice?"

Felix grinned and drew the practice sword, pointing it at Aethelbald's chin. "Do you feel brave, Prince of Farthestshore? I think I might trounce you today!"

Aethelbald's mouth turned up in a half smile, but he shook his head. "I must settle some important business first. Perhaps later."

"Why later?" Felix said. "You're here now! The business will wait for a match or two." He heard one of his attendants snort and glared back at the three of them. They assumed straight faces and pretended to be interested in other things in the yard. Felix whirled back to Aethelbald and said in a lower voice, "They don't think you'll practice with me again. They think you were just making a fool of me yesterday and are now bored of me."

Aethelbald eyed them, then turned back to Felix, pushing aside the wooden sword still pointed at his face. "What do you think?"

"I think you're scared to spar with me! I think you're afraid I'll beat you this time!"

Aethelbald shook his head. "Baiting doesn't work on me, Prince Felix," he said and started across the yard.

Openmouthed, Felix watched him go, then suddenly brandished his sword and called, "Fine! Be a coward!" Listening to the snickers of his attendants, he turned and, growling like a hurt dog, lunged at one of the practice dummies so hard that it nearly fell off the pole. "Don't need you anyway," he muttered, rolling his shoulder muscles and twisting his neck. He took first position and prepared to spring at the dummy again.

"A fine stance," a thickly accented voice cried. "You have surely been trained by a master, Prince Felix."

Felix paused, his sword arm suspended before him. Prince Gervais stood at the edge of the yard, his fists planted on his hips and a long sword sheathed at his side. Felix nodded curtly and completed his lunge, less vigorous than the last one but more precise. He smiled, tight-lipped, admiring his own work.

Gervais applauded. "Very nice, young sir," the Prince of Beauclair cried. He stepped into the yard, removing his sword belt as he did so. "Tell me, Felix, have you another practice sword? I should be honored to spar with you if you are willing."

Felix looked at the smiling prince and recoiled at the idea of a match with him. Every movement Gervais made was full of a dancer's grace, just the sort of form Felix's own master had been struggling to beat into him over the last few years. But his attendants were watching and whispering to each other again. Felix felt his hackles rise, but he said, "I'm willing if you are, Prince Gervais."

Gervais smiled at the boy, a smile that Felix wanted to smack off his face, and called to one of the guards. "Bring me a weapon." He set aside his own sword and took the wooden one offered to him. Felix watched him stretch a few moments, and his heart sank. Even in his stretching exercises, Gervais had the look of a master.

The two princes took positions across from each other and saluted. Immediately after, Gervais's sword arm extended, his torso inclining forward, his hand rising to shoulder level as he advanced. His movements were so quick and fluid that Felix could only just parry and leap back, avoiding a touch by inches. His heart quickened, pounding in his throat as adrenaline rushed through his veins. Their swords crossed, wood thunking heavily on wood. Felix parried three times, a fourth, and then felt the slap of the sword on his leg. It hurt, and he bit back a curse behind a grimace.

"Good," Gervais said, still smiling. "You are skilled, young prince, most skilled. Again?"

Felix could not refuse in front of his father's guard and his sneering attendants. He saluted the prince, their swords crossed again, and this time Gervais broke through his defense in a moment, touching him hard on the shoulder. Felix turned away, cursing under his breath, his ears red with embarrassment.

"Come, you cannot be finished," Gervais cried. "You are doing so well, Prince Felix."

Felix could hear the laughter behind his voice, and the blood roared angrily in his head. He saluted, assumed first position, and this time was quick enough to go on offensive first, surprising the other prince for a moment. But Gervais laughed even as their swords met, and the next moment Felix felt a hard slap against his thigh.

"Indeed, you will make a fine swordsman someday," Gervais said. "Again, Prince Felix?"

Nothing in this world seemed half as important as permanently removing that grin from Gervais's face. But Felix knew after three encounters that he couldn't hope to touch the Prince of Beauclair. They crossed swords again.

"When I defeated the Count of Elbeuf," Gervais said, "the most famous swordsman in his demesne, I performed just this maneuver." He feinted, Felix fell for it, and the next moment was struck hard on the arm. "Again, Prince Felix?"

Felix ran through his mind any possible ways he might decline and yet retain an inch of dignity, and found there were none. He saluted, and they engaged.

"When I encountered the Baron Dronhim of Milden," Gervais said, "I tried this."

Felix attempted to parry but was too slow, and the wooden sword hit his other arm. He wondered how many bruises his attendants would count and snicker over when they helped him to dress that evening.

"Again, Prince Felix?"

"A moment!" Felix panted, turning and stalking a few paces away to catch his breath. He placed a hand on his side, where a cramp was developing. Closing his eyes, he growled between his teeth, "If she marries that goblin's son, why I'll . . ."

He opened his eyes and saw Aethelbald standing a few yards away, arms crossed. Aethelbald looked at him, his mouth a straight line across his face, and raised his eyebrows.

Felix drew in a deep breath and turned back to Gervais. "I'm ready, prince," he said and saluted.

Gervais smiled that brilliant beam of his and saluted back. Then he lunged. Felix's feet moved in the intricate pattern he'd practiced yesterday, a little clumsy but just quick enough, and his sword arm darted out. He staggered at the end but turned his head to watch Gervais's wooden sword fly through the air and clatter in the gravel behind him.

Even the attendants stopped whispering.

Felix leapt forward and smacked Gervais, who was still recovering his feet, hard on the thigh. "Touch!" he cried. "Match!"

Gervais swore roundly and backed away, rubbing his thigh. "What did you do?" he demanded.

Felix grinned at him and shrugged. "I disarmed you! Another, Prince Gervais?"

Gervais swore again, under his breath this time, and went to retrieve his own sword from the edge of the yard, leaving the wooden sword where it lay. "Enough for today, Prince Felix," he said. "Perhaps again tomorrow. We shall see."

He buckled his sword belt about his waist and strode from the yard without another word, passing Aethelbald. The Prince of Farthestshore put out a hand to arrest him and said something too low for Felix to overhear. But Felix did not care. Inside he was bursting, and it took all his concentration to maintain a cool air as he scooped up Gervais's practice sword and went to put it away.

"When I defeated the swaggering prince of Beauclair," he whispered, smiling fiendishly, "I used *this* little maneuver. . . ."

Una spent most of the rest of the day inside working at her tapestry. It felt safer inside. Safer from what, she could not say, but safer for sure. Nurse was discerning enough to sense that her princess was in a delicate state of mind and let her alone, though she did notice that Una tangled her thread rather more than usual.

Una hardly saw her work. She kept reliving the events in the garden that morning and found, to her frustration, that she could not enjoy the memory of Gervais's romantic song, overshadowed as it was by Aethel-bald's rudeness.

How dare he take her hand like that? Pretending concern! As if she wouldn't know if she had damaged her own hands.

Monster hopped into her lap and started chewing on her thread. Una watched him do it without seeing until he had unraveled half an armored bean man. Coming to herself suddenly, Una growled, "Monster, you beast!" She tossed the cat over the arm of the chair, then set to embroidering with more will than ever, determined to dwell on Prince Gervais.

He would speak to her father, wouldn't he? Of course he would. Why waste any time? He loved her, so he would talk to Father, and things would all be settled by suppertime.

Granted, he hadn't actually asked for her hand, not in so many words. But how else could a girl interpret such a song as Prince Gervais had sung to her in the garden?

Una tried to stop the frown that pulled at the corner of her mouth, but it slipped into place anyway. Her thread tangled again, and she pulled it so tight that the poor embroidered man's face twisted grotesquely.

Tonight there was to be another dinner. Gervais was a man of such nobility and prestige that one state dinner could not possibly suffice. There would be another dinner, and all the court would be gathered, and her father would announce her engagement. The applause would be thunderous; she could feel blotches sprouting at the thought. Prince

Gervais, of course, would take it all in stride. Everyone would cheer, and he would smile, and . . .

I wonder what Prince Aethelbald will think.

Her thread broke when Una tugged too hard, and she was obliged to find her little scissors. She began snipping with more energy than was altogether necessary.

I don't care what Prince Aethelbald will think.

He would leave, of course. Tomorrow morning, presumably, after the announcement was made. He would march into the Wood, just as peculiarly as he had come, and she would never see him again.

"And that will be for the best," she muttered as she put a new knot at the end of her thread.

"What's that, Miss Princess?" Nurse asked, looking up from her needlepoint dragon.

"Nothing."

Una started adding silver to the helmet of her newest soldier, a fierce-looking fellow who brandished a slightly crooked sword at the scarlet thread flames billowing toward him. But she did not see the exciting scene before her. Instead she stood once more in the Rose Garden, listening to the song as clearly as if Gervais still sang it. She felt the tightness of breath when the dashing prince stood so near. And she still felt the pound of her heart when she recognized Aethelbald coming up the path.

I wonder what he thought when he saw us together.

But of course she didn't care about that.

That evening Nurse allowed Una to wear her second-best dress, which was thankfully a little less cumbersome than the best dress. Una made hardly a sound as Nurse put her together and styled her hair. She needed to look exceptional for the dinner, and while she did not feel very pretty in her finery, she would have to trust the Parumvir fashion experts, for tonight her engagement would be announced.

When Una came to the dining hall, she found it locked up, no sign of a feast or festival anywhere. Frowning, she made her way to the smaller private dining room used by her family most evenings. The footman standing at the door opened it to let her enter, and to her surprise Una found only her father and brother in the room, already eating.

"What are you all made up for?" Felix asked around a mouthful.

"Well, I . . ." Una did not finish but quietly slid into place. A servant set a plate before her, and she started cutting her meat in silence. Only after she'd cut each piece in half several times over did she dare raise her eyes and ask, "Will Prince Ger . . . Will the princes not dine with us this evening, Father?" She hoped her voice didn't tremble as much as she suspected it did.

Felix, who was sipping coffee, snorted and burnt his tongue, cupped a hand around his mouth, and bawled for water. During his uproar King Fidel could not speak and Una was left to wonder. But when her brother finally quieted, her father turned to her and said, "Prince Gervais left for his own country early this afternoon."

Una's heart stopped a moment. She put a napkin to her face. Left? Already? After only just expressing his feelings to her that morning? She pressed the napkin a little harder to her mouth. Perhaps she had not encouraged him enough? Perhaps he had thought she did not return his affections?

"Will he come back?" she asked.

"I should hope not," Felix said, gently touching his tongue with thumb and index finger.

Una frowned at her brother. "What do you mean? You liked him well enough last night when you were talking of hunting and sport and such things!"

"My opinion has changed since," Felix said, squinting at her. "Where have you been all day that you haven't heard?"

"Haven't heard what?"

"About his—"

"Children!" Fidel interrupted. "Felix, this is not common knowledge, and while I know that it soon will be, court gossip being what it is, I would rather you were not the principle source." He turned to Una.

"Certain news reached my ears late this morning concerning the behavior of that young man."

Una could feel the red blotches rising and dancing over her nose. Had he heard of the song in the garden? Was that somehow improper behavior? It had seemed innocent enough. "Why, Father, I—"

"It appears that Prince Gervais is currently banished from his father's house for enormous gambling debts," Fidel said quietly. "He is not permitted home until he can pay them. Pass the salt, Felix, please?"

Una's mouth opened and closed again.

"Marriage to a rich princess is a fine way to fast money," Felix said.

Awkward silence filled the room, broken only by the sounds of Felix cutting his meat.

"Are you sure?" Una asked at last in a small voice.

"Quite," King Fidel said. "I had heard rumors of his habits before now, of course, but the evidence presented this morning was enough to convince me that I did not want him singing any more love songs in my garden."

"Did he do that?" Felix asked, looking up from his plate.

"But what evidence, Father?" Una demanded. "A man should not be presumed guilty, and what could possibly—"

"A promissory note written out to one of Farthestshore's knights," Fidel said. "Gervais owes Aethelbald's servant quite a sum, which he is unable to pay."

"Aethelbald," Una whispered.

"Signed and sealed with Gervais's signet ring." Fidel shook his head. "The poor boy did not try to deny it but packed up this afternoon with hardly a word. I think the thumping he got in the practice yard may have knocked some of the silver from his tongue."

Felix chuckled quietly to himself.

Una's mind, however, could fix on one thing only: Prince *Aethelbald's* knight. Who but Prince Aethelbald himself would bring this information before the king? Una glared so hard at her coffee that it almost reboiled. "May I be excused, Father?" she asked and rose without waiting for a reply.

"You don't want your meat?" Felix called after her, but Una did not hear.

There were no servants in the hall, so she stopped and leaned against the wall, her fingers pressed to her temples. This was not how things were supposed to happen! Gervais was supposed to propose. She was supposed to accept. They were supposed to marry and . . .

Her spinning thoughts jarred to a halt. Did she *want* to marry him?

Of course she did. She was in love with him, wasn't she?

Her thoughts worked up speed and spun on while tears gathered in her eyes.

"Princess Una?"

She looked up. Prince Aethelbald stood before her.

"Are you unwell, princess?" he asked. "Should I summon—"

She knew he was speaking, but she could not hear for the roaring in her ears. A bundle of words gathered in her throat and burst out in a mad jumble. "What did you could your business *dare* you!" Her eyes burned. "Never want to speak why did you can't *stand* you!"

"Princess?" He took a step back, his face full of hurt and confusion. "Are you—"

"Don't pretend you knon't dow—don't know—what I'm talking about!"

"I don't presume to know, but I could probably guess," he admitted. "Prince Gervais—"

"What business of yours I'd like to know. What business, well?"

"Princess, I never claimed—"

"How dare you blacken his name how dare you to my father!" Una wanted desperately to spit out elegant barbs, but all that came out was an emphatic, "Don't want you mister noble go away not your business!"

If nothing else, her body language was unmistakable. Prince Aethelbald took another step back and bowed. "Princess, I understand—"

"You don't!"

"—your distress, but permit me to defend my—"

"I don't want your paltry defense!" she tried to say, though it came out, "I paltry don't want you!" and she turned on her heel and stormed away.

He followed behind a few paces and spoke quietly. "I did not go to your father, Una. I spoke to Prince Gervais on behalf of my servant to whom the prince owes a great sum. I urged Gervais to speak to King Fidel himself and admit his position, as any honorable man would."

Una gathered her skirts, tilted her chin, and rushed up the stairs to her rooms, leaving Aethelbald behind.

Una passed her evening imagining all the brilliant things she should have said to Aethelbald but didn't, but jolly well would next chance she got, so help her! They were most of them verbose, all of them witty, and each would have fallen flat if stuttered, but she didn't consider that. She penned them in her journal and practiced them in her mind until they rolled perfectly off her imaginary tongue and Prince Aethelbald, cowed, crawled into his place.

The thought did nudge the edge of her mind now and then that perhaps Aethelbald had been right. After all, he hadn't spread rumors. Gervais had done a fine job of blackening his own name.

But she refused to dwell on these thoughts, for she might have come to the conclusion that she owed Aethelbald an apology, and that could not possibly be true.

Nurse was no help.

"Spoiled, money-grubbing wastrel," she muttered as she tidied the princess's room. "Thank heaven Prince Aethelbald called him out, the scalawag scamp."

Una, who sat at her window looking out at the rising moon and writing out the final touches on an exceptionally fine verbal dart, turned on Nurse with a frown. "That's not what you said about him yesterday. Yesterday you thought him fine and clever."

"Well, perhaps he is fine and clever," Nurse said, "but that doesn't change the rest of him. And the rest of him is a scalawag scamp with no thought for anything but his own pleasure!"

"He did speak to Father himself, though," Una insisted. "That took courage, don't you think? Only a fine man would be willing to admit his own shortcomings so humbly."

"I'm not saying he's devoid of virtue, but that doesn't make him less of a shyster, a two-faced . . ."

The flame of love was well and truly smothered in Nurse's breast.

Una turned back to her window with a heavy sigh and gazed out to the darkening horizon. "Did he really love me, Nurse?" she asked. "Gambler, debtor, or otherwise, do you think he really loved me?"

"Phfff, what does it matter? Whether he did or not, he loved himself more. Hoping to marry you for money, the scoundrel. . . ."

"Maybe he loved me, though, and didn't care about the money? Maybe my fortune was only an extra blessing?" Una's brow puckered. "Do you think that's possible?"

Nurse shook her head. "Think what you like if it makes you feel better, but I say good riddance to him even so."

Una slumped, her chin in her hand, and absently stroked Monster, who was curled in her lap and purring, unconcerned whether or not the world crumbled to little pieces.

Maybe I wasn't worth loving more than himself?

The moon seemed a little less romantic than before.

9

THE FOLLOWING MORNING, Una's head ached like nobody's business, and she tried to feign illness as an excuse to stay in bed. Nurse
would have none of that.

"But my head is splitting in two!"

"It's doing a remarkably neat job since I can't see so much as a
seam."

"A history lecture would kill me today, Nurse. Truly it would!"

"I don't doubt it. Now, up!"

Was there a time, Una wondered as she plodded to her tutorial, when
she had actually wished for more excitement? Not even a week had passed
since the Twelve-Year Market had seeped out of the Wood like so much
mist before retreating again, leaving in its wake rather a lot of hassle and
confusion. If only that wretched Prince of Farthestshore hadn't come,
she might even now be celebrating her engagement to Gervais!

And well along the road to marrying a gambler and debtor.

"Preeeowl?" said Monster, tagging her footsteps.

Una sighed down at him. "I won't be grateful, cat," she said. "That Aethelbald had better just take himself and his suit and hightail it back to wherever he came from, because I will not be grateful, heaven help me!"

But she thought it best to discard all thoughts of giving the Prince a tongue-lashing. No, a frosty reserve should achieve the same result and perhaps prevent her from sounding like a fishmonger's wife. She took her seat in the classroom, vowing a vengeance of absolute silence with all the solemnest oaths she could invent and refusing to look at her brother as he tried to pass her notes.

Monster sat at her feet, sniffing and twitching his whiskers. As the tutor shuffled through his notes, gave that first introductory "Ahem," and began his lecture on the Imposter's War and the building of Oriana Palace, the cat made a slinky exit.

Monster passed through the halls of Oriana, his tail high as a banner, and the servants made certain not to get in his way, being under strict orders from their princess to "treat him nice." Thus in that small way, Monster received the respect due a lord, and he accepted this as his right, scarcely deigning to acknowledge those he passed.

He made his way to the barracks and the out-of-the-way quarters where the Knights of Farthestshore had taken up residence. Though as knights they should have been housed in finer chambers within Oriana itself, they knew how uncomfortable their otherworldly presence made the palace folk and chose instead to keep quietly to themselves, avoiding even Fidel's guards.

Massive Oeric and the smaller knight, Sir Rogan of the grass-green eyes, sparred together in the yard. They parted as Monster passed right between them, rolling their eyes but bowing as he went, though he could see neither gesture. The dark-skinned knight, Sir Imoo, sat on a bench nearby polishing a long dagger, and he rose at Monster's approach and bowed as well. Only the Prince of Farthestshore, also seated and watching Oeric and Rogan fight, did not rise. To him alone did the cat make reverence.

"Good morning, Eanrin," said the Prince.

"Good morning, my lord," said the cat and, after putting up his nose to gauge the height, hopped up onto the bench. "Pray continue," he said to Oeric and Rogan, and they returned to their sparring. Sir Oeric's sword was wooden, but the smaller knight used a real blade. Even when he made a hit, there was no chance of its piercing Oeric's rock-like hide.

Monster groomed a paw some moments while the Prince continued to watch his knights. Then the cat said, "My Prince?"

"Yes, Eanrin?"

"If you don't mind my saying so . . ."

Aethelbald waited, then gently prodded, "Go on."

"What you lack—and I mean this in the most respectful sense, you understand."

"I'm listening," said the Prince of Farthestshore.

"What you lack," said the cat, "is confidence. For while you rule the vast stretches of the Far World and master the Wood Between with a powerful hand, from the boundaries of the Netherhills to the stretches of the Final Water and beyond, you simply don't have the first idea when it comes to women."

Sir Imoo, intent on his knife, snorted but turned it into a cough.

Prince Aethelbald said, "And what would you suggest?"

"I may be but a humble house pet," said the cat, "but if there is one thing in which I hold complete confidence, it is the conviction of my own desirability."

"Spoken like a true cat."

"No matter how antagonistic the object of my current affections may be, a well-timed purr, a sweet trill, an expertly hunted and scarcely nibbled gift will work magic every time! Consider, my Prince."

Aethelbald raised an eyebrow. "You suggest I take up mousing?"

"Shrews work well too. I leave toads for Prince Felix. On his pillow."

"And we all know how great is his affection for you," muttered Sir Imoo.

Monster acknowledged him with a sniff. "Exactly! And if all else fails, my Prince, you can sing. Every princess loves a chap who will serenade her from the garden on a moonlit night. I do it myself every full moon, filling the night air with the dulcet sounds of my voice!"

"Until the housekeeper throws cold dishwater at you," said Sir Imoo.

The cat flattened his ears. "That old hag is tone-deaf."

The prince met Imoo's gaze over the blind cat's ears, shaking his head slightly. Then he said to the cat, "Eanrin, much though I appreciate your concern—"

"I live only to serve, my Prince."

"—I think you must let me make my suit in my own way."

"By circumnavigating the girl at every turn? Mrreeeowl! Is that the spirit that won the undying devotion of Gleamdren the Fair, Queen Bebo's golden-eyed cousin?"

"And when did you actually win Lady Gleamdren's devotion? Last I'd heard she was not speaking to you."

"A minor setback."

"For the last thousand-odd years."

"But I sensed a distinct softening in her demeanor when I visited Rudiobus last century. She looked at me once."

Aethelbald smiled. "She would have found it difficult to throw her shoe at your head without looking at you, Eanrin."

"Ah yes. You heard about that, eh? The true sign of thawing heart, I tell you! The more antagonistic they seem, the more certain you can be that they are struggling in the deepest throes of turbulent emotion! Believe me, my Prince, I know about these things. Am I not the most celebrated romantic lyricist of all the ages? You can be certain your lady-love is secretly pining away for you, and her sharp tongue and icy face are mere masks to disguise the depths of her feelings! It is your task— nay, your *duty*—to take every opportunity to remind her of your ardent love. Bring her flowers. Write her sonnets. I'll write them for you if you wish, and you needn't tell her. It's sure to work. She'll get so exhausted refusing you that she's bound to give in eventually!"

Silence followed, broken only by a *thunk* of the wooden sword and Sir Rogan's yelped, "Ow!"

Then Prince Aethelbald said, "Eanrin."

"My Prince?"

"Why don't you go chase a ball of yarn."

Then it was three weeks later, and summer arrived in a blaze of glory, full of sunshine and buttercups and balmy afternoons.

Una's mood did not match.

One such afternoon, Una tossed aside her embroidery, grabbed her journal, and escaped outside, ignoring Nurse's calls for her to mind the sun and not burn her nose and did she remember her hat?

"Bother the sun, and bother my hat," Una muttered, slipping into the hall. She wanted nothing more than to be left alone and wished for all the world that she could disappear. Yet that was impossible. As she hurried down the hall, she passed innumerable footmen and maids, all of whom bowed or bobbed curtsies as she went by. On her way downstairs she crossed paths with an elderly courtier and his wife, neither of whom she knew, but both of whom bowed and greeted her with, "Good afternoon, Princess Una."

She remembered once, when she was younger, reading an adventure tale in which the princess heroine had disguised herself and crept out of the palace and into the countryside on a grand and glorious quest. Granted, this had led to rather a lot of unpleasantness for the princess, but Una had been inspired nonetheless.

That very afternoon she had commanded one of her maids to loan her a gown, rubbed ashes from the fireplace all over her hands and face, and taking up the maid's bucket of dirty water, stepped boldly from her chambers.

The first footman she had encountered had bowed low and asked, "May I help you, princess?"

Una had given up disguises since then.

Out in the gardens, sunlight greeted her, and she tipped her unprotected face up to enjoy its brightness. Let her nose burn! At least it would disguise any blotches.

What she desperately needed, she thought, was half a moment to herself to sort through some of her thoughts. That moment would not happen in her chambers, nor anywhere within Oriana's walls. Neither were the gardens a suitable place for a girl in need of quiet, for gardeners and their clipping shears abounded, giving her sulky looks as she passed, as though daring her to think she served any useful purpose while they and their ilk labored in the summer sun. She nodded to them and hastened on her way, trying not to call attention to herself.

Clematis and trumpet creeper bloomed bravely against the heat, climbing the southern wall. Una did not want to walk among them today. Flowers, she found, lacked their former romance, ever since a certain serenade in a certain garden. She picked up her skirts and hurried down the path. Blossoms arched with special elegance over Southgate, which was small compared to the main gate on the western side of the palace. Southgate was trafficked only by servants, grocers, and gardeners.

Today as Una approached the gate, she heard shouts, rough and angry. The sounds startled her, and she slipped behind a shrub and wondered if she dared continue her present course. The shouts grew louder.

"Oi! If you don't let me through, I'll be certain it gets back to your superior officer, and you'll wish you'd never—"

"Right. As though you'll be on chatting terms with my superior officer. Listen, mister, we don't let just anyone come trampin' through here, and anyone who tells you otherwise—"

Una peered over the shrub and saw two guards at the gate. Guards always stood watch there, but she'd never noticed them until today, for Southgate was such an unobtrusive corner of the palace. But now both guards were growling and struggling, big hands clamped down hard on the arms of the most outlandish character Una could remember ever seeing.

He was dark complexioned, but his outfit dominated any other impression he might give. He was dressed in bright yellow with stripes of red and blue running at all angles throughout the costume. The collar and sleeves were cut in odd triangles and, of all things, had little silver bells tied to the ends of them. Una blinked several times and pulled back behind her shrub.

But the stranger had already seen her.

He lunged forward, almost breaking free of the guards, shouting and holding out a hand. "Lady! Fair lady!" he cried. "You seem of a gentle nature. Tell these blackguards to unhand me—"

Una ducked away, taking another path before the guards spotted her. She heard several angry shouts and the sound of blows. "And take your hat with you!" one of the guards bellowed.

The iron clang of the gate shutting rang in her ears. Una hurried down the path between snapdragons and lilies, wondering what sort of man could induce the palace's ever-lenient guards to shut the gates in his face. It felt almost like an invasion or something from a history book. What a terrible thought!

But rather romantic in a way.

Una smiled a little to herself as she made her way deep into the gardens, away from the palace and the gates.

White marble statues of old kings and queens of Parumvir stood at regular intervals down the paths of the seven-tiered garden, with the occasional legendary hero standing bravely between trimmed hedges. On the seventh tier, nearest the edge of Goldstone Wood, was even an old marble statue of the Bane of Corrilond, a long and serpentine dragon. The body was somewhat startling, curling as it did down the side of the path, then arching at the neck so that the jaw could open wide enough for Felix to stick his head inside, as he often did when he and Una walked together. The expression on its face was hardly menacing; it reminded Una of Monster yawning.

It was a quick walk from the top tier to the seventh if one took the cobble stairway cutting directly down and didn't stop to explore the various levels. Halfway down the hill, the gardens ended abruptly, swallowed up by Goldstone Wood.

Una loved the gardens of her home, but much more she loved the Wood.

To be sure, horses refused to step into its shadow, and men and women trembled at the thought. But to Una, the Wood had always been a place of solitary comfort, filled with memories of her childhood, and these days providing the one place where she knew she would not have to face anyone.

She stepped into it now and breathed deeply. Goldstone Wood smelled old. Not musty or antique. Certainly not like Nurse's smell of dried lavender, nor even like the smell of the aged books in the library, with their spidery handwriting in faded ink. The Wood's smell altered according to the season. Now, in early summer, when Una stepped into the shelter of the trees, she took a deep breath of rich, green air, full of health and a hint of some nameless spice that carried up from the sea below.

She crunched through last autumn's dead leaves while greener growth swung at her from low-growing branches. There were no paths in Goldstone Wood, nothing but little deer trails. Una, however, followed landmarks with ease and never lost her way, not between the gardens and the Old Bridge.

She moved quickly through the forest this afternoon. The glory of summer surrounded her, but she could not appreciate it as she should have. There in the shadows of the trees, Una found herself half remembering, but unable to quite grasp, her dream.

Every night the same dream, or dreams so similar that they may as well have been the same, plagued her. Yet every morning when she woke up, she could remember nothing more than a vague uneasiness and a tightness on her finger where her mother's ring gleamed. But the ring slid off and on as easily as it ever had, so she did not remove it.

Gervais's departure surely was the cause of her restless nights, she decided as she approached the Old Bridge. Eventually her heartbreak over him would pass and she would sleep again, but in the meanwhile she must simply endure it.

She stepped onto the bridge. How long had it been since last she'd been there? She missed her younger days, when she and Felix ventured this way and played their silly games. Smiling, she remembered the day they had found and rescued Monster, who was now so much a part of her life.

Una sat down, removed her shoes, and put her feet in the water, enjoying the cool trickle. Then she took out her journal and nub of pencil and wrote:

I'm not going to forgive him. It's my choice. He drove Prince Gervais away, and even if that has proven for the best, it was none of his business. So I won't forgive him, and that's that.

She stopped writing, for her thoughts took her no further. If only she could express what went on inside of her, she might find some relief. But no inspiration came, and she sat in silence for many long moments.

A wood thrush sang in the branches above her. She looked up and fancied she caught a glimpse of its speckled breast. It opened its mouth, and a series of notes trickled forth like water; then it flickered out of sight into the forest beyond the Old Bridge. Yet its silver-bell voice still carried back to her. She listened and suddenly thought perhaps there were words.

She turned to a fresh page in her journal and wrote quickly:

> *I listened long to your story,*
> *Listened but could not hear.*
> *When you chose to walk that path so overgrown,*
> *I remained alone with my fear.*

The thrush song went silent, then suddenly burst out again, farther away this time, deep in the forest.

Once more Una wrote as fast as words came to her mind:

Cold silence covers the distance,
Stretches from shore to shore.
I follow in my mind your far-off journeying,
But I will walk that path no more.

The thrush song ceased, and she stopped writing. She read over the lines and scratched her head with her pencil. A smile slowly filled her face. These verses were, she dared hope, good. What they meant exactly she could not guess. There were so many meanings in life, and so few of them meant anything. Why did life have to be so very confusing?

Nevertheless, Una had written verses for the first time in weeks, and perhaps not even Felix would sneer at these.

Crackling leaves caught her attention, and her heart jumped to her throat. The noise came from the far side of the Old Bridge.

Never in all her years of playing in Goldstone Wood, playing on this very bridge or on the near side of the stream, had she seen or heard anything beyond the bridge other than the occasional bird and, of course, Monster. She leapt to her feet, staggering a little, and backed away, her bare feet leaving wet prints. She peered into the shadows of the Wood beyond the bridge.

A figure stepped into view, head bent, watching its own footsteps. It came to the clear spot right before the bridge and looked up.

"Prince Aethelbald!"

He startled, stepped back, shook his head, and looked again. "Princess Una?" Swiftly he slipped down to the streambed and splashed across rather than crossing the bridge. Water poured from his boots as he climbed up the near bank, and he beckoned to Una. "Princess, what are you doing here? Please come off the bridge!"

She clutched her journal close to her side and licked her lips. "I . . . I could ask the same of you." She had not spoken with him since the evening of Gervais's departure. On a few occasions he had made some polite attempt at conversation, but true to her vows, she had snubbed him. The memory of Gervais's sudden departure and her subsequent embarrassment was still too fresh in her mind. She raised her chin and tried to speak grandly. "I mean that this is my father's wood. What are you doing tramping around in it? Does my father know?"

Aethelbald beckoned again. "Please, Princess Una, come off the bridge. This is not your father's wood, and I need no permission. But you—"

"It is too," she snapped, backing away from him. "It grows in his kingdom; therefore this is his wood. I have every right to be on my father's land, haven't I?"

He glanced at the forest on the far side of the bridge. "Have you crossed over?" he asked.

Una blinked. "Over the Old Bridge? Of course not."

The Prince let out a long breath. "You remain on the near side?" His hands were outstretched, as though he wanted to pull her off. Afraid that he actually might, she stepped from the planks onto the leafy bank.

"No one crosses the Old Bridge," she said.

"Good."

She looked down at the dirt and grass clinging to her wet toes. Aethelbald stepped closer to her. She wanted to ask him why he was there, what he had been doing on the far side, the far side that no one went to—but for some reason the words would not form in her mouth. She could not ask, no matter how she might wish to, and she chewed on her tongue, frustrated.

Yet Aethelbald was visibly relieved. "This side belongs to your father," he said. "Stay over here, princess. But, tell me, do you often come to this place alone?"

"Of course I do," she said. "I told you, this is my father's wood and perfectly safe."

"You've never met anyone here?"

She glared at him. "Not until today." She paused, then added almost as an excuse, "Felix comes with me. Sometimes. He used to."

"Ah," Aethelbald said. He cast one last glance back across the Old Bridge, pursed his lips, and looked at her again. His gaze lit upon her journal, and he half smiled, indicating it with a nod. "You come here to read?"

She hugged it closer. "No."

He noticed then the pencil in her right hand. "To write, then? Are you a writer?"

"Sometimes," she admitted.

"Stories? Poetry?"

"Poetry."

"I did not know you were a poet." He spoke with a smile that surprised her with its warmth and interest. She looked down at her feet to avoid it. "Do you seek to follow in the footsteps of the great Eanrin of Rudiobus?"

"Lights above, no!" she said quickly. "I wouldn't dream of comparing myself to his genius."

"Well, that's a relief in any case," said the Prince, and he smiled again, though she, glancing up, couldn't quite read his expression.

He asked, "Perhaps you would one day recite a piece?"

She did not answer. Deep down inside Una wanted to. Other than Felix, who didn't count, no one had ever inquired about her poeting attempts before; none had ever been curious to read her pieces or asked her to perform them.

But she kept her mouth tightly shut.

Aethelbald looked at the ground at her feet, his jaw working as though he was trying to say something. At last he said, "May I—"

"If you're thinking to ask about my hands again—no, they're still not burned."

He blinked, and all trace of a smile left his face. "I was going to ask if I might escort you home."

Shame scratched at the back of her mind. How could she be such a shrew? But she drew herself together and shook her head.

"You will stay here alone?"

"Yes." And as an afterthought she added, "Thank you."

"It grows late."

She shrugged, which wasn't a particularly elegant gesture, but for the moment she didn't care.

He sighed and took a few steps uphill toward the gardens, then paused and looked back at her. "Don't cross over."

The next moment Aethelbald was gone.

Una blinked at the spot where he'd been. Strange. For though she knew he had simply disappeared among the foliage and trees, part of her thought he'd vanished into thin air—one moment present, the next moment not. Her brow wrinkled as she tried to recall their encounter. She knew they'd spoken of poetry. Was there something else? It was muddled in her memory, probably due to her fluster at speaking to him after so many weeks of silence. How awkward to meet him out here!

She huffed a short laugh. It could almost have been a romantic meeting if he had been anyone else. But it would appear she was doomed for the prosaic.

Una lingered in the forest, until she was quite certain Aethelbald was gone, before stepping back onto the Old Bridge to retrieve her shoes. Then, as the sun began to disappear behind the trees, she too made her way back to the tiered garden. Somehow she felt better than when she had fled from her room that afternoon. She couldn't quite put her finger on it, but something had changed, something important.

She smiled as she stepped from the trees into the lowest tier of the garden and made her way up the path. The sun was sinking swiftly now, and Nurse would be irate with her for staying out so long. But this evening she could look over her new verse and know she had accomplished something all her own. Perhaps life made very little sense, but perhaps it wasn't all that dreadful either.

She was up in the second tier, following the path close to the wall, when she heard a sound like rocks scrabbling against each other. Startled, Una glanced up and down the darkening path but saw nothing. She heard the sound again and looked up just in time to see a dark figure on top of the wall leap down on her.

10

U NA SCREAMED as both she and the dark figure tumbled into the garden path, the princess squashed beneath. Bells tinkled faintly, then a hand slipped over her mouth as an urgent voice hissed in her ear, "Oh, hush. I'm so sorry! I beg you, please, quiet!"

She screamed again, the sound stifled by the hand, and struggled. The body on top of her shifted so that she was not so heavily pinned, and she got an elbow free and tried to make use of it. Her attacker dodged, still keeping his hand clamped over her face, and whispered again, "I say! Really, I'm sorry. I had no idea you were down here. Terribly rude of me, I know, but I can't help making an entrance it seems, no matter how I try."

His voice sounded vaguely familiar, though she could not place it. It was not a threatening voice, so she relaxed a little in his grip. He let her sit up. "Are you quite calm?"

She nodded, though her breath came in short puffs against his fingers.

"All right, I'm going to let you go. Please—"

She leapt up as soon as she was free and whirled on him, her feet skidding on the gravel path. In the sunset's ruddy glow she saw a strange yellow costume crisscrossed with gaudy stripes. He jumped to his feet as she did, and she opened her mouth, taking in a deep breath, more than prepared to scream for all she was worth if he moved one step toward her.

But, to her great surprise, he took a look at her face and collapsed onto all fours at her feet. Una stepped back in alarm, but he spread his hands toward her, crying out in a choked voice, "Please! Can you forgive this lowly worm, O gentlest of maidens, for his unforgivable rudeness, dropping in on you, so to speak? Will you forgive him or strike him dead with a dart from your eyes? Oh, strike, maiden, strike, for I deserve to die— No! Stay!"

He rose onto his knees, covering his face with his hands as she stared. "I do not deserve such a death!" he cried. "Nay! It would be far too noble an end for so ignoble a creature as you see before you, to die from the glance of one so fair! No, name instead some other manner for my demise, and I shall run to do your bidding. Shall I cast myself from yon cliff?"

He leapt up, and she gasped and backed away, but he sprang to the pedestal on which stood the marble statue of her many-times-over great-grandfather, Abundiantus V, whose head was turned to look over a marble shoulder. He seemed to glare directly down at the strange young man who wrapped an arm around his stone waist in a familiar manner, balancing beside the old king.

"She says I must die," the stranger told the statue, waving a hand toward Una. "Will you mourn for me?"

King Abundiantus looked severe.

The stranger turned away with a sob and looked out across the garden. "Farewell, sweet world! I pay the just price for my clumsiness, my vain shenanigans. My grandmother told me it would come to this. Oh, Granny, had I but listened to your sage counsel while I was yet in my cradle!"

He made as though to jump but froze with one leg in the air, arms

outspread, and glanced at Una. "Farewell, sweet lady. Thus for thee I
end a most illustrious career. The siege of Rudiobus was hardly a greater
tragedy, but then, Lady Gleamdren was not such a one as thee!"

He gathered for another spring but stopped himself, catching hold
of King Abundiantus's white fist. "I don't suppose my end could be put
off until tomorrow, could it?"

"I—" Una began.

"No!" he cried. "For you and your wounded dignity, I must perish at
once. Go to, foul varlet! Meet thy doom!" With a strangled cry, none too
loud but bone-chilling, he flung himself from the pedestal, somersaulted
across the path, and lay still at Una's feet. His left arm twitched.

Una gaped.

The stranger raised an eyelid. "Satisfied, m'lady?"

Una, much to her surprise, laughed.

His name, he told her, was Leonard, and he was an out-of-work
jester.

"A jester?" Una said.

"Yes." He, still lying on the ground, waved a hand in a grand, sweeping gesture. "Singer, storyteller, acrobat, and clown. Also known as," he
coughed modestly, "a Fool."

Una shook her head, smiling with a wrinkled brow. "You may get
up if you wish, Fool."

"Thank you, m'lady." Leonard sprang up and began brushing gravel
and dirt from his already much-soiled costume, ringing a dozen silver
bells as he did so.

Una looked him over. Her heart still raced from her scare, but it
was difficult to remain fearful of such a funny-looking creature. "What
possessed you to jump on me from the wall?"

He grimaced. "Yes, about that . . . I'm sorry?"

"Is that a question?"

"I suppose so. I'm trying it on for size. Usually I find that 'sorry'
isn't enough, so I don't often bother with it anymore. You seem like the
forgiving sort, however, and I thought I might risk it."

Una covered her mouth to hide a giggle. "Why were you climbing the garden wall?"

"They wouldn't let me through the gate," he said.

"They don't let just everyone through, you know," Una said. "Not through Southgate. You can come through Westgate every third and fifth day of the week if you seek an audience with the king. They wouldn't toss you out then."

"Ah, but I'm not some commoner coming with a petition. I have special papers on me, a letter of recommendation from King Grosveneur of Beauclair himself."

"You're come from Beauclair?"

"Indeed, m'lady, directly from Amaury Palace, whereat I did most brilliantly entertain the monarch of said kingdom!"

He twirled his hand elegantly as he spoke, but Una did not notice, for she was studying the buckles of her shoes. "Did you see anything of the prince while you were there?"

"Prince Gervais? No, I believe he is not currently, uh, welcome at Amaury, though I am not privy to the details."

"Oh. Certainly." Una shrugged, still looking down at her shoes, but the jester went on speaking.

"I have ventured here from the court of Beauclair to seek employment with the king of Parumvir," Leonard said, "if he will hire me."

"Hire you to clown?"

"That and sing and spin stories and perform acrobatic feats of wonder; though my singing I would wish on few, my storytelling has put many a mighty lord to sleep, and my acrobatic skills are feeble at best. But my clowning . . . Ah! Do not so soon dismiss the talent that lies therein, O ye maiden of doubt! There, in the masterful arts of tomfoolery, lurks the full measure of my genius."

He swept her a bow, catching the strange, bell-covered hat from his head so that his dark hair stood on all ends about his face and nearly touched the ground as he bent double. When he straightened again, he caught up something. "Is this yours, m'lady?" He held out her journal.

"Oh yes," she said, taking it. "Thank you."

"A book of sonnets perhaps?" he asked, smiling winningly. "Stories of romance and adventure?"

"Oh no," she said. "It's just, well . . ." She smiled back, surprised at how easy she found it to talk to this strange character. "Actually, it's my own work. I . . . I write verses now and then."

"Do you indeed? Excellent!" he cried. "I've written a song myself; it's not a very useful piece for my line of work, however. Jesters aren't supposed to sing melancholy bits."

"I like melancholy songs," Una said.

"Do you? Then you would adore this piece. Composed in the immortal spirit of the great Eanrin himself, it is bound to bring tears to your eyes! A pity I am a jester. If I were other than I am, I would sing it for you."

Una narrowed her eyes. "Well, aren't you presently out of work?"

"Yes."

"Then you aren't a jester. You are an unemployed gentleman and therefore free to sing melancholy songs, yes?"

The jester nodded and rubbed his chin. "How deftly the lady wields the double-edged sword of logic!" He slapped his knee. "For that, fair one, I give you this most melancholy of melancholy carols ever caroled in these parts." He struck a pose. " 'The Sorry Fate of the Geestly Knout.' "

Una giggled, but he raised a hand to shush her and, his face drawn as though in great pain, he sang:

> *"With dicacity pawky, the Geestly Knout*
> *Would foiter his noggle and try*
> *To becket the Bywoner with his snout*
> *And louche the filiferous fly.*
>
> *"But to his dismay, the impeccant Glair*
> *Would kibely watch from the Lythcoop.*
> *Our poor little Knout felt her pickerel stare,*
> *And allowed his own delectus eye droop.*

"Ah, sad Geestly Knout! How he'd foiter and bice,
But his noggle wouldn't nannander right,
And that impeccant Glair, like bacciferous ice,
Feazeled his snout with a single bite!"

Ending with a flourish, Leonard wiped a tear from his cheek, and Una laughed out loud. He raised an eyebrow. "The lady laughs! Ah, what a world in which we live when the innocent laugh at the sufferings of Knouts, geestly or otherwise."

"Whatever does it mean, though?" Una asked.

The jester looked still more affronted. "If art must be explained, it is hardly worthwhile, is it?"

Una laughed again heartily. When she recovered her breath, she shook her head. "Sir Leonard the Jester, the hour is late and I must return home. Why don't you join me? My father would welcome you, I am certain, and a bed for the night might be found for you. Unless, of course, you have somewhere else you must be. . . ." She blushed at her boldness and was almost relieved when the jester shook his head.

"I fear I must decline your offer, sweet maiden, for tonight I seek the home of the King of Parumvir himself, Fidel by name." He swept his hand up to indicate the palace looming above them on the top of the hill. "His fools of guards—and I say fools in the basest sense, for I defy you to find a sense of humor among the lot of them—refused me admittance, but I hope to present my reference papers to a steward or housekeeper this evening and perhaps gain an audience with the king on the morrow. It is high time I found employment again, for my raiment is threadbare and my stomach empty. So you see, fair one—"

"Oh, but King Fidel is my father," Una said. "Yes, and I'm sure he'd give you work if you want it; we don't have a jester at court."

"Your father? Then—" The jester looked her up and down, taking in her simple day dress, the leaves in her hair, the dirt on her shoes. Then he looked again at her face, and his own face lost all trace of jesterliness. "Your Highness! Princess! I must ask your forgiveness in earnest now. I am an oaf and a clod. I should have seen from your eyes, your manner, that you were royalty." With those words, he bowed a real bow, and a graceful one at that.

Una felt the red blotches appearing on her nose and was glad the light was dim. "It's quite all right," she hastened to say. "No, how could you have known? Think nothing of it whatsoever."

He smiled a sweet smile, not at all flashy. In this attitude, despite his garish clothing, Leonard seemed almost normal. "Does your hospitable invitation still stand, princess?"

"Of course. Please, do come," she said.

"In that case"—he offered his elbow—"allow me to escort you home."

11

Servants and courtiers stared as Una led the outlandish young man through the palace, but she ignored them. "This way," she beckoned to Leonard and hurried through the corridors. She realized that she must be far too late for supper, so she escorted the jester to the sitting room, where her father usually retired for a few minutes of peace in the evenings. But Fidel was not there.

Frowning and a little embarrassed, Una bade the jester stay put while she hunted up a servant. The first man she came across was the palace steward, a somber fellow without a hair out of place. She caught him by the sleeve. "Where is my father?"

He coughed and straightened his cuff. "His Majesty is in conference in his private study, Your Highness."

"In conference? On a full stomach?" This was out of character for Fidel. "With whom?"

"The Prince of Farthestshore, Your Highness." The steward's tone implied that he had far more important business to attend to than Una's curiosity, so she let him go.

"Aethelbald," she muttered and frowned. She had almost forgotten their meeting in the forest earlier that evening. Had she said something, anything, that she wouldn't want Aethelbald repeating to her father? Would she be due a lecture come the morrow? She sniffed, frustrated, and twisted her mouth. Why couldn't Prince Aethelbald let her alone for once?

Though, she had to admit, there was some chance they weren't discussing her at all. Somehow this thought was still more galling.

She returned to the waiting jester and found Leonard contemplating a series of portraits in the hall where she had left him. They were not very good pieces; or rather, Una hoped they were not. If they were accurate, then her ancestors had been distinctly lacking in forehead and tended toward greenish complexion.

But the jester, when she neared, was not looking at a depiction of one of her ancestors. Instead she found him studying a small piece of far more ancient work. The figures in this painting, though no more proportionate than the paintings of Una's grandsires, were gracefully worked, with life in their limbs and expressions on their faces. Three men stood on the shores of a black lake; one of the three wore a crown upon his head while the other two were bound in chains. Otherwise, their faces were identical. In the center of the lake lay another man upon a golden altar that rose up out of the water. Beside this altar stood a woman, her body bent over and her hands over her face as though she wept.

Una must have seen the picture a thousand times without ever pausing to look at it. Glancing at it now, she thought it ugly. Yet the jester appeared captivated.

"Leonard?" She spoke several times before finally touching his sleeve.

He startled but immediately masked his face in a smile. "You're back."

"Do you like the picture?" she asked

"Not at all. A vile piece—wouldn't you agree?"

But his gaze wandered back to the painting as though drawn

unwillingly. "I believe I have met him." He pointed to the man lying on the golden altar in the center of the lake. Though the figure was tiny, the artist had intricately painted a skull-like face surrounded by black hair.

Ghoulish, Una thought.

The jester laughed and turned abruptly away. "Reminds me of an innkeeper who tossed me out on the streets after a performance in Lunthea Maly."

"You've seen Lunthea Maly?" Una gasped, forgetting about the ugly painting and allowing Leonard to lead her from it, though she realized after a few steps that she should be the one leading him. "You've traveled to the Far East?"

"I dwelt four years in Lunthea Maly, the City of Fragrant Flowers, which indeed is as fragrant as squashed daisies left rotting in the bottom of a wheelbarrow on a summer's day." He gave her a roguish wink. "I have even performed within the great halls of the Aromatic Palace, home of his Imperial Majesty, Emperor Khemkhaeng-Niran Klahan of Noorhitam himself!"

"You performed for an emperor?"

"He gave me a peacock, he was so pleased by my foolishness." Leonard coughed modestly. "Of course, his grand vizier showed up on my doorstep the following morning to reclaim the bird, declaring the young emperor rather too enthusiastic in his gift giving. But it's the thought that counts, yes?"

With those words, the jester's stomach let out a terrific rumble, and he clapped his hands to his middle and looked embarrassed. "Forgive me, m'lady. I have not eaten a full meal in many weeks, I believe. Since I left Beauclair."

"Come to my father, then," Una said, taking his arm. "He'll hire you, and I promise he'll pay more than the thought of food for your performances."

"One can always hope," the jester said with the doleful air of one who didn't often hope anymore. But Una led him to her father's study, determined to see him situated in Oriana Palace, at least for a time.

The hall in which her father's study was located was empty except for a gentleman attendant, who stood just outside the door, covering a yawn with the back of his hand. He pulled himself upright at Una's approach, though he sneered as he took in Leonard's odd motley.

"Wait here," Una told the jester. He leaned against the window opposite the study door, his hands behind his back, shifting his feet. She nodded to the still-sneering attendant and motioned for him to depart, then knocked on the door.

No one answered. Inside she could hear the rise and fall of voices and remembered that her father was in conference with Prince Aethelbald. She hesitated, wondering whether to knock again, when suddenly her father's voice rose, and she heard through the heavy wood:

"That's nonsense, sir, utter nonsense, if you'll forgive my saying so."

Prince Aethelbald replied but spoke in that frustratingly low tone of his, and Una could not make out a word. Her father responded. "She's my own daughter. I would see that for myself, don't you think?"

Una's heart thudded to a stop in her throat. She felt wicked for eavesdropping, but somehow she couldn't drag herself away from the door. Instead she strained her ears.

Aethelbald's words were still indiscernible, but Fidel said, "We are in no danger. Southlands can burn to dust for all I care; it still means nothing! Parumvir has never been a temptation to their kind." Another pause during which Aethelbald spoke, and then Fidel again. "You do what you think best, Prince Aethelbald, but leave me and mine alone. I don't doubt that you believe every word of your warning. You're an honest sort and a good man. But you don't know Una, not as I do."

Una backed away from the door. She desperately wanted to press her ear to the keyhole and catch every word.

But part of her was afraid.

What she feared she could not name. Yet as she listened to her father's voice, she became aware of a tightness on her finger. Her opal ring pinched again, and her finger swelled up around it. She twisted it, trying to loosen the pressure.

Leonard came up behind her. "Princess?"

He was given no chance to continue. The study door opened and

Prince Aethelbald emerged, head down and hands clenched at his sides. He saw Una and stopped, his eyes first darting to her hands, then to her face. He opened his mouth, and Una thought he was about to address her.

Then he became aware of the jester behind her. He closed his mouth and, without a word, hastened down the hall and away.

Fidel came to the doorway. "Una!" He spoke sharply and his face was gray. But the next moment he forced a smile onto his face, and his voice was kind when he said, "What in the world have you dragged in this evening, child?"

Una drew her gaze back from following Aethelbald's retreating form and smiled at her father. "It's a jester, Father."

"It is, eh?" Fidel gave Leonard a once-over and raised an eyebrow.

"*He* is indeed." The jester offered the king a graceful bow.

Fidel nodded and crossed his arms. "Another lost creature lugged in from the Wood, Una? Does this one just need a good meal and a bath as well?"

"Heaven help us, he'd be grateful enough," the jester muttered.

"Oh, but more than that!" Una stepped over to her father's side, hugging his arm. "He's ever so amusing, Father, and we haven't had a jester in ages. Do you think we could hire him perhaps? He's out of work and needs a position, and he's really too funny for words!"

"Peace, girl," her father said, putting up a hand. Then he turned again to Leonard. "Who are you, and from where have you come?"

Leonard bowed elegantly after a foreign fashion that Una had never before seen. "I am called Leonard the Lightning Tongue, Your Majesty, professional Fool of no mean skill," he said. "I come from many places: Noorhitam and Aja, Milden and Shippening. Most recently Beauclair's Amaury Palace, whereat I endeavored to amuse the court of King Grosveneur. But originally, Southlands."

His gaze locked with Fidel's. If the king wondered in that moment whether or not certain words he'd spoken behind his closed door had carried out into the hall, if he concerned himself with whether or not the jester had overheard, his face did not reveal as much. Stiff masks in place, each regarded the other, giving nothing, taking nothing.

But Una heard her father's voice in her memory, harsher than she was used to hearing it: *"Southlands can burn to dust for all I care."*

She lowered her gaze, twisting her hands before her. Then, to break the interminable silence, she said, "Ask to see his papers, Father. He says he brings a recommendation from King Grosveneur."

Leonard produced the desired document for Fidel's perusal, and the seal and signature were genuine.

Fidel nodded and grunted. "I'll put you up for the night," he said. "I do not host spectacles for my court in the same manner as Grosveneur, nor is Oriana Palace a scene of revelry on the scale of Amaury. But you may entertain my family this evening, and you and I shall discuss a long-term engagement once you've gone through your paces. Agreed?"

"Willingly, Your Majesty," Leonard said with a deep bow.

Una returned to her room for a light supper and a not-so-light scolding from Nurse, paying neither much heed in her eagerness to be off to her father's private sitting room for Leonard's first performance. Nurse told Una that she looked a sight and forced her to sit at the vanity while she pulled twigs and leaves from her hair, and Una did this with as good grace as she could manage, holding her supper in her lap and eating while Nurse worked.

Her meal and toilette completed, Una escaped Nurse's ministrations and once more hastened down the stairs. The door to the sitting room had been left open for her, and she saw the glow of the firelight and heard Felix talking to someone inside.

But she paused in the hallway.

The strange picture of the dark lake caught her eye.

She frowned and stepped nearer to study the face of the figure sleeping on the golden stone. The scene was from some legend, she knew, but she could not remember hearing it referenced in any of her tutor's lectures.

The hallway was deeply shadowed. Servants had placed candles in the wall sconces, but there were none near this particular piece. Nevertheless, the gold paint on the stone caught what light there was, making the painting seem brighter, the faces of the two chained men on the shore frightened, the king crazed, and the woman by the stone ready to break in two with sorrow. The sleeper with the white face was like stone.

Southlands can burn to dust.

"Princess Una."

She turned and found Aethelbald standing in the sitting room doorway. Though she hoped he wouldn't, he came toward her down the hall. "Princess, it is dark out here. Come in by the fire."

Una did not move save for her eyes, which darted from the painting to Prince Aethelbald and back again. "What were you discussing with my father earlier?" she asked in a whisper.

He bowed his head, searching for the right words. Then he put out a hand and took one of hers. "Princess, please, will you allow me to—"

She stepped around him, snatching her hand from his grasp, and hastened into the sitting room. Her father dozed in a comfortable chair, and Felix sat cross-legged before the fire, playing a complicated game of his own invention with sticks and marbles. He often asked Una to join him at the game, but since he had a tendency to change the rules to suit his convenience, Una rarely agreed. Monster, however, curled up by the prince's side, his head turning to follow every click of marble and sticks, as alert as though he had eyes with which to see Felix's game.

Monster chirped a greeting when Una entered, raising his pink nose. Una scooped him up and took him with her to sit in a chair opposite her father. Aethelbald followed her into the room, shutting the door softly, but remained back in the shadows. Una could feel his eyes watching her, but she refused to turn his way. Instead she gazed into the flames, stroking her cat's head.

"I believe I have met him," the jester had said of the white-faced sleeper in the painting.

Strangely enough, Una felt that she had as well. Where and when, she could not guess. The feeling preyed upon her. Monster purred, but the sound did not soothe.

The door opened and the jester slipped into the room.

"Ah, yes," King Fidel said, coming out of his doze and nodding to Leonard. "I'd almost forgotten. I asked you to entertain us tonight, didn't I?"

"Quite so, Your Majesty," Leonard replied. He was clad still in the boldly striped yellow costume and somehow looked more ridiculous than ever in the context of the familiar sitting room. He carried a lute not unlike Prince Gervais's.

Una, glad to quit the privacy of her thoughts, plopped Monster onto the floor and got up to greet Leonard. "I told you I'd get you a job, didn't I?" she whispered, smiling.

"Don't count unhatched chickens," he whispered back. "Your father has declared little need for a full-time Fool, and I may yet find myself out on my ear." He began tuning his instrument, which plunked sourly in his hands. "But I should not have this opportunity were it not for you. I hope I can properly repay your kindness. He would not have given me a chance but to please you."

"It does please me," Una said. "But make him laugh and you'll be hired on your own merit."

"I shall endeavor to oblige, m'lady."

"Una," King Fidel said around his pipe, "come sit by me and let the jester play."

Una obeyed.

Leonard finished his tuning and struck a deep minor chord. "Hark!" he cried, assuming a sinister pose and strumming the same chord again. "Hark unto the tale I must relate. This is no tale for the faint of heart!"

Felix looked up from his game of sticks, trying and failing to seem uninterested.

"This is no tale for timid womenfolk, no tale for young children or babes in arms."

He strummed again, a deep *bloooome*.

"This is a tale to make your blood race, your head spin, your eyes cross and recross."

Blooome!

"This is a tale of darkest terror in the face of deepest inconsequentiality."

"Huh?" said Felix.

Una giggled.

The jester continued to play and half sang, half told his story. His singing voice was deep and not beautiful. But he sang with spirit, and the point was the story not the melody.

> *"There was a lady of fairest face and vapid mind*
> *Who one day sat a-knitting.*
> *A-knitting, a-knitting, ho!*
> *Who one day sat a-knitting."*

He told how a dark monster, a fiend of evil form, set upon this lady while she sat alone in her chambers one evening. He told of her horror as she faced the beast. He told of her attempts to flee, but the creature blocked her path. She tried to hide, but again and again the monster foiled her plans. Once she bravely took up a weapon to slay the beast, but to no avail, and found herself at the end of her means, standing upon a silken chair as her nemesis crawled toward her.

At the last possible moment, her hero came in the form of a portly maid, who squished the creature with a handkerchief and proceeded to revive her lady with smelling salts.

Una and Felix were both gasping with laughter by the end, not so much for the story itself as for the way the jester told it, with exaggerated expressions of fear, outrage, courage, and beastliness, leaping about the room even as he strummed his instrument. King Fidel chuckled heartily, and when she glanced his way, Una saw Prince Aethelbald grinning.

"Excellent." King Fidel applauded with his children as the jester played the final sour chords. "Sir Jester, we are glad indeed to have you among us. If you are half as skilled at mopping floors as you are at spinning stories, we may just find ourselves at an agreement."

An eyebrow twitched on the jester's face, but he swept the hat from his head and bowed. It was an elegant bow, Una thought. Courtly, even.

12

IN HER DREAMS THAT NIGHT Una walked a path she did not recognize through a desecrated garden.

Once these grounds must have been beautiful. The sweep of the hill, the remains of elegant shrubberies and groves, bespoke care and artistry. But all was grim and wasted about her, all the land one great grimace of pain. No growth grew higher than Una's knees before it was chopped and trampled, as though some brute force could not bear to catch a glimpse of thriving green and had blasted all to grays and blacks. Even the sun, where it shone through an iron sky, appeared as a red scar overhead.

She walked the path she did not know, approaching a great palace she did not recognize. It was not Oriana but some other structure of foreign build. What once may have been elegant minarets were now crumbled towers, giving the appearance of having been chewed. Stones that may have been rich with color were filmed over with ash.

As she looked at it, Una felt hatred rise in her soul. What a wicked place this must have been, what an evil house to deserve such ruin. Never had she loathed a place so much.

Yet her steps took her forward.

He waited in the doorway, the man with the dead-white face.

"Princess," he said as she drew near, "you have come to me."

She opened her mouth to answer. But instead of words, a scream filled her throat and poured out like rushing water. The sound filled her inside and out, a blinding, numbing, dreadful noise.

"Where are you?" His voice roared, dark beneath the white shriek of her scream. "Where are you? I've waited long enough!"

Una woke in a sweat. The ring on her hand pinched, and her fingers burned. Sitting up, she tore the coverlet away; it seemed to cling and suffocate her like a snake squeezing her in its coils. Shuddering breaths gasped out of her, and she rubbed her face with her burning hands.

"Preeowl?" Monster nosed his way out from under the quilt and tried to insinuate himself into her lap. But Una pushed him away. Drawing a long breath and trying to calm her heart, she slipped out of bed and staggered to the table with the pitcher of water.

It was empty. The maid must have forgotten to refill it.

"Dragon's teeth!" She pulled open the curtains. The window was already ajar, but the summer night offered no cooling relief. She felt tears sting her eyes and rested her head for a moment against the window frame.

Never before had she remembered her dreams on waking. But tonight the vision stayed in her mind as vividly as if she still walked in that blighted garden. As vividly as if she gazed even now into the eyes of the white-faced man.

Memories of other dreams trickled in on the edge of consciousness as she stood there looking out on the garden. She did not understand them, but she wondered now how she could have forgotten. Her fingers throbbed, and she longed for water.

The moon burst through a cloud and shone down upon her face.

Suddenly, even more than water, Una yearned to walk in that light, to breathe it in and feel it cool her inside.

"Meea?" Monster put up a paw and touched her knee.

"Go away," she said, glaring down at him. She hastened across the room to her wardrobe and withdrew a bedgown from its depths. She put it on and slipped from the room.

A few servants stood at various posts in the long halls of Oriana, but most of them dozed so late in the night. Una moved past without disturbing them and made it all the way out to the gardens without encountering a single waking soul. No lanterns were lit on the garden paths, not at this hour. But the moon was bright, and her eyes adjusted to its light enough to walk the familiar paths. The gravel path hurt her bare feet, but she scarcely noticed for the pain in her hands.

Monster trailed behind her, a silent shadow.

She did not walk far. She did not need to. Breathing in great gulps of moonlight, Una felt the heat slowly leave her. The tightness of her ring lessened. But when she looked at her hands, she was surprised to see scarlet burn lines across her fingers. Even in the dimness of the moon's glow, the raw red was discernible. She clutched her hands into fists.

Farther down the tiered garden, a wood thrush sang. Its silver voice floated on the warm air and ran like water around her. She turned toward the sound and gasped.

Prince Aethelbald walked toward her, up the garden path. The moon cast his shadow before him.

He saw her at the same moment. He stopped, and Una could not see his face in the shadows. Drawing her bedgown more tightly around her, she waited for him to either come or go.

"Preeowl?" Monster loped ahead of her, scampering to Aethelbald's feet. The Prince knelt down and stroked the cat's head, murmuring something that Una could not hear. Monster flicked his tail and gave several chattering squawks. Then he dashed off into the bushes as though he'd suddenly heard a mouse. Una felt abandoned by her pet as Aethelbald straightened and continued up the path to her.

"Princess," he greeted her, and she prepared for the questions—"What are you doing here? Why are you up at this hour?"

But instead he said, "I am leaving."

Leaving? Her brows drew together, and she clenched her fists as she wrapped her arms about herself. Somehow Una could think of nothing to say.

"I must go at once," he said.

Slowly she nodded. Aethelbald showed no sign of making good his word and dashing off immediately but stood a long while in silence before her. At last Una managed to whisper, "Why?"

"One of mine is threatened," he said, "far away south. The danger has been mounting, but soon it will be unbearable. I must go before it is too late."

"Do . . . do as you must, Prince Aethelbald." Una looked down at her feet and drew another shaky breath. The pain in her hands was agonizing. She thought she might scream.

Aethelbald reached out and took one of her hands. This time she did not pull it back but allowed him to turn it palm up. The burns showed ugly in the moonlight. Gently Aethelbald touched the wounds, and though something in Una urged her to run as far away as she could, she stood silent, unmoving. His touch was soothing, and some of the terror of her dream withdrew.

"Una," he said gently, "I do not want to leave you. I go because I must."

Again she tried to speak, but her tongue was thick in her mouth. Her frown deepened, and her fingers curled as though forming claws.

"I will return to you."

She took a step back, but he did not release his hold. Setting her chin, she tried to drag her arm back, but still he held on. Then her eyes flashed and she glared up at him. "I . . . I don't want you to return!"

She regretted the words the moment they left her mouth. But they were gone beyond recall now. Hurt flickered over the shadows of his face, but he held her hand just a moment longer.

"Nevertheless, I will come back for you."

His eyes were kind, but they frightened her. Why had she thought to venture out alone at night? What could possibly have possessed her? Some idiotic dream? The images flooded out of her mind as swiftly as they had flowed in, and she was left feeling deeply embarrassed, conscious only that she stood in the moonlight before the last man in the world with whom she wanted to stand in moonlight.

"Please, Una," he said, "let me tend your hurts before I go. . . ."

She hauled her hand away and backed up so fast that she stepped on the edge of her bedgown, nearly pulling herself down. The hem ripped, long and loud, and she knew she would be in for another scolding from Nurse when the damage was discovered. Angrily she snapped, "I have no hurts, Prince of Farthestshore! I don't know what you're talking about! I am perfectly well, my hands are perfectly well, all would be perfectly well if only you would leave a girl alone for once! Can't I even take a stroll without you hounding my footsteps? Go already, if you're going to! I wish you'd gone ages ago! I wish . . . I wish you'd never come!"

Tears sprang to her eyes and dripped down her cheeks, and she just knew he could see them. Dragons eat him! She whirled about to go, but even as she rushed toward the garden door, she heard the crunch of his boots on the gravel as he hastened up beside her.

"Una," he said, and put out an arm to block her path. Aethelbald did not touch her, but she drew back as though bitten. "I love you, Una," he said. "I will return to ask for your hand. In the meanwhile, please don't give your heart away."

The next moment, he was gone.

Una stood alone by the garden door, gazing out across an empty garden. In the east, the sky was just beginning to lighten, though many stars gleamed overhead.

She returned to her stuffy chamber and crawled back into bed. Before falling asleep, she glanced at her hands. There was not a mark to be seen. Burying her face in her pillow, she fell asleep.

Hours later, the Prince of Farthestshore and his three knights were gone. When Una made what she hoped were disinterested inquiries over breakfast, her father informed her that Aethelbald had taken his leave of Fidel the evening before and set out from Oriana before dawn.

"I guess you finally drove him off," Felix said, glumly stirring his oatmeal.

"I did no such thing. I merely made myself clear. And what do you care? You didn't exactly treat him as the favored guest!"

"I don't care," Felix shrugged, but his long face suggested otherwise. He imagined returning to his fencing practice in company with his attendants, and the thought gave him no pleasure. "Let him go, I say. It's not like we ever *needed* him."

"No," Una said. "No, we certainly never needed him."

But she had no appetite that morning.

Weary after her restless night, Una excused herself from lectures and returned to her rooms. As she turned into the east wing, where her chambers were located, she spotted a servant hard at work, mopping. She paused in surprise as recognition slowly caught up in her tired brain.

"Leonard!" She shook her head and stepped down the hall toward him. "I hardly know you without your costume. Where is your hat?"

The jester, looking singularly unjesterly in a baggy brown smock, dropped his mop with a splash and straightened. "Princess Una." He gulped. "Hullo. Yes, I've come to quite a state, haven't I?"

"What are you doing?" Una demanded with a laugh.

He smiled back, but his smile was forced. "It would seem I am unable to earn my bread with full-time foolery. I must harden myself to the rigors of the baser tasks a man can stoop to, such as mopping the floors of those who . . . Well, it is employment, isn't it? A fellow must be grateful."

"Oh," Una hastened to say, "please, I didn't intend to make fun. This is only temporary, anyway, isn't it? You won't have to work like this for long, I'm sure."

Leonard raised an eyebrow. "You are kind to your humble servant, m'lady." He nodded curtly, then stooped to retrieve his mop.

"No, truly, I am sorry," Una said. "You really are a wonderful jester, you know, and I'm sure you'll find work—"

"I have sufficient work, obviously. And don't you think it odd for a princess to apologize to her cleaning staff?" He bowed and turned away. His arms worked furiously back and forth, pushing the mop.

Una, having never before been brushed off by one of the servants, could think of nothing to say. She hurried down the hall, shaking her head and wondering why she felt embarrassed.

But before she'd gone far, Leonard called after her. "M'lady?"

She stopped, surprised, and looked back.

The jester stood with both hands on the top of the mop stick, rubbing the back of his leg with the opposite foot.

"M'lady, I don't think you should accept the Prince of Farthestshore's suit," the jester said. "When he returns. If he returns."

Una drew herself up. "I don't see what business it is of yours, my good man." She spoke coolly in what she thought of as her regal voice. But the red blotches crept over her nose anyway.

Leonard stared boldly back at her for several moments before averting his gaze to study his feet. "Of course, a floor scrubber's opinion counts for nothing, m'lady."

Una hastened on to her rooms.

13

ANOTHER SUITOR announced his intention of paying his respects at Oriana Palace.

"Iubdan's beard, they're thicker 'an flies in July, these wooers of yours, Miss Princess!" said Nurse.

"Who is it this time?" Una asked. She scarcely glanced up from the *Bane of Corrilond* tapestry when Nurse entered the room bringing word. She found herself less able to work up any measure of excitement over the matter than before. So far suitors had afforded her more distress than anything.

"The Duke of Shippening," Nurse said. "A powerful man, master of Capaneus, the greatest port city on all the Continent!"

Una paused with her needle pulled partway through a bean man's eye. "The Duke of . . . But Nurse, he's older than Father!"

"A sturdy age, practically the prime of life."

"*Practically?*"

"Close enough, anyway. And his estates are—"

"He's been called the largest man south of Beauclair!"

"As I said, he is quite wealthy—"

"Regarding his girth, not his riches!"

Nurse sniffed. "Good health is always desirable in a spouse. Why, my Uncle Balbo was a man of no mean scope, but he always . . ."

Una ceased to hear Nurse champion the virtues of famous Uncle Balbo as she stared in horror down at her needlework. The bean man she was currently working had his mouth open in a silent scream as he fled the onslaught of the flaming threads. Una felt her own face mirroring his expression. "The Duke of Shippening?" She closed her eyes. "Why me? Why couldn't some other princess be blessed with such suitors?"

Before Nurse had quite run out of steam for her monologue, Una leapt up and fled the room, deaf to Nurse's cries of, "Where are you going now, Miss Princess? If you go off in that Wood of yours and come back a mass of burrs, just see if I'll—"

The door shut, and Una hastened down the hall, hardly knowing where she went. For all the grandeur of Oriana Palace, with its hundreds of rooms and sweeping corridors and pillared halls, she felt trapped like a bird in a cage. Not even the gardens seemed welcoming once she got out into them, for rather than enjoying the summer beauty, she felt aware only of the walls rising all around. So she gathered her skirts and made once more for her beloved Wood.

Five weeks had passed since Prince Aethelbald had taken himself away, and summer was bursting with full glory, including gnats and bugs. But as soon as she stepped into the shadows of Goldstone Wood, the insects disappeared and the heat of the sun passed into coolness. She followed familiar landmarks down to the Old Bridge.

The Duke of Shippening?

All romance seemed to have vanished from life in one fell swoop. She might as well give it all up now and begin preparing herself for the role of spinster princess of Parumvir—

"Ouch! That *was* my foot."

Una screamed and leapt back. "Oh, Leonard! It's you!"

Sitting in the shade of a spreading oak was the jester. He was propped with his hands behind his head and his feet spread out before him, facing the stream and the Old Bridge. He drew back one foot and rubbed it.

"Did I step on you?" Una asked. She felt the blotches leaping into their accustomed places and self-consciously covered her face with her hand.

"No," said the jester. He rose politely, dusting dirt and bracken from his trousers, then bowed with all the courtesy of a lord. "You kicked me. Hard. Like unto broke the bone!" But then he saw the distress on her face and shook his head. "No, m'lady, you scarcely touched me. You appeared so set on your path, I feared if I didn't speak up, you might walk right on into the stream and drown without noticing."

"Without noticing you or without noticing drowning?"

"Both, probably." He grinned. "Do you come here often?"

Una nodded. She found herself reminded suddenly of her meeting with Aethelbald in this same spot, many weeks ago now. But she shook that thought away. Aethelbald was gone, and if all went as she expected, he'd never return. She folded her arms and regarded the jester. "What are you doing out here?"

He inclined his head. "You mean, of course, don't you have a certain amount of mopping or sweeping, or some such menial task you could be attending to as we speak?"

"I didn't—"

"But in fact, m'lady, this humble riffraff has already completed his quotient of demeaning labor for the morning and was given the afternoon off to practice his foolishness. And he needs the practice badly enough, for he is beginning to fear that he shall have to give up this brilliant career."

"What? Why?"

"Why? She asks me why?" Leonard picked up a handful of acorn caps and started juggling them as he spoke. "Three times," he said, "three times I witnessed the princess yawn last night as I sang. Not once, not twice, but thrice! And yet m'lady asks me why."

"Don't be silly," Una said.

"Can't be helped. It's my job."

"But I didn't yawn when you sang, Leonard!"

"Then why did you cover your mouth with your handkerchief? I saw it with my own eyes!" He bowed his head, the picture of dejection, but continued juggling the acorns at lightning speed.

"I was trying to keep from laughing too hard!" Una said, her eyes darting as they tried to follow the progress of the acorns. "I was. So you see, you must continue your brilliant career, jester. Where would my amusement come from if you abandoned it?"

He looked up. "Do I indeed amuse you, m'lady?"

"You amuse me vastly." She shook her head. "Silly, how could I not be amused? Why, you've gone and tied bells to your elbows and knees. Just when I thought you couldn't look more ridiculous!"

"I am droll, though, am I not?" With that he tossed the acorns up in the air with feigned clumsiness; a trick which he must have practiced a thousand times, for it took skill to make each one, though they appeared to fly at random, land on his head, one after the other. He made a different face as each struck, and Una had to laugh.

"You snicker at me," he said, shaking a fist at her, "but I know that you are secretly jealous. 'Ah!' the lady sighs, 'if only *I* could wear bells upon my elbows, then my life should be complete!' "

"Heaven forbid," Una said. "Oriana has room for only one Fool, I believe."

"Especially so great a fool as I," the jester replied without a smile. "And what brings you down here, Princess Una?"

She sighed. "Suitors."

"You make it sound like the descending hordes. How many this time?"

"The Duke of Shippening."

"Ah. Comparable to a half dozen at least." Leonard turned and strode to the Old Bridge, but he didn't step onto it. Instead he climbed down the bank to the rocks alongside the stream and began collecting pebbles. He juggled them a few moments, then tossed them back into the stream and searched for more.

Una took a seat on the bridge and dangled her feet over the edge, watching the jester. "Have you ever," she began, then paused, considering her words. "Have you ever dreamed of one thing for so long, wanted nothing more than to have that dream fulfilled, only to find out that maybe it wasn't what you actually wanted all along?"

He juggled four stones lightly. "I believe that's called growing up." He switched to one hand, the little rocks flashing wet in the sun.

Una watched without actually seeing and continued to think aloud. "But then you find yourself lost without your dream." She toyed with her opal ring, twisting it around on her finger and watching the light reflecting in its depths. "Like half your heart is gone right along with it."

Leonard tossed the four stones out into the stream in a quick series of splashes. "Dreams are tricky business, m'lady. It's best to hold on to what you know, not what you want. Know your duty, know your path, and do everything you can to achieve what you have set out to do. Don't let dreams get in your way. Dreams will never accomplish the work of firm resolve."

Una looked at him, pushing wisps of loose hair out of her face. "What have you resolved, Leonard, that you won't stop for dreams?"

He did not turn to her but stared out at the water. The gurgling current had swallowed his stones with scarcely a ripple. She watched him fix his mouth in a frown.

"I am resolved," he said in a low voice, "to return home as soon as I may."

"Home?" she said. "You mean Southlands?"

He nodded.

"Is it far away?"

"Very far, m'lady."

Southlands can burn to dust for all I care.

Una knew very little of Southlands, far down at the southernmost tip of the Continent, a peninsula connected to Shippening only by a thin isthmus. But there were rumors about that land, particularly in the last five years. It was cut off from the rest of the Continent now, held captive by . . . The rumors were vague on that point. But the king and queen had not been seen in all that time; no one, in fact, had either come or gone through the mountain paths that encircled Southlands. And heavy smoke hung thick as death over all the land.

Una shuddered. Nurse would not permit her to listen to gossip, but she could not help but pick up little pieces of information. Southlands was so far from the concerns of her life that she had paid little heed to the rumors. But she remembered words overheard here and there.

Death. Demon.

Dragon.

Southlands can burn.

"Is it true, Leonard?" she asked, twisting the ring on her finger again. "Is it true what they say about . . . about your homeland?"

"Maybe, maybe not." He tossed a larger rock with a *gloomp* into the middle of the stream. "I don't know what they say."

A shiver passed through Una's body despite the heat of the day. "Did you escape before the rest of Southlands was imprisoned?"

Leonard looked sidelong up at her. "Does it really matter how or when I escaped, if escaped we must call it? I am here, my people are there. My friends. My family. So I will return."

"Can you do anything, though?" Una knew she should not pry when the jester so obviously did not want to talk about his life, but the questions came anyway. "Not in five years has anyone succeeded in crossing to Southlands alive. Don't you think you should stay away for now? What could you do by returning anyway?"

"Princess Una," he replied, "you are young and sweet. You can't know about such things. I may be only a Fool, but even a Fool must see his duty, and when he sees it, he must follow through. What else can he do and still consider himself a man? Perhaps I cannot help my people. Perhaps I will live long enough to see their destruction and then perish in the same fire. But nevertheless I will go." He turned away from her and kicked another stone into the passing water. "As soon as I can put together funds enough for the journey."

"Then I think you are a very brave Fool," Una said quietly.

"If I were not a Fool, do you think I could be brave?"

They looked at each other, a silent gaze. And Una thought she'd never met a man of such firm resolution. Prince Gervais would not be so courageous.

What the jester thought she could not fathom, but he smiled slowly and at last ended the moment by crossing his eyes and sticking out his tongue so that she laughed and shook her head at him. "Clown!"

"The things you call me," he replied, dashing his bell-covered hat from his head and sweeping a deep bow. "M'lady, the day lengthens. If I do not return you home soon, questions will be asked, and do you think this humble floor-scrubber will escape a kicking from his superiors for hindering a princess in her daily schedule?"

So Una took his arm when he offered it and allowed him to escort her up the hill, through the tiered garden, and back to Nurse's well-prepared scolding. She sat quietly through the rest of the afternoon, allowing Nurse's words to skim over her head, and tried not to think the thoughts that pried at her mind.

A pity he's a jester.

But, no more of that! Get back to work and remember who you are.

Leonard had called her sweet. Did he mean it?

"Dragon's teeth!" Una muttered and attacked her tapestry with more vim and vigor than she'd given it in a long while, stabbing her finger with her needle. She was well distracted from her thoughts as she tried to keep blood from staining her handiwork.

The Duke of Shippening arrived five days later.

Not even Nurse, once she saw the man, thought Una should consider his proposal. For all her practicality, Nurse did not wish to see her beloved princess in the hands of a man more than twice her age and five times her size. But she did not express this opinion; when asked, she refused to express any opinion whatsoever. It is wise never to speak negatively of one so rich and powerful as the duke.

As for Una, she could hardly look at the man without trembling.

He joined the royal family at dinner that night, speaking in rumbling tones of Capaneus, of his vast estate, of his hundreds of serfs and acres upon acres of grounds, of hunting adventures, of tearing a wild boar apart with his bare hands—Felix's jaw dropped nearly to his collarbone as he listened—and all the other sweet details of his domestic existence.

"Yes," the duke rumbled, "life is fair and easy, I must admit, but if there's one thing it lacks, that's a woman's ministering hand. What do you say, Fidel, old boy? Where would we be without our womenfolk, eh?"

King Fidel raised a glass and said nothing. When he'd received word that the duke wished to "pay his respects," his own heart had sunk—not so much for fear of losing his daughter to this man, but because he'd known the duke since childhood, when they'd been obliged to play together as noblemen's children should. He retained vivid memories of being sat upon by the large boy, memories which had not improved with time.

"So, what do you think of all this dragon talk?" the duke asked as the meal neared its end and all his stories of himself were told out. Though he spoke to the king, his gaze rested on Una. She wished she could evaporate.

"I try not to make too much of it," King Fidel replied. "We've heard rumors of dragons before, but no dragon has ever come near Parumvir."

"Ah, but this is different," the duke said, stabbing a last slab of beef from the platter before a servant carried it off. "I've been hearing tell in Shippening that a dragon has plagued Southlands many years now. Now, Southlands is far from Parumvir, to be sure, but it ain't so far from Shippening. Trade with Southlands has been nonexistent, and one never hears from the royal family or any ambassadors. They say the crown prince, Lionheart, was killed by the creature. The others may or may not be alive—who's to know? But lately there've been changes. Word is, the Dragon has left Southlands. They say it's coming north, hunting something."

"Who says?" King Fidel demanded.

"Oh, recently a few stragglers from Southlands have made their way to Shippening, saying the Dragon is looking to procreate. It's hunting out likely prospects maybe, eh?"

"You mean it wants to mate and lay an egg?" Felix asked, whose imagination pictured dragons as overlarge lizards with forked tongues like a snake's.

The duke roared with laughter and pounded his fist on the table several times. Una lowered her head and bowed her shoulders. "Mate? Lay an egg?" the duke bellowed. "Boy, have you been reading faerie stories? Don't you know where dragons come from?"

"Please," King Fidel said, "I would rather you did not—"

"I'm just educating the boy, Majesty!" the duke cried. "Why, in these times he'd better know what he's up against. Life ain't a pretty faerie story, you know. When that dragon comes calling—"

"Stop," Fidel said.

The duke shut his mouth.

They finished eating in silence, then retired to the sitting room as usual. To Una's dismay, the duke was asked to join them, and he accepted. He sat in a chair next to Una's, lit his pipe, and proceeded to puff fumes her way, chuckling quietly to himself when she coughed. She cast desperate glances toward her father, but he was preoccupied with his own thoughts. Felix got out his game of sticks, and the room was quiet but for the clicks of sticks and stifled coughs.

At last the door opened and Leonard stepped in. He still wore his odd yellow suit—only now it was significantly cleaner than when Una had first met him, and there were patches of bright turquoise, orange, and pale pink where once had been only holes. He looked, on the whole, the product of a colorblind quilter's fancy, which was probably the intent.

He paused in the doorway, taking in the scene before him. Una smiled, but he would not look at her. His gaze rested heavily on the duke, who was dozing over his pipe. Leonard lifted a hand, struck a sour chord on his lute, and cried, "What-*ho*! A merry bunch you are tonight!"

He sprang into the middle of the room with such a clatter of bells and noise that Una dropped her needle and the duke let out an "Oooof!" as he startled awake.

"Keep it down, jester," King Fidel said. "We're glad to see you, but must you *resound* so?"

"Resound? Your Majesty, I've hardly begun to peal!" A strange gleam lit the jester's eyes, and his smile was not at all pleasant, Una thought. She stared at him, aghast, as he disregarded her father's command and strummed another loud, discordant sound on his lute. "I've written a new song," he said. "Rather, rewritten an old one in honor of our esteemed guest."

"That's decent of you, Fool," the duke said, tapping ashes from his pipe onto the rug. "I haven't heard a good song in ages."

"A *good* song I cannot promise," the jester said. "But such a song as it is, I give to you. 'The Sorry Fate of the Beastly Lout.'"

Una's mouth dropped open as Leonard began to sing a variation of the song he'd sung to her on the day they had met. Only this time he sang with a great, insincere smile on his face.

> *"With audacity gawky, the Beastly Lout*
> *Would loiter and dawdle and maybe*
> *Try his luck wenching, casting about*
> *To court a most beauteous lady.*
>
> *"But to his dismay, he was made aware*
> *That his suit was unwelcome before her.*
> *Our poor Beastly Lout felt her pickling stare*
> *'Cause his stories did certainly bore her.*
>
> *"Ah, sad Beastly Lout, how he tried to be nice,*
> *But his courting just could not amuse her right.*
> *For, you see, his great noggin was covered in lice,*
> *Which is hardly appealing in any light."*

The Duke of Shippening guffawed and slapped his knee. "Now, there's a song for you!" he cried. "Bravo! Sing another, boy! And how about a round of something to lighten the mood? The rest of you are stiff as pokers!"

This wasn't entirely true, for Felix was doubled up, trying to keep from barking with laughter while his father scowled down on him. Una had gone pale at the first line, red blotches lining her nose and cheeks.

"Fool!" the duke bellowed. "Sing again, I tell you! Set that tongue of yours to work!"

"No," King Fidel said, turning his glare on Leonard, who stood straight, his gaze fixed on the wall across the room. "I believe you are done here, jester. Good-bye."

Leonard bowed and left the room with a last jangle of bells.

"Why, Majesty," the duke cried, "I haven't been so amused in years! Is he hired on to you long term? If not—"

Without asking to be excused, Una leapt up and hurried from the room. The tune of that horrible song rang in her ears along with the duke's roar of a laugh. Tears filled her eyes as she made her way blindly down the hall.

Someone grabbed her arm, and she found herself pulled into a side corridor, spun about, and face-to-face with the jester.

"What do you think you're doing?" she cried, shaking his hand away. Her heart pounded, and she thought she would choke on the words garbled in her throat. "Insulting our how could you, you've gone and what were you—"

"You can't marry that lout," he said, his voice thick, almost menacing. Leonard looked down on her, his eyes so huge and frightening that she had to cover her face with her hands.

"I don't intend to marry that lout!" she growled, able to speak when she did not look at him. "I have no intention of marrying anyone, not that it is any of *your* business!"

"M'lady—"

"You've gone and gotten yourself discharged, you fool!"

"No!" Leonard said sharply. He took Una's hands and pulled them away from her face. "M'lady," he said, "look at me. Please. I'm not a Fool."

She turned her face away and spoke to the wall. "I don't know what else you call a commoner who insults a royal guest and gets himself—"

"No, Una," Leonard said. He squeezed her hands in his. "I am not a Fool, not a jester. I am Prince Lionheart of Southlands."

14

W HAT?"

"Please look at me, Una," said the jester. "I said I am Prince
Lionheart of Southlands."

Una blinked. Then she pushed away his hands and stepped back.
"You . . . you're a dragon-eaten Fool."

"No, I'm not." He paused, then added, "Well, yes, maybe I am. But
that's beside the point. I have been Leonard the Jester for a good five
years now, but my real name is Lionheart, and I am—"

"Prince of Southlands." She backed up until she hit the far wall. "A
likely story."

"You don't believe me?"

"No."

He set his jaw, puffing out an angry breath. "I know. You're used to
the sight of me scrubbing your floors and windows. Not a very princely
posture, eh? So what must I do to prove myself? Cut my arm and show
you how blue my blood is?"

"You could explain either why you are lying to me now or why you lied to me earlier. That would make an excellent beginning."

He removed his bell-covered hat and rubbed his hand through his hair so that it stood up like tufts of grass. "That's a bit of a story," he said and indicated the floor. "Will you sit?"

"I will not."

"This may take time."

"Then you'd better get started before I lose what's left of my interest."

His eyes narrowed and his hands gripped his jester hat as though he would like to pull it in two. "I'll try to keep it brief. I am the crown prince of Southlands—"

"We covered that."

"Shush! Let me speak." But it took him several moments of considering his words before he could begin again. At last he spoke in a low voice without looking at Una, still pulling at his hat.

"It came from nowhere. I remember the day, the exact moment, I saw the fire drop from the sky. We'd had no warning. That is . . . well, how can you be warned against something like that? Of course you hear stories of dragons, but you never expect you'll see one. They belong to the ancient history of Southlands, back before we traded with the Continent, back before we knew better than to worship and revere such monsters. Hundreds of years ago.

"But it came one fine spring day, dropped from the sky like a blazing meteor. In no time it laid waste to the surrounding countryside, set fire to the barracks that housed my father's guard, trapped my parents and eighteen other nobles inside the Eldest's House, holding them for ransom to their own people. The Dragon demanded it be brought a prime beef cow every day and instant obedience to whatever other orders it might give." The jester-prince shuddered at the memory. "It crawled about the castle grounds, destroying the gardens, burning the walls. I don't know how many people it killed with its poison breath alone. The air was thick, more putrid than you can imagine."

A memory came to Una as she listened. A memory, she knew not from where. She saw a great castle and a ruined garden, and a sky heavy with smoke and fumes. "Where were you at the time?" she asked in a whisper.

"I had gone out riding with a friend that day and was not at the castle when the Dragon descended. We'd ridden all the way to the Swan Bridge on the far south end of my father's grounds, but we saw the fire fall from there and rode back as fast as we could. When we approached, my friend was terrified by the sounds and smells and begged me to ride back to her father's estate with her rather than face that fire—"

"Her?" The word slipped out unbidden, and Una blushed.

The jester-prince smiled. "A friend, I assure you. But I refused to listen and rode out to face the monster armed only with a knife. It didn't matter. The mightiest sword ever forged by man would not pierce the hide of that great beast."

"What did it do when it saw you?"

He shook his head ruefully. "It laughed. It opened its vast mouth and roared with laughter, flames in its teeth.

" 'Prince Lionheart!' it said. 'Welcome. You wish to try your mettle on me?'

"The fumes of its breath choked me so that I could hardly breathe, and my horse, in a terror, threw me and galloped away. I was left alone, gasping and helpless. The Dragon crawled toward me, and I could not move for the burning pain in my lungs. It gazed down at me with its red eyes. It seemed like an eternity that it stared at me, its gaze burning my skin. I thought I would die; I hoped I would."

Una reached out and touched his hand. He grasped hers tightly in both of his.

"At last it said, 'You are a tempting morsel, little prince. But alas, I lost that game long ago! No, I fear I must give you up. Perhaps I shall eat you instead?'

"Then it gazed deeper still. I felt as though my flesh and bones were burned away, leaving only my flickering spirit struggling naked in the grass.

" 'Ah!' the Dragon said. 'Ah, perhaps you are not for snacking after all! You will help me, won't you? Yes, of course you will. Get up, little prince, and journey into the world. I send you to your exile. But we'll meet again, and perhaps you'll find your throne after all?' "

Lionheart's face went quite pale as he recounted the Dragon's words, and his voice altered as he spoke them. Then he was silent a long moment before he could continue. "I have thought over those words a thousand times, trying to discern some significance, perhaps some clue to the monster's destruction. But they seem as meaningless to me now as they did then in the middle of all that heat and poison." He shook his head slowly, as though trying to free himself of the memory. "That is all I can recall of that day. When I awoke, it was a week later. My friend had brought me to her father's estate in Middlecrescent. She nursed me back from a horrible fever that nearly took my life. The dragon smoke was thick across the country by then.

"That very day, though I was still weak, I packed a bag, saddled a horse, and journeyed north. In Shippening I found work as a minstrel." He smiled, rather sadly Una thought, as he mentioned this. "I've always had a knack for clowning, and I picked up a good many tricks as I journeyed across the countryside. I've worked as a jester in the various courts and manors of Beauclair, Milden, and beyond. But it was when I traveled east that I learned a thing or two about dragons."

"How to kill them, you mean?" Una asked.

"Perhaps." He looked down at his feet. "But I begin to fear I will never have the opportunity to try."

"Why not?"

"Southlands is far, far from Parumvir, especially on foot. Jesters' pay is not what it might be either, especially for one newly discharged."

"Why go on with this charade, then?" Una pulled her hand free and paced away from him. "Tell my father who you are," she said. "Tell him! He will surely supply you with equipment, with soldiers even. He will help you battle this monster, I'm sure of it. My father is a generous man. I know he—"

"M'lady," he interrupted, "what proof have I for my story? Any small token I possessed marking my heritage I was obliged to sell long ago to buy bread. My only proof is my face, which my family, should they yet live, will recognize. If ever I am able to return to them, I shall kill that monster and reclaim my kingdom. I shall come into my own as heir of Southlands at last. Only then would I have the right to speak to your father. As it is, I cannot ask him for aid, and I cannot ask him for—"

He stopped and gazed at her, his eyes intent and sad.

"Oh," she whispered.

"So you see, it is best that I leave," he said. "I cannot bear to watch these suitors of yours, knowing I have no right to . . . to pursue you myself."

"Oh," she whispered again.

"Una." He approached her, standing near enough that she felt the warmth of his breath on her forehead, though he did not touch her. "Una, I must leave. I have a dragon to fight, a kingdom to reclaim. I may not be able to return."

"I understand."

"Will you trust me?" he asked.

She didn't speak for a long moment. To her irritation, two memories flashed through her mind.

The first was of Gervais standing in the garden, singing a song he had chosen just for her.

The second was of Prince Aethelbald putting out a restraining hand. *"I love you, Una. I will return to ask for your hand."*

"Una?" The jester-prince spoke softly. She felt his gaze burning the top of her bowed head. "Una, trust me."

"All right," she said. Then she raised her eyes to him and smiled. "All right, Prince Lionheart. I trust you."

He grinned. "Thank you."

With those words he turned and strode quickly down the hall.

"Wait!" Una cried, running after him. "Are you going so soon?"

"Immediately. I must find employment so that I can save for the long journey. Una, I don't know how long it will be, and I won't be able to contact you in the interval—"

"Don't worry about me!" she said. She caught him by the arm and pulled him to a stop. "Please, Leonard . . . Lionheart. Please, before you go . . ." Hardly knowing what she did, Una took off her mother's opal ring. For a moment it stuck, and she thought it might not come off. But then it slid from her finger and she held it out to the jester-prince.

"Here," she said, pressing it into his hand. "It was my mother's. I don't know how much it is worth, but something close to a king's ransom, I should think. Use it for your journey and . . . and come back soon."

He looked at the ring, turning it to see how the light caught and burned deep inside the iridescent stones. Then he raised his gaze to Una again. Gently, he reached out and touched her cheek with a finger. "Trust me, Una," he whispered once more.

Then he left, and she did not see him again for a long time.

There is nothing like a secret to create mystery in a girl, and Una was nothing if not a mystery to all around her in the following days.

"Dear child!" Nurse cried when Una burst into tears for no apparent reason three mornings after the jester left. "Dear child, what troubles you?"

"Nothing," Una said, wiping her eyes and sighing. "Nothing. Isn't this a beautiful world, Nurse? I mean in general, you know?"

Nurse closed one eye and looked at her sidelong. "Is it?"

Una thought about it. "No. Not really." She burst into tears again, digging for a handkerchief between hiccups. Monster, sitting at her feet, meowed and touched her knee with a paw. She nudged him away. "No, it's a cruel world."

Nurse thought it expedient to bring news of this conversation to King Fidel.

"Are you certain?" Fidel asked.

"I know what I heard. I know what I saw," Nurse said.

"But what does it mean?"

"I'll tell you what it means, sire," Nurse said. "She's in love, that's what it means, and not like she was with Prince Gervais either! No, this is a more serious kind. She goes about sighing with a look of noble suffering on her face. So either it's unrequited or he is far away at present. Either way, I know the symptoms."

"In love?" Fidel wiped his brow. "If you are right, I do hope it's the latter, Nurse. If he's far away, that rules out the duke."

"The duke? Gracious, no!" Nurse said.

At that timely moment the duke himself made an appearance.

"Majesty!"

His voice boomed through Fidel's head, and the king's knees trembled a little as vivid memories of smotherment sprang to mind. But he pulled himself together and said, "My good duke, is something troubling—"

"Is something troubling me?" the duke cried, and the windows shook. "Is something troubling me, you ask? Majesty, I don't mind saying that something is troubling me right enough!" He swore roundly, and Nurse pursed her lips and folded her hands.

"I am sorry to hear it." Fidel prided himself that his voice remained calm. "Whatever your grievance may be, I hope—"

"That daughter of yours!"

"Una?"

"Whatever her name is! Why didn't you tell me she was betrothed?"

"Betrothed?" the king and Nurse cried.

The duke swore again. "You could have spared my pride by a word, Majesty. But no, just let me walk into the lion's den, my eyes wide shut, spoutin' professions of love and wedding plans and asking about the dowry—"

"Una is hardly a lion."

The duke raised a hand. "Don't try pulling that gibberish about innocent, guileless maidens with me! You set her up to this, didn't you? Wanted to get back at me for a few childish pranks, huh? Well, I'll tell you what I think!"

And he did for the next quarter of an hour, until King Fidel at last summoned his guard to escort the irate duke elsewhere.

"There goes our alliance with Shippening." Fidel sank into the thick-padded chair behind his desk, sighing. "Oh, Una. Betrothed in secret? And to whom?"

"Who could it be but Prince Aethelbald?" Nurse said.

"Aethelbald?"

"Of course. And now she's pining for him; he's been gone for weeks. Poor little dear must have been afraid to tell me for pride, she was that set against him for so long. . . ."

"Wait," Fidel said. "That does not sound like Una—and it certainly does not sound like Prince Aethelbald. He would not contract a betrothal with her without informing me. Besides, he was none too happy when he left Oriana—hardly had the look of a man newly betrothed."

"Why would he seem happy?" Nurse asked. "He was leaving his lady behind for who's to say how long? And I told you, she's got all the signs of long-suffering love about her. Perhaps she denied him, then thought better of it after he'd gone? Who else but Prince Aethelbald has been trying to woo her, I'd like to know?"

"Yes," King Fidel murmured, "so would I." He rose, his face dark with thought. "Thank you, Nurse, for your insights. Now, where is my daughter?"

Fidel found Una wandering in the gardens, dreamily gazing off into the clouds. She smiled when she saw her father. "Good afternoon, Father," she said. "Isn't it a beautiful world?"

"What's this I hear about your betrothal?" Fidel demanded, preferring not to beat about the bush.

"I am not betrothed," Una said. "I told the duke no."

Fidel stood and inspected his daughter. She did not seem particularly altered to him. Perhaps there was some trace of what Nurse called "noble suffering" or some such nonsense, but he could've been imagining that. "You are not betrothed?" he asked. "The duke seemed convinced otherwise."

Una blushed. "I cannot help what the duke thinks. You know that I cannot enter into a betrothal without your blessing."

"And you know you will have it so long as the man of your choice knows better than to eat soup with his fingers and isn't up to his ears in debt," the king said. He looked deep into Una's eyes, and she met his gaze only a few moments before turning away. "Una, what did you tell the duke to give him the impression that you are betrothed?"

"Nothing, I—"

"Una?"

Her lip twitched and she sniffed. "I . . . I told him that my heart belongs to another. He asked what that had to do with marriage, and I said, 'Everything,' and sent him on his way."

With this she burst into another one of her recent torrents of sobbing, which her father had not before witnessed. He could not recall the last time he'd seen Una cry and was entirely uncertain what to do about it.

"There, there, child," he said, patting her shoulder. "There, there. It's not as bad as all that. He will return soon, I have no doubt."

"Do you think so?" Una asked, raising her tear-filled eyes. "How do you know?"

"He spoke to me before he set out, of course," Fidel said, pleased to see how her face brightened. "He promised that he would return as soon as this whole dragon business is settled."

"He did?" Una beamed like a blaze of sunshine through thick clouds. "Oh, Father, how perfectly wonderful!"

She flung her arms about his neck, and he patted her more comfortably. "I don't know about perfectly," he said. "You gave him a pretty harsh send-off, poor man."

"What do you mean?" Una spoke into her father's shoulder.

"Well, from what I gathered, he hadn't much hope, but I am certain he will return even so, and all will be well. He gave his word."

Una pulled back from his arms and looked quizzically up at him. "I promised that I would trust him, and I'll wait for him until doomsday if necessary. How can that be a harsh send-off?"

Fidel frowned. "Perhaps he didn't understand you aright? He was rather dejected when he spoke to me. But no fear. These little misunderstandings are soon cleared away. And I will be proud to have such a man for my son." He laughed. "Anyone would be a blessing rather than the duke! But don't let on that I said so."

Una laughed as well and sniffed back more tears. "I am so glad you feel that way, Father, even if he is poor. But I just know he will succeed and regain his power! You will be proud, though not nearly so proud as I!"

Fidel's frown returned. "One moment. Regain his power? He had not lost it, last I knew. What rumors have you been listening to, child?"

"I know only what he himself told me. I trust his word."

"We are speaking of Prince Aethelbald, are we not?"

"Aethelbald?" Una blinked. "Aethelbald!" The corner of her mouth curled.

"If not, then whom have we just been discussing?" Fidel asked.

"Why, Prince Lionheart of Southlands, of course. Leonard, Father. The jester?"

15

K ING FIDEL did not take kindly to this news.

Following the initial explosion, however, he agreed to listen to his daughter's story and felt he did so with considerable grace.

"So you see," Una concluded, "Leonard—I mean, Lionheart—couldn't in all honesty approach you, could he, Father? He did the most right and most honorable thing that he knew."

The heat of shock having abated somewhat, Fidel restricted his comment to a mere, "I should say he couldn't approach me, wandering wastrel. We are fortunate he did not try to take money from you!"

Una reflected briefly on her mother's ring, but passion boiled in her breast and she cried, "Father, must you assume him false? Has he done anything to merit distrust?"

"Yes, I'll say he has! He's gone and betrothed himself to my only daughter. A penniless jester, extracting promises from a princess!"

"We're not betrothed!" Una flapped her hands in frustration. "He extracted no promises from me, but I freely gave my word to trust him."

"To trust him blindly, without proof that he really is the supposed dead prince of a dragon-ridden kingdom?" Fidel pounded fist to palm. "Would that I had him before me—"

"Yes, I trust him," Una said. "And without proof! That's what trust is, isn't it? Believing without seeing?"

"Wrong," her father growled. "That isn't trust; that's foolishness! If a man has to ask for your trust, it's a sure sign you should not give it. Trust should be earned inherently, without any verbal demands. Trust is knowing a man's character, knowing truth, and relying on that character and truth even when the odds seem against you. *That* is trust, my dear, not this leap in the dark for a man whose character you don't—"

"Perhaps I do!"

"Perhaps you *think* you do! Perhaps you don't."

Una's eyes overflowed with tears. But these weren't the passionate tears she'd been crying the last few days. These were steady, throbbing tears, hot on her face. She turned her back on her father.

Fidel sighed and placed his hands on her shoulders, but she shook them away. "Child," the king said more gently, "if you had told me that you had promised to wait for Prince Aethelbald—"

"I despise him!"

"Despise him or not, if you had told me that you promised to wait for him, I would rejoice. I know his character and trust his word and would be glad to see you trust him as well."

"I trust Leonard—Lionheart."

"You do not even know which is his true name."

"I do!" Una shook her head sharply. "He is Lionheart! He's been obliged to live in disguise, but that is no reason to distrust him. Sometimes people have to do things they do not want to do, such as hide their true names, hide their true selves. But I believe he is who he said he is."

"Which one? The jester or the prince?"

"Both! He's both, Father. I know he is, and I will trust him till I die!"

A heavy silence followed, and Fidel took the time to stifle his anger.

After all, it was not Una's neck he wished to strangle at the moment. When he spoke again, he managed to keep his voice gentle.

"Una, maybe this fantastic story of his is true. Maybe he will ride back on his white horse in triumph, a crown on his brow and a dragon's head in his sack. Maybe he will prove himself a true prince someday, a worthy husband for my daughter." Fidel took the princess by the shoulders, turning her to face him. He wiped a tear from her cheek. "But until then, Una, do not trust him. Let him prove himself trustworthy first. Please, Una, don't give him your heart."

She set her jaw, though the skin of her chin wrinkled in an effort to keep from trembling. "He loves me, Father. I just know it. That's proof enough for me. I've given him my heart. I'll wait for him." The tears streamed silently down her face, dampening her collar, but her voice was steady. "I'll wait for him, and I'll not have another."

Fidel shook his head and drew his daughter close. "Then I can only pray he will prove worthy."

Days passed, each a small eternity.

But the nights were worse.

Una woke every morning feeling as though she had scarcely slept at all and dreading even the smallest daily activities. Sometimes now she remembered snatches of her dreams, but even those memories faded after a day or two. All that remained was the heaviness, the exhaustion, and behind that a deep, nagging worry.

Few things changed over those months. Felix had his fourteenth birthday celebrated with much pomp. Monster had a less official birthday, celebrated with less pomp. Una saw and declined two more suitors, neither of whom left lasting impressions on her mind. Hours were forever, and she not once received word of her jester-prince. He did not so much as appear in her dreams.

Until one cold night, just at the onset of winter.

Una lay wrapped in quilts, holding still because the less she moved, the warmer she kept. Monster was burrowed somewhere deep, a furry lump at her feet, as near to the bed warmer as he could safely sleep. His purr had long since worn out, and silence held her room in a frosty grip.

She pretended she slept but couldn't fool herself. Her nose was frozen, but Una was too tired and too cold to lift the blankets to cover it, so she pretended it wasn't cold and failed at that as well. She wondered if the faerie-tale princesses who fell into enchanted sleeps felt like this as they lay for a hundred years, frozen in time. How boring it must be for them after a decade or two. Truly it must be—

An image flashed through her mind.

Quickly as that, the dream came and went. A face of white bone surrounded by black hair, lying upon a golden altar, frozen and still with sleep. Suddenly its eyes were open, filled with fire and gazing at her, burning to her core. As though from a great distance, she heard Leonard's voice, or perhaps a mere memory of his voice.

"It's yours! Take it!"

She gasped; her eyes flew open.

Even as she stared up at the familiar embroidered faces of the sun and the moon on her canopy, the vision hung suspended in her mind's eye, the sound of Leonard's voice filled her ears.

It was a dream. Nothing but a dream, she told herself.

She sat up, hugging her knees to her chest, and took several long breaths. As she breathed, she became aware of the burning in her hands.

This time, the burns did not go away. When at last her maid came in to stoke up her fire an hour before dawn, Una still lay awake in her bed, grimacing in pain. The burns weren't severe enough for her to demand an apothecary's attentions, but they hurt even so. Nurse clucked when she saw them and concocted a soothing ointment, which she spread on Una's fingers, then made the princess put on a pair of kid gloves to help it soak in. Una obeyed willingly enough, but when she removed the gloves later that afternoon, the burns were as red as before.

"What did you do to yourself, Miss Princess?" Nurse demanded, inspecting them and clucking still more. "Were you grabbing the fire irons in the night? You know you're supposed to let the maid do her work; that's why you've got a bell to summon her with!"

Una did not try to explain. She did not understand herself. Instead she gratefully accepted the excuse not to embroider and went to sit quietly in her window. Monster placed himself in her lap and started grooming with all the care of a dandy. Absently, Una rubbed behind his ears. His silky fur felt pleasant against the burns.

"Curious, isn't it, Monster," she whispered as she looked out across the gardens, on down to the Wood. "Curious how time works. How can a day be so much longer than a month?"

Monster twisted his ears without much interest and switched to washing his other paw.

"Where is he now, I wonder?" she whispered, stroking her cat's back. Monster started to purr and raised his haunches to welcome a scratch. "You don't suppose he has forgotten me, do you?"

Monster stated an opinion.

"Yes, well, 'meow' is little comfort," Una said and tousled his ears. "I suppose I can't expect anything, though. He said he would not be able to contact me. I wonder, how long does it take to slay a dragon? I wonder if he'll be hurt."

"Mreeow," Monster said.

"Oh, don't say that! No, he will be fine, I know it. He has learned much about dragons, you know, in the Far East. He will be fine, and he will be back by spring."

"Mreeeow?"

"I just know it, that's all."

"What are you talking about to yourself?" Nurse demanded, entering the room with a basket of mending. She was generally disposed to be short with Una these days. Although Una had ceased her random fits of sobbing long ago, Nurse still disliked the mysterious bubble surrounding the princess that she was not permitted to puncture.

"I wasn't talking to myself," Una said. "I was talking to Monster."

"Stop that nonsense and come talk to me instead. I'll at least listen to you!" Nurse settled into her chair and raised her eyebrows at Una. "Well, Miss Princess?"

"Don't call me Miss Princess," Una said. "You only call me Miss Princess when you're mad at me, and I've done nothing wrong."

"Heaven help us, if we aren't persnickety this afternoon!" Nurse cried. She pulled a long stocking with a hole in the toe from her basket. "Can't even use a nickname without offending these days . . . Where are you going? It's too late to go out walking—you hear me?"

Una did not. She'd grabbed her cloak and made a swift exit. Monster trotted after her down the stairs, trilling loudly at her ankles, but she refused to let him follow her outside. Shutting the door in his nose, she ran lightly out into the garden and down to her forest.

The evening was bitter, promising a night as cold as the last. The trees cast long and longer shadows, but a bit of orange sunlight still dappled the forest floor. Una had taken to coming out to the Old Bridge nearly every day, weather permitting. It was a sweet, solitary spot where she could sit alone with her memories. She liked to recall her first meeting with the jester, when he landed on her after sneaking over the wall, a memory that always brought a smile to her face. Who would have believed that garish lunatic would, only weeks later, steal her heart so completely? This thought made her laugh as well, but always with tears behind the laughter.

Una pulled her cloak tight about herself as she stepped onto the Old Bridge. She sat down and dangled her feet over the edge but did not touch the icy water. A brisk wind blew winter smells of wet leaves and cold earth and perhaps of coming snow into her face. She closed her eyes and, leaning back on her hands and lifting her chin into the wind, let herself dream.

"Hello, Una."

She looked over her shoulder. "My jester!" She leapt up, stumbling over her cloak. There he stood on the far side of the bridge, his foolish, bell-covered hat in his hand and his hair standing all on end. "You're back!"

"I could stay away no longer." He dropped the hat and held out both arms. "Will you come to me, Una? Now?"

She ran two steps forward, her footsteps echoing under the bridge. But she paused. "Lionheart," she said. "My prince, have you killed the Dragon?"

His arms dropped loosely to his sides. "No," he said. "No, m'lady, I am not yet a prince. I remain only your jester." He turned, and shadows from the trees crept over him. "I know you cannot love me, only a jester."

"Wait!" she called. "Leonard, come back! I do love you just as you are. You don't have to slay a dragon. You don't have to be a prince!"

"No," he said, stepping back into the darkness. "No, you cannot love only a—"

"My love, come back!"

She tried to run but fell.

She woke up.

Her breath came quickly. She closed her eyes and bowed her head. Sometimes the dreams were so cruelly real.

"Oh, Leonard," she whispered, "why don't you return?"

The orange glow of sun was almost gone, and the grays of twilight settled heavily around her. She rose to go, stepping off the bridge into the crunch of leaves and twigs on the path.

"Hello, Una."

She spun around and screamed.

On the far side of the bridge stood the Dragon.

16

HE STEPPED ONTO THE OLD BRIDGE, and the great shadows of his wings folded around him, and she saw that he wasn't a dragon. He was a man, and the wings were a long black cloak. His skin was white, white without life, like a thin gauze overlying deeper darkness. His eyes were onyx stones, but within the blackness of each stone shone red fire.

Una choked on her scream and stood with her hands pressed to her throat. She swallowed, and her chest heaved as though she'd held her breath a long while.

The man with the white face smiled, one corner of his mouth turning up before the other, and revealed beneath his lips long, black teeth. He stepped across the bridge, his tall boots knocking hollowly on the wooden planks.

"Hello, Una," he repeated.

"Who are you?" she gasped. Her feet were as if rooted to the ground.

His chuckle was deep and smooth as a cat's purr. "Oh, Una, you know me."

She swallowed again, and her breath rattled her lungs. He drew nearer, the smile still twisting the lower half of his face. His shadow, great as a tree's, fell over her like nightfall. His hair was black against his white, white face and seemed to wave and twine about his temples like flames. The air around her thickened, and her hands tightened on her own throat. Una could feel the burns sharp as knife wounds across her fingers.

His smile broadened. "Yes," he said, showing all his black teeth. "I have waited a long time for this. You have the right fire, haven't you? It is well I won the game."

She tried to speak, but her tongue pressed uselessly against clenched teeth.

He leaned forward. She felt the heat of him and thought her face would burn. His lips drew together, and his face neared hers.

In the last possible moment before she suffocated, Una jerked her head away. She drew in gulps of cool night air and rubbed her neck where her fingernails had dug into her skin.

The man with the white face took a step back and licked his lips.

"Pardon me," he said, his voice velvety soft. "I see you are not yet ready. Invite me to your home."

Her voice scraped painfully through her throat. "I don't want you in my home."

"You do," he said. "Invite me to your home."

"No." Una felt the boil of tears in her eyes.

"Invite me to your home, Una."

She pressed her hands to her mouth, but tears spilled over and scalded her fingers.

"Una."

"Will you come home to supper?" Una asked.

"Good girl," the man with the white face said.

Nurse was in the garden looking for Una. "By Bebo's crown, girl, where have you been?" she cried when Una stepped into the light of the garden lamps on the arm of the man with the white face. Nurse started when she noticed him. "Who in the— Oh!"

She gasped and drew back, her hands held out before her.

"Good evening," the man said, smiling. "Is the family already at supper?"

Nurse nodded. Una could not look at her but fixed her gaze on her boots instead.

"Good," the man said. "We shall join them. I have an invitation to dine. Lead us there."

"Princess?" Nurse spoke in a small, trembling voice.

"Do as he says," Una whispered.

Nurse led them to the door and held it for them. Una, her arm looped through the man's elbow, felt held as though by an iron chain. She did not try to resist his pull.

Monster lurked just inside and trilled a greeting at his mistress but froze still as a statue save for the tip of his nose twitching on his blind face. Suddenly his lips drew back in a snarling hiss. He arched his back and screeched a hideous caterwaul, then darted away up the hall, his tail bristling behind him as he fled.

The man with the white face smiled down at Una. "Handsome cat," he said. "Strange he has no eyes. Perhaps he could do without other things as well?"

She shook her head, her face pleading.

He laughed, patted her hand, and escorted her after Nurse to the dining room.

Only the king and the young prince were at the table that evening, seated in the glow of tall taper candles. Nurse bobbed a curtsy to them when she opened the door before scuttling off into a corner, where she crouched like a hunted animal.

"Ah, Una," Fidel said when his daughter entered. "I was wonder-ing—" His voice died when he saw upon whose arm she hung.

"Good evening, Your Majesty," the man with the white face said, bowing deeply. "Your daughter has invited me to dine."

A candle sputtered.

The king's wine glass shattered on the floor.

Fidel grabbed a carving knife and lunged at the man.

Quick as thought, the man grabbed Fidel's wrist, twisted him around, and slammed him facedown into the table. Plates and cutlery fell and smashed. Felix leapt to his feet, shouting, "Guards!"

The man with the white face silenced him with a look. Felix fell back in his chair, his mouth shaped in a silent scream even as footsteps sounded in the hall. Guards burst into the room.

"Stay back," the man with the white face said, turning slowly on the ten armed men who crowded the doorway.

He smiled, and they fell away, one of them crying, "Heaven shield us!"

"Well, Your Majesty," the man with the white face said, leaning down to whisper in the king's ear. "That wasn't very friendly of you."

"Monster!" the king barked. "Demon!" Wine from an overturned cup ran into his beard, staining his face like blood.

"Sticks and stones, dear king," the man laughed. His grip on Fidel's wrist tightened until the king's fingers went blue and he dropped his knife. The man in the black cloak hauled him upright and turned him to face his guards, who shifted and growled, hands on their weapons. "Everyone out," the man said, glancing at Felix.

The prince staggered to his feet. "No," he said weakly. "Release my—"

"Out, boy, and take the old woman with you," the man said, chuckling deep in his throat. "Do you think you won't obey me?"

Felix swayed, his eyes rolling in his head. "Father?" he gasped.

"Go, son," the king said, sagging in the man's grasp. "Go on."

Felix took one unsteady step, then another. Then he ran to Nurse, dragging her up by the elbow and out of the room.

"Guards next," the man with the white face said, his voice smooth and pleasant. "If you would be so kind?" He took a step toward them, the king held before him. One by one, the guards backed from the room, each one gasping as though great weights pressed on his lungs.

"Come, Una," the man said, turning to the princess, who stood with her back pressed to the wall, her hands over her face. "Take my arm. We're going for a stroll."

King Fidel roared and struggled, but the man in the black cloak tightened his grip still more until the bones of the king's wrist were close to snapping. "No fuss," the man said. "Come, Una."

She slipped her hand through his elbow.

The three of them, thus linked, followed the guards, Felix, and Nurse down the corridor to the great entrance hall of the castle. There most of the household was already gathered—lords, ladies, and servants alike—looking at each other in quiet puzzlement, like people in a dream, none knowing why the others were there. A little maid saw the entourage from the dining room—first the prince and Nurse, then the guards, then the king gripped by the man with the white face. She screamed and collapsed against a footman in a dead faint.

The man with the white face looked upon them all. Then he spoke a single word. "Out."

The hall filled with screams. Men and women tore and scratched at each other as they streamed through the great doors out into the yard and gardens, rushing as one body for the gates. Even the guards followed. Una lost sight of Felix and Nurse.

Soon the three of them—the man, the king, and the princess—were alone.

The man with the white face flung the king to the floor. Moaning, Fidel pushed himself to his knees, but the man kicked him down. Una cried out and tried to run to her father, but the man put out a hand, blocking her. Una grabbed the hand and bit into it, and animal sounds snarled in her throat. The man looked at her and laughed, shaking her off as if she were a small kitten. She tried to leap at him again, but a single glance froze her in place.

The man with the white face turned back to Fidel, crouched on his hands and knees. "Out," the man said. "Follow your people." He stepped forward, and Fidel, still on his knees, crawled back. "I don't need to kill you," the man said, "as long as you do as you're told."

The king crawled backward all the way to the threshold, unable to tear his eyes from the man's shadowed face. Once Fidel was outside, the man with the white face allowed him to rise to his feet.

"Una," the king cried, holding out his hands, the one blackened and bruised.

"She stays with me," the man said, stepping outside into the court-yard. Night wind grabbed his cloak and flared it out behind him.

"Never!" Fidel started forward but fell away as a burst of flame bil-lowed toward his face.

The black cloak expanded, swelling like storm clouds into vast wings. The man raised his hands, and they were talons, cruel and curved. The red in his eyes swirled and swelled until it engulfed the blackness in raging heat. Fire spilled from his mouth, and he grew and towered over the king, high as three stories, reptilian scales gleaming in the glow of his own fire. Fidel screamed and fell on his face. The Dragon's roaring laugh lashed the sky.

"She stays with me," he said, "as a testimony of your good faith not to trouble me with armies and battles! Burnt human flesh sours good air. Go now, little king. I'll let you know my good pleasure in time. Be prompt in obedience. Go!"

The king fled through the gates in a cloud of foul smoke and fumes.

The Dragon turned on Una, who hung on the door, all but faint-ing. Great red eyes pierced her own, gazing deeper and deeper, until she thought her spirit and soul were consumed in fire.

But somewhere deep in the recesses of her heart, something remained unburned. She grasped at it, gasping with the effort. The Dragon leaned closer, flames licking through his teeth, and she collapsed on her knees. Yet a small knot of peace lingered beyond the flames, cool and unsoiled. She took hold of it in her mind, clutching it close.

"He will come," she whispered.

The Dragon drew back his head, and she slumped against the door-post, her hair falling to cover her reddened face.

"Ah," the Dragon said. "I see." Smoke poured from his nostrils. "Very well. You'll be ready in time." He turned away, his tail sliding against her, knocking her back into the palace, and he crawled into the darkness of the garden, lighting the way with flames in the leafless stems and shrubs. "Go to your room, little mouthful," he called over his shoulder. "We shall see much of each other, but for now you may retire."

Una crawled inside and, with a last great effort, shut the door.

17

C AUGHT UP IN THE FLOW of people streaming through the gate, Felix struggled to break free, determined not to be separated from his father and sister. He lost hold of Nurse somewhere in the crush and could not find her again. He was helpless, pulled against his will down the road away from the palace and toward Sondhold. Nearly halfway down the hill, he spotted an opening in the crowd and darted for it. He broke from the swarm, tumbling off the road into a ditch. Mud spattered his face and thorns bit his hands, but he breathed in relief.

Shaking his head and pushing back thorns, he sat upright and tried to take stock of his surroundings. Screams battered the air around him, and he realized that they did not come only from those fleeing the palace.

Stumbling, he climbed out of the ditch and up the rough hillside until he found a large boulder projecting from the ground. Pulling himself up on top, Felix owned a view of both the palace above him and the city spread out below.

The city was in flames.

Felix felt his heart in his throat and thought it might choke him. Sondhold was under attack. Even in the harbor he could see ships' masts burning like torches. And what of Ramgrip, the old fortress built long ago to protect the city? All was dark there, cast into shadow under the glare of the fire in the city.

But who would attack Parumvir? They were at peace with all the surrounding kingdoms, had been for over a hundred years. Fidel had no enemies, couldn't possibly have them.

"Father," Felix whispered, gazing at the burning city, hearing sounds of terror that chilled him to the bone. He felt very young and very small.

Steeling himself, he leapt from the boulder and tumbled to the rough turf. He was on his feet in a moment and running toward the palace as fast as his legs could bear him. He needed to find his father.

The white walls seemed ghostly in the evening as he pounded uphill toward them. His steps slowed unwillingly, for a terror hitherto unknown rose in his breast as he neared those familiar walls. It was most like fear of the dark; a fear not of what the darkness could hide, but of everything the dark represented and the very absence of light. This was the sensation that coursed in his veins, filling him with dread as he approached his home.

In the darkness above the wall he saw suddenly two balls of fire that shredded the night sky with wicked light. Realizing that they were eyes, Felix threw himself on the ground. Horror gripped him as he cowered on the hillside, certain those eyes had seen him, certain he would be devoured.

But nothing happened.

At last he found the strength to raise his head to look. The eyes were gone. He crawled forward again, pulled himself to his feet, and made himself continue to climb. *I must find Father!* The urgent thought repeated in his head with each step, and he focused on it, trying not to think of the eyes.

Smoke drifted in the air down the hillside—dragon smoke.

"Father!" Felix called, his voice faint with terror but determined. He was near the gate now, which stood open wide. His gaze darted over the road for any sign of the king.

A body lay just off the road, a lump in the shadows only a few yards from the gate.

Felix sucked in a sharp breath and rushed to it. "Father!" Felix grabbed the king by the shoulders and rolled him over. Fidel was not only alive but still conscious, though his breath came uneasily as fumes thickened the air around them.

"Una," he moaned.

Casting desperate glances over his shoulder, terrified that the awful eyes would appear again at any moment, Felix helped his father to his feet. The prince had not yet come into his manly size, but he pulled Fidel's arm over his bony shoulders and, supporting him as best he could, started down the hill away from the palace.

"Una," the king moaned again.

"Shhh, Father," Felix pleaded.

"Is that you, Felix?"

"Yes, Father."

"We must save Una." Fidel struggled to stand on his own. He collapsed and nearly brought the boy down with him. Felix clenched his teeth and used all his strength to keep them both upright. His father was near fainting, and Felix didn't know what he would do if Fidel lost consciousness. He had not the strength to carry the king on his own.

"Come, Father," he said, murmuring encouraging words as he half carried Fidel down the hill and off the road. The rough terrain was difficult to traverse in the dark, and more than once Felix thought they would tumble headlong.

Felix recognized the boulder he had climbed before. He gently leaned his father against it. "I'll be right back," he said and scrambled up once more.

The flames in the city rose higher, particularly in the western quarter. People streamed out of it on all sides, fleeing into the surrounding countryside. Torches flashed at the bottom of the hill road. Dark figures were approaching.

Felix leapt down, praying he had not been spotted. He crawled to his father and put his arms around him, desperately trying to think. Where were their guards? Where could they go? Questions swirled in his head, but no answers came.

"You're trembling," Fidel said, his voice frail. "What's wrong?"

Felix did not like to answer when his father was so weak, but he did not know what else to do. "The city is under attack," he whispered, feeling guilty as he spoke, as though he were confessing a crime. "Men with weapons are coming this way."

Fidel growled and struggled to his feet, shaking off Felix's protesting hands. He looked around the boulder, clutching it for support. What he saw confirmed Felix's words, and he hissed curses through clenched teeth.

Felix hurried to put an arm around his father. The dark figures on the road had already covered half the distance between them. The prince could only hope they had not been seen.

"We must make for Ramgrip," Fidel whispered. "General Argus will have mustered the men by now if the fort is not taken."

"But how can we?" Felix asked. "Whoever that is coming up the hill, they're between us and the fort, and it's at least three miles to Ramgrip."

"Courage, son," Fidel said. "Argus will try to find me, but we must get off this hill. Come, help me."

Felix and his father skulked into the shadows far off the road, making their way down the southern side of Goldstone Hill. Goldstone Wood loomed near, and Felix feared his father would insist they take shelter under those dark trees. Fidel's breath came in labored gasps, and Felix found himself bearing more and more of his father's weight. The king teetered on the brink of unconsciousness.

"Mreeeow?"

Felix gasped and nearly lost his grip on the king. A slinky form emerged from the darkness and wrapped around his ankles.

"Monster!" Felix muttered. "Dragons eat you, cat. Go away!" He kicked the blind cat from between his feet. Monster came back and continued rubbing and purring frantically. Felix scowled at him. "Fine," he hissed. "You can come. But don't think I'm going to coddle you, creature."

The cat ran ahead a few steps, looked back and meowed, then slipped away into the darkness only to appear again at Felix's feet a moment later. "I'm not following you," Felix muttered. "You're blind, stupid."

"Mreaaa!" the cat squawked and sank a set of dagger-like claws into Felix's leg.

"Mreaa, yourself! Dragons eat—" Felix stopped, ground his teeth, then kicked again. The cat dodged as easily as though it could see him. It continued to pace back and forth, leading the way and looping back to make certain the prince was still coming. And Felix, rather to his disgust, realized that as he followed the cat, he found better footing in the dark.

The sounds of pursuit drew closer. Felix looked back to see torches flashing just beyond an outcrop of rocks. He saw a thicket of bushes not far ahead and made for it as fast as he could with his burden. Unable to be gentle in his haste, he dropped his father to the ground. The king moaned, and Felix winced but continued his hurried actions.

Pushing his father, he whispered, "Crawl into the bushes, quick." He could hear men's voices calling to each other, so close. "Hurry, Father!" His heart raced, and he felt he would be sick.

Don't think, he told himself. *Don't think!*

"Felix?" the king called feebly, but too late.

Felix sprang away from the thicket, running and leaping until he was several yards away. He jumped onto a boulder and shouted, "Here! Here! Over here!" waving his arms in the dark.

Three tall figures with torches turned his way. Felix leapt from the boulder and sprinted down the hill away from his father. Shouts followed him.

"Is that the prince?"

"Prince Felix! Your Highness!"

Don't think! Felix half ran and half fell in the dark down the hillside.

Two more figures appeared suddenly in his path, but his momentum was too great to turn aside. He fell into their arms, struggling and kicking, unable to free himself.

"Prince Felix?" a deep voice asked. "Is that you?"

"Let me go!" he shouted hopelessly.

"If that's you, Your Highness," the speaker said, "we are the king's men."

"Liars!" Felix cried.

"Indeed not, prince," the speaker insisted, quickly pulling back a hand when Felix tried to bite. "I am Captain Durand. General Argus sent me and my men to find you, your father, and the princess. Argus is holding the duke's men off at the base of the hill, but we are gravely outmatched. We must get you away from here."

Running footsteps told Felix that his three pursuers were catching up. Even so, he settled down in his captors' grasp. "The duke?" he asked, panting.

"The Duke of Shippening," Captain Durand said. "He has attacked Sondhold in full force without warning. We are undermanned at Ramgrip. General Argus will not keep him from the palace long. Where is your father, prince? We met many people fleeing from the palace, but they could give us no word of the king."

A shout interrupted whatever answer Felix may have given. Five horsemen rode up. By the torchlight, Felix could see that one of the riders supported King Fidel in front of him. The king clung weakly to the pommel of the saddle, but his eyes glittered when they fell on Felix.

"Bring him to me," he commanded, his voice quavering.

Durand and the other soldier holding Felix's arms escorted him to his father. The king took hold of the front of Felix's shirt and, with surprising strength, lifted him to his toes. He glared fiercely into Felix's eyes.

"Don't you ever try to save me again," he growled, his voice tight with anger. "I will not have you risk your life for me. Understand?"

Felix swallowed hard and nodded. Fidel let him go and sagged back into the arms of the rider.

"Give him a horse," Durand said. One of the five horsemen

dismounted and hoisted Felix into the saddle in his place. "Ride to the garrison in Dompstead," the captain said. "General Argus will join you there as soon as he can. I fear we will be forced from Sondhold before the night is through."

Fidel rallied himself one last time. "Una?" he breathed.

"Do not fear, Your Majesty," Captain Durand said. "We'll find your daughter."

Without another word the horsemen started down the hill at a trot. Felix clung to the horse's mane, but the beast seemed fairly sure-footed in the dark.

"Mreeeow?"

The prince heard the small cry and pulled his horse up short before he'd ridden ten paces.

"Your Highness," Captain Durand said. "What are you—"

Ignoring the captain, Felix leapt from the saddle. Monster materialized from the night at his ankles. He scooped the cat up, draped him over his shoulder, and scrambled back into the saddle. Monster's claws dug painfully into his shoulder, but Felix didn't care. He urged the horse to catch up with the others, holding on to the cat with one hand.

18

A s she came slowly awake, Una's chest felt as though it had
been burned hollow, and her eyes stung. An overwhelming sense
of nightmare surrounded her. When at last full consciousness crept in,
she could only plead with her own mind. *No, please. Please, be a dream.*
Just another bad dream.

But it was no dream. She realized that she must open her eyes. She
did and found herself lying on her back in a dim and dusty enclosure,
gazing up at tight, crisscrossed ropes. A moment later she recognized that
she was under her own bed and vaguely remembered crawling beneath
it the night before. She rubbed her face, which was crusty with dried
tears, unbent her cramped limbs, and pushed herself out from under
the mattress.

The silence oppressed her, for she had never before heard anything
like it. Always there had been some form of chatter or clatter in the
background, servants hurrying hither and yon, coachmen calling in the

courtyard, Nurse's prattle, courtiers and dignitaries—Oriana Palace was always full of sound.

Now all was deathly quiet.

Slowly Una got to her feet. The room was so dim, she could not tell if it was morning or evening. She went to her window and put her hands to the curtains. As she pushed them back, swirling smoke, black and dreadful, filled her gaze. She pressed her nose to the window, trying to see out. Here and there the smoke thinned, and she caught glimpses of the garden, charred and burning.

A heavy movement to the right drew her eye. She glimpsed a great black wing.

Pressing her hands to her mouth, she let the curtain fall back into place and stumbled away from the window into her shadowy room. She stood a moment in the middle of the chamber as though frozen. Then she whirled and darted to her door, wrenched it open, and slipped into the hallway. She closed the door softly, afraid of making noise in that awful silence.

The vast, empty palace loomed about her. She crept along the wall, down the corridor, and turned a corner into another hall, then on to a tall window, which afforded a view all the way down the hill into Sondhold. One could even see the market lawn from this vantage point.

Una looked.

Through the screen of smoke, far down below the hill, Sondhold burned.

Her city! Una clutched the windowsill for support. Her home!

"Father." She found herself screaming, her voice echoing down the long empty passages. "Father! Felix! Nurse!" She sank to her knees, still clutching the windowsill. Panic seized her, and she succumbed to sobbing without control.

"Leonard," she whispered.

Only the silence answered.

"Dragon!"

Una startled at the voice in the courtyard. She could not guess how long she'd been prostrate on the floor. The hysterics had passed, but she had not moved. Who was there to care if she did not?

But now as the bellowing voice echoed in the courtyard, she scrambled up and tried to peer through the smoke. These windows did not offer the best view of the yard. She picked up her skirts and rushed through the empty halls to her father's study, with its windows that looked out on the gates and across most of the courtyard.

She came to his door and, from habit, raised her hand to knock but stopped herself. Shaking her head, Una stepped inside. The room was dark as night, for the drapes were drawn. She flung them open and found a fairly clear view before her.

The Duke of Shippening sat on a nervous gray horse in the middle of the smoke-filled yard. "Dragon!" he barked. A handful of soldiers wearing the Shippening uniform lingered by the gate, apparently too frightened to venture farther in. The duke, however, knew no qualms. "Dragon!" he cried. "Come out!"

The great front door of the palace opened. Una's heart went to her mouth as the man with the white face and the black-red eyes stepped out into the yard.

He's been inside.

She thought she might faint but grabbed the window frame and made herself watch the scene unfolding below.

"There you are," the duke cried, spurring his horse across the ashy stones to move closer to the man. The horse tossed its head nervously but seemed more afraid of its master, for it did not bolt though the whites of its eyes showed. "I've been calling forever. Where've you been?"

"I am here now," the man said.

"So you are," the duke conceded. He dismounted and marched up to the man, his face red and swollen like a tom turkey's. "Where is she?"

"Who?" the man asked.

"You know who I mean." The duke swore, his voice reverberating. "Did you let her escape like you did her father and brother?"

"If you mean the princess," the man said, idly rubbing his fingernails on his sleeve, "she is inside."

"In the dungeons?"

"No."

"What's to keep her from waltzing out of there as easily as the king and that puny prince did, I ask you? A fine job you did holding your end of our bargain. 'You take the city,' said you, 'leave the royal family to me.' Well, I've taken the city sure enough, but where's the royal family? All escaped to Dompstead by now."

The man with the white face gave the duke a look that sent a chill through Una's heart, though the duke seemed not to notice. "The princess is inside," the man said.

"Give her to me, then," the duke said.

Una's grip on the window frame tightened.

The man with the white face snorted and turned his back on the duke.

"You promised!" the duke cried. "You promised she'd be my wife and the throne would be mine legitimately!"

"That cannot be as long as the king and his male heir are alive," the man said over his shoulder, striding toward the gardens. "Finish your job by them first. She's not ready yet anyway."

"Not ready yet?" the duke thundered. "What's she got to be ready for? She's mine, Dragon. You promised! Give her to me!" He ran after the man in the black cloak and grabbed him by the shoulder. The man turned, and suddenly he was grown twice, three times, six, ten times larger, until his body, black and scale-covered and gnarled, towered above the duke, and Una smothered a scream in her hands and leapt back from the window. She closed her eyes, her hands wrapped over the top of her head, willing herself to wake from this nightmare.

But the voices in the courtyard went on.

"I remember every word I ever spoke to you, duke." The Dragon's growl filled Una's head. "I do not forget my word so soon."

"Then fulfill your promises!" The duke shouted like a petulant child, to all appearances oblivious to the fact that he shouted up at a fifty-foot monster.

"Time!" the Dragon said, and Una fell to trembling at his tone. "These things take time. But if that cringing prince of Southlands was right, it will be well worth the wait."

Prince of Southlands?

Una's hands dropped to her sides. "Leonard," she breathed. She crept back to the window.

The duke stood in the vast shadow of the Dragon, his legs widespread, his arms crossed. The Dragon gazed down on him, his enormous eyes mere slits of fire in his black face. He looked as though he should like very much to swallow the duke whole, but both the duke and the Dragon knew he would not.

"I don't care about any bargains you made with Southlands," the duke said. "Our deal is all that concerns me."

"You have not yet fulfilled your part," the Dragon said. He snapped his wings, and the soldiers by the gate cowered in terror on the ground, but the duke stood firm.

"I would have if you hadn't let them go!" he cried, shaking his fist.

"The king and his son are nothing to me," the Dragon said. "They are your concern. But if it will ease your mind, I will send one of my own to help you in your task."

"Swear it!" the duke demanded.

The Dragon showed his fangs in an awful smile. "By the fire in the very marrow of my bones."

The duke, satisfied for the present, made a bow. "I'll return soon," he said and turned on his heel. Fire licked from the Dragon's mouth, but the duke caught his horse and left the courtyard unscathed, his men trailing behind him like so many whipped dogs.

Una crept from her father's study back into the dark hall. Fear choked her, fear in the recollection that the Dragon could change form and enter the palace, could be inside even now.

But he had not given her to the duke. Not yet.

And her family was still alive.

Why does he not come?

"He will come," she whispered, rubbing her upper arms. "He will come. I trust him. I know he will come." She tiptoed down the hall, clinging to shadows. Nothing moved, not a sound reached her ears but her own breathing. The Dragon's voice ran over and over in her head.

"If that cringing prince of Southlands was right . . ."

She froze, and her hands went to her mouth.

Leonard had gone looking for this monster. This very same beast had destroyed his kingdom. And Leonard had gone hunting for it.

If that prince was right . . .

He'd found it. Of course, they must have met, Leonard and the Dragon. Leonard had gone hunting, and he'd found what he sought, but—

Her heart lurched to her throat, then plummeted down to her stomach. "Leonard!" she gasped. New fear rose, spinning inside her so that she could hardly stand. She found herself at the door of her own chambers. With a stifled cry she flung the door wide. She staggered blindly in the dark to the glass doors that led to her balcony and wrenched them open.

Ash and smoke rolled over her, blinding and choking. She put a hand to her mouth and rushed out onto her balcony. The garden below was like a battleground, stripped and burning, small bonfires crackling at intervals. All the white statues were coated in ash.

But she saw none of this. She leaned out over the railing and, between coughs, shouted, "Dragon!"

"Is that you, little mouthful?"

She grabbed the rail for support. The next moment the Dragon's head reared up out of the smoke and Una found herself eye to eye with her captor. He regarded her through red slits of pupils. "See what a well-trained puppy I am, coming at your call?" Fire streamed through his teeth, and Una thought she would die of fear. "Come, Princess Tidbit," the Dragon said. "Don't keep me in suspense."

"What . . . what . . ." She covered her face and bowed her head, unable to speak.

"It's about that prince of yours, isn't it?"

Una jerked her head up. "What has become of him?"

"He's the one who'll come for you, isn't he?" the Dragon purred. His enormous tail twitched in the rubble. "The one your heart holds so dear, so pure." His eyes flickered crimson in the swirling ash.

"What has become of him?" Una demanded again.

The Dragon laughed a billow of flame and turned. He crawled away into the wreckage, trailing laughter and smoke.

"No!" Una pounded the railing with her fists. Her voice came out in choked, furious barks. "Dragon, answer me! What has become of my jester?"

"Your jester?" The Dragon looked over his wing. "Your jester is dead."

Una doubled over as though struck in the gut. "Leonard," she breathed, sinking to her knees. "You killed him. I knew it. You killed him!"

"I? No, not I," the Dragon said. "No, Prince Lionheart killed your jester. Jesters aren't much use in reestablishing kingdoms."

Hope, weak but alive, fluttered in Una's heart. It hurt like a knife, but she clung to it even so. "Lionheart is alive?"

"If you want to call it that," the Dragon said.

"You've seen him?"

"We met on the road between here and Southlands. I chose not to kill him. I'd not killed him the first time we met and saw no use in changing my mind. We made an agreement. Since I am through with his land, I promised to spare his life if he would do me a favor in return. He was willing enough to agree, for he knew I would kill him otherwise. He is back in Southlands—returned triumphantly a few months ago, I believe."

"He's alive," Una whispered.

"Yes, yes, he's well too, if that comforts you. He's betrothed to some baron's daughter, I hear—a childhood friend of his. A splendid match, they say, and such a happy couple."

Una's face lost all color, and the world tilted on end.

"He told me of you and your kingdom when we met," the Dragon said. "I was intrigued by what he said, thinking perhaps I would at last find what I have long sought. And I have not been disappointed. I knew that prince would be useful to me."

His words filled her mind like poisonous fumes. Bitterness clutched her throat, and she gagged. Blindly, she felt her way with her hands across the balcony, back into her chamber.

"The jester is dead, little princess," the Dragon called from the garden ruins. "There's only the prince left."

Una crawled into her closet and crouched in the shadows, gasping and holding her head.

19

The king's small escort thundered into Dompstead, Felix taking up the rear, for he found it difficult to ride with a cat slung over his shoulder. As they arrived at the garrison, Felix saw his father whisked out of sight before the prince had a chance to dismount. His one glimpse of Fidel's face filled him with dread.

Monster leapt from his shoulder and darted into the shadows. Felix cried out and tried to give chase, but someone grabbed his arm.

"This way, prince," a soldier said, all but dragging him into the fort. Felix, too tired to argue, allowed himself to be hustled down a dark corridor and between soldiers—none of whom recognized him, and few of whom would have cared if they had.

"This is your father's room," the soldier said, and disappeared the next moment, leaving Felix in an unlit, deserted hall outside a shut door. Felix tried the door handle, but it was locked. He put his ear to the door and heard voices on the other side, but no one answered his knock. He crossed his arms and slumped with his back against the door.

After what seemed like hours, he heard the sound of footsteps. A young officer, hardly older than Felix himself, appeared with a lamp in one hand and a stool in the other. "I was sent with this for you," he said, holding the stool out to Felix.

"Thank you," Felix said. "Can you tell me when I may see my father?"

The officer shrugged.

"What of Oriana?" Felix asked, placing the stool on the ground. "What of General Argus?"

"I know nothing, Your Highness," the officer said.

A voice at the end of the hall shouted, "Captain Janus! Captain!"

The officer bowed. "Excuse me, prince." He was gone the next moment, along with the lantern light. Felix settled onto the stool and waited.

The night crept on painfully slowly after the terror of the evening. The voices continued to rise and fall on the far side of the door, but though Felix knocked at intervals, no one would answer him. Another officer came by after an hour or two and offered Felix a room and a bed, but the prince refused. One physician hurrying from the king's chamber tripped on Felix's outstretched legs, cursed him roundly, and then realizing he was the crown prince, endeavored to make amends by telling what was happening inside.

Dragon poison.

Felix had heard of such things before, of course. In stories and legends, principle characters often suffered such poisoning if they breathed in too much dragon smoke. Many a pathetic tale had been told involving such a death for a hero or his love.

Some who breathed in the poison did not die, however. Some became empowered by it and went on to accomplish mighty deeds. But those were always the villains of the tales, men or women who saw beauty in terrible things, who found dragon poison as pleasing as perfume.

Felix shivered. His father would never be one of those characters, not in any tale.

But some who survived dragon fumes were not evil. For instance, the legendary bard Eanrin, who wrote *The Bane of Corrilond* epic, was supposedly present at the destruction of that kingdom, and he must have been exposed to dragon poison. Yet he neither died nor turned evil but was a hero who figured in a hundred tales, most of which he had written.

"So Father won't die," Felix told himself. "He's too good to die like that."

Dragon poison.

Felix shuddered from deep inside himself all the way out. He leaned his head back against the wall, closing his eyes. At first his tired mind jumped around without thoughts, slipping instead from a sense of color to color. Then suddenly a picture of burning eyes filled his mind, eyes that pierced through darkness and gazed at him over the palace wall.

He startled and barely caught himself from falling off his stool. He'd been asleep, he realized, and shook himself. Down the hall, pale light came through a solitary window. Felix got up and strode to the window, looking out on the practice yard of the fort. Soldiers gathered in small groups here and there, talking in muffled voices. Many were cleaning weapons. Some were sparring. Dark clouds gathered in the sky to the north. Felix realized after a moment that they were clouds of smoke.

"Prince Felix?"

A physician stood in the doorway of the king's chamber, looking up and down the hall. Felix trotted back to him and asked in a breathless voice, "How is my father?"

The physician smiled and patted the boy's shoulder. "He will be well, I believe. I am, I confess, no expert in these matters, but my colleagues and I are of the opinion that His Majesty did not breathe in enough of the fumes to cause permanent harm. He is dizzy and weak, but he should—"

"May I see him?"

"It might not be best for Your Highness to look on him now," the physician said. "His Majesty does not appear—"

Felix growled something unintelligible and pushed past the physician into the chamber. It was a small, dark room with a low ceiling and a tiny fireplace in one corner. A cluster of black-robed physicians was gathered at the foot of a narrow bed on which the king lay.

Despite protests from the physicians, Felix stepped up to the head of the bed, knelt down, and took his father's hands. Tears sprang to his eyes at the sight of Fidel's face, so gray and lined. He had aged ten years, twenty perhaps, in one night.

"Father?" Felix whispered.

The king's eyes opened, and he turned to look at his son. "Felix," he said. His voice was weak but, to Felix's great relief, sounded stronger than it had only hours before. "Where is General Argus?"

Felix blinked. He'd expected something a little more tender from the beloved father for whose life he'd feared these last hours. "I . . . I don't know," he said. "I've not heard if he's come to Dompstead. I've been so worried—"

"Go find him," Fidel said. "Bring him to me, and don't let these fools"—he waved at the cluster of physicians who stood clucking on the other side of his bed—"stop you. You're a prince, remember. Now go!"

Feeling more like a page than a prince, Felix hopped up and hurried from the room, avoiding the disapproving glares of the physicians. He stood a moment in the hall, unsure which way to go or to whom he needed to speak in order to find news of General Argus. Shrugging his shoulders, he turned right down the hall, came to a dead end, retraced his steps, and wandered until he found a door out into the yard.

Several hours later General Argus came to Fidel's sickroom. The king was out of bed and dressed, sitting by the fire. He nodded when the general entered and bowed.

"Where is the prince, Your Majesty?" the general asked.

"I sent him to find you."

The general raised an eyebrow. "I would be hard to find. I did not reach Dompstead until a few minutes ago and came directly to you."

"I know," the king said. "But the boy needed something to occupy his mind, and a fool's errand seemed as good as any. What news do you bring from Sondhold?"

The general hung his head. "The city is lost, sire. We were surprised, outnumbered—"

"I need no excuses," the king interrupted. "Did you see the Dragon?"

"No, sire, we did but hear rumor of it. I saw the duke, however. It was Shippening. His army came out of the Wood and set upon the city."

"Out of the Wood?"

"Indeed, sire, impossible though it may seem."

"What of Una?" the king asked.

"I have seen or heard nothing of the princess, Your Majesty," Argus said.

The king's fists clenched. "We must save her." He rose to his feet, swayed, steadied himself, and repeated, "We must save her, Argus. Now."

"Your Majesty," Argus said, "I have sent word to garrisons all across Parumvir. Men are coming to help us. But meanwhile our position here in Dompstead is all too vulnerable. With the men I have, I'm not sure I can protect you sufficiently."

"What are you saying?" Fidel asked.

"Sire, I must beg you to pull back. I lost too many men yesterday. We are weakened beyond belief, and you say there is a dragon involved as well?" Argus shook his head. "I beg you, my king, you must retreat to one of your northern fortresses, away from here at all costs."

"No."

"Go into hiding until we have a chance to rebuild."

"No."

"If we attack now, we will be destroyed. We're not strong enough, sire."

The king turned his back on the general, gazing deep into the fire. "He warned me," he muttered. "He warned me of this very day. And now the beast has her. What's to stop the rest of his prediction from coming true? My own daughter." He clutched his side as though in pain but waved off Argus's offered arm. "We must save Una," he said. "Before it's too late."

"Your Majesty—"

"Send Felix to the north," Fidel said, strength returning to his voice. "Send my son, but I cannot go as long as that monster holds her."

"Sire," Argus spoke gently. "We have no assurance that she is yet living. I . . . I fear it may not be so, and you must accept that she might be—"

"That would be almost too much to hope for," Fidel said. "No, we must save her or know for certain that she is dead. I will not leave otherwise. Gather your men as quickly as you can, Argus. We will return to Oriana."

It wasn't true, Una decided.

She crawled out of her closet hours later and sat down at her vanity.

It couldn't be true.

Hunting up matches, she lit a candle and set it off to her right. As though it were any other evening, she took up her brush and ran it through her tangle of hair—twenty strokes, fifty, one hundred.

It isn't true, she told herself. *The Dragon is a liar. Leonard wouldn't forget me.*

She changed from her ash-covered dress into another ash-covered dress.

I promised to trust him.

She poured cloudy water into a bowl and tried to wash her hands.

How can I be worthy of his love if I do not trust him now?

She looked at her face in the mirror, deathly white, streaked with soot, eyes wide and tearless.

"I will trust him," she said.

Felix gave up searching for General Argus and instead occupied himself hunting for Monster, whom he'd not seen since their arrival the night before. This search was also unsuccessful, and he realized partway through the day that he had not truly slept in well over twenty-four hours. The instant that realization struck, he was overwhelmed with exhaustion. He sat with his back against the wall of the barracks and, ignoring the glances of passing soldiers, fell immediately into deep sleep.

He was awakened by a rough hand shaking him. "Wake up, Prince Felix."

Felix blinked blearily up into the face of the same young officer who had brought him a stool last night. At the same time he became aware of a great commotion in the garrison yard—the ring of metal and the stamp of boots, officers shouting commands—which in his weariness he had slept through. "What's going on?" Felix asked, rubbing his eyes with one hand and pushing himself upright with the other.

"The king is mustering for attack," the officer said. "They will set upon Sondhold day after tomorrow."

Felix came fully awake at those words and sprang to his feet. "Where is my father? I must have a horse and a weapon—"

"A horse you have, Your Highness," the young officer said. "And a weapon. But you ride north with me this evening. Your father is sending you—"

"No!" Felix flashed. "No, he's not!" He turned and ran from the officer into the busy yard, only just avoiding being trampled by hurrying soldiers. The officer trailed behind him, shouting, but Felix ignored him. He spotted his father on the far side of the yard, standing beside a tall horse and speaking to General Argus. He darted up to him, gasping. "Father, let me help."

Fidel looked sternly down on his son. "You're not yet gone, Felix?"

Felix smothered the hurt that rose inside him and tried to make his voice firm. "Let me help you, Father. I can fight; I've been trained."

"You are riding north with Captain Janus," Fidel said.

"But, Father—"

Fidel grabbed Felix by the shoulder, his fingers pinching. "I have no time for this, son," the king growled. "I won't have you put in harm's way as well. This discussion is over."

Felix knew there could be no argument. Captain Janus approached, and the prince turned and followed him back across the yard. An escort of ten waited there with a horse for him, and Janus handed him a small sword, which he strapped to his side before mounting. Felix swung himself into the saddle and paused a moment, looking around the yard. "Monster," he muttered, sick at heart about leaving his sister's pet.

"The north road, men!" Captain Janus called, and the company set off at a brisk pace, leaving Dompstead behind.

20

THE TREES ARCHED LIKE PILLARS and their branches vaulted, loftier than a cathedral's dome and more beautiful. Moonlight streamed through their intertwined leaves and fell far below to the forest floor, the richest carpet of silver. On this carpet, a blind knight clad in scarlet knelt before the Prince of Farthestshore, who extended a hand to touch his head in greeting.

"What word do you bring?" the Prince asked.

"It is as you feared," the knight replied.

"Una?"

"Imprisoned by the Dragon within the walls of Oriana. I . . . Forgive me, but I could not keep her safe."

"There was nothing you could have done against such an enemy."

The Prince spoke the words compassionately, but the knight could sense the pain in his voice and cursed himself silently for his weakness, for how he had failed his master.

"What of her family?" Aethelbald asked.

"I did what I could for them," Sir Eanrin replied. "I saw them safely into Dompstead. But the king breathed dragon poison and is unstable in his mind. And the prince was sent north."

"Felix? You are sure of this?"

"I am."

"That I do not like. I want you to return to Goldstone Hill."

"As you wish, my Prince, but—" Eanrin paled.

"No, I don't intend for you to face the Dragon. Simply wait and listen and bring me word as you can. I must go to Felix before anything else. I fear most for his life at present."

"What of Una?"

"Her life is not at stake. Not yet." The Prince of Farthestshore closed his eyes and set his jaw. "Observe with your many senses, Sir Eanrin, but do not let yourself be seen. I will return for her as soon as I may, but I must go to Felix first. Before it is too late."

The blind knight inclined his head, then rose and disappeared. A moment later the cathedral of the forest was empty save for a lone wood thrush, singing its plaintive song.

Time did not exist in that darkened world. Day was no lighter than night, night no blacker than day. The Dragon's smoke covered all in shadow, and only his flames offered light.

Una was not as one living. If she ate, she did not remember it. If she slept, she always dreamed herself awake and on waking wondered if she still dreamed.

Once she dreamed herself out on a wide and empty plain, red as blood under a black sky. Far on the horizon she saw a figure, tall and straight, striding toward her. Her heart thrilled, for she knew that form. "My love!" she cried, joyfully extending her arms.

Then her heart stopped.

Sudden terror replaced her joy, terror that grew as the figure neared. For she saw in his hand an upraised sword and knew it was intended for her.

"No!" she screamed, and woke into the nightmare of reality.

Her bedclothes were grayed with ash. She pulled them back, coughing at the smoke that lingered throughout the palace and wondering for the hundredth time why she had not suffocated long ago.

Whenever she woke, though she could not guess the hour, Una went through her toiletry rituals as though beginning a new day. But no matter how she searched, clean water was nowhere to be found, so she bathed her face in a grimy trickle still in the bottom of her washbasin.

This time, after her attempt at washing, Una sat down at the vanity, gazing sadly at her ash-smeared face, and began once more to brush her hair.

The silver glimmer of the sword flashed through her mind.

She recoiled, dropping her brush. Slowly she realized the flash was not from the sword of her dream. In her mirror was a gleam of reflected sunlight.

Una turned on her stool to look behind her. There, more brilliant and beautiful than anything she could have imagined, a sunbeam shone through her window, cutting through ash and smoke, and fell in a pool on her floor.

She tripped over herself rushing to the light. She collapsed on her knees and lifted her face and hands, gazing at the whiteness that seemed to wash away all the filth. Tears ran down her cheeks, cool and cleansing. She let them fall on her hands and watched them gleam in the sunlight.

Far away a silver bell-like voice sang. She recognized that voice, the first she'd heard from outside since her imprisonment: the voice of a wood thrush. Clear as the sunlight, its song washed over her heart. Una rushed to open the window, hoping to better hear the thrush.

But smoke rolled in, and she heard instead the Dragon growl from somewhere on the castle grounds, "Is that you, little mouthful?"

She shut the window. The light was buried once more in gloom and shadow, but Una returned to her vanity, a smile on her lips. Words formed in her head, and she whispered:

"Beyond the final water falling,
The Songs of Spheres recalling,
We who were never bound are swiftly torn apart.
Won't you return to—"

She broke off, her breath coming unevenly, swallowing smoke. "He will come," Una told her reflection. "I trust him."

She buried her face in her dirty arms.

If there was one thing Felix had learned in all his years as Prince of Parumvir, it was that being a prince brought no advantages whatsoever.

"Stop!" he cried, reining in his horse when he and his escort were no more than six miles outside Dompstead.

"No, Your Highness," Janus said, slapping the rump of Felix's horse and startling it back into motion.

"I say!" Felix grabbed a handful of mane to keep his balance. "Stop, I say! I cannot go any farther."

"Your Highness, we have scarcely begun," Janus said, showing no sign of halting. "You cannot yet be tired."

"That's not what I mean," Felix snapped. "I cannot go a step more away from my father. I cannot abandon him in this hour."

"Obeying and abandoning are hardly one and the same," Janus said. "Keep up, Your Highness."

"He's my father!" Felix protested.

"And he's commanded you to go north with us."

"I'm your prince!"

"Whom I have been commanded to escort safely."

"Without my father here, I am your superior."

"Yet your father's word is superior to your own, Your Highness, whether he is present or not."

So they continued, and Felix lapsed into silence, hating every step that took him farther from Oriana Palace, from his father, from Una.

Where is Una? He thought of her trapped in the palace, surrounded by dragon fumes, and tears sprang to his eyes. He sniffed and wiped his face, hoping none of the soldiers could see him weep. How long could one be exposed to dragon smoke before it took serious effect? His father seemed to be recovering—he'd certainly not lost his force of will. But he'd been in the smoke for only a few minutes. How many hours now had Una been trapped in the palace?

Assuming she was still alive.

Felix felt as if it had been years since the Dragon had come to Oriana, and he himself seemed much older than he had been. Certainly too old to be sent away north like a useless little child.

"Captain Janus," one of the men said, "there are riders coming quickly up behind us."

Every man slowed and looked over his shoulder. Felix squinted into the mostly set sun and, sure enough, saw a cluster of horsemen galloping toward them up the road.

"Are they ours?" Janus asked.

"Cannot tell from this distance, sir."

"You," Janus said, pointing to one of the men at his side, "reconnaissance. The rest of us will continue. Come on."

Felix could hear urgency in the captain's voice, though it never once rose in pitch. His heart rate sped up as he nudged his horse into a joggling trot behind Janus, and he kept looking back over his shoulder to watch the approaching horsemen and the one soldier riding back toward them. The fourth or fifth time he looked back, he saw the solitary soldier pull up his horse, wheel around, and start galloping headlong after them.

"He's coming back!" Felix cried.

"They're after us," Janus shouted. "Fly, men!"

Wind rushed in Felix's ears as the horses broke into a thunderous gallop up the darkening road. He looked back only once, in time to see the solitary rider ridden down by the strange horsemen. He glimpsed upraised swords and faced forward again. His horse galloped just behind

Captain Janus's mount. He wanted to look back but knew already from the shouts of his escort that they were being gained upon.

Suddenly Captain Janus turned his horse off the road, galloping madly to the left toward Goldstone Wood. Without a thought Felix followed, and the two of them broke from the company, fleeing across the short field and up a hill. The Wood began at the top of the hill, dark and menacing in the twilight. Captain Janus reined in his horse at the edge of the forest and leapt to the ground. "We cannot ride through here in the dark, Your Highness!" he cried. "Dismount. Make haste."

Felix slid from his horse, looking back to the road. Several horsemen, whether part of his escort or not he could not guess, were halfway across the field. He slapped his horse to make it run, then turned and followed Janus into the trees.

Low branches and brambles clawed at him, but he ran as fast as he could, his heart beating double-time in his breast. He lost sight of the captain but plunged on, making so much racket that he could not hear whether he was still pursued, though often he could have sworn someone was just a step behind him. He turned several times, expecting to see someone reaching out after him, but all was dark behind as well as before him. The trees became smudges of shadow. Several cuts burned across his face where branches lashed him, but fear drove him forward.

At last, exhausted, Felix stopped and collapsed against the trunk of a thick tree. His breath came hard and painful in the cold air. For a time, breathing took up all his attention. Then as he slowly found himself able to take a normal breath, he realized how silent everything was around him. Placing a supporting hand on the tree, he pulled himself to his feet.

He stood in the midst of Goldstone Wood, and he was alone.

"Captain Janus?" His voice sounded thin and childish on the crisp air. He coughed and tried to deepen it. "Captain Janus?"

Felix took a few steps in the dark, walked into a whole new snarl of brambles, and spent another several moments untangling his arms and legs. Mad and muttering, he pulled back, shaking his head. "Hullo?" he called again and did not care how little his voice sounded.

Something crackled off to his left, and he thought he heard a voice calling his name. "Felix! Felix!"

"I'm here!" Felix cried, stepping in the direction of the voice. "I'm over here! Hullo?"

"Prince Felix," a voice spoke near at hand. "Do you want them to find you?"

Felix turned. "Captain Janus?"

A dark shape stepped out from behind the tree against which Felix had leaned a moment before. Felix could just discern that it held a hand out to him.

"Come, prince, we must go."

Felix took a step, then stopped. He felt for the sword at his side. "Are you Captain Janus?"

"Don't you recognize my voice?" the captain asked.

"Yes, but—" Felix started to slide his sword from its sheath, but before he could draw it, the figure lunged. Felix ducked behind a tree, narrowly escaping the cold blade of a sword that clanged against the trunk. He heard a hissing curse and drew his own sword. Backing away from the tree, he stood with his blade between himself and the tall figure.

"Traitor!" he cried. "Are you working for the duke, Captain Janus?"

The captain laughed a thin and reedy laugh, and Felix suddenly smelled smoke on the air. "I serve only my Father," the thin voice said, and it no longer sounded like Captain Janus. Sweat poured down Felix's brow. He saw his opponent raise his sword, and felt his own body assuming a position he had practiced countless times in the yard at home.

The dark figure lunged. Felix's feet moved almost of their own accord in the complicated step, his sword arm darting out at just the right moment. He felt the nick of a sword touch his arm, but he was quick enough. His enemy's sword flew high, crashing through the branches and landing somewhere in the darkness as the disarmed man, surprised, stumbled forward onto his knees. Felix leapt forward, his sword upraised, but hesitated to strike the exposed back before him.

His enemy, still on his knees, turned, and Felix found himself gazing into two bright yellow eyes like those of a snake.

"Fool!" the thin voice hissed.

The next moment Felix was flat on his back, slitted pupils mere inches from his own face. Claws pierced through the cloak on his shoulders, down into his skin. He screamed. The figure above him hissed, and Felix gagged as thick fumes poured into his face. He writhed and managed to free an arm, but claws tore viciously at his chest. He screamed again.

"Felix!"

The yellow eyes disappeared, and the heavy body that pinned him was suddenly yanked away. Felix rolled over, clutching his chest, and felt the warmth of blood on his hands. He could not see but rather heard the scuffling of two bodies in the dark near him. The world blazed red in the light of a brilliant fire. He saw two men, both unarmed, one taller than the other, and flames poured from the mouth of the shorter.

"You!" the fire-breather roared.

The taller figure, weaponless, charged through the flames. Felix heard a screech, high and terrible. Then his eyes closed, and the flames disappeared as unconsciousness overtook him.

Aethelbald watched the small dragon disappear into the night sky. He turned and hurried back to the clearing, which glowed in the smoldering fires that lingered in patches. He spoke a word, and the fires died as though struck out by many beating hands.

Aethelbald knelt beside the boy. "Felix?" he whispered and, receiving no answer, quickly inspected the prince's wounds. His eyes narrowed. He removed his cloak and wrapped it tightly around the young prince, then gently picked him up.

Holding Felix close, he spoke a single word to the silent Wood. "Open."

The gates to Faerie parted.

21

Una woke from convoluted dreams, coughing. Smoke hung more thickly in the air every moment. Yet, while it caused much discomfort, stinging her eyes and annoying her lungs, it did not smother her.

When the coughing spasm ended, she groaned and leaned her head heavily into her hand. She'd fallen asleep at her vanity with her head pillowed on one arm, resulting in a cramp down her neck. Her dreams had been awful—dark and smoke filled—yet now she wished she could crawl back into them. Anything to escape.

She guessed it must be evening, for the shadows in her chamber were deepening into blackness. When she raised her head from her hand and looked into her mirror, Una could scarcely discern her own features. She fumbled across the top of the vanity, found matches, and lit a candle. The flame's red glow lit up her pale face, casting strange shadows under her eyes. A layer of black ash covered her skin. She rubbed at her cheek but merely smeared the grime in deeper. The whites of her eyes gleamed unnaturally in the glass. She felt oddly frightened of her own reflection and turned away, shivering.

A door slammed.

The sound, somewhere far below her, perhaps on the ground floor, echoed up through the empty halls of Oriana. It was faint, but in that heavy silence it battered her ears like hailstones on window glass. Her heart stopped.

He's inside.

She leapt to her feet, knocking over her stool. Her foot caught in her skirts, and she stumbled, catching herself on the vanity, rattling the little glass bottles. The candlelight flickered. Una froze, one hand gripping the top of the vanity, the other clutching her skirts, and strained her ears.

She heard nothing but her own breathing, sharp and quick.

"It's all right," she whispered. "It's all right. He doesn't know where you are. He won't find you."

But he could. He could go through every room in the palace, and if she stayed where she was, he would find her eventually.

She grabbed the brass candleholder and, cupping her hand to protect the flame, hurried to her door. She pressed her ear against it but again heard nothing. So it was either play cat-and-mouse through the dark halls of Oriana or sit like a rabbit in a trap.

Una put her hand to the doorknob. It creaked as she turned it, but the door swung open quietly enough. She held the candle out before her, but its glow could only pierce some of the shadows in the hall beyond. Nothing moved; no sound reached her ears. She stepped into the hall and closed her door most of the way, afraid to shut it completely for fear of the latch clicking. Every sound was dreadful to her, even her own breath coming in tiny puffs. She stole down the hall, shielding her candle flame with her hand, and turned the corner into the next.

A shadowy form stepped before her.

She stopped in her tracks, her heart leaping into her mouth. The candle wavered and sputtered.

Slowly she found her breath returning. Her own reflection stood before her in the tall, dark window. It was a ghostly shape, oddly contoured in red. Una licked her dry lips and hurried on down the corridor, avoiding looking at window glass as she went.

She reached the door at the end of the corridor and paused there, her hand on the latch. A stairway lay just beyond, leading down to the floor below. It was a servants' stair, one she rarely used, but she dared not take the main staircase. She stood a moment, listening. Her ears were her only ally in the darkness, and they told her nothing.

But he was inside the palace.

Her mind worked frantically. Una could not simply wander through the corridors and empty rooms, hoping to elude him. She needed to hide—somewhere safe, deep inside the palace. Immediately she thought of her father's treasure hold, down below the basements. It was the deepest, most secret spot in the castle, and she knew where her father kept his key.

Fidel had shown her the key in its secret drawer in his desk a few years before. There was only one key and one lock, for the treasure hold was always guarded by eight armed men at a time. No one had ever succeeded in penetrating it. As far as Una knew, no one had yet bothered to try. Surely it would be a safe place if she could but retrieve the key.

She stepped into the narrow stairway and hurried down it, holding the candle carefully before her to light each step. These were older steps, made of stone, the tops worn from frequent use. She had to be careful as she descended the spiral. Each turn she made was an agony, for her imagination told her what to expect in the darkness around every bend. But there was nothing, and she reached the door at the end of the stairs.

Her heart hammering, she stepped into the hall. This hall also had a row of tall windows, and she turned her face away from them, not liking to see her own pale figure tiptoeing in the reflected world beside her. Her feet made no sound on the thick rug, and she made her breaths as light as possible. All was silent.

A few turns later, she came to her father's study and stepped inside, shutting the door softly. Here she breathed in momentary relief. The room was dark, full of strange shapes. Gilded candle sconces on the wall gleamed in her candle's glow. But the dragon smoke had not penetrated so thickly here. It still smelled like her father.

Una set her candle down on the desk and felt around for the secret drawer. Her hand bumped a sheaf of papers, knocking them from the desk. She gasped and tried to catch them, but they hit the floor and scattered. She stood as though paralyzed until the sound cleared from her ears, replaced once more by silence. Taking a deep breath, she reached with trembling fingers to once again feel for the secret drawer. She found it and fumbled a moment with the little mechanism. It sprang open with a snap, and her fingers found the key. It was three inches long, made of iron. She held it tightly in her fist, as though merely by possessing it she was rendered safe. Then she slipped it into her pocket, retrieved her candle, and returned to the door.

Una paused with her hand on the latch. How she longed to stay there, in the comfort of her father's study! If only she dared crawl into his big chair and curl up there, breathing in his smell. Perhaps it would be enough? Perhaps she needn't dare those dark halls again?

But no, it was not safe. Like a mouse she wished to crawl deeper and deeper, to bury herself in darkness so no one could possibly find her. She had the key and must go.

Una crept back out and darted down the hall, around another bend, then another, coming at last to a long back staircase that led down to the basements and below. She'd never used it herself, having never before ventured into the storerooms. As she opened the door, dank air rose to meet her. Shivering so that her candle flame danced back and forth, she stepped into the stairway and started down.

Somewhere overhead, a door slammed.

It was upstairs, probably on the same floor as her chambers. He must know now that she was not in her rooms. She strained her ears, unable to breathe.

Nothing.

Panic billowed inside her, and she gathered her skirts in her free hand and started down the stairs, nearly running. But these steps were even more worn with age and use, and she slipped, tumbling forward.

She put out her hands to catch herself, one grabbing hold of the metal stair rail, the other pressing into the wall on the other side.

Her brass candleholder bounced on the steps. The flame went out, and the candleholder continued clattering and ringing all the way down into the darkness.

She choked on a scream and continued down the stairs, faster now, gripping the rail and the wall to support herself in her descent. All was pitch-black, so Una could not see the steps before her, and many times she would have fallen if not for her death grip on the railing. As though in a dream, she felt she could not run fast enough; weights pulled her feet back, restraining her. A sharp cramp shot through her side, up through her rib cage, but she did not slow. Down the stairway she wound, past the main levels of the palace, far past the basements. Her hand brushed doors leading into the primary storage rooms, but she knew these were not the sanctuary she sought. Only when she reached the bottom of the stairs did she stop.

There was no door here, only an opening carved into the rocks of Goldstone Hill, leading into a fairly wide passage. Una slipped into the opening, still keeping one hand on the wall, and followed the passage to its end. The air was stale, and the stones that she could not see under her feet were rough, but terror of discovery drove her on. She came to the door at the end of the passage, felt around in the darkness, and found the lock attached to a large chain that held in place a heavy bolt across the door itself.

She'd have to lift the bolt in order to enter the king's treasure hold.

She realized in that moment that she would not be able to lock herself in.

"Princess?" The voice in the stairway was deep and terrible. "I know you're down here."

She fumbled in her pocket for the key, pulled it out, and tried to insert it in the lock. It wouldn't go in, her fingers trembled so.

"Come out, princess. There's no use hiding."

The key slipped from her fingers and clinked on the stones below. She knelt and felt around in the darkness, desperate to find it. Light suddenly poured into the stone passage, casting her shadow sharply onto the door before her. Shielding her eyes with her hands, she turned and saw the figure standing at the end of the passage, holding high a lamp.

"There you are," he said.

"Duke Shippening!" she gasped.

The duke stepped into the passage, his face lit from below by the red glow of the lamp. A long knife hung at his belt. "A merry chase you've given me, wench," he growled. "What possessed you to come down here? Thinking to lock me in the dungeons?" He snorted a laugh and advanced across the stone floor, his hand held out to her. "Come here, girl."

Una crouched on the floor. There was no escape but by the way she had come. Her eyes were wide like a hunted animal's in the lantern glow.

"Come here," the duke said. "You're leaving with me. I've waited long enough, I think."

"No," Una said, shaking her head.

"What? You'd choose that Dragon over me?" He snorted again. "Well, that ain't an option. You're coming with me, going to make me king. Legitimate, even."

"No."

He reached out a great hand like a bear paw and lunged. Una ducked and darted under his arm, propelling herself with her feet, her hands scraping the floor. But she tripped on her skirts, and the duke grabbed a handful of hair and pulled her back. She screamed.

"Let her go."

Una and the duke looked to the end of the passage. The Dragon stood there in human form. His obsidian eyes locked with the duke's, and fire glowed behind his gaze.

"What for?" the duke growled. "She's mine!"

The Dragon did not answer, did not move. But the duke obeyed, his fingers slowly uncurling from the tangle of her hair. Released, Una crawled away from him to the space between the Dragon and the duke. She curled up, her hands over her head, her back pressed into the wall.

"Get out."

"She's mine, Dragon!" the duke cried, trembling in rage. "You promised her to me to make me king!"

"She's not ready."

"Ready for what? She doesn't have to be ready for nothing! She just has to live long enough to put me on the throne."

"Get out."

The duke strode forward until he stood over Una, his big boots stepping on the edge of her skirts, but he did not touch her. "I've already done with the heir. The king is nothing without his son, and she's next in line! I've waited long enough. When will you fulfill your end of the bargain?"

"When you have fulfilled yours."

The duke swore and lurched forward until he stood eye to eye with the Dragon. The duke snarled like a wild animal in the Dragon's face. "I'll get the king. But you'd better give me what I ask in return, demon!" He disappeared up the dark stairway, taking the lantern light with him.

But the passage was not dark. Una looked up and saw light, fiery and hot, glowing from the eyes of the Dragon.

"Up, little mouthful," the Dragon said. "Back to your rooms."

Una slid up along the wall and, keeping her gaze on her own feet, moved to the base of the stairs. She felt the heat, the horrible heat, emanating from the Dragon's body as she passed him. She proceeded up the long stairs, in an upward journey that seemed an eternity. The Dragon followed soundlessly.

At last she reached the main level and stepped out of the close darkness of the stair into the spacious darkness of Oriana's empty halls. She went on down the hall, not waiting to see if the Dragon followed her. In three steps, she paused.

"My brother?" she whispered.

The Dragon's voice, disembodied, full of heat, hissed in her ear. "Killed this evening, not two hours ago."

Una ran. Across the hall she fled, around a corner to the main staircase, up two flights to her chambers. She burst into her room, slammed the door, and crumpled to her knees.

"Felix!" she cried.

Morning came. The sun cut a single beam through the dragon gloom and shone in a pool just inside Una's window. Una, leaning against her bedroom door, watched it settle there. With an effort she pushed herself to her feet and crossed her room, kneeling at last in the little circle of light. She tilted her black-smeared face, and tears rolled down her cheeks. She caught them on her hands and watched them trail through the grime. More tears came, and more. She leaned forward, her hair hanging in tangles about her, and sobbed desperate and awful sobs.

"Felix," she whispered. "Felix, little brother!"

Sunlight warmed the back of her head and the silver song of the wood thrush flowed down the ribbon of light. It broke through the dragon smoke and slipped through the window to gently touch her as she wept.

> "Beyond the final water falling,
> The Songs of Spheres recalling.
> When the senseless silence fills your weary mind,
> Won't you return to me?"

Something deep inside her trembled. Una breathed deeply and her sobs lessened, though tears still fell. "He will come," she murmured, looking at her hands in the gleam of sunlight. "He will come back to me. He will make things right."

The sun moved on and disappeared. The thrush song grew fainter, then was gone. Dragon fumes drew in about her, thick and suffocating once more. She got up and went to her vanity. She took up a heavy, shell-edged comb and ran it through her hair, but it caught in the tangles. Though she pulled painfully, the knot wouldn't give. With an angry cry, Una threw the comb into the mirror.

The mirror cracked.

The day passed in a haze of smoke. Una sat still on her stool, looking at nothing while her thoughts wandered this way and that, confused in the fumes. She thought of Felix, his wicked grin and ready laugh, thought of the pranks he used to pull, the games they had played together by the Old Bridge when she was his Faerie Queen and he her faithful gremlin. Every nasty thing she'd ever said to him rang back clear as yesterday in her mind, and she cursed herself repeatedly.

But as the day wore on, the poison in the air drove thoughts of her brother into deeper recesses of her mind, removing all good memories and leaving only the pain of loss. She shook her head violently, pressing her burned hands against her temples.

Slowly, the images of Felix flowed from her mind, and now Una thought of Leonard.

She pictured him as she'd last seen him, clad in his Fool's clothes but his eyes so serious. She tried to recapture every word they had spoken, but many of them had faded. She found it difficult to remember his face. She could recall every expression, every smile or frown—Oh, that dear smile and still dearer frown! But the features were faded and vague.

"I am forgetting him," she admitted at last. Evening was coming on, but she lit no candles. "I am forgetting him."

A scream squeezed out of her throat. "No. Please don't take his memory from me!" Una leapt to her feet, her fists pressed to her temples. "I won't forget; I won't! He said, 'I shall kill that monster and reclaim my kingdom.' And he promised to return, didn't he?"

A new picture sprang to her mind unbidden, a picture of a young maiden, fresh and sweet. Her hair was adorned with flowers, and her eyes were alight with joy. Una saw her, this strange girl, more real in her mind than her memories of the jester. And she saw her smiling at Leonard.

"No!" Una shook her head fiercely. "No, he promised!"

"Una, trust me," he had said.

"I remember his words. They're as good as a promise, aren't they?"

"No, little princess."

The deep growl echoed hollowly inside her.

"No, little princess, he didn't promise, did he?"

Her windows burst open and hot air rushed in on her neck. She wrapped her arms about herself, bending double as poisonous air enveloped her. Gagging and choking, she turned to face the window.

The Dragon's head reared in the darkness outside, his red eyes piercing the dreadful whorls of smoke and flame.

"Come," the Dragon said. "Come, speak to me of your jester-prince. I am curious to know more of this story."

22

GOLDEN LIGHT FILLED FELIX'S VISION—golden, and blue as well. He blinked, but the world remained a blur of colors. A pain like fire burned in his shoulder and chest. He closed his eyes, grinding his teeth. When he opened his eyes again, his vision was clearer. He saw a pattern of golden leaves above him, crisp against a backdrop of blue. At first he thought it was a mural, but then the leaves danced softly back and forth as though touched by a breeze, and he realized they were real. Or almost real.

He tried to sit up, but searing pain shot from his heart to his shoulder, then up his neck. Gasping, he fell back and found that his head lay cushioned in something downy. A moan escaped his lips.

"You are awake."

He heard the voice but could not turn his head to view the speaker. It was a soft voice, low and sweet. A gentle hand pressed against his forehead. "You are still feverish," the voice said.

"Who are you?" Felix asked. His lips were dry, and his voice cracked.

"I am Dame Imraldera," the voice said. "Lady of the Haven." A damp cloth as soft as his pillow pressed against his face and across his dry mouth. "My Prince brought you here and asked me to care for you."

"Your what?" Felix's brow wrinkled as he tried to put together memories. "Where is here?" He could recall flying across the dark road on his horse, could remember wandering through tall trees. A vision of yellow eyes flashed across his mind, and he flinched back into his pillow. "What's happened? I . . ." His voice tightened with panic. "Where am I?"

But the low voice hushed him, and the cloth wiped his brow. "You are safe now, Prince Felix. The Prince of Farthestshore has brought you to one of his Havens. You must rest and try to trust me. You have been pierced by dragon claws and have taken in a good deal of poison. But I can heal you."

Dragon poison.

Felix felt his face wrinkling up as he tried to suppress tears. He was too old to cry, for pity's sake! He choked out his next words, hoping the strange woman could not hear the tears in his voice. "My father? Una?"

"My Prince will care for them, child. Sleep now."

The damp cloth touched his eyelids one at a time, and he slept.

Una gathered her skirts in her hands and stepped through the window onto the balcony. The glow of the Dragon's eyes created a path for her to follow through the murk and cast her shadow sharply behind her. The heat of his gaze threatened to melt her, yet Una went on, compelled beyond her own wishes or control.

She came at last almost under his jaw and sat down in the circle of her skirt.

The Dragon closed one eye and turned his head to regard her with the other. "Who would have guessed the fire could be found in one such as you?" he said. "How delicious!" His long black tongue licked out. Una shuddered but could not look away.

The Dragon settled himself comfortably, adjusting his vast wings to wall her in on both sides, intensifying the heat. "Now, little mouthful," he said, "tell me about your jester-prince. Yes, I have met him, but he revealed only so much of himself to one such as I." He smiled, and flames flickered behind his eyes. "I am curious to know what this Lionheart showed you. Speak, Una. Why should we have secrets from each other?"

Una felt her throat was too parched to utter a word, but when she opened her mouth the words poured out of her like the sudden rush of water from a crumbling dam. She forgot herself and to whom she spoke in the relief of letting her thoughts flow freely. She scarcely noticed the Dragon's prompting questions, for each direction he prodded her speech seemed so natural, exactly what she wished most to speak of next. Trivial details slipped in with the most poignant moments, yet all seemed equally important. As she spoke, Una found she could picture Leonard's dear face almost as clearly as if he stood before her, and she never once wondered whether that might be the Dragon's work.

"He was so fine," she found herself saying over and over. "Unlike any other young man I've met. He knows the meaning of hard work, yet does not run from it like other princes might. His is a life of purpose and direction. Who can compare to him? Prince Gervais? That silly fop with whom I fancied myself in love? Not likely! I see now how cheap was his suit and how cheap was my affection for him. How can a charming personality compare with a noble character? Like my plump parade pony with my father's war horse."

"So you loved Lionheart's princely soul, eh?" the Dragon asked.

"No, not at first," Una said. "At first I did not even notice it. But I loved him anyway, perhaps even from the first day I met him. He . . . he made me laugh so! He was self-deprecating yet proud, foolish yet witty. I never laughed so much as when I was with him. I was never so happy before."

"You loved him for making you laugh?" The Dragon chuckled. "How delightful."

"I did," she said, "but I did not realize it until later. No, when I began to think of him at all, I stifled those thoughts as foolish. Not until he spoke to me on the night he left . . . spoke to me in a voice I had heard only once or twice from him, altogether unlike his jolly self. . . ." She lost herself in reverie, and although her skin gleamed with sweat in the dragon heat, Una felt cool and distant.

"He spoke of his trials, of the dangers he had endured and had yet to endure. He spoke of his quest to kill . . . "

"To kill me," the Dragon said.

"Yes, to kill you. To kill you, to reclaim his kingdom, to put things right for his people . . . So brave, so good is he! But you see, with such a vision before him, how could he let himself be distracted?"

"Not even by you, little princess," the Dragon murmured.

"Not even by me."

"His goals were far greater than his love for you."

"Of course, as it should be."

"You wouldn't want to get in his way."

"Never. He would not be the man I loved if he were to turn aside for me."

"And so he asked you to trust him."

"Yes, and I do trust him."

"And you gave him your heart."

"My heart is his."

"But he never gave his in return."

Una's lips parted. No words came out.

The Dragon lifted his head and barked a great laugh. "Foolish girl, what kind of exchange was that? You gave him your heart for nothing, and now you have nothing, do you?"

She bowed her head, her hair hanging down to her lap. "I required no promise from him."

"But he took one from you. Such a noble soul, wouldn't you say, this Prince Lionheart of yours?"

"He is," she said. The air was thick and bitter in her nostrils.

"Then that leaves only one alternative," the Dragon said. "You, little mouthful, are not worth a promise. You are not worth his heart."

"I—"

"Either he is not what you thought, or you aren't," the Dragon said. "What other choice could there be?"

"I trust him."

"Then your trust is misplaced, for he has forgotten you. He no longer owns his own heart, for he gave it to another and keeps hers in return. Did I tell you how lovely his betrothed is? I saw her the day I first met your prince. She came from the gardens to drag him away when he fainted for dread of me. Plucky little thing, she was. Beautiful too."

"I—"

"You know what I think?" The Dragon snapped his wings, and Una cowered down before him. "I think you are worth far less than you fancied yourself. Not what he mistook you for, are you? Look at you—a crying, sniveling wretch, dirty and ugly. A princess? Hardly."

Una pressed her forehead to the stones, squeezing her eyes shut.

"He probably realized his mistake the moment he was away. 'Foolish fellow,' he said to himself. 'Why, you don't even know that girl! What made you think such a passing fancy could be real love?' "

"I trust him," Una whispered.

"As soon as he saw that lovely girl in Southlands, one of his own people, his old friend . . . Ah! Then he knew what love was meant to be. He could trust her. She would not be so stupid as to give her heart to a stranger."

"He—"

"A stranger who would dispose of it as soon as it best convenienced him."

Una gathered herself together, clenching her hands against the burning pain that pulsed from her fingers, up through her arms, and into her head. She tried to stand, couldn't, so instead she forced herself to look up into the Dragon's huge face.

"I don't believe you," she said.

"Don't you?" The Dragon leaned down until his breath whipped her hair across the stones. "But what would you say in the face of proof?"

"You have no proof. You are a liar."

"Am I?" His voice dropped to a low, insidious hiss. "Be that as it may. But look you here and then tell me if I lie."

He raised his gnarled hand, turning it upward, clutching something. Slowly his claws uncurled, and Una saw what he held in its center.

An opal ring, the stones gleaming with inner fire, reflected the light from the Dragon's eyes.

Una could not speak.

"Oh, princess," said the Dragon, "if he could only see you now. How he would count himself blessed to have escaped so weak, so puny a creature as you! How he would congratulate himself on having made the right choice. Your heart or his life. Some men might have dithered, but your Lionheart is a man of resolve. Isn't he, Una? Strong and steadfast of purpose."

The great hand closed once more, and Una's vision filled with smoke. She closed her eyes, her knotted fists scraping against the stones beneath her.

"Poor little Una," said the Dragon. "You are heartless now, aren't you? No better than a dragon yourself."

She crawled backward, and he let her go. She inched her way from his looming presence until she could stand again. Then, shoulders rounded, she retreated to her dark bedroom, closing and latching the window behind herself. The dragon poison whirled in her brain, dizzying and horrible; Una could not think and could not breathe.

"Leonard," she whispered. "Why don't you come?"

She fell upon her bed and cried as she had never cried before. With each tear that fell, Una felt her soul shrivel.

Fidel surveyed his troops in the gray of early dawn. Hardly more than one hundred men remained from the garrison at Ramgrip. Combined with the regiment from Dompstead, they made a brave front as they lined up for battle on the hills outside Sondhold. General Argus sat on a big horse beside the king, disapproval etched in every line of his face. They were no match for the forces from Shippening.

A messenger rode up and saluted his king and commanding officer. "The duke's men are gathered just over the next rise," he said.

Argus nodded. The information was not new. He turned to the king and said in a low voice, "We'll be routed, sire."

"Perhaps," Fidel said.

"They are more than twice our numbers," Argus said. "Sire, you know we cannot hope to win."

Fidel did not reply. Winning a battle was not foremost on his mind. If they could but distract the duke long enough, that was all he asked. A group of five men, hand-selected by him, were to slip into Oriana Palace while the attention of the duke—and hopefully of the Dragon—was diverted. Perhaps they could find the princess and steal her away.

Argus knew the plan but hated it, for he could see no hope of success. "Please, Your Majesty," he said one last time even as the sun gleamed on the horizon, desperately trying to break through the atmosphere of smoke. "Please accept your loss and run while you still can. We can gather our resources, given enough time, and come back to punish this dog as he deserves! But not today."

"Felix is safe," Fidel said. "I must see my daughter now as well."

He spurred his horse, trotting away from the general down to the front line of soldiers. There he nodded to a lieutenant, who raised a golden horn to his lips. The clear note rose in the thick air, and as one man, the troops stepped forward to meet the duke.

Una woke from bitter dreams to see the beam of sunlight break through the ash and smoke and shine upon her floor. She sat up in bed and looked at it glittering on the dust.

In her breast something burned.

"No more," she whispered.

She climbed from her grayed blankets and left the room. The long, silent corridor seemed like a great throat swallowing her down and down.

She stumbled twice on the stairway, gripping the rail for support. At last she reached the entry hall. The door swung open at the slightest pressure, and she stepped into the courtyard.

All was ruin and rubble. Stones, charred black, piled where once had been graceful walls and statues. The trees were burned to smoldering stumps, and the smoke rising from them was venomous.

Una walked amid the ruins, and the ash swirled about her feet. She walked as in a dream, slowly but surely, guided by some unknown force.

The Dragon met her at the gate.

"Yes, princess," he said, breathing smoke upon her. "Your fire is right. You are one of my kin."

"Yes," she said, her eyes tearless and sad.

"But not completely." He smiled. "Come closer, and I shall finish the work for you. Come here, mouthful. Your heart belongs to me."

The princess stepped toward him, her face upraised.

"Lean closer," he said. "Let me kiss you."

The blood rushed in her veins, throbbing in sudden panic, but the princess stood on her toes, reaching up to the Dragon. She felt the brand of his kiss on her forehead.

She fell back, crying out in agony, but the cry changed to a roar, hideous and deep, bursting from her breast and out her throat in flames and smoke. Her hands hit the ground, but instead of hands, terrible scales and claws scratched and tore the stone to pebbles. Ebony wings beat from her shoulders, and more flames burned her mouth, burned the ground, scorching everything around her black.

"What have you done to me?" she cried. Her voice was harsh with fire.

23

THE DRAGON WATCHED the young dragon roll upon the ground, slapping her wings against the burning rubble. He said nothing, only watched while furnaces smoldered in his eyes.

At last Una lay exhausted, her sides heaving, her fire momentarily spent. The Dragon approached her, his fangs gleaming in a monstrous smile.

"My daughter," he said, "what a fine fire you have inside! Five years now I've searched for you, and I might have passed you by, such a puny creature you are. But I pride myself on having recognized you at last."

The dragon that had been a princess opened an eye. It glowed dully, though fear rimmed the edges and dilated the pupil. "What have you done to me?" Her voice was rough as gravel underfoot.

"What have I done?" The Dragon flared the black crest on his head in pride. "I've released you, my sister, my child! I've allowed you to become what you truly are, what you have been all this time. Now you may embrace the freedom of your spirit unbound!"

Una moaned, and her eyes rolled back in her head.

"You know it is true," the Dragon said. "You've known all along, deep inside."

"What am I to do?" the young dragon asked, pushing herself upright.

The Dragon opened his mouth to speak, but at that moment a horn sounded not far off, beyond the gate, across the fields, and over a hill. Its golden note broke clear through the heavy air, and both dragons turned to the sound, the elder with a snarl and a burst of flame, the younger with a new light in her eye.

"My father!" she rasped in her burning throat.

The Dragon hissed and raised himself to see over the high stone wall. "The fool," he growled. "I warned him, didn't I?"

The young dragon, wings flailing, struggled to her feet and also peered over the wall. Through a haze of red, she saw the lines of King Fidel's army advancing, armor and weapons gleaming dully in the light of torches, for the sun could not pierce the Dragon's gloom.

"So be it," the Dragon said. "Wait here, little sister, until I've dealt with these gnats."

He drew himself together; his powerful haunches propelled him upward and his great wings struck the air until, catching a current of wind, he soared high into the smoke-filled sky. Down below, the Duke of Shippening's army lined up just outside the city, while Fidel's men marched stoutly forward. It was a pathetic sight, the ragtag troops of Parumvir in the weak advancing position against the larger and more securely stationed men of Shippening. There was no need for the Dragon to become involved. But the furnace was hot in him now.

He rose like a black sun, fire pouring from his gaping mouth, and the army halted. Screams filled the air, both from Parumvir's men and those of Shippening. King Fidel's horn sounded again, and the army moved forward once more, but the Dragon's shadow fell upon their hearts.

The Dragon circled them, a vast vulture, as the fire grew inside him that his black scales glowed red and flames leapt from the corners of his eyes. He opened his mouth, aiming at the front line of soldiers.

But another fire struck him in the face, harmless yet startling. He turned, surprised, in time to see the young dragon hurtling toward him on frantic wings. She collided into him, her talons clawing into his side. His tail whipped around at the impact and lashed her closer to him, and the two fell, grappling together. The Dragon, too taken aback to fight, pushed her away before they hit the ground, and caught himself on an updraft. She, unskilled with her wings, struck the earth and lay dazed.

"Foolish sister!" the Dragon barked, flames shooting out the sides of his mouth and curling over his head as horns. "What insanity was that?"

Una lurched up, breathing heavily. "My father!" she gasped.

"Idiot!" The Dragon spat at her. "*I* am your Father!"

"No!"

"Yes, dragon!" he cried. "I am your Father. I am your brother, your mother, all your kinfolk now!"

"No!" She leapt into the air again and flew at him. He knocked her aside with a single stroke. The young dragon recovered herself in the air and charged again, spitting fire and sparks. The Dragon caught her in his strong forelegs and bit her neck fiercely. She roared and clawed at him, but he worried her, shaking his head back and forth, then flung her from him. She hit the ground, her wings beating the earth into clouds of dust.

The Dragon settled nearby, slithered up to her, and cuffed her across her face. She rolled away, and he cuffed her a second and a third time.

"There, little sister!" he roared, his fire reddening her scales. "Test my authority, eh? Test it again!"

He lunged at her and tore into her already bleeding neck. The young dragon screamed, blue flames spewing from between her teeth. With strength she did not know she possessed, she broke away and took to the air. This time she fled as fast as her wings could carry her, higher and farther into the sky.

The Dragon raised his head and bellowed a roar that shook the earth for miles. Then he lowered himself on all fours and looked around. The king's army was in retreat, leaving the land behind calm, black, and deserted.

The Dragon looked over his shoulder and watched the young dragon disappear south into the haze of his smoke. He smiled and licked his lips. "Perfect."

"To the king! To the king!" Argus cried.

Few listened to him; most of the men fell back in the ranks, running over each other in their haste to flee what they'd already known to be a hopeless battle. The sight of the Dragon had been enough to destroy what courage remained in them, but two dragons were beyond reason. They fled in terror while King Fidel sat on his horse as though frozen in the middle of a sea of running men.

Cursing, Argus spurred his horse forward, cutting through the flood of screaming soldiers until he reached the king's side. "Sire!" he cried.

Fidel did not answer. Argus grabbed the bridle of the king's mount and dragged the champing horse over the hill after the routed army. Fidel sagged in his saddle, his face expressionless. They had no sooner passed out of sight of the Duke of Shippening's army than the king toppled from his saddle and landed heavily in the dirt. Argus reined in his horse, leapt down, and ran back to catch up his king.

"Una," Fidel moaned as Argus wrapped his arm over his shoulders. "She's lost."

"But you're not lost yet, sire!" Argus growled through gritted teeth. He barked to a passing lieutenant, "Are there no loyal men left in Parumvir?"

The lieutenant stopped in his flight and called some of his own men back to him. Together, they bore the king from the deserted field.

24

Una burned inside. She wished she would burn to death, but she did not die. She only burned.

Higher and higher she flew, above the black smoke and still higher. At last she burst out above the gray clouds into blinding white sunlight that struck her eyes like daggers. She screamed in pain, sinking back below the clouds, and continued flying south.

Her wings carried her far, over landscapes she did not recognize, hills and valleys of Parumvir dotted with flocks of sheep that, if her shadow fell across them, stampeded in panic. Their sheepdog guards fled as well, abandoning their flocks to run, tails tucked, for the nearest shelter.

Una flew on. The sensation of flight was lost on her, for her mind was consumed with her burning: the throbbing burn at her bleeding neck and the boiling burn in her breast.

It might have been days, years, centuries later, for all she knew, when she began to regain some of herself. The fire inside her died even as the sun set on the horizon, and she found it more and more difficult to catch the updrafts with her hideous wings. When at last she could go no farther, she descended like a falling stone. An empty farmer's field presented itself to her view, and she tumbled into it. Her legs, unable to support her weight, collapsed beneath her.

At first she lay still, not thinking, hardly breathing. Then slowly, painfully, thoughts crept in. What was she? What had become of her? Where could she go? Who could help her? The questions rang loudly in her head, and panic stirred up the fire in her breast.

No! No fire! She whimpered and squeezed her eyes shut.

A child's scream filled the air.

Una's eyes opened, and she scrambled to pull her ungainly limbs under her. Pushing herself to her feet, she watched a little girl, screeching like an angry kitten, flee the field up a hill. Answering deep-throated shouts rose moments later. Una sat up on her hind legs and saw peasants running from barns and cottages—women carrying children away, men with pitchforks and scythes charging toward her, shouting and menacing.

Terrified, she tried to scream, but a monstrous flame billowed from her throat instead. Smoke spilled out and covered the ground at her feet. The peasants stopped. Some flung themselves down on the ground while others turned and fled. Three sturdy men, one bald and white bearded, brandished their flimsy weapons higher and continued charging, screaming like barbarians.

She took to the air even as the nearest peasant, armed with an ax, stepped into the field. Her shadow swept over him and his two companions as she left them and the field far behind.

The flame roared in her head. *They believe I'm a monster,* Una thought, snarling even in flight. *That's what they think of me. Idiots!* Flames licked between her lips. *Mindless creatures. I should burn them all!*

She shook her head violently as she recognized her thoughts. *No, that's not who I am. This is a lie; this isn't me. This is his work, but I am still inside.*

Deep down inside herself she searched. Red ash covered everything, every thought, word, or deed. But as she rooted around in her soul, she thought she could still see traces of the princess.

It's all a lie. Just a lie!

But the fires were stoked inside her once more, and she flew on. She flew over flat green lands she did not know, not the hills of her own country. Night came on, and a silver moon glimmered high above. She landed at last beside a quiet river and crawled into it. The river bubbled and steamed about her. Moaning, she turned on her side to bathe her neck wound. For a moment, cool water sent an icy thrill through her body. But that moment passed, and the burning returned threefold. She would have wept, but the fire had consumed all her tears. Instead, exhausted, she propped her chin on the shore, keeping her nose just out of the water, and lay still. The moon gleamed down on her, highlighting the rough contours of her unsightly frame.

When she woke, her fire was low, and Una found herself once more in the body of a girl.

Fidel sat in the dark in his small room at the garrison in Dompstead, for he refused to let servants in to light his fire. Numb, he stared into shadows. Voices carried through the door from the hall, and Fidel recognized General Argus's voice above the rest.

"I must see the king!"

"He will admit no one—" Fidel's attendant protested, but Argus interrupted with a roar.

"Let me pass. We must flee this place before the duke arrives. We haven't much time. Let me speak to him."

"Sir, we have our orders."

"Hang your orders!"

There was a scuffling in the hall; then a new voice spoke. "Word for the king . . . concerning his son."

"Tell me," Argus demanded.

Low voices murmured, but Fidel did not wait for the attendants to decide whether the message was important enough to disobey his command and let the messenger through. He got up and, staggering in the dark, opened his door.

The attendants, the general, and the young soldier who brought word of his son all looked up as though caught in some sin.

"What news do you have of Felix?" Fidel demanded.

"Please, sire," his senior attendant said, reaching out protectively to the king. "You must rest—"

"What news?" Fidel roared, slapping the attendant's hands aside and grabbing the young soldier viciously. "What news of my son?"

The soldier, white as a sheet, babbled, "I was with the company that rode north, Your Highness. We were attacked, set upon by Shippening soldiers—"

"My son?"

"Lost, sire."

Fidel's grip slackened, and he sagged back, caught and supported by several of his attendants. "Dead?" he whispered.

"I do not know," the soldier said. "I fear so. We were slaughtered, Your Majesty."

Fidel, in a weak haze, noticed suddenly how haggard and weak the young soldier was, saw the wound crusted with blood on his shoulder.

"We were slaughtered," the soldier repeated. "Captain Janus led the prince away, but we could not keep up, and they disappeared into Goldstone Wood. When we came to the Wood there was—" He hung his head, and his voice choked suddenly. "A dragon," he said. "Not large, but we were unprepared."

The soldier, hardly more than a boy, shivered and swayed on his feet. General Argus put a supporting hand under his elbow. "I alone escaped," he continued. "I was wounded and fell into a ditch. I believe I fainted." His voice was low with shame. "When I woke, I searched the Wood but found only my . . . my comrades. Dead. All except Captain Janus." He shuddered and whispered, "Burned."

Another soldier who stood aside from the group spoke up, drawing the king's attention. "We discovered Janus's body," he said, "just out-side Dompstead. He was dead before the company left for the north. Whoever it was who rode with your son was not Captain Janus but an imposter."

Fidel closed his eyes. Everything within him was still, the stillness of death. "Take me inside," he murmured, and his attendants assisted him back to his room, beside the dark fireplace. One of them started to build a fire, but the king said, "Leave me," in a tone that made no room for argument.

But Argus stood his ground in the doorway. "Your Majesty, the duke will come. Probably this very evening. We cannot protect you here. Dompstead is unprepared for defense."

The king did not answer, and the attendants tried to force Argus from the room.

The general nearly shouted in frustration, "We must get you away from here!"

Fidel looked up, and murder flashed through his eyes. "Leave me, Argus. Now."

The general cursed as a man should never curse before his sovereign but allowed himself to be pushed, still cursing, from the room. The door slammed.

Fidel sank into darkness and felt the dragon poison in his blood sucking him deeper. "My children," he whispered.

The attendants stood in the hall, pale as ghosts, and listened help-lessly to their king's weeping.

Heavy drizzle hung in the air, dampening the streets of a small town and the spirits of those who walked in them. This time of year, all one could expect in Beauclair was rain, rain, and more rain, with the occa-sional sleet for added interest. It put everyone in such a sour mood that even friends refused to make eye contact with friends.

Into this town Una stepped on unsteady feet, uncertain anymore of her own limbs. If a wind blew, she felt a lightheaded whirr inside, as though her small frame would be lifted and blown away like dandelion fluff. Her dress was torn, hanging in loose tatters on her body, little protection from the cold and rain. She felt conspicuous, but no one took notice of one solitary girl, intent as they were upon getting to their various destinations and out of the wet.

At a signpost, Una recognized that she had been following the Wide Road, the primary highway that merchants and other travelers took between Parumvir and Beauclair. The town she entered was, from what she could tell, built in the Beauclair style, and she guessed that she must have crossed the border.

She had never in her life traveled so far from home, yet here she stood in the middle of a strange town, utterly alone. She wanted to crawl into a hole and cry for fear and loneliness. But there were no tears, not even now that her fire was low.

She stood in the middle of a cobbled street, looking this way and that. Surely there was somewhere she could go for shelter? Warm light poured through the one large window of an inn at the end of the street. The sign, creaking mournfully in the wet air, sported a crude sketch and read: *The Rampant Dragon.*

She grimaced.

But perhaps they would let her warm herself at the fire? For though Una could feel her own fire deep down inside, it was faint, and outside she was cold and desperate for comfort.

The door of the inn was firmly closed against the bitter night. She knocked smartly, then stepped back, tucking her hands under her arms, hunched over in the cold.

A thin, grizzled man looked out, around, and finally down at her. His face darkened.

"What d'yer want?"

"Please, sir," she said, her voice raw and hoarse, "might I sit a spell by your fire?"

He eyed her. Rain, coming heavier now, dripped down her face and off her chin, plastering her long hair to her shoulders. But part of an ugly red scab on her neck still showed. Her skin was white as a ghost's, her eyes wide and frightened. But as he looked into those eyes a moment longer, he drew back behind his door. "Eh, git 'long wit yer," he growled. "Dars talk o' dragons abroad, en I b'ain't takin' no risks. Git, yer hear? No dawdlin'."

"Please, sir—"

He slammed the door in her face, shutting out her glimpse of warmth.

Wet and miserable, she sank to her knees on the doorstep, leaning her forehead against the soggy wood. "Please!" She raised a fist and pounded. "Do I look like a dragon? Please, just for a moment!"

"Git, I said!" the innkeeper called from the other side and refused to answer her again.

She turned and pressed her back against the door, drew up her knees, and wrapped her arms around them. Maybe her fire would drown and she would just die?

How long she sat, she couldn't say, but she was startled from a half sleep by the sound of hooves. Looking up, she saw a company of twenty-some horsemen squelch into town. Their bridles and gear were all blue and silver, and one of them wore a cloak with the royal insignia of Beauclair emblazoned on the back.

The company pulled up before the inn, and stableboys darted out to take the horses while the men dismounted. The sullen and soggy leader stumped to the inn door, nearly stepping on Una before he noticed her.

"Out of my way, girl," he growled, nudging her none too gently aside with his boot, then pounded on the inn door. "Ho, innkeeper! Open for your prince!"

"Prince Gervais!" she cried, scrambling to her feet. "Gervais!"

The prince took no notice of her. The door swung open, and the grizzled innkeeper bowed until his head nearly touched his knees. "Yer Highness is most welcome," he said, ushering the prince in by the fire.

"Oh that yer would grace my 'umble 'stablishment! I b'ain't able to 'spress the honor—."

"Spiced cider. Now," the prince said, flinging aside his wet cloak and holding out his hands to the flames. His company gathered around him. Unnoticed, Una slipped in with them, lingering in a shadowed corner of the room.

"And may I 'quire," the innkeeper said as he and his servants carried in twenty-odd mugs of hot cider for the prince and his men, "what brings Yer Highness to these 'umble barts? May I venture dat ye is aimin' for Parumvir to hunt deh dragon 'bout which we've heard tell?"

The prince took a long draft from his mug before answering, "You guess well, old man. Such indeed is my intent." He leaned forward, closer to the fire, gazed into its depths, and muttered, "I intend to collect that bounty money; heaven help me if I don't!"

One of Gervais's men pulled his chair up beside the prince and spoke in a low voice. Standing near in the shadows, Una heard each word.

"Your Highness."

"What?"

"We cannot go on," the man said. "You know that."

"Yes, we can."

"Your Highness, please. It is yet a full day's journey to Parumvir, many more till we'll reach the capital. By all accounts the king has fled his own city, and the Duke of Shippening has taken up residence. For all we know the dragon won't be there when we arrive; perhaps he was never there at all."

"Oh, he's there all right," Gervais said. "I know it. He's got to be."

"Your Highness—"

"Have you any idea what the bounty on a dragon's head is?" Gervais snapped. "More than you'll ever see in a lifetime!"

"Only if you succeed in killing the beast."

The prince growled something indecipherable. His man shook his head. "Give it up, Your Highness. You knew it was a fool's errand when you first heard of it two days ago."

"I need that bounty, Andre," Gervais said. "It's that or the widow."

"Then go back to the widow before she chooses one of her other ten suitors. You could still win her, even after leaving abruptly as you did. But not if you continue this chase any longer."

Gervais growled again, but his man pressed his case. "You know what she said. She will choose a new husband on the eve of her birthday. You have only three days, but you could yet win her if you return now. You are the favorite."

"Lucky me."

"You'll not find the dragon in that time, prince, and even if you do, you'll still have to face its fire."

"I'd rather that than the widow."

"The widow is a guarantee." The man took Gervais's arm and shook it. "All your debts paid! Is that not worth something?"

The prince sank his head into his hand, slumping deep in his chair. "If only I'd succeeded with that princess in Parumvir."

"But you didn't. Nor with the count's daughter, nor even with that heiress in Milden. Face it, sire. The widow is your last hope."

Gervais did not answer but remained slouched, gazing into the fire.

Una heard all this in silence as she sank farther back into the shadows. *How quickly you've forgotten me, Prince Gervais.*

Something deep inside smoldered.

No!

She closed her eyes, trying to stop it, but the heat built, increasing every moment in pain and intensity. She slid away along the wall, determined to find the door before anything burst inside her.

"Oi! I thought I told yer ta git?"

The innkeeper appeared before her. She tried to duck around him but fell over a stool. He reached out and grabbed her roughly by the arm, dragging her to her feet. "Little dog!" he cried, his fingers pinching into her arm. "Little beggar! I'll tech yer to—" He struck her across the face, hard.

Una screamed, clutched her cheek with her hand, then, snarling like an animal, wrenched her arm free. The fire pounded in her temples, burned in her chest. She hesitated a moment, turned, and flung herself at Gervais's feet. Her wet hair spattered about her face, and her white skin shone luminous in the firelight. He gave a yelp, but she cried, "Prince Gervais, do you know me?"

"Know you? Get away from me, girl! Who are—" He started to his feet.

Hearing the scraping of swords being drawn, she lunged forward and grabbed his hand.

"Gervais, I am Una, Princess of Parumvir. Remember? Remember me, prince? Remember how you sang to me? I need help. I need mercy. I—"

Gervais shook himself free and stepped back, shouting, "Unhand me, girl! I don't know you!"

"Please!" Una cried even as the innkeeper caught her roughly under the arms and dragged her back. "I'm lost! I—"

"Forgive me, sire," the innkeeper said, hauling her back toward the door. "Don't know 'ow she git in 'ere."

Una struggled in his grip, broke free, and staggered toward the prince. "Please help me!" she cried, but several of his men stepped between her and him.

One of them struck her again across the cheek that still smarted from the innkeeper's blow. "Out, rat," the man growled as she hit the floor. "How dare you speak to a prince in that way? Out with you!"

The fire roared to life. It burned through her veins, pulsing like blood as the innkeeper grabbed her again. Her eyes caught the scornful face of Gervais. "You forgot me!" she cried, and flame burst from her tongue. The men fell away in surprise and terror, and the innkeeper screamed and fell back as though he'd been burned. Fire flooded from her mouth and poured down to the floor.

"She's a dragon!" Gervais cried, snatching up his sword. He ducked around her flame, leapt over the prostrate innkeeper, and grabbed her by the hair. He yanked her head back, exposing her throat, still white and smooth. At the sight of his upraised sword, she clawed behind her, trying to catch hold of him.

He struck, but the blade could not pierce her hide.

She twisted in his grasp, felt her hair tearing from her scalp, and slashed at him with cruel talons. Gervais let go and jumped back only just in time to avoid her attack. "Catch her!" he cried. "Don't let her escape!"

Five or six of his men leapt upon her, and Una did not try to swallow her flame as she struggled through their grasping hands. She felt her body expanding, felt her fire building. She shook the men off and ran for the door, bursting into the rainy street just as her wings spread wide.

"My bounty!" Gervais rushed after her, his sword gripped in his hand. "Come back, dragon, and face me!" he shouted.

She turned. Their gazes locked. His eyes widened.

"You forgot me," she snarled, and her mouth opened.

A run of silver notes pierced her mind as though from a great distance.

Una, where are you?

Rain poured from heaven, steamed off her great body, and rolled from her muzzle. The fire in her eyes dulled to embers.

"Please," she whispered, gazing up into the sky. "Please don't forget . . ."

The next moment, her shadow passed over *The Rampant Dragon* and disappeared into the dark clouds.

Gervais breathed again, then coughed on the fumes that surrounded him. He sat down in the mud of that empty street, dropped his sword into the muck at his side, and cradled his head in his hands. "It's the widow for me," he muttered, so miserable he almost wished that dragon girl had succeeded in cooking him.

"Who was she, anyway?" he wondered.

25

IN THE DARKNESS OF HIS CHAMBER, King Fidel heard as though from a great distance cries in the training yard, the sounds of officers barking commands, but he could not understand their words. He was lost, numb. He knew he would have to gather himself and venture out again soon. But the dragon poison was thick in his veins, and he could not move. If the duke was coming, let him come.

"Your Majesty."

Someone spoke behind him, though he had heard no one enter the room. He recognized the voice, however.

"Your Majesty."

"How did you come here?" Fidel asked.

"Through the Wood." The shadowy figure stepped before the king and knelt at his feet. "I bring you news."

Fidel shook his head. He could not see the features of the face turned to him, but he reached out and patted a shoulder. "I can bear no more just now, Prince Aethelbald," he said. "You were right. My son is lost to me, and my daughter—" He choked on his own words, and his hand shook on the Prince's shoulder.

Aethelbald bowed his head. A long silence hung between them, broken only by the king's shuddering breaths and the cries out in the yard. Aethelbald reached up and took the king's hand. "Felix is safe," he said.

"What?" The king's voice broke.

"Felix is safe in my Haven on the Borders between this world and the other," Aethelbald said.

"My son?" Fidel whispered.

"Yes, Majesty."

Fidel's tears fell heavily down his face, and he could not speak for a moment. "You are of their kind," he murmured at last. "I wasn't sure what to believe before. All those old wives' tales come to life, come out of the Wood. It was too fantastic. But you are of the Far World, aren't you?"

"I am, Your Majesty," Aethelbald said.

Fidel took hold of both Aethelbald's hands and held them in a tremendous grip. "You are their Prince," he cried. "You have saved my son!"

"Yes, Majesty. My faithful servant Dame Imraldera tends him even now. He has been grievously poisoned, but he will live."

"Blessings, blessings on you, good Prince!"

Aethelbald kissed the king's hand, then lifted him to his feet. "Now you must go," he said. "The duke comes, and many good men will die needlessly to defend you if you stay. I am sending Sir Oeric and two more of my knights to guard you on your journey north. General Argus has made everything ready for your departure."

"Yes." Fidel nodded and straightened his shoulders, but he felt old and weak. "Yes, what you say is good. Aethelbald, my daughter . . . I saw her, saw what she has become—"

What strength remained to the king seemed to flow out as he spoke. He sagged forward, and the Prince caught him.

"You were right," Fidel breathed. "You were right all along, and I should have listened to you. I should have protected her."

"Fidel."

The king looked up. In the darkness he could just see the glint of Aethelbald's eyes.

"Fidel," the Prince said, "you could not have prevented this."

"Don't try to comfort me. I know my own guilt."

"Yes," the Prince said, "you are guilty. You made mistakes. But even so, you could not have prevented what happened." He held the king upright, made him stand, and pushed back his shoulders. "Now you must go on. Lead your people. The duke will try to find you while you are yet weak. You must hide, and you must grow strong once more. Have courage, good king. Have hope. Your son is safe."

"And my daughter?"

"Have hope," Aethelbald repeated. He let go of the king and stepped back into the shadows. "I will find Una. Now go."

The room was silent again, empty. Fidel went to the door to call his attendants. As he put his hand to the latch he heard the strangest sound, faintly, just beyond the din in the yard. It sounded like birdsong.

Few people saw her pass. Una developed a dragon's talent for traveling unnoticed. The burning never eased, but she gradually became accustomed to it until she did not notice it anymore. Her wounded neck healed into a rough scar in a matter of days.

She flew south, through Beauclair, through the Duchy of Milden, flying blindly. She did not eat or drink, for her fire burned and gave her strength without other sustenance.

Not until she crossed the borders of Shippening did she know the aim of her flight.

"Southlands is not far," she told herself. "Only a few days more."

She doubled her speed, tucking her knobby limbs close to her long body until she formed a long black ribbon from nose to tail, snaking through the sky.

The Red Desert loomed to the east, immense, dry, and hot. Una shuddered when she looked at it. It reminded her of the ocean, vast and unsearchable. Yet the ocean was full of life, while the desert was a landscape of death.

A world of dragons, she thought.

Closing her eyes to the sight, she flew on her way.

Gervais forgot me, but Leonard never will.

"Una, trust me," he had said.

She would trust him. And she would find him.

Everything burned and smothered, though now and then a soothing, cool breeze broke through the heat. Felix drifted in and out of consciousness, mostly alone. He felt trapped in a constant dream of fire. Sometimes the woman with the gentle hands was present, and her voice comforted him through the haze.

One night he woke fully for the first time, though the heat of fever still seared inside him. It was late; he could see stars shining through the gently moving leaves above his head. He sat up and looked around the strange room, which seemed no more than a clearing in the Wood. The bed on which he lay grew up out of the ground, rooted like a tree, and the sheets were soft petals and leaves held together by invisible threads. He pushed them back and swung his legs over the side.

On unsteady feet Felix crossed the room, following a trail of moonlight. There were neither walls nor doors nor windows, only trees growing all around, yet ivy draped these so thickly that he seemed as enclosed as he'd ever been in his own rooms in the palace. He felt around in the ivy until he found a thinner place, then pushed through, out of the clearing.

Trees stood on either side like walls in a corridor, and moonlight shone on the path like a carpet unrolling at his feet. Felix followed it. Tiny pricks touched his arms and face like biting bugs. He slapped at empty air, and the little pricks stopped. He followed the moonlight, his fevered eyes scanning the trees and the arch of branches over his head. Stars glimmered between the branches like candles in sconces. He could not tell whether he walked in a forest or in a grand manor house.

Something gleamed before him. The moonlight seemed to flow down the path to this one spot and stop there, pooling into a small pond of light around an object suspended between the branches of two young birch trees. Felix, stumbling a little, made his way to the end of the corridor and looked upon the object.

It was a sword.

Silver and moonlight and strength, all forged into a weapon.

It filled Felix's gaze. In his fevered state he felt a tremble of cold fear rush through him as he looked upon it, yet it was beautiful. He longed to touch it but could not move his hands.

"It belongs to my lord, the Prince."

The soft voice he knew spoke behind him. Felix turned slowly and met the gaze of a young woman. Her face was full of moonlight. She smiled. "Go back to bed, young Felix."

Felix looked back at the sword, frowning. "Why does he not carry this sword?" he whispered. "It is so beautiful. . . . A sword such as this, it could kill the Dragon."

A gentle hand touched his arm. "He will take it up when the time is right," Dame Imraldera said. "Come, Felix. Come away."

He resisted her urging. But a sudden roar just beyond the wall of trees filled his ears. He jumped back in terror and clung to the woman, who put her arms around him. "Don't be afraid," she said. "It cannot come inside."

Felix's breath came in short, panting gasps. "What is out there?"

"The world of Faerie," she said.

The roar, deep and harsh, inhuman yet not quite animal, filled the air again, and something scuffled on the other side of the trees. Felix trembled, but Imraldera remained calm. "It cannot come inside," she said. "You are in the Prince's Haven. Nothing may come inside without his permission."

Felix leaned heavily in her arms, sick with fever and fear. "Come," she said. "Let's get you back to bed." She led him back down the hall, and Felix felt more peaceful, though the strange creature still snuffled and roared just beyond the trees. When they stepped back into the clearing-bedchamber, all sounds from the other side were silenced. Felix let the woman cover him in the soft sheets. Sleep descended upon him.

"Why does he not use the sword?" Felix whispered before he slipped away.

"He will at the proper time," the young woman replied. "Sleep, Felix."

From Shippening, Una flew across the Chiara Bay and the thin isthmus that attached Southlands to the Continent, then on over the ring of mountains that encircled most of the country. She beheld Southlands for the first time.

It was a strange country, far stranger than Una had expected. Beneath her lay a flatland scored by deep gorges filled with dark forest. Like green-black rivers, these gorges cut the stretches of tableland into vast islands. Connecting these islands, bridges stained by dragon smoke yet still white and beautiful soared in elegant arches.

As a child she had heard tell of the acclaimed Southlands bridges but had never been able to envision them for herself. She could well believe the legend that they had not been built by the hand of man, for what man could design such marvels? They crisscrossed, gleaming high above the dark forests below, connecting the cities and towns of Southlands, providing communion among the people that would otherwise have been impossible, unless men dared brave the forests below the plateaus.

On the plateaus, Una beheld cities of glorious towers and minarets such as she had never seen before, and the colors that presented themselves to her eyes were beyond her experience. They were familiar in some senses—green, red, or blue. But the shades were different, the hues bolder, more intense than anything she had before seen. And the frequent patches of blackened land, charred and smoking still, only made the colors seem brighter beneath the blue of the Southlands sky.

She thought of her homeland, last seen shrouded in dragon smoke, devoid of color. And her fire burned bitterly in her breast.

On and on she flew across the strange countryside, hardly knowing where to search. But at last, as she passed over the largest and most beautiful of the bridges, something caught her eye.

The desecrated castle.

She recognized it from her dream: the enormous, fire-ravaged structure surrounded by ruined gardens of skeletal tree stumps and ash-blown shrubberies. It was restored some now, not so decayed as it had appeared in her dreams. Several of the towers were being rebuilt, and much of the ash had been cleaned from its stones, revealing the colors beneath. But she recognized it as the hateful palace of her nightmares.

And she knew that here was Lionheart's home.

Before the great castle was a city, the greatest of all the cities she had yet seen. It bore deep black scars from many fires among the streets and tall buildings. Nevertheless, as she flew high above it, she could feel the excitement of teeming life below her.

She could not land anywhere near for fear of being seen, so she chose instead to take shelter in the deep ravine beside the plateau, beneath the black covering of forest. The trees grew so thickly there that they blocked out the sun, for which she was grateful. The ground trembled as she landed, but other than the sounds she made as she crawled through the brambles of the forest floor, all was silent. There was a sense of deadness in the air of the forest. And beneath the deadness, a smell of life that was not life. She smelled it through her own smoke, and it made her shudder.

Una crawled to the edge of the forest, where the land began to slope up steeply and the trees ended in an abrupt line, and gazed up to the white arc of a bridge high above her. She realized suddenly that she had flown for many days without rest. Her wings and limbs quivered, aching for respite.

"I cannot rest," she told herself. "I cannot rest until I find . . . I must find him. But how can I do so in this state?"

She looked down at her claws, huge and black and gnarled. "He won't even recognize me. Leonard . . . how could you love a monster?"

A growl rumbled deep in her throat, and flames slid between her teeth. With a vicious snarl, she opened her mouth and let out a billow of fire on her own limbs, then turned her head and blew more fiercely on her body and wings, wishing she could burn herself away and be no more.

When the smoke cleared, Una looked again, and one hand was that of a princess. The other was scale-covered and cruel.

26

THE DRAGON FIRE that sustained her had sunk low in her breast. But Una felt it there still, where her heart should be. "No," she whispered, clutching the front of her gown. "Let it die. Just let it die."

She knew it would not.

She practiced walking among the tall forest trees, struggling to carry herself upright and lift her feet. Her movements needed to be less awkward if she was going to pass unnoticed in the city. The sun rose high above her, but the air was icy. She welcomed the fierceness of winter air against her skin, however, desperate to cool the burning that pulsed through her. Her left hand seemed to suck the light into its dark scales and render it blackness. She covered it with her human hand, tried to tuck it under the folds of her tattered garments. The left sleeve of her dress was still mostly intact, and she pulled it low over her knuckles.

"I must find him," she told herself, looking out from the shelter of the forest up toward the city. "Or at least have word of him."

The thought filled her with fear. The Dragon's words came to mind: *"Betrothed to another."*

She stepped out of the trees. "It's not true," she said. The place on her finger where her mother's ring had once sat felt strangely bare. Una clenched her hands, human and dragon, into fists. "I trust him."

Fire burned her throat, but she swallowed it back.

The climb was long and hard, particularly now that she was unused to her small human body. She discovered a path that progressed steeply up the otherwise sheer rock face, and she followed it, sometimes bent double to use her hands as well as her feet. The muscles in her arms shook with effort, and often she had to stop and breathe deeply, closing her eyes.

The sun set and the moon rose. Somehow, the white face of the moon was more terrible to her than the sun's golden rays. The moonlight was icy, and she thought she would freeze on the outside even as she burned to death within. She lay down upon the trail, exhausted, her arms over her face to shield her from the moon's eye, and slept a tormented sleep.

When Una woke she did not open her eyes but kept her arms over her face, feeling the sharp scales of the left one biting into the skin of her cheek. She did not want to face the sun nor the rest of the climb. Birds sang their morning chorus, and she cursed them bitterly between her teeth.

A jangling bell sounded in her ear, startling her from her stupor of misery. She sat up, every part of her body aching from a night spent on rocks, and looked up the path.

A goat stood not many paces above her. It flicked its ears and winked its yellow eyes at her, then voiced a disapproving, "Bah!"

"Good morning to you too!" Una snapped, drawing up her legs and scowling at the goat. She pressed her forehead into her knees, once more blocking the sunlight and wondering where she would find the strength to continue her long climb. Perhaps she would not try. Perhaps she would simply stay put until the sun and the moon burned her away to nothing and the fire inside her went out.

"Oh!" a voice said. "There *is* someone!"

Una startled for the second time that morning and blinked up the path once more. Beyond the goat another figure appeared. At first she could not tell if it was male or female, for the person's face was shrouded in a linen veil and the voice that spoke was very soft and hard to discern. But on second glance, Una determined it was a girl, a small one with hunched shoulders and a hand put out to touch the rock wall on her right.

"Beana told me someone needed help down here," the veiled girl said, moving around the goat. "Shoo, Beana."

"Bah!" said the goat.

"Who are you?" Una asked. Her voice was harsh in her mouth, but she hardly cared.

"I am nobody," the girl said. "Who are you?"

Una shook her head and gave no answer. She buried her face in her knees again.

"Have you come from the Wilderlands? Are you trying to climb to the Eldest's City?" The girl drew closer until she stood over Una. Her voice was easier to understand now that she was near; she spoke with the strong accent of Southlands.

Una did not look up but shrugged her shoulders.

"You are weak and worn." There was a long pause, then, "And I see that you suffer."

Una felt a hand touching her scale-covered arm. She snapped upright and pulled it away from the veiled girl's grasp. "Leave me alone!"

"Please, m'lady," the girl said humbly. "I am not one to judge you. Will you look?"

Frowning and cringing away, Una lifted her face to see the hand the veiled girl extended to her. To Una's surprise, she saw that the hand was gray and hard as stone, and tipped with long claws. She looked up at the veiled face and could just discern eyes through a slit in the linen. "Are you . . . are you like me?"

The veiled one shook her head. "No, m'lady. But let me help you even so."

Hesitantly, Una reached up and placed her awful hand in the awful hand of the stranger. She was surprised at the strength in the veiled girl's grip as she found herself pulled to her feet.

"You go to the city?" the girl asked.

Una nodded. She allowed the girl to put her arm across her shoulders and support her as they began to climb the trail. The shaggy goat turned about nimbly and led the way, sometimes pausing to bleat an irritable "Bah!" as she went.

The sun was high by the time they came to the plateau above. Una shook herself free of the veiled girl. "Which way to the city gates?"

"I can take you there myself," the veiled one said. "I serve in the Eldest's House. I know the way."

"Serve in the Eldest's House?" Una felt the fire flickering inside her. "Have you seen . . . That is . . . have you heard tell of . . ."

"Yes, m'lady?"

Una shook her head and moved away from the girl. She couldn't bear to know. Not yet. No, she must find him, that was all, and he himself could tell her all she needed to know. "Thank you for your assistance," Una said, turning her back on the girl. "I will find my own way."

"Please, m'lady—"

"Leave me alone!" Una cried. And with a strength she had not realized she still possessed, she started running, running across the open land to the city before her, fueled by a fire inside and a keen desire to leave the stranger and her ugly goat far behind. When at last she dared look back, she breathed in relief to see she was not followed.

Her path took her directly to the city gates. She covered her hideous arm as best she could and slipped into the ranks of plentiful commoners. She still felt out of place, for everyone about her was brown and clad in brilliant colors and bangles and scarves. She took shelter behind a great mass of a woman with curly red hair and an enormous voice who kept shouting to those around her in such a thick accent that Una could not hope to understand her. Shielded by such a person, she doubted she would attract much attention. Unless the guards looked close and saw the remnants of silver threads in her tattered clothes, Una could pass for the most innocuous of peasants. But her dragon hand—what could she do with that? Once more she tucked it into the folds of her gown.

"Hey there, young miss!"

It took Una a moment to realize the guard spoke to her. She blinked and pointed to herself, raising her eyebrows in a worried line.

"Yes, you!" the guard barked. "You're totterin' like a drunkard! You been samplin' the wine a'fore the festival?"

Una, who could scarcely understand a word he said, so thick was his accent, tried to shuffle past, hiding her hand, her eyes fixed on the feet of the red-haired woman before her.

"Eh, I asked you a question!" the guard said. He grabbed her right arm sharply as she passed and whirled her about to face him. She gasped in pain as his fingers dug into her skin. She twisted her other arm behind her back, hiding it as best she could. Then she gasped again when she found herself looking into dark eyes very like those eyes so dear to her memory. For an instant she thought her journey over, her beloved found.

That instant passed.

The guard dropped her arm as though burnt and backed away, his eyes widening. He shook his head and growled, "Move 'long, girl. Eh, scat!"

Una ducked her head and scurried into the city.

The streets were crowded, but it was not the sort of crowd caused when people leave their work and shops, lock up, and make for home, as would be usual for that time of day. Una had been out in the city back home enough times to know how the routine should look and feel. Rather, this crowd was a festive one, full of laughing tension edged with joyous frenzy. The people she passed were giddy, as though they had not known happiness in a long time and this new taste of it intoxicated them. They shoved and jostled, but all in fun and good spirits.

It frightened Una. Every time someone bumped into her, they turned with a smile and a bright "Sorry!" on their lips. But when she met their gazes, their lively voices turned to murmurs and they backed away hurriedly. Each time, Una wanted to hide her face, to crawl under a stone and disappear. She lowered her eyes, pulling her hair around her cheeks as a hood, and went on. She kept her left hand tucked under her arm, hoping that no one would see it.

Once a woman ran by with a wild laugh and accidentally pushed Una off the street, into a dark alley. Una, glad for momentary relief from the crowds, leaned her back against the wall and sighed, pressing a hand to her burning chest. "Let it die," she murmured. "Oh, let it die. I must find him."

A clatter at the end of the alley caught her attention. She turned and saw a tiny orange kitten, tail high, trotting toward her. "Monster," she whispered, though she knew it wasn't her pet. She knelt down, holding out a hand.

The kitten halted. Its ears went back and its tail bristled. It let out a tiny snarl and a hiss, turned, and dashed into the shadows.

Una rose and stepped back into the street. Setting her jaw, she pushed and prodded her way through the crowds, stepping on feet and using her elbows as needed. Everyone seemed to be making their way uphill, so she focused her energies on going that direction too. Somehow, she felt she would find answers there.

Leonard, I'm coming. Wait for me.

In all the babble around her she made out a few words: "The crown prince." "The Lady of Middlecrescent." "The crown prince."

Una felt the flame in her chest flare every time she picked out those words. The crowd became so thick, she thought she would suffocate, and she screamed, "Wait for me!"

People backed away from her in surprise. The crowds parted, and she passed through the last street into the city square at the crest of a low hill.

The square was filled with more people than Una had ever before seen. Ribbons and banners were strung between buildings and poles and, near a fountain in the very center, musicians played and young people danced. All around her she heard the murmurs, "The crown prince! The crown prince!"

She saw a great house on the far side of the square, toward which most of the people seemed to be pressing. It had huge double doors, once white, now grayed from heavy smoke, and above was a balcony large enough to hold an entire company of soldiers. The house, she guessed, must belong to the mayor, and on that balcony the people expected soon to see the reason for all their merrymaking.

She pushed her way forward, and people, after a glance at her face, let her through without a word. She stood at last just under the balcony where the fevered excitement had reached a zenith.

"Excuse me," she said, touching the sleeve of a burly man, a butcher by the stains on his hands and fingernails. "Is the crown prince expected soon?"

"Yes, miss," he rumbled in the jewel-like tones of Southlands, shrugging off her hand and stepping back. "Why else do you think we're here?"

"To celebrate his betrothal?" Una asked, reaching out to grab the butcher's sleeve again, afraid he'd escape before answering.

"His wedding, miss," the butcher said, using both his strong hands to shove her away. "Don't you know he marries Lady Daylily, the Baron of Middlecresent's daughter, at the week's end?"

Una let him go, and he disappeared into the crowd. She turned her gaze up to the balcony. "It's not him," she whispered. The flame inside hurt so badly! "It's not my Leonard."

Suddenly a great shout filled the square. Una wanted to clap her hands to her ears but dared not expose the scales on her left hand. She could not tear her gaze from the spot at the front of the balcony, between two flags, where she knew he would stand.

Then there he was.

She hardly recognized him clad in blue and scarlet, rich clothing fit for a prince. A crown of silver graced his head where once had sat a bell-covered hat. His face, so comical, so expressive, was now bearded and solemn even as he smiled down on the people. He was thinner, older, sterner.

But he was her jester.

"Prince Lionheart! Prince Lionheart!" the crowd cried, and there was love and pride in their voices.

"Leonard," Una whispered.

The prince raised a hand to salute the crowd, then reached behind and drew someone up beside him. She was radiant, smiling, dressed in elegant fur wraps against the winter chill. She seemed ready to burst with joy as she waved to the people and clung to her prince's hand.

"The Lady of Middlecresent! Lady Daylily!" The crowd redoubled its shouts, and the musicians struck up a lively tune so the young people could dance again to express their joy.

Una clutched her stomach. The fire rolled inside her, and she felt she'd be sick as she watched the beauty accepting smiles from the prince. Her jester. Her Leonard. Sobs and fire choked her throat. Without hope that her voice could be heard in that joyful din, she raised her right hand to her face and shouted, "Leonard!"

The noise did not decrease; the festive mayhem did not abate. But the prince stepped away from his lady, leaned over the rail, and searched the seething masses. His gaze met Una's.

He gasped.

Blood like lava pounded in her veins, and she panted with the terror of it. For Una felt, in that moment when she saw the look on his face—not a look of joy or delight, as she had so long dreamed of seeing when at last reunited with him, but of pure surprise and, an instant later, pure horror—that she would burn him alive with the heat of her eyes if she could.

"Una." His lips formed her name, though she could not hear him. His hands tightened on the rail, and he shook his head and looked again. She gazed up at him, all the sorrow in the world on her pale face, and he knew his eyes did not lie.

The lady touched his shoulder and asked a question. Startled, he turned to her and made a hasty reply. Then he vanished from Una's sight, leaving the lady standing alone.

Una could not look at her but turned away, waiting. She knew he would come. This time, he would come.

27

U<small>NA!</small>"

She turned around, and there he stood. His crown was gone and he wore a cloak to hide his rich clothing, but she would know him in a thousand.

"Leonard," she whispered, her voice drowned in the din around them.

He stepped forward, his eyes intent on her face. "Una, what . . . what has happened to . . . What are you—"

He grabbed her hand, and she kept the other tucked out of sight as he drew her aside, elbowing his way through the crowd, which did not recognize him and which was only too glad to get away from the pale, foreign girl. Lionheart half sheltered her with his cloak, as though trying to hide her from prying eyes, or perhaps to protect those eyes from seeing her. He brought Una through the worst of the crowds, then pulled her down a narrow side street where few people walked. He took another turn and another. Neither tried to speak; both moved as quickly as they could.

They came at last to the outskirts of the city, where few houses stood and a trickle of a drainage stream flowed quietly under an unguarded footbridge. At the bridge, Lionheart halted and let Una go. He threw back his hood so that she could see his stern face. His hair stood all on end, just as she remembered.

"Where is your father?" he demanded.

"I do not know."

"You are come alone, then? How did you get here? Why was I not given advance notice of your coming?"

"No one knows," she said.

Prince Lionheart shook his head. "You can't do that. You're a princess. You can't travel all the way from Parumvir to Southlands by yourself!"

"But I did."

He stared at her, studying her face. "What has become of you, Una?" he asked, and she could hear fear lying just beneath the surface of his voice.

"I could ask the same," she whispered.

"No, I mean it," Lionheart said, shifting on his feet. "There is something odd about your face, something not—"

"Again, I could say the same," Una replied, and a tiny smile lifted a corner of her mouth. "That beard . . ." She reached out a hand to his face, but he caught it and pushed it away.

"This is no time for jokes," he said.

Una drew back and wrapped her arms about herself, still keeping the scale-covered hand hidden. "Then it is true," she said. "You have killed him."

"Killed whom?"

"My jester."

He stared down at her a long moment, a number of dark expressions sliding across his face. "I don't know what you're talking about," he said.

"Oh, Leonard!" She tried to touch his arm, but he turned away and stepped back.

"I'm not Leonard, Princess Una," he said. "I thought I told you that."

"Where did you go?"

He raised an eyebrow and refused to meet her gaze. "Here, obviously. Back to Southlands."

She shook her head. "You know what I mean."

"I don't!" he snapped. "I don't know what you're talking about, and I'm not sure you do either. You aren't speaking rationally."

"Leonard—"

"That is not my name, and I wish you wouldn't use it!" He pinched the bridge of his nose, frowning. "I did exactly what I told you, went exactly where I said I would, back . . . How long ago was that? Many months! I left your home and traveled directly down here, just as I had purposed while enjoying your father's hospitality."

"And you fought the Dragon? Killed him, even?" Una stepped closer to him and reached out again to touch his hand, but he pulled away, tucked his hands under his arms, and leaned against the bridge railing. She forged ahead. "Please tell me, my prince. Tell me how it happened."

"The Dragon was gone by the time I arrived," he said, "leaving my kingdom in ashes, my people rendered near helpless with fear, my father near crazy with sorrow."

"You never saw the Dragon?"

The prince still would not meet her gaze. "Don't think it's been easy. I maybe didn't fight a monster, but the work I've had to do, the blood, sweat, and tears I've poured into rebuilding my people, and will have to keep pouring out for years to come before we'll ever reach our former—"

"You never saw the Dragon?"

"Aren't you listening to me? It was gone by the time I got here."

"That's not what he said."

"What?"

"He said you made an agreement, that he wouldn't kill you and would let you return home if . . . if what? What was your side of the bargain?"

"Una, your voice . . ." He stared down at her, and fear raced across his face, but he hid it the next instant. "What are you saying? Of whom are you speaking?"

"You know whom I mean." Una stepped close and grabbed his arm with both her hands, but he yelped and shook her off.

"You burn!" he said. "Una, are you ill?"

She pulled her hands close to her sides, her fists clenched. "Yes," she whispered. "Yes, I am. What was your side of the bargain, Lionheart? When the Dragon agreed not to kill you?"

"You're babbling nonsense," he growled. "I've made no bargains with anyone. I came here, just as I told you. Why don't you listen?"

"No bargains?" Una spoke to the boards of the bridge. "What about the bargain you made with me?"

Lionheart did not answer. The drainage stream trickled underneath them laboriously, as though any moment it would dry up altogether.

"You asked me to trust you," Una said. Her voice quavered, but no tears came to her eyes. "You asked me to trust you, Lionheart."

"I shouldn't have said that," he said. "I must have forgotten. But I should never have said that or anything of the kind to you." He rubbed a hand down his face and shook his head. "And your ring, the one you so generously lent me. I'd almost forgotten that as well. I will pay you back for it, I promise."

Dirty promises!

Flames raged inside her head, but Una bit her tongue and struggled to suppress them.

"You promised you'd return," she whispered.

"If I did, I shouldn't have. I should have known my obligations would keep me here."

"And her?"

Lionheart lowered his head, trying to look her in the eyes, but she turned away. "I am going to marry her, Una. I had no right to say any of those things I said to you. I am ashamed of any implications I made. They were foolish, thoughtless—"

"Which gives you the right to unmake them now?"

The sun disappeared behind a cloud, casting the world below into shadows. But Una's world burned red.

"You asked me to trust you."

"I take it back!" he cried, flinging up his hands. "Things change, Una. People change. Can't you get that into your head? My promises to her are good, unlike any I might have made to you. I made them after winning back my kingdom, under my true name, not in disguise as a . . . as a Fool. As a lackey cleaning the dirty floors of those who should have been my peers! I am not ashamed of any promises I have made to her."

Una stepped back as though struck. "You are ashamed of those you made to me?"

"Una—"

"You are ashamed of me?"

"Don't put words in my mouth!" he barked. "I am ashamed of that whole period of my life, that degrading, despicable—"

"You never fought the Dragon," Una said and gasped suddenly.

He shook his head. "No, I didn't, and there's no shame in that either. I must do what's best for my kingdom. That includes not being devoured by monsters. Can you understand that? My people need me alive, not roasted."

Fire flickered in her throat. "You never fought the Dragon."

He spoke through clenched teeth. "I told you, Una, sometimes plans change. I'm sorry, but—"

"I'm sorry?"

"Is that a question?"

"I suppose so. I'm trying it out for size. Usually I find that 'sorry' isn't enough, so I don't often bother with it anymore. . . ."

"It isn't enough," she whispered.

He shook his head, exasperated. "I can't help that."

"You never fought the Dragon."

"No, and I won't."

"You never fought—"

She swung her scale-covered arm at him, swiping with curved claws. He cried out and dodged aside, knocking her arm away, and she staggered forward on the bridge, bent double. The flames inside her burst through.

Lionheart shouted and fell flat, then pushed himself back on his hands and elbows as a pair of black wings rose and overshadowed him. "Una!" he shouted.

A dragon head reared up, roaring in pain and anger. Eyes like lava turned on him, and the gaze burned.

"You never fought the Dragon," the monster spoke, and smoke rolled from her tongue. "Will you fight me now? Will you kill *me*?"

He lay paralyzed in her shadow, a dry scream trapped in his chest. She leaned in, her fiery eyes threatening to engulf him, to burn him to embers. But her voice wavered. "Won't you try, my prince?"

He covered his face with his arms, turned, and tried to crawl away. She placed a great claw on his back and pushed him to the ground. The bridge creaked and groaned. "You killed him," she growled. "You killed my Leonard, Prince Lionheart, killed him as cruel as murder. But you won't fight the Dragon. Coward!"

She felt his stiff body relax under her claw in hopeless certainty of death. She opened her mouth and felt the flames building inside to bellow forth and consume him.

Una! Where are you?
Behind the roaring of her fire, she heard a voice, small and silver.
A thrush song.
Una, I'm coming for you.
Wait for me.

She raised her head and let the flame burst out and burn the sky. Then her great wings opened and carried her up and up, into the deepening twilight.

Lionheart rolled over and lay upon the bridge, gasping, unable to make his lungs draw a complete breath, gazing up into the empty sky.

28

Felix walked from his bed on unsteady feet across the white stone floor to stand at the edge of his chamber. It was open to the outside world, high upon a great mountain, and looked out across a landscape altogether foreign to him.

"The Far World," he whispered as he gazed upon things he had thought existed only in tales. Strange mountains jutted like teeth across a hazy horizon while a river, sinuous as a snake, cut through miles upon miles of forest.

He'd seen mountains before, of course, and forests and groves and rivers. In fact, he'd seen these very same mountains, these very same forests, this very same river, for they were the Northern Mountains, Goldstone Wood, Goldstone River. But he stood now in the Far World of Faerie, and everything was different here—bigger and stranger, more wild and more beautiful. Felix leaned heavily against a white sapling that felt strangely like marble under his hand. He looked at it but could not tell if he supported himself against a column or a tree. He shook his head, which was clouded and uncertain. His knees shook, whether from weakness or from fear he could not guess.

"Your fever has broken at last."

Felix turned, looking over his shoulder. The woman with whom he had spoken a few times now stepped through a leafy curtain, bearing a silver tray that held a tiny silver bowl and a thin silver pitcher. She wore a long lavender tunic and billowy trousers of light green beneath, after an old and foreign style that Felix had never before seen. A filmy scarf draped over her hair, which was black, and her eyes were blacker still. As she came closer, Felix frowned. At first he had thought her not much older than Una, but now he guessed that she must surely be far older, though her dark features were smooth and soft like a girl's.

Dame Imraldera smiled and set the tray down on a small white table beside his bed, then poured water from the pitcher into the bowl. "Are you thirsty?"

Felix shook his head but after a moment's thought changed his mind and nodded. He reached out for the bowl she offered and looked at it. "Will it . . . do anything to me?" he asked.

She laughed. "If you're afraid it will doom you to an eternity as my slave or something along those lines, no, it will not. It is water, nothing more."

He sipped it and found that it was water, but the woman was wrong to say it was nothing more. It was light and clear, like nothing he'd ever tasted—perhaps most like the drops of honeydew he and Una used to suck from honeysuckle flowers. He downed it greedily, but when he reached the end felt that it was enough and did not ask for more. He handed the silver bowl back to the woman. "Are you a Faerie?" he asked.

She shook her head, still smiling. He liked her smile, he decided. Her teeth, he noticed with some surprise, were just the tiniest bit imperfect. Were Faeries allowed to have crooked teeth, even if it made them somehow more beautiful? "Mortals cannot see Faeries within the Wood," she said.

"I can see you," he said.

"But you cannot see the Faerie attendants around you."

Felix blinked. He looked quickly over his shoulder, as though he might catch a glimpse of some winged creature if he were fast enough. And while he thought for half a moment that something flashed in the corner of his eye, the room, for all he could see, was empty except for him and the woman. "Then you are not a Faerie," he said. "But you can see them?"

"I can."

"Then you're not mortal?"

She smiled, flashing those white, slightly crooked teeth. "Will you allow me to check your wounds, Prince Felix? You have been sick with fever these last many days, and I'm not sure I should even allow you up. But I will as long as you won't fuss as I check your bandages. Agreed?"

Felix hesitated and glanced back across the wide view he had been observing before she entered. He blinked. Then he cried out in alarm and leapt back.

The vista of mountains and vast expanses was gone. His view was now simply of trees and more trees, close and surrounding him. "What in the name of Iubdan's sin-black beard—"

The dame touched his shoulder, making shushing noises. "Prince Felix," she said, "come away from that window. The sight will only distress you."

"But . . . but I saw . . ." He struggled to find the words to express himself. "I was up on a mountain, and I saw all the Far World. . . ."

"Hardly *all* the Far World, young one!" the woman said, chuckling quietly. "I'm sorry, Prince Felix. This Haven, you must understand, rests in the Halflight Realm between your world and Faerie. Sometimes it will show you the world beyond; sometimes it will not. It is strange and uncomfortable, I understand. . . . Long, long ago I once saw as you see. But please trust me when I tell you, you are safe. You are safe in the Prince's Haven, and you are safe in my keeping."

Felix turned to her and saw that her eyes were kind and, he thought, sincere. He went to sit on the edge of his bed, which was softer than goose down, and the woman peeled back his shirt and—clucking like Nurse and shaking her head—decided to change the bandage on his shoulder.

"It was a deep wound," she said, taking a roll of soft gauze from the folds of her robe and cutting the old bandage away with a tiny knife. "A lot of poison seeped in, and I feared infection."

"Am I all right?" Felix asked, watching her uneasily. Everything she did looked as though it should hurt him, yet her fingers were so gentle that he felt no pain. Still, he winced back uneasily from the knife.

"You will be," she said. "But you must listen to me and do as I ask, or things may go the worse for you."

He scowled a little. "I'm not a baby," he muttered, low enough that he didn't think she would hear. But the corner of her mouth lifted, and he knew she had.

"What did you say your name was?" Felix asked once she had finished applying the new bandage.

"I am Dame Imraldera," she replied.

"And you are Aethelbald's servant?" Felix shook his head. "You people have the strangest names."

She laughed outright at this, and Felix blushed. "Perhaps not so strange as *Felix*," she said, "though I think your name suits you. And the Prince is my master, yes. But he is more than that to me. He rescued me from . . . from an evil such as I will not describe to you here and now." A dark expression passed across her face as she remembered, but she shook it aside. "He rescued me, and now I call him my brother as well as my lord. I am the keeper of this Haven, which belongs to him." She gave him a reassuring smile.

But Felix did not feel reassured, and his head hurt. He looked down at his hand resting on the soft blankets of his bed. "How long must I remain here, Dame Imraldera?"

Her smile disappeared, as though the sun dropped out of the sky and behind a dark horizon. "I do not know, Prince Felix," she said. "It may be that you can never leave."

"What?" Felix jumped to his feet. "What are you saying?" he roared. "Of course I must leave! I can't stay in this Faerie place forever! What about my father? He needs me. I have to go back!" He ran to the edge of his strange room and discovered that the forest was gone and once more he stood on the edge of a precipice. Far below him the river snaked by, a silver thread. He gulped and paled, backing into the room. "I have to go back," he said. "There must be a way out of here."

"Of course," Imraldera said, coming up beside him. She was shorter, but when he looked down at her he felt almost as though he looked into the face of his own mother. He blinked back tears, hating himself for crying.

"My father," he said, his lip quivering. "He's in trouble, you understand. And he sent me away to protect me, but I'm afraid he'll need me, and then I won't be there, and . . . and what if he thinks I'm dead? What will he do then? As it is he's worried sick about my sister, Una. Don't you see? I've got to go back!"

Imraldera touched his shoulder gently. "Please come sit again, child. My Prince has gone to your father. All will be well."

"I'm not a child." Felix sniffed and rubbed his nose with the back of his hand but allowed himself to be led back to bed. He sat on the edge of it, scratching his left ankle with his right foot. "What about Una?" he asked.

Imraldera did not answer but poured more water into the silver bowl. "Drink this."

Felix obeyed and felt sleep weighing down his eyelids. "Dame Imraldera?"

"Yes?"

"What happened to me in the Wood? Why was I brought here?"

"A dragon, Prince Felix. He breathed poison into your mind, made you see what he wanted you to see. Such is their way, such is the power of their venomous breath. And when he tore you, the poison of his claws sank deep inside of you. I have extracted most of it, but some I may not be able to get out, and if you leave the safety of our Haven, an infection would set in."

"Is there a chance you can get it all out?"

"There is always hope, Felix."

Felix lay back on his pillow and turned his face away from her. Sleep claimed him soon after.

The flames were so hot, and the young dragon flew and burned and flew and burned. The fire would not die, and she could not escape it, so on she went, aware of nothing but the burning. She did not notice the passage of time, neither the rising nor the setting sun. Her world was all flame, which sometimes built up so horribly that it burst from her mouth, leaving a trail of smoke in her wake. The people she passed over cowered in terror as her shadow darkened their lands, but she did not see them. Nothing but fire and ashes filled her mind.

At last—she couldn't say how much later—some of the flames began to wane. Her vision cleared, and she looked down to discover where she had come.

Below her stretched the vast expanse of the Red Desert.

World of dragons.

When she looked west toward the setting sun, she could still just make out a green stretch of land. But east, where twilight deepened, all was barren.

She flew on, feeling strength leave her body as the fire cooled inside. Soon she would have to rest. But if she rested, she might have to think, and that would be unbearable.

On the horizon, great stones that might once have been pillars but were now blasted beyond recognition stretched ragged hands toward the sky. The dragon flew toward them. Soon they loomed over her, towers of rock, and with her last burst of strength she propelled herself in among them, taking shelter in their shadows. Her wings crumpled, and she collapsed on hard stone.

She woke in sunlight. A small ray gleamed through a crevice in the rubble above and shone down upon her face. She groaned and tried to turn away, for the light hurt her eyes. Sand and stone scraped painfully against her cheek. Surprised, she reached up and touched her face and found that it was smooth and scaleless once more.

But then the dragon girl looked at her hands. Both were covered in scales, and talons tore into the rock on which she sat. She stared at them, numb, unsure what she felt. The sun shone full upon her now, causing her skin to glow white, almost translucent. Yet her hands seemed to absorb the light.

She stood and felt dizzied by the lightness of her human body. Her clothes were more tattered than ever, exposing her legs and her dragon arms. Her sleeves, which had disguised most of her scaly arm in Southlands, were in shreds.

Looking around, she found herself in an alley of stone vaulting high above her to a narrow opening through which only small patches of sunlight could creep here and there. A twisted path stretched before and behind her. Steadying herself with her right hand on the wall, she followed the path forward. More patches of light gleamed down at intervals, but she avoided them, sliding instead through the shadows. She had no idea where she went or why, and neither did she care.

The realm of dragons.

A shape moved in front of her. She gasped, surprised but not afraid. She felt she could not be afraid anymore.

It moved again, and she stood silently and waited.

"Who are you?" a young man's voice spoke, disembodied in the dark. A crack of light fell between them, hiding both in deep shadow.

"No one," she answered and leaned against the wall.

"Are you a sister?"

"I don't know." She pressed herself into the rock, for suddenly, though she wasn't afraid, her knees went weak. "Are you going to kill me?"

"Perhaps," the voice said. "You sound small. Are you?"

"I'm not big," she replied. "Not now."

"I think you are a sister," the voice said. "Step into the light so I may be sure."

The dragon girl could think of no reason not to obey. She pushed herself from the wall and, shielding her eyes with one clawed hand, slid forward into the light. It warmed her clammy skin not unpleasantly.

"Ah," the voice in the shadow rasped. "Sister."

A hand, thin and spindly, took hold of one of hers and pulled her forward, out of the sun. She did not resist, though she half expected to have her throat slit any moment. When nothing of the sort happened, she opened her eyes and found herself looking into a pair of slitted pupils on a long, pale face. Her vision adjusted slowly in the dark, and she thought perhaps the face was young, but shadows sagged under the yellow eyes and in the hollow cheeks.

"Have you a name?" the yellow-eyed stranger asked.

"No," she answered.

"Neither have I," he said. "Come with me. I'll show you home."

She followed, led by the hand. They made slow progress, for he seemed to understand her weariness and adjusted his stride to hers. Like her, he avoided the sunlight where he could. But sometimes there was no choice but to pass through a beam, and she then glimpsed a pale young man not much older than herself, all angles and edges, with a greenish cast to his skin.

"Where are we going?" she asked at length.

"To the Village," he said.

"How long have you lived there?"

"I forget. Long and not long." He was silent a moment, and their feet gritted in the sand.

"No one understood me before, you see," he said. "Tried to control me. But I showed them."

She did not answer.

"Here they understand," he said. "No chains, no obligations. That's what I like."

She remained silent.

He squeezed her hand almost encouragingly. "And you?" he asked.

"Forgotten," she said.

"They always forget us at first," he said. "But they won't later. He will show us how to make them remember."

Again she did not answer. But strangely, part of her understood what he said.

They came to the mouth of the tunnel, and she found herself looking down into a vast, dimly lit cavern. Red fires smoldered here and there, but no sun infiltrated these black walls. In the darkness arching above, she could almost discern signs of elegant architecture long left to decay, as though once upon a time this cavern had been a feasting hall of extravagance beyond anything she had ever seen. But that may have been no more than a trick of the light, and this cave nothing more than a natural cavern torn into the desert rocks.

In the dimness and smoke she could see many shadowy forms moving about. Some were upright but moved heavily. Some were bent double and seemed to be carrying invisible burdens. Some, like her companion, skittered here and there between the fires, swift as young snakes. She saw rickety buildings of wood and more solid structures of stone, but not many of either.

"Welcome to the Village," her slit-eyed companion said. "Come. Come down with me."

She followed him, still holding his hand, down a narrow path from the mouth of the tunnel to the cavern floor below. She felt ill at ease, stepping out of the closeness of the tunnel into that great, dark openness. Soon they were surrounded on all sides by shadowy figures hurrying hither and yon in the dark, though she could not tell where they hurried or why. Simultaneous sensations of heat and cold emanating from them overwhelmed her senses, and she was uncertain whether she was hot or cold herself. She clung to the hand of the stranger who led her but found no comfort there.

A heavy shoulder knocked into her, and she stumbled up behind the yellow-eyed boy. "Hey, watch your step," he growled, but not at her.

The person who had jostled her stopped and turned. Man or woman, it was impossible to tell in the dark, but the frame was huge and the voice deep and rocklike.

"What have you there?" the giant asked the yellow-eyed boy.

"A new sister, just arrived. She is forgotten."

"Ha!" the giant snorted. "They'll always forget you, small one, no matter how pretty your little pale face may be. They'll always forget you. Unless you *make* them remember. But then . . . Ah, then they do not forget so soon!"

The giant laughed from deep in her gut, and the sound sent ripples of fear through the dragon girl's veins. She gasped in relief when her guide tugged and led her swiftly on.

"She was a queen once, long ago," he said when they were well away.

"She?"

"Yes. And all this—" he extended his arms as though to take in the cavern—"all this that you see and beyond, all this desert that we call our home, this was once her kingdom. But for a chest full of rubies, her lover betrayed her to her enemy. Long she languished in the dungeons of her own palace, waiting to be executed. Then our king found her. She was willing enough, and her fire was so great that the whole palace and everyone inside burned to nothing within the hour. Then she set upon the land itself. Many no longer believe the vast kingdom of Corrilond ever existed, she wasted it so beyond recognition or recall."

"Corrilond?" She shook her head. "The Bane of Corrilond? But that is a legend five hundred years old!"

He did not seem to hear but continued speaking in a low voice, nearly a whisper. "Nothing but charred ruins. Great cities, shining Destan, luminous Aysel, and the magnificent Queen's City of Nadire Tansu . . . all gone. Now there is nothing but desert as far as the eye can see."

He paused then and whispered, "I saw it, the Queen's City, before it was destroyed. When I was young I traveled there with my uncle, and it was more beautiful even than the halls of Iubdan Rudiobus! And I saw it destroyed, and smelled the stench of burning death." He turned to her. "Although her name has been forgotten, the last queen of Corrilond never will be. Would you like to see the rubies, the dirty treasure for which her lover sold her?"

She did not respond, but he led her across the cavern to a still darker cave on the far side. He grabbed a red torch on the way, and it threw their shadows weirdly on the stone walls. Her dragon arms, gnarled and hideous, seemed to cast darker shadows than the rest of her.

"Here," her yellow-eyed guide said. He blew on the torch. It flamed more brightly, and her eyes were filled suddenly with the glitter of innumerable jewels, mountains of gold and silver, crowns and coronets, goblets and platters, ropes upon ropes of pearls, and gilded mirrors. She could not breathe, for the air was heavy with the weight of riches.

Her companion let go her hand and stepped over to a nearby chest. He plunged his hand inside and lifted up a fistful of rubies, which cascaded and clinked between his fingers. But with each jewel that fell, she heard a scream, sometimes high, sometimes low, all filled with terror, so faint and far away that she almost missed them.

"What is this place?" she whispered when the last ruby had fallen and the last scream faded to nothing.

"The Hoard," he replied. "This is where we gather our offerings for our Father. Whenever we venture out, we bring back something for his pleasure. Sometimes we bring him meat. Mostly we bring him gold."

She shuddered and backed away. "Those screams . . ."

"Eh? Oh, that." He shrugged. "You'll not notice them before long. Most of us don't. Unless we want to. Some of us enjoy them." He smiled, and his slit-eyes glinted. "Come. I must show you one more place."

She did not want to take his hand again, but he grabbed her and all but dragged her from the Hoard's cave back into the cavern. Weaving his way through the shadowy figures, her guide led her to the very center of the cavern. There sat a giant stone throne.

It was covered in blood.

"This is his throne," the yellow-eyed boy said. "This is where we worship him, our lord, our master. Here he sits and judges us. And if he deems us worthy, we live. But if we have failed him in any command, he devours us."

The dragon girl felt a shiver run through the boy's arm. "Devours you?" she whispered.

"*Us*, sister. Yes, such is his right, for he is our Father. Sooner or later, we all fail and give our blood to him."

She stared at the yellow-eyed boy in horror. "Why do you not flee this place?"

He turned slowly to look at her, his slitted eyes boring into her face. "There is no other way for us," he said. "We are his children."

"But you said there were no chains here!"

"Only those I have chosen for myself," he replied, setting his jaw. "I choose to give him my blood when he demands it. It may be a hundred years from now. Perhaps it will be tomorrow. Meanwhile, I live free."

She stared at the throne, and the smell of dried blood filled her nostrils until she gagged.

The yellow-eyed boy watched her, a smile on his face. "Now you know your end, little sister. You stand at your beginning. We shall see how long until the two meet. In the meantime, let your fire burn and you'll not long be forgotten in the outside world."

She pulled her hand free and ran through the darkness, through the shadow people, away from that awful throne. She ran until she hit a wall and fell back on the floor, stunned. There she wrapped her dragon arms over her head and curled into a tight ball.

Realm of dragons.

My home.

29

A T MIDAFTERNOON, Prince Lionheart stood beside his father's throne to hear the news of his kingdom. Court was held in a small assembly hall, as the great throne room of the Eldest's House had been burned to the ground by the Dragon. King Hawkeye, aged and shriveled by too much exposure to dragon smoke, still ruled Southlands, but more and more he deferred to his son's opinion on matters.

It was known among the court of the Eldest that the Council of Barons watched Prince Lionheart with a wary eye, uncertain whether or not they could trust his leadership after his five-year absence. But Hawkeye, by his deference to his son, made as clear as he could his desire that Southlands trust Lionheart. Soon, it was rumored, Hawkeye would step down from the throne altogether and pass the crown to his son.

This cold afternoon in midwinter, Prince Lionheart listened to reports from various landowners. Much of the land surrounding the Eldest's City was still wasted after the Dragon's invasion. Few fields had been left unspoiled. This made all the more important in the coming year a good crop yield in other portions of the kingdom.

He stood in deep contemplation of the report one of his barons had just finished making when the herald announced, "Prince Aethelbald of Farthestshore."

Lionheart looked up and saw a man he recognized approaching from the doorway. Aethelbald—he had met him at Oriana Palace. He winced as he always did when reminded of that place.

"Greetings, Prince," King Hawkeye said as Aethelbald neared the throne. "You have journeyed far, have you not? Farthestshore! I cannot remember the last time I beheld a man from Farthestshore."

Aethelbald bowed low before the king. "Long life to Your Majesty," he said. "Yes, I have journeyed far." He straightened, and his gaze locked with Lionheart's. "Greetings, Prince Lionheart," he said.

Lionheart nodded. "Strange that we had no word of your coming, Prince Aethelbald."

"Not so strange," Aethelbald said. "Few would know the paths I take."

"Do you travel with a large company?"

"I travel alone."

At that, the courtiers of Southlands turned and whispered to each other. A prince, traveling alone? And where did he say he was from? Farthestshore, of all places! Surely this was some sort of hoax.

Lionheart spoke loudly to drown out the murmur. "Do you seek lodging? Allow us to treat you to the hospitality of Southlands."

"No," Aethelbald responded. "I seek a word with you, Prince Lionheart. In private, if I may."

Lionheart felt a heavy stone drop in his stomach. He knew of what the Prince wished to speak with him. Had Aethelbald not been one of Una's suitors? He hid a grimace by coughing but in that extra moment could think of no excuse to deny Aethelbald his request. "Very well," he said. He bowed to his father. "If you will excuse me, Father?"

Hawkeye nodded, and Lionheart withdrew, beckoning for Aethelbald to follow him. Two of Lionheart's attendants stepped into line behind them, but as Lionheart opened the door to a smaller audience room, he bade them to stay outside. He made room for Aethelbald to precede him into the room, walked in behind him, and shut the door. They stood in an antechamber of impressive size, with various maps adorning the walls and heavy curtains on the windows. They were new curtains; the old ones had reeked of dragon smoke.

Lionheart took a seat on a large chair, almost a small throne, on the far side of the room. He did not offer a seat to Aethelbald. "At your pleasure," he said.

Aethelbald stood in the middle of the floor, his arms crossed over his chest, not in a hostile manner but as though he didn't know what else to do with them. The effect was almost awkward, but he looked Lionheart steadily in the eye. "Have you seen Princess Una?"

Lionheart gulped. Something in him did not like the directness of the question, and he did not wish to answer. Perhaps it was Aethelbald's quiet tone, firm and nonthreatening, that set his teeth on edge. "Princess Una of Parumvir?"

"The same."

He shrugged and kept his gaze steady against Aethelbald's. "What makes you think I would have seen her?"

"You have heard of the situation in Parumvir?"

"Yes. Dragon-ridden. And the capital is controlled by the Duke of Shippening now, is that right? A great pity. I liked King Fidel. He was kind to me during my . . . my exile." Lionheart drew a long breath. "But that is all far from here, and I have much to occupy my mind in my own kingdom."

"Una is missing."

Lionheart raised an eyebrow. Even mention of the girl's name made his heart beat uncomfortably. His hands and part of his face still burned from his encounter with her. "So I understand," he said.

"She fell in love with you." Aethelbald hardly moved as he spoke, and his gaze did not shift.

Lionheart found himself wanting very badly to look away. "What makes you think that?" he answered, trying to look incredulous.

"I guessed."

"Well, if it bothers you, I have no intention of—"

"Answer my question," Aethelbald said. "Have you seen Princess Una?"

Lionheart could not hold his gaze a moment longer. He looked down at his fist resting on the arm of the chair. "Yes, I have. She came here not even a week ago, alone."

Aethelbald was silent.

Lionheart fought the urge to squirm in his chair and managed to maintain his cool tone. "At first I wondered how she had come here by herself. But . . . she explained in no uncertain terms."

"She came to you as a woman?"

"Yes. But I saw the change."

Aethelbald did not reply. The silence was so long that Lionheart at last looked up and saw that the Prince was turned away, his head bent.

"See here," Lionheart said, clenching and unclenching his fist. "I am sorry about what became of her. I am. But there isn't a solitary thing I can do about it now, is there?"

Aethelbald did not speak.

"A lot of things happened during my exile." Lionheart grimaced. "Most of them I wish to forget. Una was kind to me when I needed a friend, and . . . and I appreciated her kindness. Perhaps I implied more than I felt, but that is hardly—"

"Did you?" Aethelbald asked.

Lionheart took in a deep breath. No reproach lurked in the Prince's tone; he merely asked the question. Lionheart thought for a moment that he hated the Prince of Farthestshore.

"There was too much . . . simply too much to do when I came back," Lionheart said. "I couldn't very well leave, could I, when my people needed me here? Not all of us are free to go chasing across the countryside after dreams or monsters, Prince Aethelbald. Some of us have responsibilities that must come before our own desires."

"And there was your bargain to consider," Aethelbald said, nodding.

Lionheart opened his mouth, then shut it again. "I don't know what you're talking about," he muttered at last.

"But you do, Prince Lionheart," Aethelbald said. To Lionheart's deep disgust, the expression on his face was not condemning but pitying. "I know the Dragon better than you think. I know the game he plays and the bargains he drives."

Lionheart stood and crossed his arms over his chest. "That's none of your concern, Prince Aethelbald."

"In that case, let me bid you good day," Aethelbald said and started to turn away.

"What do you propose to do now?"

Aethelbald paused. "I journey to the Red Desert."

"Are you mad?" Lionheart shook his head, then took another look at Aethelbald's face. "You are mad, but I see that you're serious." He sighed. "Do not think that I am unconcerned about all of this, Prince Aethelbald. If there is anything I can do to aid you in your quest, please accept my help."

Aethelbald's eyes narrowed as he looked at Lionheart. "Come with me," he said.

"What?"

"Come with me, Prince Lionheart. Come to the Red Desert and help me rescue the princess."

"You . . . you cannot seriously . . . " Lionheart turned away. "You do realize, don't you, that you cannot enter the desert and survive? Those who have crossed beyond sight of its borders have never returned. You will die there. I cannot abandon my father and my people for certain death, as you well know."

"Then I bid you good day," Aethelbald said. Lionheart heard his footsteps heading for the door.

"Wait," Lionheart said. The footsteps stopped. "I will send men with you. I will select them myself—strong men, loyal." He faced around, gazing at the back of Aethelbald's head. "It is all I can give you."

Aethelbald did not look back. "Thank you, Prince Lionheart," he said and left the room.

The attendants in the hall put their heads in, but Lionheart waved them away. "Shut the door," he said. When it clicked shut and he was alone, he slowly took a seat once more.

"I did what I had to do," he said to the empty air before him. "What other choice could I make?" He sank his forehead into his hand and shut his eyes tight. "What other choice was there?"

She felt as though she had always lived there. How long had it really been? Whether days, weeks, or mere hours, she could not guess. The dragon girl sat against the wall in the shadows for what seemed like an eternity, watching the vague figures drifting, shuffling, sometimes crawling between points of red fire. Now and then a new flame would flare, casting more weird shadows along the cavern floor and walls, or an old flame would flicker away and die. On the whole, the scene before her did not change except that eventually her eyes became more used to the gloom.

Finally she stood, still pressing her back to the wall. Long moments passed and she did not move, but none of the shadow figures took notice of her. Her hands against the rock for support, she started to slide along the wall, making her way slowly around the circumference of the cavern. She met no one as she went, for none of them came near her.

She found at last the path leading its winding way up to the mouth of the tunnel above. She looked up uncertainly, somehow unable to take another step.

A figure skulked past her. She leapt back, cowering in the shadows, but the figure did not seem to notice her. It staggered up the path, falling against the wall as it went, stumbling to its hands and knees, crawling, rising, and stumbling again. Even as she watched, when it was halfway up the path, it burst into flame. A small dragon, trailing fire, rushed forward and vanished into the tunnel.

"Do you wish to burn?"

Drawing in her breath, she turned to find yellow eyes gleaming at her.

"Do you wish to burn?" the boy with the yellow eyes repeated. He came around and stood before her, leaning his shoulder against a boulder between her and the path. "I do."

"I . . . I wish to leave," she said, afraid what he might respond.

"You may," he said. "We often go out from the Village. Last time, I traveled all the way to Parumvir at the command of our Father. I scorched a dozen soldiers, scorched them to cinders on the edge of a wood." He tossed back his head and barked a short laugh. "What a fire that was! But I want bigger things next time."

"Must you return here when the burning is over?" she asked.

Yellow eyes blinked at her. "Where else would we go? This is our Father's Village."

She looked beyond him to the tunnel. "Do you never walk in the towns of men?"

"I did a little at first," the boy said, shrugging. "But men disgust me. At first I liked to go to towns— they did not provoke me so fast. But they recognize us soon, no matter what. Their hearts fear us even if they don't know why. I hate their fear. Nothing incites my fire more. I find I can scarcely enter a town before the fire bursts out of me now. So I come here when I need quiet. Here among my family."

She did not answer. Instead she slipped past him and started up the path, picking her steps.

"Wait."

She paused but did not look back. The boy came up beside her and held something out. It was a hooded robe, black and made from some animal hide. The boy wore one just like it.

"Take this," he said. "It's dragon skin. Cover your white hide. We don't like to see so much exposed humanity when we aren't burning. It's repulsive."

She took the robe and slid it on, covering the tatters of her dress. The sleeves were long and hid her dragon arms. As the folds of hide settled on her sparse frame, she realized that she could not leave the Village. Where could she go?

She turned back and hurried down the path, away from the yellow-eyed boy, back into the smoke-filled cavern. Keeping to the outer fringes, away from her kinfolk, she found a boulder and slid behind it. Even then she did not feel hidden. She leaned her head back against the rock and wished she could cry.

Why don't you come for me?

Her fire sputtered like coals newly stoked but did not flare to life. Instead a great heaviness pressed her down. She rocked herself back and forth, her eyes closed, and images came to her head, images of a bell-covered hat and a comical face smiling at her. She let herself slip into dreams.

Captain Catspaw and his eleven men stood in the courtyard of the Eldest's House beside their horses. Not half an hour ago, word had come for him and his men to prepare for a long journey. *"A journey where?"* he had demanded, but the messenger had shrugged without answer. Now Catspaw and his men waited as Prince Lionheart paced before them, his face stern and set. A strange man in rough, brown travel clothes stood off to one side.

Prince Lionheart indicated him with a sweep of his hand. "Obey this man as though he were your own prince," he said. "Follow wherever he may lead you."

Catspaw blinked and adjusted his hold on his horse's bridle. "Your Highness," he said, "where do you send us with this stranger?"

The prince glared at him. "Your only concern is to obey, captain," he growled. "But know this: You follow this man for the honor of Southlands, for the honor of your king. Do as he says; go where he asks. He will lead you to . . . to a great treasure."

Captain Catspaw nodded. "And we are to bring back this treasure? For Southlands, Your Highness?"

Prince Lionheart did not answer. Instead he turned to the stranger. His voice was tight but loud enough for each man to hear. "Is this all I can do for you?"

The stranger was silent.

Prince Lionheart set his jaw. "In that case, I wish you well in your endeavor."

The stranger reached out and placed a hand on Prince Lionheart's shoulder. "Come with us," he said.

The prince shook himself free. "You know I cannot."

The stranger bowed. "Then farewell, Prince Lionheart. We will meet again in coming years. But for now, farewell."

Prince Lionheart made no answer but walked away, leaving Catspaw and the men with the stranger.

The stranger approached them and spoke in a quiet voice. "I am Aethelbald of Farthestshore," he said. "Will you follow me?"

Catspaw and his men looked at each other, eyebrows raised, but Catspaw answered, "We will follow you, sir."

"You will wish to turn back."

Catspaw frowned and swallowed hard, but he replied, "We will follow you. For the honor of Southlands."

Aethelbald shook his head. "That is not enough."

Without another word he turned and walked from the courtyard, out through the front gate. The men, trading more puzzled looks, mounted up and started after him.

"Excuse me, sir," Catspaw said, bringing his horse up beside the stranger. "Will you not be wanting a horse?"

"No, thank you, Captain Catspaw," Aethelbald said.

Catspaw blinked. He couldn't remember giving the stranger his name.

The twelve men on horseback followed the one man on foot. "Farthestshore," Catspaw muttered to himself as he went. "I've heard stories about that place since I was hardly up to my father's knee."

The other men murmured under their breath as well. None of them liked the idea that stories such as those might prove real. Yet the strange man who led them did not seem fantastic in his person. He walked quietly out of Southlands's capital and across the country, heading north. When he did speak to them, his voice was pleasant and calm. But as he led the way, the men began to notice how strangely he kept in front of them, always walking at the same pace. No matter whether the men trotted, cantered, or walked their horses, the stranger remained ahead of them without seeming to quicken or slacken his pace.

All day, Aethelbald led them away from the city. They crossed over the shining King's Bridge to a farther plateau and on through villages and farmlands. But when they neared the edge of that stretch of tableland, Aethelbald did not lead them toward the next bridge. Instead he walked to the edge of the cliff and then disappeared over the edge.

The company gave Catspaw bewildered looks. But Catspaw was under orders, and he barked a sharp command to his men. "Follow him!"

So they spurred their horses on and found that the Prince of Farthest-shore walked a path that led down into the gorge, a path wide and easy enough that the horses made no complaint about following him. The men, however, were much more nervous, and they were more nervous still when they reached the edge of the dark forest below.

No one entered the Wilderlands. It was an unspoken rule throughout Southlands. The bridges were life and the Wilderlands forbidden since the ancient days before words were written down or the Eldest's House was built. No one climbed down to the Wilderlands below unless banished in cruelest punishment for the most vile of deeds.

Yet the Prince of Farthestshore did not slacken his pace as he passed into the shadows of the forest. The men shivered as they followed him, and icy tremors, not entirely unpleasant but strange, passed through each of them. None of them spoke as they moved single file through the trees. Each one's vision on either side was blurred and distorted, almost as though he wore blinders. The passage of time was uncertain, for the sun hardly seemed to move overhead as it gleamed through the trees. They walked in a straight line, never turning or inclining either to the left or to the right. Suddenly they were out of the woods again, and their vision cleared.

Catspaw swore under his breath as he recognized where they were. Somehow, without crossing the isthmus, he and his men stood on the Continent, many days' journey from the Eldest's City, in the hinterlands of Shippening. He looked over his shoulder and saw a dark wood very like those of Southlands, but he knew it could not possibly be the same.

"Sister o' Death!" one man at his elbow hissed. "What miracle or magic is this? How'd we cross the Chiara Bay without so much as wetting our feet?"

Captain Catspaw did not answer but stared at the solitary figure standing before him and at the landscape beyond. The Red Desert stretched before them, great and hot, a nightmare come to life.

"Captain?" One of his men urged his horse up beside him and whispered urgently, "Are we going in there?"

The captain spurred his horse so viciously that the poor creature startled, and rode up beside the Farthestshore man. "Sir," he said, his voice only just respectful.

Aethelbald looked up at him. "Yes, captain."

"Where are you taking us?"

The stranger indicated with his chin. "That way."

"Into the Red Desert?"

"Yes, captain."

Catspaw quietly swore again but bit back the first few remarks that sprang to his lips. At last, sucking in a deep breath, he said, "My men have seen enough of dragons, sir."

Aethelbald did not answer.

The captain spoke through clenched teeth. "If you have a death wish, I beg you would not drag us along with you."

"I have no death wish, Captain Catspaw," Aethelbald replied.

"Look, sir," the captain said, glancing uneasily at the vast expanse of sand, dry as bone, stretched before him, "we do not know you, do not know your kind. Perhaps you are aware of something we are not—"

"I am," the stranger interrupted. "And if you will follow me, I will see that you come to no harm."

"That's a pretty promise," the captain snorted. "But it won't hold up against dragon fire. I've seen what one dragon can do! We all have. Maybe you think all those stories and legends we've heard were exaggerated, but I assure you they are not. Far from it! We have all of us breathed in dragon fumes and lived under the shadow of dragon smoke for five long years, and it's a miracle any of us is alive. That being said, sir, you cannot expect me to lead my men into the heart of dragon country."

"I do not expect you to lead them," Aethelbald replied. "I ask all of you to follow me."

"To what purpose?" the captain cried, and he heard his men murmuring their agreement behind him. "At least give us a reason for this suicide!"

"Is not the command of your prince enough?" Aethelbald asked.

"No, sir, I must say it is not. Prince Lionheart is young. And he escaped those five years living under that demon's eye."

"Very well," Aethelbald said. "I will not ask you to follow me by his command, captain. But I ask you to follow me even so."

"Why?"

"As your prince told you, we seek a treasure from the heart of the desert, from the very center of the Dragon's kingdom. It is more dangerous than you can imagine, and one false step will mean death for you or much worse. But if you walk behind me and do not stray from my path, you will remain unharmed. You have my word."

Catspaw looked into the stranger's eyes. Something inside him stirred, and he felt as though, yes, perhaps he could follow this man. Had he not led them already down a way so strange that they would never have believed it existed? Had he not brought them farther in one day than they could have traveled in ten?

His horse quivered beneath him, and the captain looked up and gazed once more at the Red Desert stretching on to the farthest horizon. His heart quailed at the sight. He closed his eyes and would not look again at the stranger. "You ask too much," he growled and turned his horse sharply away. "Come, men," he ordered and started back at a canter the way they had come.

The wood was gone. The bleak countryside of the Hinterlands stretched out before them, and beyond that the Chiara Bay, dividing them from Southlands and home. The captain looked back once over his shoulder, saw the stranger watching them. Then Aethelbald turned and strode into the desert, where he vanished.

The captain faced forward again, cursing viciously under his breath. "Let the fool kill himself. Why should we die for him and his confounded treasure? Dragons and dragon fire, a man can only stand so much!"

30

THE SOUND OF RUNNING WATER sang sweet music in her ears. She opened her eyes. Leaves, golden against blue sky, arched high above her. Wooden slats pressed into her back and her head. Her hand felt around and found the edge of the boards. Turning her head, she looked around. Trees, their graceful branches swaying in a gentle breeze, filled her gaze. She lay on the Old Bridge in her dear Goldstone Wood.

I'm dreaming.

She did not care.

Carefully, so as not to wake herself, she sat up. Her chest expanded to take in a great gulp of light, clean air. She was Una, Princess of Parumvir. This was her home.

With a laugh that filled her whole body with feathery lightness, she jumped from the bridge and splashed into the water, soaking her skirt up to the knees. It was cold, bitingly cold, and delicious to feel. She spun around, searching the trees. Sunlight gleamed through branches, spattering the ground with touches of gold. Beyond the light, shadows thickened. "Where are you?" she whispered.

He would come any moment. It was her dream, after all. He would come to her here.

The brook trickled between her wet feet, and the tree branches crackled together in a breeze.

No one came.

"Where are you?" she said, louder this time. She climbed back onto the Old Bridge, water dripping from her, and shivered a little in the cool air.

No one answered.

The sun began to sink behind the trees, and still she waited. Golden light disappeared, and the gray of dusk settled around her, yet no one came. She sat on the bridge, holding her knees, and whispered to herself:

> *"Twilit dimness surrounds me.*
> *The veil slips over my eyes.*
> *The riddle of us two together long ago,*
> *How fragile in my memory lies!"*

A silvery voice sang above her head. Raising her chin, she searched the branches for the wood thrush. The notes spilled into the evening.

> *"Beyond the final water falling,*
> *The Songs of Spheres recalling.*
> *We who were never bound are swiftly torn apart.*
> *Won't you return to me?"*

She bowed her head, pressing it into her knees. "Where are you?" she whispered.

Where are you?

"I'm here. I'm waiting for you still. I promised I would. Won't you come find me?"

I am coming. Wait for me.

"Oh, Leonard!" Were tears actually in her eyes, or did she dream those too? "Leonard, I am waiting. I'm still waiting!"

No. Wait for me. *I will find you.*

Something rustled in the brush behind her.

I will find you.

She turned sharply.

"Leonard!"

The trees vanished, as did the stream.

A pale, sunken face with yellow eyes peered down at her from over her sheltering boulder.

"There you are, sister. I found you."

A fortress hidden within the rugged crags of the Northern Mountains stood dark in the night, only a few windows lit by candles. One path led through the treacherous reaches of the mountains to the fortress's gate, which remained tightly shut. Standing guard upon the wall above the gate were two knights, one with skin like midnight, whose eyes gleamed brighter than candles in that darkness; the other with hair like fire and green jewel eyes, who could not seem to help smiling even as the night wore on in undisturbed silence.

At last his black-skinned companion asked, "Why do you grin so, Rogan? What can you find so amusing on such a windless, cold night?"

The green-eyed one smiled all the more. "We shall have action before dawn, Imoo! After all these weeks standing watch in this remote piece of nowhere, we shall see battle once more!"

"What makes you think that?"

"I smell it, my friend!" Rogan touched the weapon at his side. "Can you not?"

The other man shook his head, but inside he found his heart

beginning to hope. He did not like this world beyond the Borders. It was far colder than his own country, and after several weeks of guarding King Fidel of Parumvir in this isolated place, he had begun to think the cold had seeped into his bones and would stay there permanently. Not a pleasant thought.

"If only Oeric would return," Sir Imoo said. "It has been two days since he left—I would have thought he'd be back here by now. If only he would bring us word of the outside world! I feel I shall become like one of those before long." He indicated the stone watchmen carved and set within alcoves of the fortress wall. There were two of them, solemn figures from legends of Parumvir's past. It was the custom for statues of these men to stand guard over the king's fortresses, but Imoo found them uncomfortable company in the long watches of the night.

Sir Rogan remained merry. "He will return tonight, Imoo. And he will herald attack, and we shall test the sharpness of our blades upon our enemies!"

Imoo shivered and stared hard into the gloom of the mountain trail winding down beneath them, searching for any sign of truth to Rogan's words. The green-eyed knight started to hum to himself and soon began to sing a bloodthirsty song. His jewel eyes shone like those of a cat ready to pounce but ever so patient for the right moment.

At last Imoo said, "He comes."

Rogan drew his sword.

The yellow-eyed boy grinned down at her, his eyes gleaming like struck matches. Angry at losing her dream, the dragon girl snarled, "What do you want?"

"There's been a disturbance in the tunnel," he said. His teeth glinted in the light of his own eyes. "Someone's been discovered in our lands, not a brother or sister. He wandered in here on his own and was taken without a fight. How foolish is that? They are bringing him to the Village. Come, let's go see!"

Reluctant yet also interested, she climbed out from behind her boulder and followed the yellow-eyed boy. A great crowd, hundreds of shadow figures, gathered thickly near the mouth of the tunnel. They jostled and fought each other, and spurts of flame flared up at intervals. But everyone's eyes were fixed on the tunnel mouth, curious about what was coming. The yellow-eyed boy led her off to one side and showed her where to climb to a ledge from which they had a clear view. She settled onto the narrow outcropping and waited.

Suddenly, there he was.

Her eyes widened and her breath stilled. She did not hear the shouts from a hundred dragonish throats, did not take in the swift surge of heat and anger. Her gaze was filled with Prince Aethelbald standing in the mouth of the tunnel over the dark cavern, held by two enormous men with black talons. He was unarmed, yet his face was, she thought, serene even in the harsh red firelight.

"Who are you and how dare you cross our borders?" the Bane of Corrilond, who stood forefront in the mob, demanded.

"I seek a princess," he replied. His voice rang clear among the harsh snarls that rose in response.

"A princess?" The Bane of Corrilond spat. "We have no princess here. We are all brothers and sisters, not princes and princesses. And you have not answered my question. Who are you?"

"I know who he is."

The dragon girl started in surprise to hear the rasping voice of the yellow-eyed boy beside her.

"Who is he, then?" the Bane of Corrilond asked, turning red eyes toward the ledge where the two sat.

Instead of answering, the yellow-eyed boy slid from the ledge and elbowed his way through the crowd and up the path until he stood face-to-face with the captive.

"Hello, Prince of Farthestshore," he said.

"Hello, Diarmid," Aethelbald replied.

"What do you call me?" The yellow-eyed boy snorted. "Is that a name?"

"It is your name."

"Funny thing, that. No wonder I forgot it. I have no name now, Prince. How long has it been since last we met?"

"Five hundred years by the Near World's count."

"Only five hundred? I thought perhaps more. Seems like an eternity since last I really burned!"

"What is this?" the Bane of Corrilond cried, coming up beside the yellow-eyed boy. "Is this one of your former kin?"

The yellow-eyed boy laughed and flung an arm around Aethelbald's shoulders. "This is the Prince of Farthestshore, my one-time master of yore!" He spat the word with a spark of fire. "The selfsame master who, five hundred years ago, tried to undo the gift our father bestowed upon me. He tried to quench my fire!"

The people of the cavern roared as in one rage-filled voice. "Burn him!" some cried. "Tear him! Bleed him! Enemy of our father!"

The dragon girl gripped the stones of the ledge so hard that blood trickled from her fingers. Her dragon kin writhed in fury below the tunnel mouth, and more flames rose in the darkness until the whole cavern glowed. The yellow-eyed boy laughed again and pushed the Prince to the ground, eliciting approving shouts from his comrades. The two big men who had dragged Aethelbald in grabbed him and pulled him to his feet. He shook one of them off, but three more reached in and seized him so that he could not move. The yellow-eyed boy stepped forward and took Aethelbald by the throat, grinning cruelly, fire dancing in the corners of his mouth.

"Wait."

The Bane of Corrilond's voice filled the cavern, and her kin quieted before her. She hauled the yellow-eyed boy back from the Prince. He bared his teeth at her, but she ignored him, gazing instead into Aethelbald's stern face. "Wait," she repeated. "We must save him. How often do we come across such fair and fresh meat? What more worthy gift could we offer our Father?"

The dragon folk murmured in agreement, but the yellow-eyed boy licked back flames. "He's no good," he spat. "He'll not take the fire and would taste bitter to our Father."

"We shall see," the Bane of Corrilond said. "In the meantime no one harms him. Throw him in the cage."

The dragon girl watched as the dragon folk pulled Prince Aethelbald down into the cavern, the crowd jeering and jabbing him, threatening him with fire. They dragged him underneath her ledge, and he raised his eyes and saw her.

"Una."

She saw his mouth form the word. Her name.

Covering her face with her gnarled and scale-covered hands, she turned to the wall. The din of dragon voices filled her ears and did not let up for hours.

31

THE CURTAINS WERE DRAWN, admitting no outside light. But the long drapes caught the glow of the brands in the fireplace and reflected it back until the room was all red and shadows. Lionheart, having retired from his father's court for the day, sat quietly in those shadows. He'd given orders to his attendants to admit no one, not since his brief interview with Captain Catspaw and his men.

"Cowards!" Lionheart had shouted at them as they clustered before him.

"Forgive us, Your Highness," Catspaw had said, cringing away. "We did our best, but we could not—"

"Could not? Would not, you mean. Has the honor of Southlands no claim on your hearts? I promised Prince Aethelbald the help of twelve loyal men, and this is how you serve me?"

"Please, Your Highness—"

"Out of my sight!" the prince had snarled, and the captain and his men had crept from the room, slinking like frightened cats. When they had gone, Lionheart had ordered his attendants from the room as well and, muttering curses under his breath, had drawn all the curtains and pulled his chair up close to the fire.

There he had sat—how many hours now, he could not guess. But the fire was almost dead, leaving behind only the popping embers. The room grew colder, but Lionheart did not move to put a log in the grate, nor did he summon his man to do it for him.

"Cowards," he growled again.

Shameful, those men. You should punish them. Rid yourself of those who will not serve you as they should.

"I should rid myself of those weasels," Lionheart muttered. His fingers tensed, relaxed, then tensed again.

You cannot afford to keep them in your service, my prince. They will only hinder your work.

"I cannot afford to keep men like those in my service."

Rid yourself of them as soon as possible. Just as you did the girl.

Lionheart covered his face with both hands. He drew in a sharp breath, like a sob. "Get out of my head!"

Oh, my sweet prince—

"GET OUT!" he roared and leapt to his feet. Hardly knowing what he did, he reached into the fire, took up a handful of the scalding embers, and flung them into the darkest corners of his room. "Get out! Go away from me!"

Silence crept in around him. Deep and black and dark.

Then suddenly his mind's eye filled with a vision, a memory of two red eyes, ovens of fire. He had crouched, a quivering wretch, in the shadow of that Beast, and a fiery voice hissed in his head:

"Give me her heart, Prince Lionheart, and I will let you live."

"No!" he whispered, closing his eyes. But still the memory played before him, as vividly as though he were caught forever in that one moment in time. He groveled before a great, black king. "No!"

"Your life for her heart. It is an easy enough exchange. Then you may return to Southlands, reclaim your crown, rule your people. But give me the heart of this princess, your love."

"Leave me in peace!" Lionheart pulled at his hair with his burned hands, desperate to free himself of the memory.

"It is the only way, Prince Lionheart. What other choice do you have?"

"It's yours. Take it!"

The memory faded; the fire died away. Lionheart stood again in the silence of his chamber, which was cold and black as a crypt. He felt tears in his eyes but blinked them away and dropped his head heavily to his chest.

A woman's voice brushed his consciousness again—subtle, serene. A seductive voice speaking from far-off reaches, without fire, without warmth, like a sunless day.

You did what you had to do, Lionheart.

"I did what I had to do."

There was no other way.

"No other way."

Now take my hand and walk with me, Prince of Southlands, and I will show you what it means to see your dreams realized.

He raised his head and for a moment caught a flashing vision of white, white eyes and a black hand extended to him. Then it was gone, and his chambers were silent once more.

"I did what I had to do," Lionheart whispered, a shiver running through his body. "There was no other way."

Behind the walls and ramparts where Imoo and Rogan stood, in the ancient, moss-grown keep of the fortress, high in a private chamber, Fidel sat by candlelight, reports and papers spread out before him. He should pack them away and go to bed, he knew—should have done so hours ago. But he also knew that he would not sleep, and as long as sleep eluded him, he might as well work.

Three weeks now, Fidel had lived tucked away in this remote fortress, far from the comforts of his palace. Strategically it was the safest place to which he could flee, for the mountain pass was narrow and it would be difficult for any attackers to penetrate the defenses General Argus had arranged under the direction of the three Knights of Farthestshore. Fidel did not doubt his own safety.

The papers before him contained figures on supplies and the needs of the troops that were gathering from various reaches of Parumvir. The country had not come together for war in many years, and Fidel suffered agonies as he realized just how defenseless they had become during the generations of peace.

Somewhere outside among the cold mountains, shouting voices rose in the air.

Fidel pulled another sheaf of papers toward him. Commanders of various garrisons had sent reports, and some sent pleas for assistance that Fidel was unable to give. The world was falling apart, yet what could he do to stop it? He'd sent word to allies in Beauclair and Milden but so far had heard no response.

Fidel cursed and pounded the tabletop with the flat of his hand. "What can I do against the Dragon? There are no heroes left in this day and age who can fight him."

The shouts outside increased, and a horn blast rang clearly. Fidel, pulled from his thoughts, pushed his chair back and went to the window. He cupped his hands in order to see through the dark glass. Torches flickered below him in the fort yard. Risking the cold night air, Fidel opened the window and leaned out to get a better view.

The clang of sword on sword filled his ears, the shouts of commanders and even General Argus's voice booming in the night, "To the king! Find the king!"

"Shippening," Fidel breathed and drew back from the window. In the same moment he heard pounding on his door, and Sir Oeric burst in.

"Your Majesty," the knight said. "The Duke of Shippening—"

"Impossible!" Fidel roared and with a mighty swoop knocked all his papers and the candle from his desk. *"Impossible!"*

"Please, sire," Sir Oeric said. He stood like a great boulder in the doorway, and his drawn sword had blood on the blade. "My brethren can deal with the duke, but we must be certain you are safe. If you will come with me . . ."

He stepped over the piles of papers on the floor and took hold of the king's arm, for Fidel had slumped heavily against the wall. The king looked up into the knight's white-saucer eyes, and suddenly his own haggard face hardened and he knocked Sir Oeric's hands away. "Away with you! I'm not some old dotard, not yet!" He straightened his shoulders and took down his own sword from where it hung, ever ready, beside the door. He strapped it about his waist and stormed from the room into the hall.

There was no escape; he knew that. If Shippening had breached the wall, there would be no escape for any of them. Fidel made his way down the stairs, hearing the sounds of battle from the floor just below.

"Please, Your Majesty!" Sir Oeric cried behind him. "Not that way!"

He whirled on the knight, drawing his sword as he spoke. "Away from me!" he cried.

"Your Majesty," Sir Oeric said, looming huge above him on the narrow stair, "I am charged by my Prince to keep you safe. You must come with me."

"I'll not abandon my men here!"

"But, Your Majesty—"

Fidel did not hear what else the knight might have said, for in that moment he heard a scream, a voice that he recognized. He whirled and continued down the stairs into the hall below and threw himself at the first man in Shippening garb that he saw. His sword came away red with blood. He turned and blocked another attack, then drove his blade home. He looked through the haze of the torchlit hall, his mind numbed by the din of battle, and his face went suddenly pale.

General Argus lay against the wall, blood soaking his front, a young aide fighting desperately to defend him. With a roar, Fidel lunged across the hall to the general's side. "Argus!" he cried, dropping to his knees.

The general raised his eyes and tried to speak, but no voice came. Fidel gazed down at him for what seemed a small eternity, but the press of battle forced him to his feet again. He stood back-to-back with the young aide near the door leading into the yard. A crush of men poured through—men of Shippening. Around him were some of his own people, but they were far outnumbered.

Fidel raised his sword and shouted, "To me, Parumvir!"

Men gathered at each side and rushed forward with him into the onslaught. But there was too little room in the hall. They were crowded together and could hardly raise their swords without cutting each other. The men of Shippening pushed them back, and when Fidel, panting, leaned against the far wall, the number of those who stood with him was greatly reduced. Blood oozed down his right hand, and he felt his face to find more blood and a long, stinging cut on his cheek.

Sir Oeric appeared beside him. "Sire," he growled through sharp fangs, "with all due respect, I insist that you stay back with your men."

Even as he spoke, more Shippening soldiers spilled into the hall. Breathing hard, Fidel could only watch them coming, but Sir Oeric brandished his sword. "Stay back," he repeated, then charged forward alone into the attack.

For a moment he seemed to be swallowed up by the enemy. Then, bit by bit, Fidel watched in amazement as the men of Shippening fell away, fleeing the hall, spilling back out into the yard in the face of one man's defense. Soon only the fallen soldiers of Shippening remained in the hall, their blood mingling with that of Parumvir's men. Fidel, sword in hand, ran to the door and looked out into the yard.

Men of Shippening flooded through the gates and over the walls. Alone in their midst stood the three Knights of Farthestshore. And as they fought side by side, the enemy could not draw nearer to the fortress keep. For the first time since the alarm was sounded, Fidel found his heart lifting. They would survive the night after all. He shouted in defiance of the Duke of Shippening and charged forward with his faithful men at his heels. Emboldened, they threw themselves with renewed vigor at their attackers, driving them back across the yard, back over the walls.

Fidel stood beside the knights, his face full of triumph as he turned to them.

But they stood pale as three ghosts. Sir Oeric said in a low voice, "He has come."

The next moment, like two great suns in the night, the eyes of the Dragon appeared in the darkness between the walls at the great gate.

The green-eyed knight cried out in dismay, but even as he did so he charged into the Dragon's very face. "Rogan!" Sir Imoo shouted and ran after him. A great burst of fire, roaring like a hurricane, burned the night, and the second knight only just fell away in time to avoid the fate of his brother.

Then the Dragon passed through the gates, and with one sweep of his claw he sent Imoo flying across the yard, where he struck the wall and fell like a crumpled reed doll upon the stones.

Sir Oeric placed himself before King Fidel, but though he was great and tall as a giant, he seemed but a tiny child before the black majesty of the Dragon.

And the Dragon, as it looked down upon him, laughed.

"Well met, sir knight!" His voice was full of fire, and Fidel felt the poison of his breath wafting over him. "It's been a while since last I set eyes upon you. Found yourself a name yet, goblin?"

Sir Oeric did not reply but stood protectively over the king, his sword arm upraised.

The Dragon laughed again, a thunderous sound. Fidel dropped his own sword and fell to his knees, and even the knight stepped back and cringed away as sparks flew and burned his skin. "I owe you too much to crisp you to cinders," the Dragon said. "I do not forget a service rendered, however unwillingly. If not for you, little knight, I might yet be bound to the Gold Stone! So no, I'll not kill you now. But you will have to stand aside and let me take the little king."

"Go to the hell prepared for you, Death-in-Life!" the knight spat, his deep voice strangely thin before the monster's might.

"In good time, little goblin," the Dragon said, raising the crest on his head. "If you'll not oblige me, I may send you there before me."

"You cannot!" Sir Oeric declared. "My life is not yours!"

But the Dragon smiled. "And who's to stop me?"

His tail, sinewy as a snake, thick and strong as an oak, lashed out, and the end of it wrapped about Sir Oeric's waist, lifting him from his feet. With a snap like a whip, the Dragon flung the knight from him, over the wall and into the darkness, laughing as he watched him fly. Then he turned his burning eyes once more upon the king. His vast body dwindled, the wings shrinking and folding into a long cape, and his burning eyes, no longer set among scales, were instead set in a face of white skin stretched over a skull of black bone.

In the body of a man, he stepped over to the king, who fell upon his face before him.

"Greetings, King Fidel," the Dragon said. "It's time to come home."

The cage sat off to one side of the bloody throne. The cage itself was stained with the blood of countless captives, but it sat in such a dark corner that some of its hideousness was hidden. One could smell it, even so.

No other dragon folk were near the cage now, having at last lost interest in its new inhabitant. The dragon girl could see Aethelbald sitting cross-legged in the back, his eyes closed, his head bowed to his chest. She gulped and took in a deep breath, pulling the sleeves of her robe down over her dragon arms. When she opened her mouth to speak, no words would come. Cursing herself, she turned to go.

"Una?"

She froze as though paralyzed at the sound of her name. It hurt to hear it, like a knife in her mind.

"Una."

His voice was low and, wonder of wonders, kind. Her chest felt dull and empty as her fire sank inside.

"Una, come back."

Keeping her face hidden by the hood, she crept up to the cage. He stood at the bars, gripping them with both hands. As she neared, he reached a hand toward her, but she remained out of reach.

"Why did you come here?" she whispered.

"To find you."

She knew that but could make no sense of it. "When the Dragon returns," she said, "they are going to kill you."

"They will kill you too."

"I know."

"It will not be a good death," he said.

She turned away from him, clenching her dragon hands into fists so that her own claws pricked her scaly palms. "All I love are lost to me," she whispered. "My brother is dead. My father may be as well. And my—" She clenched her teeth, for the flame rising inside burned her throat.

"Your brother is alive," Aethelbald said.

She stopped breathing. "What?"

"Felix is alive, Una. The duke's plot did not succeed, and your brother was only wounded. He is receiving care. He is alive."

All the world was still, around her and inside—a stillness without serenity, a silence without calm. "Felix," she whispered. Then she hissed through her teeth like a snake. "He may as well be dead, for I am dead to him, dead to all of them!"

Aethelbald reached out to her. "Una—"

"That is no longer my name!" she snarled.

"That name is precious to me," he whispered.

"More's the pity for you, then."

"Little sister."

She gasped and stepped back at the Bane of Corrilond's growl.

"Little sister," the giant woman said, grabbing her shoulder with a massive hand. Claws pricked her skin. "Were you, perchance, the princess sought by this handsome Prince? How fitting. So you weren't entirely forgotten, were you?"

The giant bent down and snarled in the girl's face. "But he's not the right one, is he?" She chuckled harshly. "You gave your heart to another, and this one can never help you now. Poor little sister. And poor little Prince! You see, don't you, that there is no redeeming our kind." She turned to him and showed sharp fangs in a hideous smile. "But perhaps this will stir up a fire in your own breast, noble Prince? Jealousy makes a fine flame. How does it feel to not be good enough to win her heart, no matter what you risk?"

Aethelbald slowly shook his head. "Woman, I fear you have long since forgotten the meaning of love."

The Bane of Corrilond hissed, then glared down at the girl. "True love does not exist, little sister. I learned that lesson centuries ago. You would do well to learn it now."

With a flame in her mouth, she disappeared into the darkness. Moments later, a fireball roared to the ceiling of the cavern, and a massive red dragon raced up the path to the tunnel and vanished, gone to spend its flame on the desert night.

The dragon girl, her breath coming in short gulps, looked down at an object clutched in one scale-covered hand: a cold iron key plucked from the Bane of Corrilond's robes.

32

A SWIFT BREEZE FLOWED THROUGH the branches of the Wood, skirting along the tops of the trees, then wrapping about the trunks, flowing faster than water as it went. It came at last to a grove of white aspens and shook the branches in a wild rustling before dying away into nothing.

Felix sat upon the edge of the bed in the white room that had been his since he arrived at the Wood Haven, patiently allowing Dame Imraldera to check his bandages. She clucked to herself as she always did while cutting away the old dressings. But when the trees made their soft susurrus above them in the strange vault that was neither ceiling nor forest, she paused and looked up, a strange expression crossing her face.

"What's that look for?" Felix asked, watching her.

"What look?" She blinked and turned back to him.

"That faraway, no-longer-paying-attention-to-what-you're-doing look. Like you were suddenly a thousand miles away."

"No, no!" Imraldera laughed. "I am very present."

"Good, because you've got a knife in your hand." Felix added, "What's wrong?"

"I was listening, that's all."

"To thin air?"

She laughed again and went back to work on his bandage, wrapping the soft gauze around his shoulder. "Remember, I can see and hear what you cannot, Prince Felix."

"Oh yes." He shuddered. "How many are in this room with us now?"

"You have at least five attendants at all times. They minister to your needs even as you sleep, keeping off Faerie beasts who would do you harm."

"Beasts?" Felix looked around his chamber. He had grown used to it with time—how much time he could not imagine, for it was impossible to measure time in the Halflight Realm—but suddenly he remembered how open it was, and he saw more of the forest than he did of the white walls. And he remembered the bestial roar he'd heard the night he walked the moonlit hall. "I'd forgotten. Are there many beasts in the Wood?"

"More than you can imagine," she said. "The Far World is not a safe one."

Felix snorted. "Then why are you keeping me here?"

"Because the Prince's Haven is safe, and his servants, your attendants, will let no harm befall you." She patted his shoulder and tugged at his shirt. "There, you are done. Button yourself up and lie down again."

"I don't want to lie down," Felix said, buttoning his shirt. "I've been lying down for ages—probably a good hundred years at least."

"The best way to heal is to rest."

"I have been resting." He got to his feet and paced to the other side of the room, which once more overlooked the wild landscape of Faerie, so oddly familiar yet so foreign. He could see the Northern Mountains from here, though back home he knew they were much too far away to see. Strange that they seemed simultaneously much closer than he knew them to be but also ten times more distant. He knew he stood in Goldstone Wood, yet from where he stood, the Wood seemed to stretch out for miles upon miles, an ocean of trees, much more vast than he had ever believed the familiar forest he had always known to be.

And the Goldstone he knew had never held wild beasts.

"Dame Imraldera," Felix said, "when can I go home?"

He turned around to speak to her and saw her standing with her back to him, her head turned so that he could see her profile. Her mouth was open, her brow puckered, and her eyes stared again at an empty space in the air.

"Dame Imraldera?"

"Felix," she said, turning to him suddenly, as though she hadn't heard him call her but needed him quickly. "Felix, I've just received word of your father."

Felix's stomach dropped to his feet. He felt dizzy watching the expression on her face and reached out to grab a tree for support. "What?" he demanded.

"He has been taken. By the . . . the Dragon."

"Alive?"

"Yes."

Felix sank to the ground, too weak with relief to stand. Alive! His father still lived. Capture was not the end; capture could be fixed. Dead he could do nothing about, but capture . . .

Imraldera moved to his side and bent down to touch his shoulder. He looked up at her sharply. "You must let me go," he said.

"Felix, I—"

"You must. He's my father!" Felix felt tears burning his eyes and pounded his fists into the hard dirt beneath him. "You cannot make me sit here a minute more when my father's life is in danger!"

"Felix, there is nothing you can—"

"Don't tell me that," he cried, knocking her hand away from his shoulder. "He's my father. That counts for something. I can help; I know I can."

"The Prince will—"

"Aethelbald isn't here." Felix took in a deep breath, trying to calm himself, to speak like an adult rather than a child in a tantrum. "When was the last time you heard from your master? Honestly."

She bowed her head, her hands folded before her. "Not in a long time."

"See?" Felix scrambled to his feet. Though he stood half a head taller than the woman, he felt like a little boy pleading with his nurse to let him go out and play in the mud after a shower. "See, you can't know that Aethelbald will do anything. You can't know where he is. But *I* am here, and *I* can do something! You know Faerie, don't you? Isn't it true that there is power in blood ties that . . . that sometimes can overcome foes much too great otherwise? Isn't it true, Dame Imraldera?"

"Felix," she said gently, taking his hand and stroking it as though trying to soothe a baby. "Felix, if you leave here now, the poison—"

"Will it kill me?"

"Not immediately," she admitted. "Perhaps not for many years. But someday, Felix, yes. If you do not stay and receive the full healing I can give you, the poison will pump through all your veins, will work its way into your heart. And you will die, young prince. Whether in a year, in ten years, or in fifty, the dragon poison will kill you."

Felix shrugged, shaking his head angrily. "A year? I can save my father and be back here long before then! I will return immediately—I promise—and you can finish your treatments then."

"But, Felix—"

"You'll always have some excuse, because you don't want me to go." Felix pulled his hand from hers and stormed across the room. "You don't want me to go because you think I'm too young, you think I'm useless, that I can't do anything. But I *can*, I tell you. I can save my father!"

"Felix—"

"What?" he snapped. "Don't try to comfort me; I don't want it."

Imraldera stood quietly in the center of the room, her hands still folded. "I cannot keep you here against your will," she said. "If you desire to go, I will send you back across the Borders. Your attendants will protect you until you pass through, but once you're on the other side you will be truly alone. And, Felix, I will not be able to make you return to me."

Felix looked up. "But you will let me go?"

"I will."

He leapt up, pounding the air with his fist, then grabbed the startled woman up in his arms and spun her around so that her tunic and flowing trousers swirled. "Thank you!" he cried. "Thank you! Thank you!" He set her down, both of them staggering from the momentum, and kissed her smartly on the cheek. "You will see," he said. "I'll save him, I truly will. And I'll come back before the year is out, fit as anything, and you can do whatever you need to!"

Imraldera, tears in her eyes, backed away. "Oh, little Felix," she murmured. "I hope that you will."

But he did not hear what she said, for he was busy shouting to the thin air, "Attendants! Invisibles! Can you get me some real clothes? Something other than a nightshirt? And boots and things. And a sword! Don't forget a sword! A sharp one!"

In that moment, as the dragon girl stood with the key clutched in her hand, watching the trail of fire that marked the Bane of Corrilond's departure, she was thankful that she no longer possessed a heart, for she knew it would beat through her chest. Glancing over her shoulders, certain that at any moment one of the shadowy figures would stop its aimless wandering to apprehend her, she slid the key into the lock. The metal on metal clanged so horribly, she thought she would die on the spot. She shook too much to turn the key.

A strong hand slid between the bars and covered hers. "Let me help," Aethelbald said.

She removed her hand from under his and quickly pulled the sleeves of her robe lower. Had he noticed the scales?

He turned the key, and the lock clicked open. The door creaked as he pushed, and she started and turned this way and that, certain of attack.

"Don't be afraid," Aethelbald said, sliding from the cage to her side. "Most of them do not care enough, caught up as they are in their own burning. We need fear only one of them now, for most have spent their anger on me and already forgotten." He reached for her hand, but she refused, so he gently took her elbow instead. "Come, Una. You must know the way out."

She took two steps, but fear of the hundreds of shadows, her dragon kin, overwhelmed her. "They'll kill us both," she breathed. But she did not care what they did to her.

"They won't, Una." He leaned close to whisper in her ear. "Trust me."

At those words, she shivered and pulled away. But Aethelbald's hand remained on her elbow, and somehow she felt able to step forward again.

They passed through the shadowy figures, and to her surprise not one of them looked their way. She and the Prince might as well have been invisible. Startled by this, she found herself looking more closely at the figures than she had before. She discovered that most of them did not walk toward any particular destination: They paced. Some of them paced the whole length of the cavern, turned, and paced back again. They walked with their gazes fixed on the ground just beyond their feet, and as they walked they muttered quietly to themselves. Sometimes fire licked between their teeth or in their eyes. Sometimes they would stop and spit a small flame toward the ceiling. Then their pacing would continue, getting faster all the time, until finally they burst into flames and rushed from the cavern out into the desert, venturing to unknown destinations. They would return eventually, and if not, who cared? All were too busy in their own pacing to notice.

She herself had not noticed until now.

They reached the mouth of the tunnel unhindered. "There," she said, trying to pull her elbow from Aethelbald's gentle but firm grip. "There's your way out. Follow it quickly."

"Not without you."

"I can't go," she said, hanging her head.

"Then neither can I."

A flame burst up in her chest and into her mouth. She forced it back as best she could. "You must go. They'll kill you."

"I'll die before I leave you," he said.

How she hated him in that moment! Hated him enough to swallow him whole—hated him for his heart, which she coveted; hated him for loving her as she could no longer love her jester-prince; hated him for not being her jester; hated him for all his stupid, noble self-sacrifice, so wasted on her.

Hated him because she knew she could never deserve his love.

"Come, then," she hissed and hurried into the tunnel, leaving behind the cavernous village of dragons.

Just for the moment, she told herself. *Just until I slip away from him. For I belong in the Village and must return.*

It was night outside, she realized. No sunlight found its way through the cracks in the tunnel ceiling. Her eyes were used to the dark, though, and she did not stumble. Aethelbald's steps hesitated here and there, but he seemed to follow her lead without question. Several times there were twists in the tunnel or it split, and she was uncertain which direction to choose. She quietly selected, using the best reasoning she could, but finally she was forced to admit, "I am not certain of the way."

"I remember," Aethelbald said.

She realized then that she had not been leading him at all but that he had been guiding her with gentle pressure on her arm. Of course he would know the way. He had come here to find her, hadn't he?

She yanked her arm free from his hold. "You lead, then," she said. "You don't need me."

"I don't wish to lose you in the dark, Una," he said, his voice soft. "Please, walk before me."

She turned her back and went forward down the path, keeping out of his reach. This stretch of the tunnel was straight and even, and she did not need his assistance. Soon she saw light ahead, white light unlike the red flames she was accustomed to. It had been so long since she'd seen it that she almost didn't recognize it for what it was: moonlight.

"Oh," she breathed, and something inside her that she did not know still existed stirred. She stepped up her pace and hurried to the mouth of the tunnel, hardly noticing the crunch of Aethelbald's boots behind her.

"Wait, Una!" he cried, but she ignored him and ran from the rocks out into the open air. The desert stretched around her in all its barren loneliness, but above—ah, above! There the sky vaulted from a light blue on the horizon up to greens and deeper blues, all the way to the deepest violet-indigos in the highest regions, where innumerable stars glittered, pure treasures unsullied by blood and greed. And the moon, its light engulfing any stars within its sphere, shone as a brilliant crown of white, more lovely than words.

Fire forgotten for a moment, the dragon girl ran forward, stretched out her arms, and spun about, her face tilted to watch the stars twirling above her.

She heard Aethelbald's urgent voice. "Una!"

"Good girl, sister."

Even the moonlight betrayed her.

A spindly hand grabbed her arm, and she gasped in pain and surprise. Two yellow eyes gleamed above her. "I thought she might be the princess you sought," the dragon boy said. He forced her down and pinned her to the sand, twisting her right arm behind her and pressing a knee into her back. Her dragon claws tore uselessly at the sand.

"Let her go." Aethelbald stepped from the shelter of the tunnel into the moonglow. "Your fight is with me. She is nothing to you."

"Did you hear that?" the boy with the yellow eyes hissed. "You are nothing, you who once were a princess!" He chuckled. "But you are wrong, Prince of Farthestshore, if you think I have no grievance against her. She would betray us for you. Us! Her kinfolk who took her in and taught her, who gave her a home. She would betray us for you, a stranger. Worse, an unwanted suitor!"

She felt the dragon boy's cold hand slide around her throat, felt the prick of unsheathing talons.

"Let her go, brother," Aethelbald said, his voice low and menacing. "Fight me instead. I am weaponless, you see."

"Unlike before, eh?" The yellow-eyed boy spat, and flame flashed by her face. "You think he will help you, little princess?"

She began trembling, with fear or rage she could not say.

"He offered to help me too, long ago. I was young and foolish then, frightened at first by the change worked in me by our Father. And he, my noble Prince, my master, set his servants upon my trail, and they tracked me down until I was too weary to flee. Then he came to me himself. He came to me, claiming that he wished to help me. Hounded down, exhausted, I agreed to accept his aid and made myself vulnerable before him, swallowed my flame. But you know what he did?"

He spat fire again, singeing her hair. She screamed and struggled, but his hand tightened on her throat. "Not a step closer, Aethelbald, or I'll snap her neck in two!" the yellow-eyed boy cried. "You know what he did, little princess? He took out his sword and tried to run me through. I submitted to him, and he tried to kill me! I trusted him, and he betrayed me!"

Smoke and ash filled her mind, blinding her eyes.

"Diarmid," Aethelbald said.

"Death-in-Life eat your eyes!" the yellow-eyed boy screamed, and hot cinders burned the girl's neck. "That is no longer my name!"

"You should have trusted me, Diarmid," Aethelbald said. "But trust is not found in you, I fear. Not so with her. She longs to trust."

"He'll force you into anything, little sister, as he tried to force me," the yellow-eyed boy said. "He's more manipulative than you can imagine! Don't listen to him or—" He cried out and fell from her back, struck in the head by a large stone. She scrambled free of him, and smoke poured from her nostrils.

Roaring, he leapt at her again, his face contorted. But Aethelbald caught him and knocked him into a sprawl. The two of them rolled in the sand, fire spilling from the boy's mouth, catching Aethelbald's cloak aflame. He snatched the cloak off and flung it over the boy's head, then turned to find her.

She felt the transformation taking place. *No. Not in front of him!* she screamed inside, but the fire burst from her.

"Una! No!" Aethelbald caught her about the waist and pressed her to him so that she felt the beating of his heart against her cheek, and for a moment she thought the change would fade, would stop.

But, in a painful wrench, she pushed free from him, screaming, "Don't look at me. *Please!*"

Flames from the mouth of a yellow-eyed dragon struck her full in the face, and the heat of them completed the work of her own fire.

Mighty wings tore at the night air, and she raised her heavy body up onto two legs. Whirling with surprising agility for her size, she sent a burst of fire into the yellow eyes of the other dragon. It roared in laughter rather than pain and swung at her with its claws like a sparring cat. She gnashed her teeth at him and flamed again, then leapt into the sky, pushing and pulling with her wings, leaving the yellow-eyed dragon and the Prince far behind. Only a harsh voice followed her.

"Burn, sister, burn! Don't let him quench your flame!"

33

THE DRAGON LANDED HEAVILY in the sand in a faint, and moments later it dwindled into the form of a pale girl.

Waves slowly licked up the shore, inching closer until they pulled at the girl's hair and tried to draw it back with them. Still the girl remained motionless. If she didn't move soon, she might drown; humans were such fragile beings.

Hands reached from the waves and took hold of the girl. Cradling her, they turned her so that her head rolled out of the water. The dragon maid moaned and her brow puckered, but she did not wake.

It didn't matter. The hands were patient, as patient as the old sea. They held the girl's head out of the water, and the owner of those hands thought many thoughts. Dragons were vicious creatures, or so it was supposed. Yet, looking down at that white face, one could not be afraid.

"Poor creature," a delicate voice murmured. "Poor little thing."

The voice began humming to itself. The humming turned into singing, gentle as the water lapping the shore.

"Twilit dimness surrounds me,
The veil slips over my eyes.
The riddle of us two together long ago
How fragile in my memory lies."

The pale girl's face softened, and her dragon hands relaxed. The sun sank behind the water, and the dragon girl's shadow grew longer and longer behind her. At last she moaned, stirred, and her eyes blinked open. Her body tensed and her gaze darted about, but the next moment she calmed again. "Is someone there?" she asked.

"Yes."

"I cannot see you."

"No."

"Are you real?"

"Very real."

"But I cannot see you!"

"Not with those eyes."

A long silence followed. The gentle hands stroked hair back from the dragon girl's forehead, and the girl breathed deeply.

"You sang my song," the girl said after a long silence.

"It was written on your face, in the scales on your hand."

"Are you Faerie?"

"Some call me that."

"You aren't human," the dragon girl said.

"Neither are you."

The girl sighed. "Not anymore." Her mouth trembled, but she composed herself. "Have you a name?"

"Yes."

"May I know it?"

"You'll not be able to pronounce it with your tongue."

"May I hear it anyway?"

The voice sang a quick succession of notes, soft and fast as a thrush's song, but more wild and wet and deep. Unlike a human voice, this voice sang multiple notes at once, sweet chords and harmonies as well as melodies.

The pale girl closed her eyes and sighed. "That is a beautiful name."

"And your name?"

The girl shook her head. "I've lost mine."

"What was it, then?"

"Una, Princess of Parumvir. But that was before . . ." She held up her dragon hands, clenched them into fists.

"I am sorry."

"No," the dragon girl said. "No, it is just as well. This is what has been inside all along. It is just as well it came out. This way I can deceive no one. They all know what I am—even . . ."

"Yes?"

The pale girl sat up, and the gentle hands let her go. "Even the one who loves me. Even he has seen me for what I am." Her voice was low and heavy but tearless. "He'll not love me now."

Another long silence fell between them. The dragon girl turned this way and that. "Are you still there?"

"Yes."

The sun painted the clouds above vivid orange against a purpling sky. The dragon girl looked up and watched the colors change and listened to the silence and the water.

"Una?" the voice spoke at last.

"Yes?"

"Who is this one who loves you? Tell me more of him."

The pale girl tucked her dragon hands under her wet robe. "He is a prince, a true prince," she said. "Kinder than anyone I have ever met . . . merciful and kind." She bowed her head, and her long, dripping hair covered her face. "Why am I speaking this way? Why am I saying any of this? It is foolishness. It is all foolishness now—so very late! If I had realized, if I'd had eyes to see, perhaps it would be different. I was such a fool. I thought I loved Leonard passionately; I thought I longed for his return."

She put a hand to her eyes, wishing tears would come, though they would not. "But it was not Leonard's voice I heard. All along, when the Dragon's darkness was all around me, when I thought I would melt for the heat of my own flames, it wasn't Leonard's voice I heard. Not once. It was the Prince of Farthestshore. It was for Aethelbald I waited. If I could have seen it just a little sooner, perhaps things could have been different, but now . . ."

She cursed bitterly between sharp teeth and pounded her fist in the sand. "It's all just foolishness, and you are probably just some foolish dream of mine as well! Just as I dreamed Gervais cared for me, just as I dreamed my father could protect me, just as I dreamed Leonard would return, would be true—but it was all false!" She wrapped her arms over her head, pulling her hair with sharp claws.

"Una."

The girl shook her head and squeezed her arms tighter.

"Una."

"What?"

"I like the name. Your language is so harsh and sharp on my tongue that I rarely speak it. But Una is soft."

The waves pulling back to the sea drew the voice away even as it asked, "Do you wish to be Una again?"

"Oh, it is too late," the girl moaned. "I am trapped with this fire inside me. My heart is gone! It is too late for me now."

The sea was pulling faster now. The voice came from a distance. "The dragon must die," it said.

The girl looked up, her eyes darting about. "What?" she called. "I cannot hear you. What did you say?"

"The dragon must die if you are to live. That is your only hope." The voice lingered above the water, then disappeared.

"Wait!" The girl leapt to her feet and rushed to the edge of the waves. The sun reddened the water to lava, and the sky darkened like smoke. "Wait, please!"

Sea gulls flew overhead, squalling with each other. The dragon girl stood alone on the beach, gazing out across vast stretches of dark water.

Then, from far below, deep under the sea, a voice, or perhaps a chorus of voices, weird and wild, rose and murmured among the waves.

> *"May my heart beat with courage*
> *Before this torrent of shame,*
> *May I find the warm sweetness of forgiveness*
> *Between the ice and the flame.*
>
> *"Beyond the final water falling,*
> *The Songs of Spheres recalling,*
> *When the senseless silence fills your weary mind,*
> *Won't you return to me?"*

Strange and inhuman as those voices were, they brought the Prince of Farthestshore's face vividly to mind. She bowed her head and wished again for tears, but they had long since burned away. When the moon rose high, the dark shape of a dragon lifted into the air, casting a hideous shadow on the sand far below.

"Whatever you do," Dame Imraldera had said just before Felix left the safety of the Wood Haven and returned across the Borders into his own world, "do not cross the Old Bridge. If you forget everything else I have told you, Prince Felix, do not cross the Old Bridge, neither coming nor going. Ford the stream instead. Do you hear me?"

He had heard her, so when at last he crossed from the Halflight Realm into the familiar Wood he had known all his life, he remembered what she had said. It was strange to feel the difference, crossing the Borders, for though the landscape about him did not alter, the air itself did, and he knew he was back in his own world once more.

A thrill rushed through him at being back where he belonged, and he hurried through the darkness of the Wood, hastening uphill as fast as he could go. He came upon the bridge and the stream, and realized that this was the first time he had ever been on the far side in all his years playing under these trees. But he remembered Imraldera's words and did not cross the Old Bridge itself; instead he splashed through the icy water and tried not to flinch as water soaked down his boots and froze his feet.

He made his way up well-worn trails that he knew like the back of his hand; then the trees thinned around him and he neared the edge of the Wood where Oriana Palace's gardens began. He slowed his pace, creeping more cautiously from shadow to shadow. His eyes searched each low-growing shrub and bramble, darted to inspect each tree trunk in case some Shippening sentry should be stationed near. But he saw and was seen by no one as he crept to the Wood's edge and gazed from the safety of the trees up the garden path to his home on the crest of the hill.

Smoke hung in the air, rising from somewhere in the courtyard. The whole garden reeked of dragon smoke, and Felix gagged at the smell.

Quick as thought, he darted up the seven tiers of the garden, slipping from statue to shrub, still watching for those who might alert the Dragon or the duke to his presence. But no warning shout rattled his ears, no arresting cry. He came at last to the topmost tier, where once flowers had bloomed, up near the palace itself.

From this position he could hear the sounds of men in the courtyard, which was just out of his view. He could see lights in some of the upper rooms of the palace and knew that the duke and his men must have taken up residence inside. His father, he guessed, would be down in the basements—perhaps even locked away in the ancient, long-unused dungeons. Felix shuddered at the thought, and his hand slipped down to feel the hilt of the sword at his side, his own weapon returned to him when he had left the Haven and stepped out of Faerie.

Crouching in the shadows under an enormous burned shrub, Felix considered his options. He daren't stay in the garden overnight, not with the Dragon walking the grounds. But the Shippening men had taken over the palace. How likely was it that they would be using the servants' quarters in the south wing? He could slip in there and hide until he discovered where they kept his father. But how could he get in when all the doors were undoubtedly locked?

"Meaaa?"

Felix startled and bit his tongue hard. "Ow!" he growled and glared at the little form crouched beside him. "Monster, you dragon-eaten beast, bother you and all your next of kin!"

The cat raised its sightless face and rubbed a cheek against Felix's ear, purring madly. Felix pulled his head away from the tickle of whiskers. "How did you get all the way back up here, animal? Did you come looking for Una?"

The cat continued to purr.

"Useless creature," Felix muttered, turning back to survey the palace. "Wish you could show me a way inside."

The cat slipped out from under the juniper bush and trotted to the palace. Felix watched his slinky golden form jump to a windowsill and slip through the windowpane like magic. Felix blinked, surprised. He scrambled up and ran from the safety of his bush across the yard to the window. When he reached it, he found that one of the panes was broken. Monster sat on the other side, smiling a smug cat smile. Felix put his hand between the shards of broken glass and found that he could just reach the latch inside. He undid it, and the window swung open.

The next moment he was in the kitchen, crouched beside the big fireplace, breathing in sharp relief while Monster rubbed across his knees.

The Dragon watched the kitchen window click shut. He turned and trod on silent feet deep into the night shadows. Why alert the duke? He would find the boy in good time, and in the meanwhile, why not let the young prince hope? Hope is such a beautiful dream that dies such a hideous death.

"Death-in-Life," the Dragon whispered to himself—and smiled.

Dame Imraldera sat in the white room before the window, the silver sword held across her knees. She waited, watching the moon rise over the vast stretches of the Wood. She sat without blinking, still as a statue.

"He's here! He's come!"

Little voices whirled about her head and tiny hands touched her face and motioned behind her. Imraldera rose and turned. "My Prince?"

"I am here." Aethelbald stepped into the room. His clothing was worn and burned, his face lined with care. "I have come for my sword."

34

THE DRAGON PRINCESS landed on the beach, well outside the city. Smoke billowed as thick as thunderclouds overhead, turning the ocean a stormy black. Her once beautiful city was a mass of rubble and fire, made all the more terrible by the memory of what it had been. She found herself thankful once more that she had no heart, for it would have broken in two at the sight.

On reluctant feet she crawled along the seaside up to the road, hardly noticing the difference when her body lost its grand proportions and again became that of a girl. Only when a foul-smelling wind blew, threatening to knock her off balance, did she realize and look down at herself. Her shape was human, but her hands and feet were scale covered, and she could feel scales on her neck and chest. Her fire flared cruelly at the sight of her own ugly limbs.

"No. I don't want it anymore," she hissed between sharp teeth.

But something inside her hissed back, *How will you live without it now? What do you want instead? Food? Water? Such weakness!*

The dragon girl felt the heat boiling up inside her and knew she could not stop it. It was her life now, the very foundation of her existence.

"Very well," she murmured, and fire danced on her tongue. "Very well, but only a little more. I won't need it soon. But for today I will burn."

The fire grew as she neared the ruins of her city. Many of the buildings still stood, but they were darkened with ash, standing like lost orphans amid the wreckage. The destruction here was much greater than she had seen in Southlands. She felt she'd burst with fury at the injustice.

Good, the voice inside her murmured. *You need your fire hot for this.*

She picked her way down the smoldering streets, her dragon feet impervious to the heat and jagged edges of broken stone. She fixed her gaze on the hill above the city, where the walls of the palace still stood, and she could see the high gables and windows of her former home, ghostly gray against the smoke-darkened sky. The road up Goldstone Hill was long and deserted. Bit by bit, she picked her way to the palace gates, breathing in great gulps of dragon fumes. Each breath fed her own fire, which was by now a raging furnace in her chest.

The palace gates lay in twisted ruins on the ground. She stepped through the melted and broken metal and gazed again on the scorched grounds of her home.

Men of Shippening filled the yard, marching down the burned steps from the front door into the courtyard. On their shoulders and in their arms were her father's treasures. More treasure, gold and silver and jewels, lay scattered about like discarded rubble. Intent on their task, none of the men noticed her standing quiet as a shadow in the ruins of the great Westgate.

She felt fire rise like bile in her throat.

"Hello, my child."

Slowly she turned to her right and faced the tall man with a face as white as leprosy and eyes as black as death. He stood leaning with his shoulder against the wall.

"Welcome home," he said, revealing fangs in a smile.

Late in the morning, after a sleepless night in hiding, Felix crept through the servants' wing, Monster twining between his feet and purring but otherwise quiet. Felix tried to kick him away, but the cat returned each time. "Fine," Felix whispered, glaring down at the cat. "But you've got to be quiet, understand?"

Monster flicked his plumy tail.

Felix put his ear to the door that led from the servants' wing into the main hall of the palace. He could hear the tramp of feet coming and going, the voices of officers growling orders and soldiers responding.

"The duke has ordered it all cleared out by nightfall. Look lively. Watch where you're stepping—do you want to break that? It's worth five times your life, man!" This from a voice more distant, yet bellowing enough to carry down the hall through the door to Felix's ears. Two more voices followed, muttering but near enough to be heard.

"Why do we need to empty the storehouse?" the first one said. "He's taken the palace, hasn't he? Practically taken the country. Why does he need to loot a treasure store that is already his?"

"Erh," his companion snorted. "S'ain't the duke's orders we're following. I'd stake my life it's that . . . that *other* one's doing. We're looting for him, and he'll take it all, and how will we or anyone stop him, I'd like to know? He'll leave the duke a crown here all right, but a penniless crown in a penniless kingdom. And d'you think the folks of Parumvir will stand for our duke one moment more once *himself* has flown back to wherever he belongs?"

Their voices faded. Felix cursed and flexed his fingers over the hilt of his sword. Looting his father's treasure store! He wanted to burst out upon them, sword flashing, knock them flat, strike them . . . But what good would that do?

He needed to find his father. That's all that mattered now. They would worry about treasure later, but for now he must find a way to the king. But how could he slip down to the dungeons when the only stairway leading that way was currently trafficked by those Shippening thieves? And with the palace halls crawling with his enemies, Felix dared not so much as open the door to the passage in which he hid.

He knelt down, and Monster jumped onto his knee. "What am I going to do, beast?" the boy whispered.

At that moment a new voice boomed through the hall. "Drop what you're doing and go! Out to the courtyard at once, you dogs!"

Monster jumped from Felix's knee, growling as the clatter of many priceless items dropping to the hard floor and the metallic whisk of many weapons being drawn echoed in the hall. Footsteps pounded and disappeared as the great front door boomed shut.

Cautiously, Felix cracked open the door and peered out from the servants' passage. The hall was empty. Monster slipped between his feet and trotted forward, but stumbled across the treasures that he could not see littering the floor. He stopped and lowered his nose to sniff at a jewel box lying open at his feet. Felix stared up and down the hall. He had not even known that his father owned all these beautiful things. He looked toward the door, shut and silent. Faint noises sounded from the yard beyond, but he hardly cared for those.

When he looked back up the hall, it was empty too, as was the narrow staircase leading down to the treasure store and to Oriana's old dungeons.

Clutching the hilt of his sword and taking courage in its familiar heft, Felix slipped from hiding and raced to the dark staircase.

The stairway was utterly black, save for the light of a few lanterns hung on the walls by Shippening soldiers. Felix swallowed hard, wishing his heart would settle back in his chest where it was supposed to be, and started his descent. Once, long ago, he had been taken to view the ancient dungeons. Memories of the heavy iron chains and the cave-like rooms still crept into his nightmares now and then. He hated the thought of his father in such a place but did not doubt that the duke would keep him there.

He reached the door leading to the dungeons and found it unlocked. He stepped first into the guardroom. Much to Felix's relief, a lantern hung from the ceiling. He climbed onto a stool in order to take the lantern from its hook, then approached the tunnel that led deep into the rock of Goldstone Hill to the dungeon cells. His courage faltered as he gazed into the blackness.

"Father?"

Darkness swallowed his voice.

"Preeeow." Monster rubbed against his calf. He reached down to stroke the cat's back, but Monster slipped from beneath his hand and trotted into the tunnel.

Gulping, Felix followed the cat, calling every few steps, "Father?"

The third time he called, he heard a moan from a cell on his left. He held his lantern up to a tiny wooden door with bars near the floor, through which food could be passed. Monster crouched at the bars, his tail twitching. "Father, is that you?" Felix said.

"Felix?"

The voice was faint but unmistakable.

"Father!" Felix crouched down and looked through the bars, but the light from his lantern showed him nothing. "Father, it's me. I'm here to rescue you."

"Felix, you fool!" His father's voice growled through the darkness. "Why did you come here?"

Felix blinked, hurt at his father's tone. But he saw a thin white hand reach between the bars, and he took hold of it in both of his. "I had to come, Father."

His father's hand squeezed briefly, but his voice came harsh from the other side of the door. "Go away. Now! Get out before those men return."

"I have to free you first," Felix said. Then he stopped and sat up, letting go of his father's hand. He had overlooked an important detail: the dungeon keys.

A shout rang through the courtyard. The dragon girl turned, startled, and saw the Duke of Shippening at the top of the front steps, gesturing toward her and bellowing, "Quick, men! Surround her! All of you!"

The men at work hauling the treasures dropped their burdens, drew their weapons, and rushed toward her. She was surrounded in a moment, one pale girl in a forest of a hundred swords. She stood quietly with her head bowed and did not meet their eyes.

"Let me through!" the duke bellowed, and a ripple moved through the many-layered fence of soldiers as they made way for their overlord. He stood at last before her, his arms crossed, looking down on her.

"Your looks ain't improved much, wench, and I'll tell you that straight." The duke puffed heavily through fat lips. "Well, 'tain't no difference. He was right anyway. He said you'd come back if we captured your father."

Her head jerked sharply, though she did not look up. "My father?"

"Wouldn't let me kill him yet. Said it would be a waste of good bait." The duke reached out and grabbed her chin roughly. "My, but you're an ugly thing, like a lizard you are! But you'll do, little princess. Now I'll send your father to join your dead brother, and with you as my wife, no one will contest my claim to the throne!"

She raised her eyes to his face, and the duke found himself looking into bottomless depths of molten heat. He screamed as though burned and backed away into his circle of soldiers who, frightened, also stepped back, raising their weapons higher.

The Dragon's laugh rolled like heat lightning over their heads. The men of Shippening fell away, parting so that a path cleared between her and the Dragon. Their eyes locked across the distance.

"You are much too honest, my child," the Dragon said, smiling so that she could see the fire between his teeth. "Look at you. Even now you look more dragon than human. Most of my children hide it better. You will not be able to walk in man's world like that."

"I am not your child," she growled.

He shook his head and strode with a catlike tread down the path between the soldiers until he stood over her. "Of course you are," he said. "My own pretty child."

"Dragon!" The Duke of Shippening's voice quavered, but he coughed and spoke again. "Dragon, honor your promise now. Give her to me."

"Honor *my* promise?" The Dragon turned a slow gaze upon the duke. "I don't recall you honoring yours, Duke Shippening. Did you bring the king here? My memory seems a bit hazy on that score. I could have sworn that was *my* doing."

"You have no use for her," the duke said. "Give her to me, as we agreed!"

The Dragon turned his slow smile back down upon the girl. "Your last brave suitor is most ardent. At least one of them still wants you, little princess."

She did not break the Dragon's gaze as she spoke. "Duke Shippening, leave my father's house immediately." Her voice hissed with fire.

"Wh-what?" the duke cried.

She turned to him, and her stare could have melted his eyes had he stood closer. "Leave my father's house."

The duke paled and stepped back, his hands before him. One by one his men had slipped away, loath to remain so near the Dragon and the strange girl, and now the duke found himself horribly alone. He sought his one ally. "Dragon?"

The Dragon laughed again, turned on his heel, and started toward the sagging front doors of the royal house. "Come with me, daughter. I would have you bear treasures back to my Hoard. I have been considering how I should best transfer them. Your coming is fortunate. There is much more inside, down in the vaults to which you so kindly led me. Once you have borne them to the Village, you will await there my return."

"Stop," she said.

The Dragon paused on the threshold and looked back over his shoulder.

She raised her chin. "You will not enter my father's house again, nor—" She choked on the flames in her throat. "Nor will you touch his goods with your dirty hands."

An evil laugh filled the courtyard as the Dragon threw back his head, shoulders heaving. "Foolish child." He showed every tooth in an awful smile. "I am your Father and this is my house now, remember? So of course I shall enter and take what belongs to me. And you will help me. Come, girl, before I lose my sense of humor."

Within three paces she lost all human semblance and was in full flame, fire bursting from deep inside her, hotter than she had ever before burned, so hot that the stone steps of the palace began to melt, and she focused all on the spot where the Dragon stood. The black figure disappeared in the onslaught of blue and red fire. Screams from dozens of soldiers were soon drowned out in the awful roar of her fire. The world was nothing but flame; nothing but heat filled every sense.

At last she stopped and staggered back, poisonous smoke filling her eyes. But even as she stood blinded she heard the Dragon's laugh again, fuller and deeper than before.

"Was that all you had inside?" With a sweep of his arm he cleared the smoke, revealing himself unsinged upon the melting steps. "I misjudged you. I thought your flame far greater than that!" He opened his mouth, his jaw dropping grotesquely to his chest, and his own flame billowed forth, sweeping over her.

She stumbled back as though struck with a mace, turning her massive head away. At first her dragon hide absorbed the heat. But soon she felt a change. The fire became so hot, it penetrated under her scales to her soft flesh, and the scales themselves burned and melted.

She screamed. A high, inhuman, hideous scream that shattered glass, then rose in intensity and horror. As she screamed she struggled to escape, but the inferno surrounded her no matter where she turned. She thought she could bear no more, but it went on and she did not die.

When the Dragon swallowed his flame, he towered over her, black and monstrous, his crest upraised like a kingly crown, his wings arched behind him.

"Foolish sister!" he roared, snarling down on her smoldering frame. "You thought to kill your king, your Father? I *gave* you your fire! Do you think you can use my own flame against me?"

He smacked her, his claws tearing into her burnt flesh. She screamed again and crawled away, her torn wings beating feebly on the ground.

"Try it again, dragon!" He struck her a second time and a third. "Burn me! Let your flame build up and smolder inside as you smolder outside. Come on, dragon!"

Where the strength came from she could not say, but with all that was in her she pushed herself to her feet, sucked in a great gulp of air, and took to the sky. The Dragon King laughed at her flight, sending more flames after her, but he did not follow.

"Go!" he shouted. "Finish yourself off! I'll find you later and gnaw your bones, my child! I'll gnaw and burn your bones!"

35

S HE COULD NOT FLY FAR, for her wings were shredded and disintegrating like burned leaves. The young dragon fell from the sky no more than a mile from the city and lay where she had fallen on the sand by the sea. Her breath came in uneven gasps, and each one caused searing pain through her whole body. She closed her eyes and slipped into darkness, knowing that she was dying.

Her mind filled with images and sounds crowding together and vying for dominance. The images were all from her life—from her very earliest memories of playing with Felix down by the Old Bridge, to much-hated lessons with her tired-eyed tutor, to Nurse's funny old face. Over the visions and collage of colors, she could hear voices, such familiar voices.

"Trust is knowing a man's character, knowing truth, and relying on that character and truth even when the odds seem against you."

"Oh, my love is like a white, white dove, soaring in the sky above!"

"I can only pray he will prove worthy."

"Oh, my love is like a fine, fine wine . . ."

"I cannot bear to watch these suitors of yours, knowing I have no right to . . . to pursue you myself."

". . . If only she'd be mine!"

"Will you trust me?"

". . . a sweet, sweet song . . ."

"Una, trust me."

"Oh, my love . . ."

"I will trust him till I die!"

At the sound of her own voice shouting those last words, fire blazed up in her mind. Such a lie! Her trust had broken, shattered along with her heart. All that was left inside burned and burned, destroying the images in evil flames, destroying the voices of her loved ones.

The Dragon's eyes, like liquid fire, swallowed her, and she choked and drowned in flames. This was death, then; this was the end of all dreams.

A wood thrush sang like a silver bell, high and sweet.

I love you, Una.

She opened her eyes unwillingly. The murmur of waves on the shore filled her ears, and gentle rain fell upon her burning skin, at once painful and soothing. Tears mingled with the rain, and those drops hurt most of all, yet she did not flinch away.

She gazed up into Aethelbald's face. He held her scorched body tenderly in his arms.

"Why do you love me?" she asked, her voice rasping in her burnt throat.

He put a hand gently to her face and wiped a hair from across her eyes. She could feel rain on her bald scalp and knew that she had little hair left. "Because I choose to," he said. When he blinked, two tears fell on her cheeks, painful yet blessed. "I chose to long ago, long before we met. When my father sent me to win you, I loved you already."

"You've made a poor choice, you see," she said. How harsh and horrible her voice sounded in her own ears. "Nothing but a dragon."

"I knew that from the beginning." All the sorrow in the world was in his face. "I have watched many dear to me fall prey to the Dragon's fire before. So yes, I knew already, Una. Yet you are my chosen love, the only one for me."

She turned her face away. "Others have told me as much. Their words were empty."

"Look at me, Una."

She would not.

"Una!"

Slowly, though the sight of his tearstained face burned more than fire, she raised reddened eyes to his.

"My words are not empty."

A sob caught in her throat, and she gasped at the pain of it, then gasped again when she realized that tears filled her eyes. They gathered and spilled, trailing excruciating paths down her blackened cheeks, yet the relief of tears was greater than the pain. She felt his arms tighten about her, and he pressed his cheek against the top of her bald head, letting her cry softly.

"My Prince," she said at last, her voice catching. "You know I cannot love you."

Aethelbald leaned back and brushed a tear away with a gentle hand. "Let me enable you to."

"No, I cannot!" she said, shaking her head. "I *cannot* love you. I have no heart . . . none."

"Then let me give you mine," he said.

"It would burn away inside of me!" She wanted to cover her face with her hands but found she could not move her arms, could not even feel them anymore. "Everything inside me burns now. Everything is fire and ash."

"As long as you are a dragon, yes."

"I cannot help what I am," she whispered. "I would if I could. I tried to kill the Dragon as I was told. I know he must die before I can be free. But I could not kill him. And now I am . . . now I am dying." She closed her eyes. "It is too late for us, my Prince."

His voice came mellow and soothing to her ears. "As long as you are a dragon yourself, you cannot hope to defeat the King of Dragons. The fire in you must die first."

"I *am* dying," she said. She could feel the minutes of her life flitting away. "I will be free soon."

"No!" he said, his voice thick with tears. "No, you cannot die while still a dragon. I will not allow it!"

"There is nothing to be done," she murmured. "I cannot change what I am. Even if I kill myself now, I cannot change what I am."

"You must let me do it," he said.

"What?"

"You must let me kill you, Una."

An evil voice screeched through her memory. *"You know what he did, little princess? He took out his sword and tried to run me through!"*

"You must let me, Una."

She felt her breaths coming harder, and each one was agonizing. "You would kill me?"

"I submitted to him, and he tried to kill me!"

"I kill you to save you," he said. His eyes pierced her with their tenderness yet also filled her with fear.

"I trusted him, and he betrayed me!"

"I am dying already," she whimpered, and more tears stained her face. "Must you kill me?"

"You will die as a dragon if you do not let me help you," he said. "Trust me, and you will die instead a princess."

"I trusted him!"

She tried once more to move but could not find her limbs. "All right," she whispered. "Do as you must, my Prince. I . . . I trust you."

Gently Aethelbald lowered his face to hers and kissed her on her charred and blackened mouth. She closed her eyes and felt she could not bear such exquisite pain or beauty.

He laid her down in the sand. Each movement and shifting of her limbs was agony, but it would soon be over. He stood over her, and behind him dragon smoke churned in an angry sky. With a metallic ring he drew his sword. She trembled where she lay.

"My Prince!" she gasped. "Will it hurt? I am afraid."

"It will hurt." His voice was heavy with sorrow, yet his eyes were full of love. "Death is painful."

Gazing into those eyes, so deep, so kind, she took in a last breath. "Do it," she said.

His sword was swift and sure. In a flash of silver, he pierced her through the breast, deep inside. She screamed as she felt the blade entering deeper, down into the furnace that was her soul, ice-cold amid the flames. Down into the darkest fire it penetrated, and the flames fled before the blade. She felt herself slipping away. Out of a heavy, twisted body, she glided into light, cool air.

Dragon claws tore at her back, pulling her, restraining her. She felt the blade twist inside, screamed again in agony.

"I trusted him, and he betrayed me!"

Last desperate flames clawed at her.

Betrayed!

Her own dragon eyes glared at her, full of hate, full of fire.

Betrayed! the dragon cried.

Then it was finished. The husk of her body lay empty, the fire gone forever.

36

THE DRAGON WATCHED THE MEN carry King Fidel's treasures from his vaults and place them in piles about the courtyard. He picked up a golden goblet. The soft gold melted at the touch of his hands, and the elegant curves sank into an unlovely lump. He tossed it back to the pile with a smile. The shape was nothing, the beauty unnecessary. All that mattered was the gold.

As the sun sank low, casting the dark shadow of the palace over the eastern courtyard, the duke came to the doorstep, his arms folded across his barrel chest. "That's most of it," he said. "Only a few chests left." His eyes spoke other things, but fear restrained his tongue.

"Good," the Dragon said. "Now you may bring Fidel and his son to me."

The duke blinked. "His son? The brat was dead long ago."

"I think you will find otherwise if you go now and fetch the king to me."

The duke's eyes narrowed. He pointed to two of his men and ordered them down to the dungeons, then waited at the top of the steps, watching the Dragon move from one pile of treasures to the next. Things were not going as he had expected when he made this bargain many months ago. Certainly he could take the throne once the king was dead, but how could he hope to keep it? Not an ounce of Parumvir's royal blood flowed in his veins, and without the promised marriage to the princess he could not hope to justify himself to the angry people of this land. The best he could anticipate would be constant battle, constant unrest, and if the Dragon took much of this treasure . . . But surely he could not carry it all away with him, or even very much?

The duke spat on the stone steps. *Curse all dragons and their bargains.*

"Unhand me!"

The duke turned at the frantic voice, and his eyes widened with surprise. The two soldiers he'd sent to the dungeons returned, one of them dragging King Fidel by his chains and the other, lo and behold, holding Prince Felix by the arm and the back of the neck. The young prince flailed and kicked viciously against the much larger man but to no avail.

"What is this?" the duke roared.

"We caught him in the dungeons, my lord," the soldier holding the prince replied. "He was with the king, tried to free him but had no key, you see. Little urchin—"

The duke grabbed Felix by the shirt, yanked him from the soldier's grasp, and lifted him off his feet, snarling into his face. "What are you doing still alive?"

Felix, white as a sheet, could not speak, suspended as he was in the air. Fidel rallied himself and raised his arms, chained together. "Don't hurt the boy!" he cried. "He . . . he's not my son, just a servant who wanted to help me, but he's nothing, really! Send him away. Don't harm him."

"Not your son, eh?" The duke drew his long dagger. "In that case you shouldn't care if I—"

"Wait."

The duke froze as the Dragon's hiss tickled his ear. He dropped the prince and backed away as though stung. The Dragon stooped down and gazed into Felix's face.

The prince stared back, then suddenly cried out and flung his arms over his head, recognizing the tall man's eyes as the same burning orbs that had glared over the wall at him the night the Dragon came.

"It is as I thought," the Dragon said, straightening and looking down on the boy cowering at his feet. "You have poison in your veins. They couldn't work it all out of you, could they, little prince? Your sister has proven disappointing, but you perhaps—"

"No!" Fidel screamed, pulling against his chains so hard that he fell on the stone steps. The soldier holding the end of his chain kicked him in the side, but the king struggled up. "No!" he cried again. "Don't touch him! Leave him alone!"

The Dragon looked at him and shook his head. "Wretched man. Your daughter succumbed to my kiss with hardly a thought. Your son will, in time, do the same. You cannot protect them. You never could."

He waved a hand to the soldiers. "Chain both of them in the yard," he said. "I will deal with them when I return. But for now . . . " He smiled, and flames wreathed his face. "For now there is no hurry, and I have a promise to fulfill. I must gnaw her bones."

His black cloak billowed into black wings, and his body became long and sinewy and horrible by the time he reached the broken gate. The men of Shippening scurried from his path like so many cockroaches scuttling into safe nooks in the rubble of the wall. He crawled over the twisted metal into the road leading down into the city.

A man stood in his way.

The Dragon stopped. His eyes slitted as he regarded the figure standing before him. The man stood in the middle of the road, his head bowed, his cloak swept back over his shoulders, a drawn sword in his hands. The blade gleamed red in the light of the Dragon's eyes. Fresh blood stained its edge.

The Dragon's tail twitched at the end. "Do I know you?" he asked, turning his great head to peer at the man more clearly with one eye. "You seem familiar."

"We have met," Prince Aethelbald said.

The Dragon drew back with a hiss at the sound of the voice. His eyes swirled with churning fire, and he revealed every fang in a snarl. Then he looked again and laughed.

"You!" he cried, his eyes narrowing to two red slits. "What are you made up as? Look at you, pathetic creature, a little man-beast! Never thought I'd see the day that you, my Enemy, would reduce yourself to such a state. You, who walk where mortals cannot; you, who bound me to the Gold Stone. Why, I could snap you up in a mouthful and still be hungry for dessert!" Tongues of fire licked between his teeth.

Aethelbald raised his bowed head, and his eyes met those of the Dragon without flinching or fear. "You cannot kill me, Death-in-Life, Destroyer of Dreams and Devourer. I know you for what you are, and none of your fires will touch me."

The Dragon licked his lips. "So said all your little knights before I swallowed them! I have no intention of returning to that prison. I am stronger now than I once was, and you . . . Ha! You are nothing but a *man*!" He smiled. "Besides," he said, "I have something you covet, do I not? Something you prize that you will never own, Prince of Farthestshore!"

He lowered his head, his hot breath beating down upon the Prince. "I have taken her already, my Enemy. I have taken and twisted her, burned her in my flames. And you, you will never see her again."

"You are wrong, Death-in-Life," the Prince said. He stepped to one side. Behind him stood a girl dressed in a simple white robe. She did not look at the Dragon but kept her gaze fixed on Aethelbald's face. Her eyes were serene, without a trace of fire.

"Daughter!" the Dragon snarled. "My daughter, my sister! You cannot live without your fire, and I still hold your heart!"

Though her breath came a little faster, Una did not answer but kept her gaze on the Prince.

Aethelbald spoke instead. "I have given her my heart. She no longer needs your fire to live. But I have come now to claim her heart from you. It is mine now by right!"

The Dragon's crest flared up, and fire rimmed his eyes. "You'll have to kill me, then, man!"

He opened his mouth, and flame burst forth. Aethelbald grabbed Una and dragged her out of the way behind a pile of rubble. The Dragon snaked down the road and climbed onto the pile, looking down on them from above. More fire poured from his mouth, and Aethelbald only just pulled the princess from its path. The rock behind them melted.

"Stay close to me," Aethelbald whispered, clutching her hand. Pulling her behind him, he ran back up the path and through the broken gate into the east courtyard. The shadows were deep on this side of the palace, and it was difficult to discern which dark shapes were piles of rocks and which were soldiers of Shippening.

Aethelbald, drawing the princess along, leapt behind a pile of rocks crumbled from the broken wall. They ducked their heads as the Dragon, his eyes streaked with fire, entered the courtyard.

The Prince let go of Una's hand.

"Aethelbald!" she cried, reaching for him.

"Don't be afraid, Una," he said, his voice strangely quiet. "Look." He took her chin in his hand and pointed her head to her left. She saw her father and brother chained to the base of a broken statue, coughing as dragon fumes rolled into the courtyard.

"Come out, coward!" the Dragon bellowed, flames leaping from his mouth.

Soldiers cried out, and some slipped from cracks in the wall and fled down Goldstone Hill. Flames spread about the courtyard, catching anything that could yet burn.

"Your father and brother will be killed in this fire," Aethelbald said. "You must set them free. I will lead the monster away." He gazed into her eyes a moment, then suddenly drew her close and kissed her, even as the air boiled and the heavens roared.

When he pulled back, he gently touched her cheek. "I will come for you. No matter what happens, I will come for you. Now go!"

He adjusted his grip on his sword and gathered himself to climb over the pile of rubble, grabbing the rocks with his left hand and pulling himself out from behind them. He leapt onto the top, a clear target.

The Dragon turned, and a burst of fire scorched the stones. Though she crouched safely on the far side, Una could feel the heat of the flames through the rocks. The Prince leapt away in time and darted across the yard, running for the gate. The Dragon, spitting more fire, turned and followed.

Una struggled to breathe amid the thick smoke and pressed her hands over her mouth. Choking back tears, she staggered across the fire-scathed yard.

"Una!" Felix shouted when he saw her coming through the haze of smoke. Fidel raised hopeless eyes, and joy filled his face at the sight of her. She fell on her knees before them beside the broken statue, and they flung their arms around her in a tight embrace.

"Look," Felix said, pulling away. He pointed. "The soldier dropped them when he fled."

Una looked and saw the ring of keys not three yards away. She leapt up and ran for them, hardly able to see for the smoke around her. She scraped her knuckles grabbing them up and rushed back. Felix was chained with only one cuff on his wrist, attached to his father's arm. She tried several and soon found the key that fit his lock, and Felix pulled himself free. But Fidel was chained with links between his hands and feet, and one about his neck that the soldier had secured to the base of the statue. Una freed his hands and feet, but each key she tried for the neck chain refused to fit.

A hand reached out of the darkness and grabbed her shoulder. She screamed as she was yanked to her feet, and the keys dropped from her hands.

"I must say," the Duke of Shippening's voice growled in her ear, "I never thought I'd be so pleased to see you alive, princess!"

She screamed again, and Felix, roaring like a young lion, hurled himself headfirst with all the force in his young body, catching the duke hard in the side just below the ribcage. The duke grunted and staggered, and Una freed herself from his grip. She swept up the keys, feeling through for the last few that she had not yet tried. She heard the scrape of a sword being drawn but did not look around. Only three keys were left untested. She fitted one in the lock around her father's neck and heard a click.

Fidel rose like a hurricane and threw the chains he held into the face of the duke. The duke caught them, but one of the links flew back and struck him across the forehead. He stumbled back.

"Felix!" the king cried. Felix, on his hands and knees at the duke's feet, scrambled up, half crawling toward his father. The duke reached out a meaty hand and grabbed the young prince by the back of the shirt, his sword upraised.

A hideous roar shook the stone. Una, clutching her father, saw the Dragon approaching, his eyes red like flowing lava, and before him ran Aethelbald, his gaze intent on the duke. He leapt forward and grabbed the blade of the duke's sword with his bare hand, pulling it from his grasp, and simultaneously brought his knee into the small of the duke's back. He and the duke tumbled onto the stones, and Felix burst free and ran to the king and Una.

The king grabbed both his children and dragged them behind the base of the statue just as streams of fire roared past them, burning the air, melting the far side of their shelter. The duke's scream pierced their ears for an instant and was swallowed up in flames the next.

For half a moment Una breathed as the fire lessened. Then with a cry she broke free of her father's grasp and ran from behind the stone into the swirling smoke and ash. Coughing, she stumbled forward but could see nothing.

Red eyes glowed above her, cutting through the darkness and ash. She saw by their light the charred bones lying upon the stones.

37

ETHELBALD," Una whispered.

She looked slowly from the bones up into the eyes of the Dragon. Fire streaming from his mouth, he lashed his tail, and it wrapped about her like a python. With a sickening lurch she rose into the air, feeling the biting cold of the wind on her face at the same time as the awful burn of the dragon scales that dug into her skin, and she lay limp as a rag doll in his grip.

They flew from Goldstone Hill down into the ghostly ruins of what had once been her city, and there, in the middle of the square that had formerly teemed with life but now stank with death, the Dragon dropped her. Una lay where she fell, curled into a tight ball, and felt the ground quake as the Dragon landed.

"See, little princess?" The Dragon's voice hissed, filling the air and echoing down the long, dark, dead streets of Sondhold. It seemed as though a thousand demon voices repeated each word, flinging them at her like knives. "See, even he has failed you. Even he burned in my fire. What good is his heart to you now?"

She pushed herself up, her hair covering her face like a veil, and knelt in the ashes, her face in her hands.

"No one withstands my fire," the Dragon said. She felt his great heavy body above her, felt she would melt in his heat. "Give it up, little princess!"

Una lifted her face and gazed into endless depths of flame.

"Give up his heart," the Dragon said, his poisonous breath tossing her hair back from her face. "Take back my fire, or you will surely die here and now!"

Lost in the black and burning night, she could find no voice.

"Take back my fire."

The heat, like weights, pressed her down into the ground. She could not breathe.

"Take it and live, my child!"

She closed her eyes.

Somewhere, so far away that Una almost could not hear it, a wood thrush sang.

She squeezed her eyes, strained to better hear. The sound—silver notes like bells in the morning—swelled. The song grew and grew, filling her head, drowning out the Dragon's voice, driving away the fumes in her mind.

I love you, Una.

Won't you return to me?

She lifted her eyes to the dark sky above the Dragon's head, above the inferno eyes.

"I would rather die," she said.

The Dragon's jaw lowered, and she felt the heat of his furnace building. But above his head she saw a tiny being on wings, singing in silver bells as it flew.

I love you, Una.

As she watched, the thrush darted into the mouth of the Dragon. Then Una saw Aethelbald, her Prince, kneeling on the monster's tongue, sword in hand. Even as flames rose in the Dragon's throat, the Prince stabbed into the roof of its mouth.

The Dragon screamed. Like the ocean in a storm. Like hurricane winds tearing a city apart. Like mountains, thought immortal, tumbling in a mighty avalanche of stone. He screamed and reared up, fell backward, writhing and convulsing, knocking down buildings and smothering his own fires beneath his body.

Una fled the market square, down to the docks and the storm-tossed sea. She flung herself into the water to escape the rain of fire, and clung to posts of a pier as waves beat over her. The roar filled her ears, and hot ash sizzled in the ocean around her. She watched the Dragon flail and flame in death agonies until she had to hide her face in her arm.

At last all was still.

In the water, Una shivered with sudden cold. Above her in the city, fire crackled and died away to nothing. A tiny wind touched her face, spraying her with light droplets, and disappeared.

Una waded to the shore and climbed onto land, her clothes heavy on her light frame. Smoke bleared her eyes and choked her, but she stumbled up the ghostly path to the market square. The demon voices were hushed into empty, gaping silence. She did not speak, hardly breathed as she went, and her footsteps made no sound on the stones. The smoke was thicker every step she took, but she would not turn back.

In the market square lay the Dragon.

His body had crushed the former city center, devastating the buildings to dust underneath him. The heat from his dead fire rose like a wall around the body, but Una fought her way through.

The Dragon's mouth was open, and his great black tongue draped across the stones. Poisonous smoke filled Una's nostrils, and she gagged. She peered between rows of teeth.

The sword remained thrust into the Dragon's upper jaw. But the blade glowed red with heat and was twisted like wire, the silver hilt melted like wax.

"No," Una whispered, shaking her head. "No, you promised."

She dropped to her knees as the heat and smoke overwhelmed her senses. "Aethelbald, don't leave me. . . . Not yet." She wrapped her arms about herself, bending so that her forehead pressed into the stone. "Please don't leave me. I'd rather die than live without you now!"

Her hands clutched her chest, feeling beneath her skin the heartbeat so strong inside her. It was his heart, not her own, but she felt it must break. "Please, my love! Don't leave me alone!"

"Una."

She would not look up but turned her face away.

"Una, look at me."

"No!"

"Una."

Strong hands reached down and took her own. Real hands, warm.

"Una, I've come back for you."

"No!" She tried to pull away, but he would not let go.

"Una, I am no ghost." One of the hands grasping hers loosened and turned palm up. She saw there two red stripes of blood, fresh blood drawn by the blade of a grabbed sword. "Does a ghost bleed?" he asked gently.

Slowly she raised her face. Kind eyes, infinitely deep and clear, gazed into her own. "I told you I would come back for you, didn't I? No matter what." Aethelbald smiled and wiped ash from her face. "Do you not believe me even now?"

"I . . ." Her voice broke with a sob, and she flung herself into his arms, clinging desperately. Aethelbald held her, stroked her hair, and murmured, "It is over now. The danger is past. I will never abandon you. I will never abandon you, Una."

Dawn found the black carcass of the Dragon. The light of the sun pierced through the fading dragon smoke, disintegrating the body to ashes. A sweet breeze carried the ashes away to the desert and scattered them across the sand.

38

Fidel stood with his son just outside the broken gates of Oriana Palace, his arm around the boy's shoulders. They did not speak but watched the fires die in the city below.

At last Felix asked, "What will we do now, Father?"

"We will rebuild," Fidel said.

"What with? Most of your wealth was burned."

Fidel squeezed his son close to his side and was silent. Again they stood and watched the dark road below them as morning slowly broke through the fading dragon smoke. Monster twined and purred about the prince's ankles until Felix was persuaded to kneel down and rub a comforting hand down the cat's head and back. And still they watched the road.

Suddenly Felix yelped like a puppy and ran down the hill at breakneck speed, and Monster careened blindly behind him, tail high above his head. The prince hardly slowed himself before he fell into the outspread arms of his sister on her way up the road. She laughed and nearly toppled over backward, but Aethelbald reached out and caught them both, steadying them. Felix, much to his disgust, found tears running down his face, and he swiped them away at first, but to no avail. Una laughed again and tried to wipe his cheek with her thumb, but he brushed her off gruffly before whirling her about in another hug.

Gently Aethelbald parted them and, taking Una by the hand, led her up to Fidel, who waited like a sentinel before the gates of his palace. Aethelbald bowed to him. "I have brought you your daughter, Your Majesty."

Fidel took Una's hand as Aethelbald offered it. He stared at it a moment, small and white in his own. Then he knelt down at Aethelbald's feet and wept.

Una, her father, and her brother were too full of joy after their bitter separation to consider the fragility of their position. They clung to each other and laughed and cried and interrupted each other and laughed and cried some more. When at last Prince Aethelbald asked them to follow him into the Wood, they did so without question, still laughing, still crying, and saying words very little worth hearing save for the glad voices in which they were spoken.

Aethelbald never once let go of Una's hand.

He led them into the shadows of the forest and onto a strange path that blurred on the edges of their vision and that seemed almost to carry them as they walked, crossing miles with each step. But they held on to each other and were not afraid as they followed the Prince of Farthestshore away from the ruins of Oriana Palace and the smoke-filled destruction of Sondhold.

When they emerged from this path, they found themselves far north along the coast and facing the city of Glencrocus.

Felix looked back the way they had come and did not see the Wood anywhere, and he shivered, not with fear so much as with wonder.

Monster, close to his heels, meowled imperiously until Felix picked him up and carried him the rest of the way into Glencrocus.

The watchers at the city gates hailed the newcomers, and when they learned that King Fidel approached, they sent out word to the mayor. What followed was a time of great commotion as the faithful people of Parumvir rushed to greet Fidel and his children and to carry them safely into the city and on to the mayor's fine house. But before the rush of servants met them, Prince Aethelbald drew Una aside.

"I must go," he said.

She did not answer, only looked at him.

"I must find my servants and see to your father's interests as well." She nodded.

"But I will return for you, Una. Will you wait for me?"

Then the crowd was upon them, and people swarmed about the princess and took her hand from Aethelbald's. She had no time to give him any answer but a smile. This she gave him even as they were pulled apart and she disappeared in the rush that carried her into the city.

And in the excitement at receiving the lost king and his children, no one noticed the Prince of Farthestshore as he turned and disappeared, vanishing onto his own strange path.

Una was bustled along through the streets of Glencrocus, losing sight of her father and brother but trusting the joyful people about her. She was nearly to the front doorstep of the mayor's house when a familiar voice grabbed her attention.

"Una! Princess!"

She looked back over her shoulder and recognized a funny old face calling and waving from the depths of the crowd. "Nurse!" Una cried and demanded that the old woman be brought to her. The people surged around them and propelled Nurse into Una's arms, and the two of them stood and hugged each other and cried.

"Come, Miss Princess," Nurse said at last with a gruff sniff. "It's not seemly for a lady of your station to be seen making so much ado over her staff. And in full public eye! What will they all think? Come inside at once, and I'll see that they fix you a nice bath, 'cause you smell a terrible something, my dear, I ain't going to lie. . . ."

Prince Aethelbald did not return for days. During that time, Felix and Una saw very little of their father but stayed together in peaceful company with Monster purring in their laps. Una found she did not wish to tell her brother of her adventures after fleeing Oriana Palace, did not wish to remember them at all.

Felix, as he sat and stroked the orange cat, frowned a good deal, for every time he opened his mouth to tell his sister all that had happened to him since their parting, the words would not come. His memory clouded and his tongue muddled, and he found he could not discern which of his adventures were real and which were dreamed.

So they spoke very little, each simply enjoying the presence of the other.

"Are you going to marry Aethelbald?" Felix asked four days after their coming to Glencrocus as they sat in Una's chambers beside the empty fireplace. Though the weather was somewhat cold, Una discovered that she did not like to order a fire in her rooms but preferred to wrap up in blankets. Felix and Monster complained noisily at this, but she was immoveable.

"Marry Aethelbald?" Una said with something like a smile. "I don't know."

Felix snorted.

"Don't snort at me, Felix. It's not seemly."

"You're going to marry him, aren't you?"

"Perhaps. None of your business if I do."

"Is so my business! Do you have any idea what kind of getup they'll stuff me into for your wedding if you get married?" He sighed. "They'll bejewel me—that's what they'll do. All the more after what's happened. Must you get married, Una?"

Una smiled again and did not answer.

"Why is this fool cat sitting in my lap and not yours?" Felix pushed Monster from his knee, crossed his legs, and folded his arms across his chest. Monster meowed irritably and started grooming a paw.

"Una," Felix said without bothering to soften the scowl on his face.

"Yes?"

"I'll miss you when you're gone. A little."

Una reached across and took her brother's hand, squeezing gently and smiling at his refusal to meet her gaze. "I love you too, Felix."

When Aethelbald returned the following day, he did not come alone. He came in company with his remaining knights, Sir Oeric and Sir Imoo, and the surviving host from the Northern Fortress—including, to King Fidel's delight, General Argus, who, though wounded, was still very much alive. The king embraced his general with great joy and was almost too distracted to pay attention to what else the Prince of Farthestshore brought with him.

The treasures of Oriana Palace, which had been scattered about the courtyard the night of the Dragon's last fire, were not all destroyed. In fact, Aethelbald and his servants bore to Glencrocus the bulk of it unscathed, and the royal treasure stores were regained. Thus Fidel was assured that, though weakened, he would have the strength and resources to reestablish his kingdom to its former glory.

But some things were never restored. The palace on Goldstone Hill, filled with dragon smoke and burned with dragon fire, was left to crumble in ruins, never to be rebuilt. And the ruins along Sondhold Harbor, though one day at last built back up as a prosperous fishing village, were never restored to the former prestige of Parumvir's capital city.

Una sat beside her father when he received Prince Aethelbald and the gifts he brought. After showing King Fidel the treasures, Aethelbald turned to the princess and bowed before her. Then he said, "I found something else as well, my lady. Cup your hands." She did as he asked, and he dropped something into her grasp.

It was an opal ring, gleaming with its own fire.

She looked up at him, and he smiled. "Courtesy of Farthestshore," he said.

"Prince Aethelbald." She dropped her gaze, cursing the red blotches as they exploded across her nose but forcing herself to speak anyway. "I would be . . . I think I should like you to keep it. If you would."

He knelt before her, and she pressed the ring back into his hands. Still unable to look at him, Una whispered, "Will you be leaving soon? Returning to Farthestshore, that is?"

"Yes," he said. Then suddenly he squeezed her hands tight, and she could feel every eye in the whole assembly pinned on her and the Prince, and she just knew they were counting the blotches, every last one. Aethelbald said, "But if you will marry me, Princess Una, I will take you with me."

She met his gaze then and smiled at him, and red blotches aside, those who watched the scene thought they had never seen their princess more beautiful.

"I'll have to think about it," she said.

Felix snorted and rolled his eyes. "Applebald!" he muttered, and all the courtiers gathered in that room sent a gale of gossip flying back and forth.

39

Princess Una of Parumvir and Prince Aethelbald of Farthest-shore were married beside the sea. Una, much to Nurse's disgust, refused to wear the ornate, many-layered gown designed especially for her by the Parumvir fashion experts. She chose instead a simple gown of white without ornaments or jewels, and rather than a crown, she wore flowers in her hair.

To salve their wounded dignity, those selfsame tailors pounced upon the Prince of Parumvir, and Felix—as he'd suspected would be his fate—was stuffed into the stiffest, most choking of lace collars, complete with little jewels dripping along the edges, a set of sleeves so puffy and slashed with scarlet silk that he thought he might tip over if they weren't perfectly balanced out by yet more dangling jewels, and a pair of shoes that curled at the toes. He nearly fainted several times during the ceremony for lack of breath.

But to his relief, no one noticed Felix in the grandeur of the company present. Sir Oeric and Sir Imoo stood to one side of Prince Aethelbald,

Sir Oeric huge and craggy as a mountain, Sir Imoo black as night with starlike eyes. Beyond them Felix saw a host of other people, some of whom disappeared in certain light, only to reappear momentarily in all their shining strangeness. Felix thought he glimpsed a black-bearded king no taller than a rabbit, who stood beside a queen of equal height with hair so long and so golden that it looked like a river of liquid gold. At one moment, he could have sworn he saw a girl in green sitting on the back of a giant frog; then a moment later he believed he saw a boy no older than five leading a white lion on a leash like a puppy. Felix glimpsed also a man with a swan's head, a flame-orange tiger, a woman with cat's eyes, and many, many more.

Except, when he blinked, he didn't see anyone but the Prince and his two knights and all the gathered people of Parumvir dressed in brilliant colors. He pulled at the tight collar around his neck and wished to heaven some horrible disease would take all the fashion experts of Parumvir and prevent them from ever designing anything again.

"There you are!" a voice whispered fiercely in the middle of the ceremony. Felix took a surreptitious glance over his shoulder toward the nonexistent crowd beyond the Prince, and saw a young woman with a dark face and darker hair and slightly crooked teeth. He thought for one moment that she spoke to him, but realized the next that she was scowling down at his feet. He followed her gaze to where Monster sat, tail curled primly about his paws, one ear cocked back as the woman spoke.

"Where have you *been* all these years, wretched beast?" the woman said, edging closer.

The cat turned his other ear back, twitched the end of his tail, then bolted off into the crowd, vanishing from Felix's sight.

Felix turned to look at the young woman again, but she was gone. Fidel, standing beside his son, nudged Felix in the ribs, and the boy quickly faced forward once more, trying to focus his attention on the ceremony. He thought perhaps he knew that woman from somewhere, sometime. From long ago perhaps, or maybe from a dream?

At last the ceremony was complete. As Aethelbald took his bride in his arms, many voices rose into the air, flying from the sea and from the wind and from all around, a thousand voices as beautiful and wild as starlight and moonlight. And they sang:

> *"Beyond the final water falling,*
> *The Songs of Spheres recalling,*
> *When the sun descends behind the twilit sky,*
> *Won't you follow me?"*

Felix, standing beside his father, looked out to the sea and almost, but not quite, saw the Faerie beings he knew swam among the waves. Their voices pricked his memory again with some lingering impression of . . . of what? A promise and a kind smile and a silver pitcher of clear water. Strange images of high mountains and shafts of light through green leaves, of a woman clothed in lavender and green. It was all too strange, and he shook these thoughts away with a frown. Perhaps he'd think of them again tomorrow.

Una, as she stood back from her husband's embrace, looked out to the ocean and for the first time saw the Faerie beings in the water, their hair glowing like fire. The sea unicorns raised their heads from the foam and gleamed like so many suns as they sang.

"Do they sing for you?" she asked her husband.

"They rejoice with me," Aethelbald said, tucking her hand through his arm. "For you are mine now. Forever."

She smiled into his eyes, and the light of the song filled her to overflowing.

ACKNOWLEDGMENTS

I cannot thank my mother, Jill Stengl, enough for the hours of critiques and brainstorming sessions she put into helping me polish this story into the best it could be. You, Mummy, went above and beyond the call of duty.

Thanks to Erin Hodge, Esther Shaver, Paula Pruden-Macha, and Edward Schmidt, all of whom read this book at different drafts and gave me honest opinions. What a blessing it is to have such friends!

So much thanks to Kim Vogel Sawyer, Jill Eileen Smith, and Elizabeth Goddard for giving this young writer a boost when she needed it.

Thank you to the rest of you who read it for fun: Peter, Tom, Jim, Ben, Abbey, Debbie, Laura, Hannah, April . . . If I've forgotten one of you, please consider your name inserted here with gratitude. All of you were great encouragements.

And I can't forget to mention my agent, Rachel Zurakowski, who believed in me and this story from the beginning. You are a superhero, Rachel.

The team at Bethany House Publishers has been fantastic through every step of this process. This has been a wonderful experience that I will never forget. Thanks to all of you!

ABOUT THE AUTHOR

Anne Elisabeth Stengl makes her home in Raleigh, North Carolina, where she enjoys her profession as an art teacher, giving private lessons from her personal studio and teaching group classes at the Apex Learning Center. She studied illustration at Grace College and English literature at Campbell University. *Heartless* is her debut novel.

THE STORY HAS JUST BEGUN . . .

COMING SOON TO BOOKSTORES

MORE

TALES OF GOLDSTONE WOOD

Timeless fantasy that will keep you spellbound.